D1594268

The Emerald Tablet

Andrew Clawson

**Get Your FREE Copy of the Parker Chase story
A SPY'S REWARD.**

Sign up for my VIP reader mailing list,
and I'll send you the novel for free.

Details can be found at the end of this book.

Prologue

Persia – 358 BC

The most powerful man in the world was dying.

The King of Kings. A man whose empire spanned continents. The heavy footsteps of his armies shook the earth. As leader of the Achaemenid empire, he had conquered the vast sands of Egypt and the warriors of Sparta, yet no man could defeat time. Until now.

Artaxerxes II sat stiffly upright on his throne, looking down on the visitor. This man did not prostrate himself, but lowered his head briefly before meeting Xerxes' gaze. A satchel hung at his side, where it had been since the visitor had set out from his home in Athens. It was covered in dust from hundreds of miles spent on ship and horseback to bring him from one seat of power to another.

Artaxerxes stood from his throne; his imposing height was made even more so by the tall golden headpiece he wore. He leaned heavily on a cane that sparkled in sunlight streaming through a colonnade, gems flashing with each step down until he stood level with his guest. "Nebrus, my friend."

"My Great King Xerxes," Nebrus said. "It is good to see you after so many years. Your vigor is inspiring."

Xerxes offered his hand, which Nebrus clasped gently. "I am old, *iatros*. I am not dead."

Nebrus smiled, gripping Xerxes' hand with warmth. "Perhaps my skills as a doctor are not what men say."

A shadow crossed Xerxes' face. "That is what we must discuss. Come with me."

Xerxes led the physician deeper inside the walls of his palace. Each soldier who stood along the walls shifted so they never showed their back to their king. A retinue of guards followed Xerxes and Nebrus as they journeyed further into the complex. Xerxes waved one hand, keeping them all at a distance so none could hear their conversation.

The towering hall they walked through changed, becoming a perfect mirage of tranquility. Nebrus studied his reflection as they passed a shallow pool fed by channels carved into the stone floor. Lush green fronds and leaves lined the walls, incongruous in this Persian desert. A sign of Xerxes' impossible wealth. Xerxes noticed Nebrus's wandering gaze.

"Beauty from another land," he said. "Not unlike what you see in Athens every day."

"Yes, my king. It is a surprising reminder of home. Though we have little that compares to your palace."

"The Parthenon of Athena is magnificent." Xerxes noted the hint of pleasure cross his guest's face. "Your mentor showed it to me many years ago."

"Hippocrates honored beauty in all forms," Nebrus said. "The human form most of all. It is what led him to study medicine. An appreciation for what the gods created."

"His wisdom taught us all," Xerxes said. He stopped as the familiar pain arced across his chest. A fit of coughing came next, muffled by the silk cloth he pulled from a fold in his robes. A servant rushed over to take it once the fit subsided. Nebrus could not miss the bloodstains.

"Take this." Xerxes removed his formal headpiece, a cylindrical hat that recently seemed far heavier than it used to be. The servant took it before vanishing behind them. "Nebrus, join me in the garden. I seek your counsel."

Xerxes waved again, leaving his retainers and guards behind as he led Nebrus into an open-air garden. Palm leaves shaded the entire area and its pools of cool running water. A well-used stone bench sat near the room's center, a place where Xerxes had spent more time of late, and though Xerxes waved off Nebrus's offer of help to sit, he took a long moment to gather what strength he still possessed.

Nebrus did not waste words. "You are dying, my king."

"Even kings must pass from this world to the next," Xerxes said. "I have seen physicians from across my realm. Others like you who studied at the feet of Hippocrates. None has proven a match for my ailments. There is one hope remaining."

"Me," Nebrus said. "And what you suspect we Greeks have discovered."

Very little surprised Xerxes. This did. "Yes. There are rumors, whispers repeated in dark hallways from the lips of deceitful men."

Nebrus touched the satchel at his feet. "The reason you have heard only whispers is I have told no one. What I have was not achieved alone. Hippocrates taught me how to be a doctor, and together we created the elixir. My teacher sought two promises from me: to do no harm, and to respect the power of our discovery."

"Which is why you are here and he is not," Xerxes said. "Your mentor was the wisest man I knew." Tiny waves formed as wind rippled the pool in front of them. "What is the truth?"

"I am not certain of its limits," Nebrus said. "We have used it only once. On a young man in Greece, a man Hippocrates believed could far exceed his own accomplishments in the art of healing. The young man had a wasting disease and would have died."

"How does he fare?" Xerxes asked. Nebrus held his eyes, unmoving. "I see," Xerxes said. "The evidence is before me." He looked anew at Nebrus. The sturdy physique. The vigor of youth. All in a man who, by Xerxes' account, was nearly one hundred years old.

Xerxes fell silent for some time. Tree leaves rustled. A passing cloud briefly covered the sun. Xerxes coughed. "You are the only man alive with this knowledge. You also must have misgivings about its power."

"I am. I do."

"Perhaps that is what Hippocrates desired," Xerxes said. He lifted his hand to encompass every direction. "I am but one man. A leader of armies and rich beyond measure. My empire stretches in all directions, unimpeded by sea or mountain. The work of several lifetimes, much of it a gift from my father, and his father before him." Xerxes' cane tapped the floor. "One day it may vanish. Become dust floating on the hot desert wind. The question now is, what impact will I have? How will I be remembered? Our actions now could reverberate through the centuries." He turned to face Nebrus. "If your knowledge is shared, what then? Only the gods know." He indicated the satchel. "Show it to me."

Nebrus reached into the satchel, removing a rectangular block of pure gemstone. Writing had been carved into the surface, and the stone reflected sunlight with a dim greenish glow. Xerxes' eyes widened. "It is magnificent. This is the only one?"

"It is."

"Then we leave tomorrow to complete what Hippocrates wished for. To be certain this knowledge is never possessed by any unworthy man again."

Chapter One

Athens, Greece
Present Day

Harry Fox was going to clear a dead man's name. The hardest part? To avoid getting himself killed in the process.

"*Próseche!*"

A motorcycle racing between the curb and traffic nearly clipped his elbow when Harry walked too close to the curb. The man ripped ahead, cutting across three lanes to make a turn before disappearing between a row of white-washed buildings. No one so much as honked a horn.

"These people are nuts," he said to no one.

Harry was used to crazy drivers. He lived in Brooklyn. His fellow Americans, though, had nothing on Athens' motorists, drivers who took lane markings and traffic signs as suggestions at best. Harry pushed through the crowded sidewalk to get farther away from the traffic buzzing past his elbow and then barreled on. He kept a tight grip on the messenger bag looped around his neck. He couldn't show up without the bag. No artifacts smuggler ever carried his purchases out in the open.

Exhaust scraped his throat. Sweat trickled down his neck as the Grecian air wrapped him in its smothering embrace. People filled the sidewalk, the crowds giving Harry cover to start and stop, step into shops, and perform other countersurveillance measures as he moved. He looked for familiar faces or people paying him too much attention. Anything that might give away somebody on his tail. No one stood out.

Harry stopped under the awning outside a food market. He studied a warehouse down the street. In thirty minutes, he had an appointment there with the seller to complete their transaction: Harry's purchase of a cultural artifact with questionable provenance. A statue of Zeus, king of the gods in Greek mythology. The statue dated from before the time of Christ and would have been welcomed by museums around the world. Such a piece was enough to draw attention across oceans, to attract an American buyer to Athens, determined to own this one-of-a-kind piece. A buyer such as Harry, who paid in cash and didn't ask questions. Two parties willing to deal without troublesome people like the authorities getting involved.

Or at least that's what Harry wanted the sellers to believe. His demand to see the artifact before completing the sale had gone unchallenged. A week after learning where to find it, Harry was in Athens and headed for the rendezvous. The buyers didn't know his identity, not unusual in deals such as this. They had no reason to be alarmed, to suspect this was anything but a chance to make money. In short, they had no idea what was coming.

His watch showed fifteen minutes until the meet. Harry reached into his bag and touched the cool metal inside. His phone rang. He closed the bag again and checked the screen, did a double-take when he saw the country code for Germany. *Why was she calling?*

Harry answered. "Sara?"

"Good morning, Harry. Hope I didn't wake you."

It was early back home in Brooklyn. "I'm in Greece," Harry said. "Is everything okay?"

"Are you buying antiquities?" she asked.

Something like that. Sara knew his work involved acquiring cultural artifacts, which was partially true. She didn't know the specifics, and Harry intended to keep it that way. "If the price is right," Harry said. He changed the subject. "Is this about my amulet?"

Harry's fingers brushed across the amulet beneath his shirt. An Egyptian artifact that used to be his father's. Harry never went anywhere without it. It was a piece that had given Harry more questions than answers, one of which Sara Hamed had helped solve.

"I certainly don't call for the conversation," she said.

Harry laughed, caught off guard. "I didn't know Egyptologists had a sense of humor."

"Spending your days with three-thousand-year-old mummies isn't funny. People with pulses are better game for that. You're busy. Is later today better?"

"I'm not busy," he said hurriedly. The Zeus statue could wait. "What's going on?"

"It's about your amulet. I learned more about it."

Harry's chest tightened. "Did you find something?"

"Do you remember what I told you about the scarabs?"

"That the same writing on my amulet was on scarab medallions given out by Mark Antony and Cleopatra. It's not the kind of thing you forget."

"True," Sara said. "The reason you had a hard time finding out what's written on your amulet is that no one has seen any of these scarabs for hundreds of years."

He recalled their conversation when Sara had dropped that bomb on him. She had been able to interpret the writing on his amulet. "You only knew it from a drawing, right?"

"Yes. There aren't any around now. Lucky for you I remember things."

When Harry had met Sara in Germany months ago, she'd done two things that he'd never forget. The first was going toe-to-toe with a bunch of drunken skinheads who had targeted Harry just for how he looked. The second, and far more important, was telling him what the Egyptian hieroglyphs on his father's amulet actually *meant*.

"That's the truth," Harry said. "What else did you learn?"

"I need a little more time to sort through all of it. Can we connect later this week? I don't want to give you bad information."

Harry clenched his hand into a fist. "You can't tell me now?"

"I need to be certain of this." He could hear the smile edge into her voice, an alluring look he wouldn't soon forget. "Come on, Harry Fox. A few more days won't hurt anything."

She was right. As badly as he wanted to know, a couple of days wouldn't matter. "I'm holding you to it," he said. "Call me day or night – it doesn't matter."

"Will you still be in Greece?"

Harry's gaze went to the warehouse across from him. "I hope not."

He clicked off, slipped the phone in his pocket, then opened his bag and removed a pistol, quickly hiding it in his waistband. Harry dodged cars as he crossed the street, first circling the entire warehouse before stopping outside a side door where he'd been told to wait. All thoughts of the amulet faded, though, when a buzzer sounded and the door lock clicked open. He reached up and touched the Egyptian piece beneath his shirt. *Watch out for me, Dad.*

Harry pushed the door open. A man's voice sounded, the words English. "Murderer's Row."

Harry breathed a silent sigh of relief. "1927 Yankees."

"World Series champs."

"Four-game sweep over the Pirates." Their agreed-upon code words exchanged, the man stepped forward so the light caught his face. It seemed the frown on his lips deepened. "This way," he finally said, pointing into the darkness behind him.

Harry stepped through the door and squinted. The other man was taller than Harry, not unusual, and he darted behind Harry to shut the door. His white shirt was practically fluorescent in the dim warehouse.

"I can't see anything," Harry said. He turned to keep the man in view. "Where are the lights?"

A switch clicked, and far overhead a series of lights flashed to life, some more brightly than others. "Follow me," the man said.

White shirt didn't mind Harry bringing up the rear as they ascended a concrete ramp that brought them to the main open floor of the vast building. A floor-to-ceiling corrugated metal wall, parallel with the two longer sides, ran down the center of this rectangular building to cut it in half. A separate wall ran perpendicular to the longer one near the back, above which rows of glass windows stretched the length of the interior. Offices, from the look of it, accessed by steel grated steps that switch-backed up in front of them. Instead of taking them, the man veered away, leading Harry to a door in the perpendicular wall.

Light spilled out as he pulled it open. Harry stopped walking.

"How many are here?" he asked. "We agreed on two."

"We are only two," white shirt said. "I see you are alone."

"My associate is outside," Harry lied. "In case I don't come out on time."

The man offered Harry an oily grin. "We are businessmen. There is no trouble here."

His accent sounded Greek. These were local boys. Which jived with what his broker had told him. "Glad to hear it," Harry said. "You don't want to upset my boss."

A tremor cracked white shirt's rictus grin, then vanished. "I see," he said. "Follow me."

One of the overhead lights buzzed as they entered the room. Thin lines of sunlight outlined a door at the rear, which likely opened to the street. An easy escape if needed, for any of them. A single table had been placed in the room's center, though no chairs were around it. An old television hung in the corner. Harry's attention went to a new man, this one standing beside the table. The guy had a mustache, and he looked a lot like the one who had led him inside. A metal case sat on the table.

Mustache man raised his arms as Harry followed white shirt inside. White shirt quickly stepped to one side.

"Welcome," mustache said. "I have—"

White shirt gave it away. His eyes didn't stop moving, never settling on Harry for more than an instant as Harry walked in. Harry's senses went on full alert, everything in clear focus, so much that he didn't miss the flash to his left, away from white shirt and almost completely hidden behind the open door.

Harry ducked, lashing a kick out at white shirt as he twisted. White shirt's knee buckled and he cried out, clutching it as he fell. Harry stepped toward the shadows to where he'd seen the flash of movement, closing the distance and getting inside the third man's reach before he sprang up, his fist headed for the guy's chin.

On the walk over Harry had reached into his pocket and found the ceramic knuckledusters he carried everywhere. He'd slipped them on as he ascended the ramp inside, then kept his hand hidden until now, when his fist smacked dead into the chin of a man stepping out to ambush him. With a sound of teeth cracking, the man toppled, and the gun he'd been holding fell at Harry's feet.

Harry kicked it away and pulled his own pistol out, aiming at mustache man. "Get down on the ground."

Mustache hesitated. White shirt tried to stand, screamed when he put weight on his wounded leg, then collapsed. Harry stepped out, away from the guy who'd ambushed him. Who was now down for the count.

"On the ground," Harry said again. The man hesitated, and Harry played a hunch. He aimed his pistol at white shirt now. "Or I shoot him."

"*Erchomai se!*" White shirt screamed it twice, and the mustached man got down.

Harry moved his pistol back to aim at white shirt. "He's your brother?" Mustache man nodded. "Thought so. Hands behind your back."

The fight had gone out of mustache man, and he kept still as Harry put a knee in his back, pinning him down so he could remove the man's belt and use it to bind his hands together. He dragged the one who'd tried to ambush him into the open, then used that man's belt to tie his hands together. The man was breathing, though he hadn't made a move the whole time. He'd be up soon, missing a few teeth and with one heck of a sore jaw, but he'd live.

"You." Harry waved his gun at white shirt, who still clutched his knee. "Take your belt off and loop it around your hands."

The man spat Greek words from between gritted teeth, none of which Harry understood. "Yeah, your knee hurts. Shouldn't have tried to ambush me. Now do it, or I'll tie your legs together. How will that feel?"

"Dirty raghead."

"What was that?" Harry asked. "I didn't catch it." White shirt didn't repeat himself. "And I'm from New York, you chump. Want to insult me again?"

White shirt took the hint, looping his belt around until Harry warily came over to finish the job. With all three men tied up, he tucked the pistol in his waistband and turned to the mustached man, who glared at Harry from the floor. "If you don't talk, I'm taking everything I can find and shooting all of you." Not quite the truth, but this guy didn't know that.

Mustache swallowed, hard. "We can still make a deal. What do you want?"

"We had an agreement. Your man over there had a gun. He was going to shoot me."

"No," mustache said quickly.

Harry raised an eyebrow. "So it was just a robbery."

Mustache hesitated, then nodded. "We were not trying to kill you."

Harry shook his head. "You guys are idiots. How long do you think you'll be in business if you pull stunts like this? And what would have happened after you robbed me? I'd have come looking for you, that's what. With friends. The kind who don't give second chances." He went to the table and reached for the square metal box. Latches clicked open, the lid flipped up, and Harry pointed inside. "You think this statue is worth robbing me for? Vincent Morello isn't worried about losing half a million dollars. But you'll spend the rest of your life running from him, and that much money won't get you guys far enough."

The guy's eyes went wide. "You work for Morello?"

Harry paused, his hand still over the open metal box. "That's right."

Vincent Morello ran the most successful crime family in New York City. He didn't have many enemies, because his enemies didn't live very long. That this crew of punks knew of Vincent wasn't that surprising. "You trying to pick a fight with the Morellos?"

"No. I'm sorry. We had no idea." Mustache stopped, seemingly puzzled. "You are not Italian."

"You win a prize," Harry said. "What's your name?"

"Luke."

"Okay, Luke. You tried to rob me." He grabbed the pistol and aimed it between Luke's eyes, which snapped shut. Harry counted to three. "I forgive you."

Luke risked opening one eye, and he saw Harry put the pistol away. "You do?" he asked.

"I do, because I need something from you."

Luke couldn't muster a response.

"This statue." Harry tapped the metal box. "How did you get it?" The man sputtered. "If you don't want to talk, I can change my mind about the forgiveness."

"No," Luke said hastily. "I got it a long time ago. Almost twenty years."

Harry fought to keep his face neutral. That lined up with what he'd hoped. "Tell me how you got it."

"I bought it from an American," Luke said. "He needed to move it quickly. No provenance."

"Why quickly?" Harry asked. "It's stolen, but so is everything you buy." Luke didn't argue. "The police must have been after the American."

"I don't know, but these men were arrested a few months before I bought it. One person at the deal was an informant."

"For the U.S. government?" Harry asked.

Luke shook his head. "No. I don't touch anything the American government is after. I heard it was the local police force."

"Local as in New York."

Luke shrugged. "I didn't ask questions."

"Who did you buy this from? Give me names."

The guy Harry had knocked out groaned. Harry waited for him to roll around, realize he was tied up, and start struggling. Then Harry whistled. The pistol was in his hand again. "Hey, you. Don't try anything stupid. Luke and I are talking."

Luke said something in Greek. "What'd you say?" Harry asked.

"I told him to listen," Luke said, then spoke to his friend again in English. "He works for Vincent Morello."

The formerly unconscious man stopped struggling. "But he is not Italian." The man squinted. "Are you?"

Harry sighed. "What is it with you guys? I'm part Pakistani." His pistol disappeared. "Those names, Luke."

"I don't know, I swear. I only saw one of them during the deal. That's it. No names."

Harry grunted. What he said made sense. "What else can you tell me? Anything." He kept his voice level, though it was an effort. *This was his best lead to clearing Fred Fox's name.*

"The only thing I ever heard is those guys disappeared. The one who sold it to me and all his friends."

"How do you know?"

"I tried to find them again. To buy more artifacts." The man's eyes went to the metal box, then back to Harry. "More statues. No one I talked to had heard from them since my last buy. They all disappeared."

"You mean someone killed them," Harry said. Luke agreed. "Why kill them?" Harry studied the flickering light overhead. "The statue's not fake, is it?"

Luke didn't respond. Harry looked down to find the fear had returned. "You were trying to sell me a fake statue? You didn't think I'd notice?"

"The statue is real." The words rushed out of Luke's mouth. "Except it's not here."

"You didn't bring it?" Harry looked to the box. "Then what the hell were you going to sell me?" Harry didn't need an answer. "Nothing. You wanted to steal my money."

Luke's eyes kept going to the metal box and back to Harry. One of the men behind him muttered something that Harry didn't catch. He turned, but nobody was moving. Both white shirt and the guy who had ambushed him were looking at the box too. Harry's gaze followed suit.

"What's in this thing?" Harry pulled the box closer to him. Metal screeched as he opened it, and the flickering bulb overhead cast dim light inside. The box was felt-lined. And heavy. It sure wasn't empty. Harry removed the knuckledusters and touched a rectangular object, smooth around the sides. "You brought a stone *tablet?*"

He lifted it out. Solid stone, about the size of a shoebox lid. "There's writing on it," Harry said. He angled it under the light. "What language is this?" Then he realized the back wasn't smooth like the sides were. He flipped it over to find the underside covered with writing. He couldn't make heads or tails of it, but one thing was clear. This tablet was old. "What is this?"

"A royal Persian decree," Luke said. "Written centuries before Christ."

"Why did you bring it?" he asked. Luke didn't respond. "You

wanted to steal my money, not sell this to me." Harry almost laughed. "Damn, but you guys are stupid. You bring a real artifact when you're trying to rob me."

At least, it looked real. Harry had no idea what it said, though the wedge-shaped letters and repeated slashes resembled Ancient Persian texts he'd seen before. Interesting, certainly valuable, but secondary. Luke and his co-conspirators had given him what he truly needed. Not the Zeus statue, but information on where they'd acquired it, which brought him one step closer to clearing his father's name. The tablet was a bonus.

"I like this," Harry said. "Tell you what. You tried to rob me. I forgave you. Now you're going to sell this to me."

Luke stared at him, dumbfounded. "Sell it to you?" he finally managed.

"Yes. Instead of the statue. Same price, minus a fee for my trouble." Harry pulled out a black felt pouch from his messenger bag. He removed two of the larger diamonds inside and pocketed them, then held out the pouch. "There. Almost half a million in diamonds. Now you didn't lose everything and I got what I needed." He didn't bother explaining what that meant. "We never see each other again. Deal?"

Luke didn't hesitate. "Deal."

"Follow me and I'll shoot you." Harry slipped the Persian tablet into his bag, went back to the door he'd walked through and left, flicking off the lights before he went out. None of the men made any noise as he made his way across the warehouse and outside, checking every direction before he slipped back into the crowds, holding his bag tight. He needed to talk to someone about an artifact deal that had gone bad over twenty years ago. After that, he had a tablet to decipher.

Chapter Two

New York City
The Next Day

Vincent Morello peered at the strange stone on his desk. "What are you going to do with a tablet?"

Barely a day after leaving Athens, Harry was back in Brooklyn explaining to his boss why he'd returned with a tablet instead of a statue.

"I couldn't leave empty-handed," Harry said.

"You negotiated a lower price as well." Vincent picked up the two diamonds Harry had set on the table. "Nicely done."

"My pleasure, Mr. Morello."

"It's Vincent. How many times must I tell you?" The head of Brooklyn's most successful Italian family, and the man to whom all the other heads of Italian mob families in New York turned for guidance was soft-spoken. He often reminded Harry of someone's grandfather. "What does this tablet say?"

"I deciphered most of it," Harry said. "It's Old Persian cuneiform, the language of the Achaemenid empire. This was written sometime during the reign of Artaxerxes II. Or Xerxes, which is how they wrote his name here." Harry pointed to the carved imagery of Xerxes' name. "It reads like a myth, though it's not one I've ever heard. The way it's written is odd, because it clearly references Xerxes II. He was a real king, but his subjects didn't revere him as a god, and this talks about things that aren't real, like a mystical elixir. Down here," he pointed to the bottom, "is the word for *tomb*. Possibly Xerxes' tomb, which is still intact today."

"Is it a story?" Vincent asked. "It does not sound like a child's tale."

"This is like no bedtime story I've ever encountered," Harry said. "The gist of it is that there's this elixir, and the king needs it because he's sick. It talks about a long journey taken to get it, a trip filled with peril. Not physical peril, but spiritual. The king has to make a choice, and if he decides incorrectly, he's doomed."

"Doomed to die?" Vincent asked. "What choice?"

Harry frowned. "It doesn't say. I don't even know if the wrong choice kills him. It says *doom*, not *dead*. In the end the king never makes a decision. It ends with a warning." He traced the final words, which he'd memorized. *"Follow the Greek's knowledge before the king's wealth to reap his reward. The incorrect path leads to doom."*

"A warning, as you said." Vincent tapped the stone. "But how much is it worth?"

"To the right buyer? I'm guessing a million, give or take. Two reasons." Harry pointed to the last lines carved on the tablet's front. "This is Xerxes' signature. I think it's real, and according to my research it would be one of only two in the world."

"That is great news."

"It gets better." Harry carefully flipped the stone over to show the reverse side. "The other signature is here, on the back."

He hadn't told Vincent about the other side. "A different story?" Vincent asked.

"It's the same general idea, but the journey is different. Same warnings about the dangerous *power*, but a new journey getting there. I'm not sure what to make of it."

Vincent pointed a gnarled finger at Harry. "You are Fred Fox's son. You will unravel the truth."

Harry grinned. "I will."

"Enough of the tablet," Vincent said. "What else did you get from these dishonest Greeks?"

Harry settled back in his chair. A shaft of sunlight fell through one of the bulletproof windows in Vincent's office, warming his face. "They bought the statue twenty years ago. That's around the time my father was framed. Right before you met him."

"They held on to this statue for twenty years?"

Harry nodded. "They said the men who sold it to them were anxious to get rid of it. The Greeks suspected the sellers knew authorities were actively searching for the statue and they wanted to unload it quickly."

"Which makes sense," Vincent said. "Your father went to jail as part of a setup. He did not know the men who hired him to authenticate the statue were dealing in stolen artifacts. Nor did he know one was an informant."

"An informant who lied and said my father knew the statue was stolen." Harry chewed his lip. How quickly life could turn on you. "Just one more guy for the cops to bust. Makes the informant's information more valuable."

"A travesty," Vincent said. "Your father was ill-used by those men. Though I would not be here today if it were not for his misfortune."

Fred Fox had been arrested as part of a stolen antiquities sting and sentenced to jail. His cellmate? Vincent Morello, boss of the Morello family. When a rival gang tried to assassinate Vincent in jail, Fred Fox had intervened to save his life. Vincent had beaten his charges shortly thereafter, had his personal attorney get Fred a plea deal for time served, and then hired Fred the day he'd walked out of jail. From that day on, Fred Fox had procured genuine artifacts for Vincent Morello. Their partnership had made them both rich. Harry had been a small child when this had all occurred, but twenty-plus years at his father's side had sparked a fire inside him to be just like his dad.

Then a year ago, Fred Fox had been murdered in Italy. Suddenly Harry wasn't just like Fred. He became Fred. The Morello family antiquities hunter.

"Not only did your father save my life, but he overcame an immeasurable loss. Your mother died while he was in custody."

Harry had only vague memories of her. Dani Fox, the daughter of an Englishman and his Pakistani wife, had only been in Harry's life for a few years. It was mostly her hair he recalled, the thick, dark hair that had tickled his face when she hugged him. But her image stared him in the face every time he looked in a mirror. He took after Dani far more than Fred on the outside. On the inside, though, he was Fred through and through.

"I don't remember much about that time," Harry said. "One day she was there; the next, she was gone, and I was with relatives until my dad came to get me. Then I met you." He still recalled the first time he'd met Vincent Morello. At the time he couldn't have imagined what it would mean in his life. Now, he was one of the few men Vincent Morello trusted. A made man in the Morello crew, with all the protections it afforded.

"Fred rarely spoke of that time," Vincent said. "I cannot imagine the pain of losing a wife and a career at the same time."

Fred Fox's career in academia had ended with the arrest. It didn't matter that he was eventually found innocent. Fred had told him once no university would even look at his resume, Ph.D. or not. Taking Vincent's job offer had been an easy choice. How else could the newly widowed man have provided for his son and also do what he loved?

"He told me you saved each other," Harry said. "He loved chasing down history."

"Perhaps." Vincent looked out the window. "Your father also required our protection. He received threats against his life in jail. I suspect the informant who framed him was the source. I was in a place to offer that protection for you both. The authorities trusted this informant. If Fred had convinced them the informant was lying, it would have gone poorly for him."

"So he destroyed my father's life," Harry said.

"Without the confidential police files, we will never know." Vincent steepled his fingers. "I tried to get the name myself. It is buried. But as you said, Fred and I saved each other, so perhaps fate intervened in a terrible way to change all our lives. You are trying to clear Fred's name another way, the only way left to us."

"The statue of Zeus is my best lead," Harry said. "If I follow that back to the source, I'll find the informant."

"Unfortunately, the Greeks' information is too vague." Vincent looked back at Harry. "I will see what I can find with my contacts in the police department. Even twenty years later, an antiquities sting that large will be remembered."

"The sellers involved are all dead," Harry said. "The Greeks believe someone killed them."

"Which makes the circumstances even more memorable," Vincent said. "I will learn who these men were, and then we will know who would want them dead."

"They said the statue of Zeus was *lost* during the bust. Could be one of the sellers escaped, then immediately sold it to the Greeks. Before whoever hired my father found them." Fred hadn't known the names of the men he was working for, the ones who had hired him to authenticate the statue. They were middlemen, cutouts for an unidentified buyer.

"I suspect the people who hired Fred to authenticate this statue before they purchased it did not appreciate what the sellers did. They found them, learned it had been sold, and finished their business." Vincent shrugged. "That is what I would have done."

Vincent's voice was flat, emotionless. Thank goodness he was on Harry's side. "Thank you for offering to ask your contacts," Harry said. "I'm sure it will take time." He looked down at the tablet. When he looked up, Vincent was watching him.

"It will," Vincent said. "Until then, what will you do?" Vincent indicated the tablet. "This is an interesting tale."

It was like he'd read Harry's mind. "It is. I'd like to dig into the story." He sat forward on the edge of his chair. "I know a scholar in the city who can tell me not just what this says, but what it *means*. My gut's telling me there's more to this than I'm seeing."

"By all means, go. Learn what you can and do what you do best." Vincent pointed to the tablet. "Uncover the past."

Harry was halfway out of his chair before he remembered. "What about the Canas? They could still try and cause trouble. Are you sure you don't want me to stay close?"

Altin Cana was an Albanian gangster in Brooklyn whose turf pushed up against the Morellos'. Word was the Cana family wanted to expand their territory into Vincent Morello's turf. No other gangs would be so dumb as to mess with Vincent, but Altin Cana was different. Ruthless in a way that put even hardened mobsters on edge.

Vincent waved a hand as though shooing a fly away. "Do not worry about Altin Cana. His men talk. Let them. They are small, and we are strong. See what truth is behind this tale of Xerxes. You have my full support."

Harry thanked Vincent before taking the tablet and heading outside. The guard sitting by the front door stood when Harry strode past. Mack was one of the few guys in the Morello crew who'd accepted him from the start. Good thing for Harry, too, because Mack was built like the trucks bearing his name.

"Harry, you beautiful man. Headed out again? I thought you made enough money last month."

Harry laughed, bracing himself as Mack bestowed one of his crushing bear hugs. Harry's feet left the ground, forcing him to hold on until he landed. "Got another artifact to look into now," he said, indicating the bag.

"That was a lotta diamonds I heard about," Mack said. "I shoulda paid attention in school. None of this door guard crap for Harry Fox, no sir. That's for chumps like Mack."

Mack was one of Vincent's most trusted soldiers. Guarding his home was an honor, and they both knew it. Harry reminded Mack of this.

"Stop it, Aladdin. Gonna make me blush." Mack winked, then pretended to primp Harry's black hair, which he'd let grow out a tad. "Just messin'. Now, if I had your looks, the girls would be knockin' this door down."

"I'll put in a good word for you," Harry said, then left before Mack decided to give him another bone-rattling embrace.

"*Arrivederci.*"

Bracingly brisk air washed over Harry's face when he walked outside. He turned down the sidewalk to pass beneath leaves just on the verge of changing with the fall season. Life with the Morello crew hadn't been easy when he'd started tailing after Fred Fox, learning a role he had never expected to inherit so soon. Harry's Pakistani ancestry didn't buy him any points with the close-knit Morellos, and even though he spoke their language and respected their customs, it wasn't until this past year, when Vincent's son Joey had truly accepted Harry, that things got easier. Guys like Mack had been the outliers. For years, Harry's friends in this crew had been few. Now Joey had his back, along with the entire crew.

Harry's thoughts turned to what secrets might lie hidden in this tablet. His instincts hadn't steered him wrong yet. There was more to this than an odd tale about an ancient elixir. Harry went off to do his thing – unlock the truth behind a mystery from the past.

Chapter Three

The Manhattan Antiquities Trafficking Unit's offices had three interrogation rooms, all in the same hallway with an old-fashioned holding cell, complete with steel bars. One of the interrogation rooms was currently occupied by a man handcuffed to a metal ring on the desk. Steel bolts secured the desk to the floor. Few people knew the district attorney's office had a dedicated antiquities trafficking team. For the man invited in today, this was the start of a short journey with one destination. Another jail cell, and a lengthy stay.

Special Agent Nora Doyle leaned against the wall outside the interview room, flipping through a file. Five years on the team and it never got old, catching an artifacts trafficker in the act. Early this morning the operation she had handled every step of the way had culminated in the arrest of the man named Ted Hawley. Over the course of several months, she had convinced Ted she was a potential buyer for a sculpture, a likeness of Roman Emperor Marcus Aurelius carved during his lifetime. The sculpture was an actual image of the man, three feet tall and two hundred pounds of marble. It had been stolen from an Algerian museum decades ago. Ted had walked right into her trap, even doing her the courtesy of bringing the statue to their arranged exchange. Nora had confirmed its authenticity, her team swooped in, and another stolen artifact was safe again.

Nora cleared her throat, opened the interrogation room door and walked in.

"Ted Hawley." Nora pulled out a chair and sat across from him. She placed the file in front of her. "You are not having a good day, Ted." He stared at the table, shoulders drooped, chin down. "Guess what I just discovered? You're on probation. For two more weeks." She shook her head. "You almost made it. So close. Now you're not only looking at ten years for artifacts trafficking, but you'll also be finishing the second half of your sentence for those theft charges now. You've already been inside for five. Looking forward to fifteen more?"

Ted didn't move. Nora let him stew for a moment. She didn't need another agent to be the good cop. She planned to convince Ted to play ball all on her own. "Unless you talk to me. If that happens, maybe I recommend we go easy on you, make the sentences concurrent. That's only ten years now. And who knows? If you cooperate fully, there could be a deal in it for you."

Ted looked up for the first time. Bloodshot eyes darted around the room, over the fluorescent overhead lights, the one-way mirror to their side, the untouched soda can in front of him, all before settling on her. Shallow breaths came quickly. "What are you saying?"

Nora tapped her pen on the file folder. "I have enough in here to bury you, Ted. How deep depends on what you say. Feel like talking?" Ted jerked his head up and down. "I thought so," Nora said. "First, tell me how you got the statue."

Ted blinked. His mouth opened and closed, but nothing came out. "I bought it. From a French guy. I never got his name."

"You have to do better than that." Nora put her pen down. "Who was he? Names, Ted."

Ted tried to stand, the chains clanging as they held him down. "You know how it is. No names. I swear, I never got one. He was French, that's all I know." His words came in a torrent. "Wait. I have a number. His phone number." Ted pointed at her file. "That will help. You can use it, track him down. You gotta have something in there about this guy."

She almost felt bad for him. Almost. "This file? It's all about you, Ted. And the prosecutor will love the easy conviction I'm taking to him right now, unless you give me something real. A phone number? Get real. That's from a burner phone that's in a garbage dump by now. It's useless."

Ted sputtered a few times. He really had nothing.

"That's too bad, Ted." She picked up the folder and stood.

His faced turned red and his eyes raced around the room. "Wait." Ted was shouting when he jumped up, only to be held fast again. A vein bulged on his neck. "I can give you something else. Something better. A guy, right here in New York."

Nora stopped halfway to the door. "I want the Frenchman who sold you this statue."

"This is bigger. A Persian tablet. Five thousand years old."

Nora frowned. "I'm listening."

Ted lowered his voice. "It happened in Athens. A few days ago."

"My jurisdiction doesn't extend to Greece."

Ted leaned closer. "A deal to sell a Greek statue. It hadn't been on the market for ages."

"What statue?" Nora asked. She needed details. Today she had backed Ted into a corner. Chances were he was trying to bluff his way out.

"Zeus," Ted said. "It was on the market decades ago, but it vanished. Then a couple weeks past, word gets around a big buyer wants this Zeus statue."

"How did you know someone wanted this specific statue?"

Ted shrugged. "From a couple of places. People talk."

She didn't argue as she scribbled notes. "Why was the statue off the market for so long?"

"A guess? Too hot, and because once people heard a buyer was out there, the seller popped up too fast. If a collector had it all these years, the whole thing would have taken longer to set up."

Which made sense and gave credence to Ted's theory. Nora could check for old cases involving a statue of Zeus. "The seller learns someone is asking for this statue; they decide it's been long enough for the authorities to have lost interest and decide to sell." Ted nodded. "I want to believe it," Nora said. "Except you told me this was about a Persian tablet."

"I'm getting there. The deal for the statue went bad. The sellers had another item with them, and the buyer saw it, decided he wanted that too. The sellers said no, so this buyer stuck them up and stole the tablet."

"What about the Zeus statue?" Nora asked.

"Beats me," Ted said. "Didn't hear about that part. All I know is this buyer stole the Persian tablet. Five thousand years old."

Nora stopped writing. "You can't even tell me if this statue exists, because for all you know it could still be with the buyers." She pushed back from the table. "This is garbage, Ted. Enjoy prison."

Ted's chains rattled once more as he jumped and shouted, "Wait, I'm not done." Only when Nora sat back down did he continue. "The statue doesn't matter. The tablet does. It's big, I'm telling you."

Nora's pen tapped again. A tablet that old *did* get her attention. But none of it mattered if she couldn't verify Ted's story. "Why?"

"It belonged to King Xerxes. It's the only one in the world, and that guy has it." He paused. "There were three sellers in Greece. Two days after this buyer took the tablet, all three vanished. Dead or in hiding."

Nora perked up. "They were selling the tablet for someone else. So, whoever took it cost the real owner money, and he was angry."

"Three disappeared guys angry," Ted said.

"The tablet must be valuable."

Ted offered a desperate smile. "That good enough for you?"

"How does this tie to us in New York?"

"The buyer who took it was from New York. He's connected with the Morellos. That's why the Greek sellers disappeared. Whoever the real owner was isn't trying to mess with Vincent Morello."

Gears turned in Nora's head. "So instead of messing with Vincent, the owner takes it out on the middlemen who lost it." Her pen scratched furiously. Ted had surprised her. "This guy should be in the city."

"You find Vincent Morello's guy, you find the tablet." A dash of color returned to Ted's face. "Do we have a deal?"

Nora pressed her lips together, breathing through her nose. "Right now? No." His face dropped. "If I can verify what you're saying and find this tablet? Maybe." Hope returned. "You're spending the next few days in jail either way. You'll hear from me if this lead pans out."

"What if it doesn't?"

Nora stood and walked to the door. "Then I hope you have a good attorney."

Only after she was inside her own office did Nora's face come alight. "This could be *huge*," she whispered to herself. There were several kings named Xerxes in Persia's history. One of them had defeated Sparta's King Leonidas and his famed three hundred warriors. Any artifact directly tied to the Persian leaders would be enormously valuable today, and recovering it would be a public relations boon for the anti-trafficking unit. They would be first in line when it came time to allocate budget money next year.

A rectangle of sunlight fell through a window and made Nora squint as she unlocked her desk drawer, sliding it open to reveal several generic cell phones. Burner phones, for when she needed to speak with people who didn't like cops. She picked one, powered it on and dialed a number. The man she needed to speak with was finicky about how she contacted him. Unsurprising, given what would happen if his boss found out he occasionally chatted with a law enforcement officer.

Five rings, then the man answered. "Who is this?"

"It's your friend from the city." The man lived in Brooklyn. To him, Manhattan was the city. It wasn't a flattering term.

A pause. "I'll call you back."

The line went dead. Nora reviewed her notes, tamping down on the voice in her head that always sounded when she used this source. Stefan Rudovic was a crook, plain and simple. An underboss in Altin Cana's Albanian crime family. Stefan was a gangster, one with whom she'd struck an alliance. He provided information. A year ago, Nora had let him off on a questionable charge, one she'd had little chance of convicting him on anyway. Better to gain a source of street-level intelligence rather than nothing at all. And at the end of the day, he was a small fish. Nora had her eyes on bigger prizes.

Her phone rang two minutes later. "Can you talk?" she asked.

"I'm good," Stefan said. "What's this about?"

Nora dove right in. "I need a name. Does the Morello family have a man who deals with antiquities? A guy who would go to Greece to buy or sell artifacts."

What sounded like a low growl came through the phone. "You're talking about Harry Fox. If someone is in Greece doing Vincent's business, it's Harry."

"You know him?"

"Not really," Stefan said. "Harry's old man used to do the same thing for Vincent. When he died a year or so ago in Italy, Harry began handling that part of the Morello business."

"Any idea if he's in the city now?"

"I don't keep tabs on the guy."

"I've heard that Harry Fox was in Greece to buy a statue of Zeus. He turned on the buyers, but didn't steal the statue. Instead, he took a Persian tablet that may be tied to King Xerxes."

Nora looked out her window at wispy clouds floating across the sky. They moved a good distance before Stefan responded. "I haven't heard anything. Not yet, at least."

He stopped talking. The silence grew tiresome. Nora sighed. "Would you ask around, see what you can find out? Sounds like

Harry Fox moves in your circles. People talk. If this happened, someone knows about it." She bit her lip. Stefan didn't need to know this, but her gut said Ted Hawley had told her the truth. "There were three sellers in Greece. Now all three are missing."

Stefan whistled. "You don't say. Either dead or hiding. Must have been a pricey tablet. I'll see what I can find. Remember this the next time I need your help."

Nora rubbed her forehead. Maybe she'd gone too far with Stefan, letting him slide on one or two occasions. *His information is always solid.* "I'll remember." The voice in her head came back, louder this time. She buried it.

"I'll be in touch," Stefan said, then clicked off.

Nora set the phone on her desk. Her stomach twisted into a small knot, the same one that always materialized when she cut a deal with people like Stefan. Sure, he was lower level, not involved in anything big. And yes, he gave her solid intelligence on black-market antiquities dealings in the city. Stefan had no qualms about selling out rival crooks. She kneaded her eyebrows. Did he benefit from their arrests? It could be Stefan was using her to clear out the competition, but Nora couldn't worry about that. She worked to get criminals off the street, to arrest the loss of humanity's record due to theft, greed and selfishness. If it meant getting her hands dirty and working with crooks along the way, so be it. Her world wasn't black and white.

Fortunately, her NYPD colleagues didn't have the same issues. To them, you break the law, you're a bad guy, and they kept records of people like that. If this Harry Fox worked for Vincent Morello, then the Organized Crime Control Bureau would know him. She picked up her desk phone and called a friend who worked there. First, learn more about Harry Fox. Then, pay him a visit.

Chapter Four

Brooklyn, New York

Stefan Rudovic slipped a coat over his shoulders and headed outside, past a chair inside the front door where a man was posted day and night. The first line of defense at the Cana family headquarters. Not that anyone in their right mind would walk through Altin Cana's front door looking for trouble. Do that and you'd never get out alive. The problem was, some of the people the Cana family dealt with couldn't find their right mind with a map and a head start.

A cool breeze gently flitted down his collar as Stefan walked several blocks, cutting across the street to a busy park where he hid in plain sight among the mothers and children. He leaned against a tree, turning his face to catch the sun's pleasant rays, looking like he had plenty of time to do nothing. In truth, he scanned his surroundings for anything out of the ordinary, a face he recognized, a person who looked, well, like him. Out of place. Only after he felt certain no one had trailed him there did he make the call.

A man answered. The voice of a man who knew things. Like where to find people who didn't want to be found. "Yeah?"

"I need to find three men," Stefan said. "Greeks. They're hiding from someone."

"What makes you think I can find them?"

"You know everyone," Stefan said. "I only want to talk; that's it. Nothing in person." Stefan gave a rundown of what he knew, adding details Nora hadn't provided based on his knowledge of the artifacts trafficking world. "There's five grand in it for you when they call me," he finished.

"Ten."

"Seven, and you're lucky I'm offering that."

The man grunted. "Keep your phone on. A man named Luke will be in touch."

Stefan turned his ringer on full blast and pocketed the phone. He walked across the street and grabbed a coffee, then came back and settled on a bench. Only a few sips remained when his phone blared. "Hello?" he said, setting the cup down.

"You trying to set me up?" A half-crazed, heavily accented voice filled Stefan's ear. "I swear, you come for me, I'll break every bone in your Albanian body, you hear?"

"Easy." Stefan kept his voice low. "I just want to talk. I hear you've had a rough week."

"That damned Morello man. What do you expect? We're not protected, like you. Must be nice to have Altin Cana watching your back."

Stefan didn't disagree. "The buyer wanted a statue of Zeus, but ended up taking a Persian tablet. What happened?"

"Why do you want to know?"

"All you need to know is I'm interested, and maybe I can help you get out of this. Whoever owned the statue can't be happy with you. If he was, you wouldn't have fallen off the map." Two children barreled past him, shrieking as they ran. "Luke, I'm your friend in this."

Stefan's use of his name caught Luke off guard. "How do you – it doesn't matter." Luke muttered something in Greek Stefan didn't understand. "You want to help? Fine, I'm not turning you away, and I know there's a cost. But you don't know everything, big shot. What's your price?"

"We have a mutual enemy. If helping you hurts the Morellos, I'm interested."

"First, we're not hiding. *We* owned the tablet, not anyone else."

Stefan almost laughed. "Smart move. You put the rumor about another owner out there. Now no one is surprised you're off the map. Easier for you to move around."

"We aren't helpless," Luke said. "We had no idea the buyer was a Morello man. I wouldn't have tried what I did."

"You tried to steal from him?" Darkness crossed Stefan's thoughts. People like Luke didn't deserve sympathy. "You had it coming, then."

"From what I hear, you are not one to pass judgment."

Stefan let that pass. "You want to get back at Harry Fox? The guy who stole from you. I can help you do it."

"How?"

"Tell me about the tablet."

Luke grumbled before responding. "I've never seen another one like it. There's a story carved on one side, and a second story on the other. No one who's seen it can say what it truly means."

"Tell me the stories."

Luke offered a tale of elixirs possibly conjured by Greek physicians, along with a murky story of following two paths, one of which led to doom. Fact or legend, it grabbed Stefan's ear.

Stefan digested it for a moment. "That's tough to follow. Are you sure that's the story?"

"More than one expert agreed," Luke said. "It's hard to tell if they are myth or parable."

"There's no end point, no conclusion?"

"It only says the person on this trail is doomed if he makes the wrong choice, and warns about a *deceptive healing power*. The back side is nearly identical. The same ending. A warning."

"Why haven't we ever heard of this?" Stefan asked, mostly to himself. "Plenty of stories have survived over time. If Xerxes II thought enough of this story to inscribe his name on the tablet, we would know about it."

"You want my guess? Like you said, it's hard to follow. I'm not surprised people forgot about it over time."

Stefan didn't argue. No reason to make Luke think this was more important than he already did. "Either way, it's valuable. I might be able to get it back for you."

"The Morellos look bad if you get it back," Luke said. "What else will it cost me?"

"Thirty percent of what you sell it for. And before you try to negotiate, that's my only offer. Either take seventy percent or get it back on your own."

Luke didn't argue. "Deal. How are you going to get it?"

"Word is Harry Fox is back in New York. It won't be hard to find him." He barreled ahead, not giving Luke time to think. "Where are you now? If I get it back soon, we need to meet for the handoff. I'll come to you."

Silence. A long wait later, Luke gave in. "Toronto. We'll be here for a few more weeks. Is that long enough?"

"Should be," Stefan said. "Keep this phone. I'll be in touch. Keep your head down until then. No telling who's listening to these calls."

He clicked off, pulled a different phone out of his pocket and dialed Nora Doyle. She answered at once.

"This is Doyle."

"It's your friend from Brooklyn. Write this number down." Stefan rattled off Luke's number. "The three missing men are hiding in Toronto. Call your Canadian friends and tell them to use that number to track them down."

"What about the tablet?" Nora asked.

"I'm working on that. Are three international artifacts traffickers not enough?"

"Let me know when you find out more about the tablet. And don't get any ideas about keeping it."

"The last thing I want is an artifact your team is after."

He hung up and pocketed the phone. Moving between running children and harried parents, Stefan retraced his steps to Cana headquarters, past the security man sitting inside and through the sprawling structure to Altin's office door. The big man looked up and waved at him to come in.

"Sit," Altin said. "What brings you?"

"Mr. Cana, I have a proposal. I have an opportunity to bloody Vincent Morello's reputation, and to make you money."

Altin raised a bushy eyebrow. His grizzled features didn't have to move much to make a loud statement. "I am listening."

"Harry Fox recently acquired an Ancient Persian tablet. Two stories are written on it, and I suspect the stories are more than just words." A bolt of energy arced through his body. Stefan folded his hands. *Focus.* "I believe it can lead us to something lost for thousands of years."

"Which is?"

Stefan was undeterred. "Even if I'm wrong, the tablet is valuable. If I get it from the Morellos, we can sell it for half a million dollars to the right buyer." A total guess, but Altin didn't know that.

"How did you learn of it?" Altin asked.

"Harry Fox obtained the tablet in Greece. I know someone close to the Greek sellers." Stefan had no desire to tell Altin Cana he had a quasi-relationship with an anti-trafficking agent. "I pay him to keep me aware of artifact movements."

"How certain are you that the story is real?"

"It could be nothing more than a story," Stefan admitted. "If so, we still have the tablet to sell."

"And the Morellos get a bloody nose." Altin shifted in his chair, his elbows finding the desk. "This is a big city, Stefan. But it is not big enough for a man like me to live beside a man like Vincent Morello. So, what am I to do?"

Altin lifted his hand, waving at the walls. "Sit in this house and let Vincent run the city." Altin shook his head. "No. Vincent is the reason I cannot expand. He sits on the other side of Brooklyn, controlling much of the city. How am I to grow my business? It is time for him to move aside. This will serve as the opening move to push the Morellos aside and show this city Altin Cana is the stronger man." He aimed a finger at Stefan. "What do you need from me?"

"Nothing yet," Stefan said. "First, the tablet. Then travel funds may be required."

"Move quickly, Stefan. Our attack on the Morellos begins with you."

Chapter Five

Manhattan

Nora Doyle's desk phone rang. A Toronto number. "Nora Doyle speaking." She listened for a moment. "You found all three? They had *what* on them? That's fantastic. No, please, prosecute them on that charge. It's all yours, Captain. I'm happy to be of service."

She hung up, then fell back into her chair, an invisible weight only she could feel vanishing. *They caught the Greeks.*

The police captain who had just called, told her about the bust. It had all gone down as planned, with Toronto police pinpointing the Greeks' location based on the cell phone number Nora had provided. Best of all, the three Greeks had been arrested while in possession of a dozen stolen Italian sculptures dating to the Renaissance. Nora was happy to let the Toronto authorities press charges against the trio. Less paperwork for her, and the Greeks faced serious jail time. She didn't need the credit.

What mattered was that her gamble of trusting Stefan Rudovic had paid off. A gamble Nora had first made several years ago when she'd had evidence to nail Stefan for trafficking in stolen goods. Stefan had tried to sell a collection of Viking coins to an undercover agent, and when Nora had brought him in and made it clear he faced federal charges, Stefan had offered to talk. Then, now, and in the future. He'd offered to provide her with information on what was happening in his world, and in return, Nora had dropped the charges.

So far, her bet had paid off in small doses, a name here or a small-time crook there. Today was different. Her commanding officer would be sure to let the district attorney know about this, the kind of international cooperation that generated headlines.

Toronto got this bust. The D.A. got his headlines. And yesterday Stefan had given Nora a name – Harry Fox. It didn't take long for her friends in the Organized Crime Control Bureau to find his address. Nora fired off a quick email to her superior informing him of the good news, though an idea buzzed in the back of her head all the while. Nora bit her lip. The idea sounded good now. Would it work? A bird landed on her windowsill and stared at her through the thick glass. *Why not?*

She grabbed her jacket and headed out. She already had one win for the day. Time for another.

Less than an hour later she parked outside Harry Fox's apartment building. On the way over she had run through different approaches in her head, testing and discarding them in short order. None sounded any better than the others, mainly because this was unlike any past recruitment. Nora had nothing to pressure Harry on. The Greeks were already going to jail, and even if he didn't know that, Nora had only Stefan Rudovic's word that Harry Fox was involved. Which was why she had come here. She didn't trust Stefan. She needed another source in this antiquities racket, and Harry Fox was the best option.

She turned off the car. Harry Fox's driver's license photo stared at her, clipped to the front of a painfully thin file. She took a breath and looked up at his building.

Harry Fox walked out the front door.

"Gotcha." Nora checked that her service weapon was holstered before jumping out, tucking her badge away as she crossed the street and hurried to catch up with him as he stood at a red light. As Harry waited for the light to change, Nora was able to step directly behind him. He was shorter than she expected. The morning sunlight glinted off a sturdy chain peeking above the back of his collar. She stepped beside him, invading his personal space even by New York standards, and he glanced over to find her looking directly into his eyes. She blinked. The light turned, and Harry walked away.

"Harry Fox."

He jerked, a puppet whose strings had been pulled.

"I just want to talk." She stayed a step away, directly alongside him. "That's all."

"You got the wrong guy." Harry put his head down and kept moving.

Nora hurried to catch up. "I know you're Harry Fox."

His eyes lingered on hers for an instant. "Never heard of him." He kept walking.

"I need your help." Nora threw an edge into her voice. "Please."

He accelerated, gained the far sidewalk and turned down a more residential street, leaving her to chase him until, as suddenly as he'd started, Harry stopped. He didn't turn around. "Who are you?"

"My name's Nora."

"Why are you following me?"

"I need your help."

"You said that." Now he turned, giving her a full view of his face. In person his skin was lighter than in the picture. He had let his hair grow, the back part curling up above the chain necklace. "What makes you think I would help you? And before you answer, remember. I have lots of friends in this neighborhood." He looked to the bodega beside them. "Senora Nunez runs that place. I've known her forever. You try anything funny, people won't like it."

Nora turned her head to see a gray-haired woman through the window. Harry waved, shouted a greeting. The woman waved back.

"I'm not here to cause you trouble," Nora said.

"Then tell me what you want."

"A man gave me your name."

"Who?"

She ignored his question. "I have an interest in antiquities."

Wrong question. "I don't," he said, and turned around.

"Altin Cana." She blurted out the name. "Does that name mean anything to you?" He whipped around. "I see it does," she said. "I need your help in dealing with his crew."

Harry didn't respond at first, and she waited him out.

"Are you in trouble?" he finally asked.

The gangster has a heart. Nora dropped her eyes. "I'm not sure."

Harry took her arm and pulled Nora up against the bodega wall. He kept his back to it. "Say I decide to help you. First, tell me what's going on. From what I hear, Altin Cana is dangerous."

"He is," Nora said. "The Cana family is involved with artifacts trafficking." No reaction from Harry. "I am as well, and I made a mistake. My work brought me into contact with them. Now I know that was a bad idea." She looked around, letting her eyes flit everywhere as her foot tapped the sidewalk, over and over. "I can't trust them anymore."

Harry's face darkened. "There's no way anyone who knows Altin Cana would tell you to contact me."

"They didn't say that," she said quickly. "Not exactly."

Harry stepped to her in an instant, getting on top of her before she could move. His innocent face turned hard in that moment. "You're lying. Last chance. Tell me what's going on or I assume you're here to cause trouble. Trust me, it won't go well for you."

Nora's back hit the wall and her blood ran hot. "Step back," she barked. Harry's eyes widened. "Now. Back up." He did, giving her space. She fought the urge to go for her gun. "The Canas are gangsters, who from what I hear have it out for your boss, Vincent Morello. When they lock horns, I guarantee you one thing: nobody wins."

Harry's mask of anger wavered. "Who are you?"

"My name is Nora. If Altin Cana starts a war and Vincent Morello loses, you're on your own. Even if Vincent wins, the Morello family ends up weaker. Who do you think is going to come knocking on his door?"

Harry's mask came back. "You. You're a cop."

"I'm an agent with the Manhattan district attorney's anti-trafficking unit, and you're going to want me as your friend sooner or later. This is your chance." Now Harry seemed uncertain. He wasn't backing off, hadn't moved. "You know what I'm saying is true. You'll need a friend, and for a guy like you there won't be anybody better than me. You want me in your corner? Answer a few questions. I'm not here to arrest you. I want information. That's it."

Harry turned to lean against the wall, his shoulder close to hers. "Impressive, you predicting my future." He smirked. "Let's say you're right: two men I may or may not know get into a disagreement, and everyone loses. You say if I talk to you my problems will be solved."

"I can't solve all your problems. I *can* make a few of them go away. If you talk to me."

Harry shrugged. "What do you want to know?"

The last five minutes had given her plenty of signals. Harry wasn't on the hook, not yet. She needed better bait. "Right now, nothing. Later? I'll have questions. You help me with answers, and I help you with any problems."

Harry shifted his weight. "A get out of jail free card?"

"Depends on what you did," she said. "I hear you deal in artifacts. Statues, sculptures, tablets." He flinched. Stefan *was* telling the truth. "You get into trouble involving that type of thing, call me. I have friends with city, state and federal agencies. If they find out you're a C.I. for me, they'll go easy on you."

"A confidential informant. I sell people out, and you save my skin. *If* I ever find myself in trouble. Who's to say you won't be the one causing it?"

"I never turn on my sources," Nora said. "Never."

Harry scratched his chin, watching traffic pass as Nora forced herself to keep still. Eventually he turned to face her, hands in his pockets as he leaned in close. She fought the urge to back away.

"Listen, Nora. I don't know anyone named Altin Cana. I don't know a Vincent Morello. I don't do anything with artifacts. Leave me alone."

He turned and walked away. Nora didn't follow when he rounded the corner and vanished. *Damn.* She kicked the wall softly. He'd almost been there. She could feel it, could sense how close he was. Harry Fox didn't seem like the kind of smuggler she usually dealt with. No, he was different, more *normal*, and she almost had him. Except almost meant nothing. Now she had burned Stefan Rudovic's tip, outed herself to Harry Fox, and didn't have a new informant or the tablet. But all was not lost. Harry Fox's reaction had given him away. He knew about the tablet. All she had to do was stay on him.

Nora ran back to the car and gunned it for her office, blue light flashing all the way. At her desk, she first put in a request to tap Harry Fox's cell phone, including a record of all activity. It normally took a few days to get anything back, so she picked up her phone and spent all of five minutes getting the Greek smuggling leader on the phone. His name was Luke. Unsurprisingly, he was anxious to talk.

"I don't know who you are, lady, but if you said we can get a deal, I'm in. What can you do for me?" Luke was almost breathless. "What do you need? Anything. Ask."

"I said *maybe* you can get a deal." Nora dangled the bait. "If you answer my questions, and if what you tell me pans out."

"I'm listening," Luke said.

"Does the name Harry Fox mean anything to you?"

Luke took a long time to respond.

"You're facing felony charges in a foreign country," Nora reminded him. "I'm with the Manhattan D.A.'s office in New York. The guys who have you are friends of mine. They listen to me. And they owe me."

Luke didn't ask *why* they owed her. "Yeah, I know Harry Fox."

"When's the last time you saw him?"

"Couple days ago."

"Do better than that, Luke."

"He came to Athens for a business deal."

"Did it involve a statue of Zeus?"

"That's right," Luke said. "Only things didn't go as planned."

"He double-crossed you." Even as she said it, the idea didn't sit. Nora's gut said Harry wasn't like that. It didn't often fail her.

"Listen, Agent Doyle. I'm shooting straight with you. We tried to pull one over on Harry. Only I didn't know who he was."

Always trust your instincts, girl. "You didn't know he worked for Vincent Morello."

"If I did, I wouldn't have done it."

"Tried to steal his money and keep the Zeus statue."

"You got it. Only this guy is some kind of Arab prizefighter and drops all three of us. He gets us all down, then realizes there's no Zeus statue. I didn't bring it."

Nora shook her head. "How did the tablet come into play?"

"I carried it in its case, told Harry the Zeus statue was inside. He opened the case and saw it." Luke laughed, catching Nora off guard. "And get this. Once he finds out what it is, the guy actually *pays* me for it. Uses the money he brought to buy the statue and gets the tablet instead." Luke grumbled. "Didn't pay half of what it was worth."

"Except he could have simply taken it," Nora said. She looked out the window, now speaking half to herself. "What kind of man does that?"

"A guy with a thing for old stories," Luke said. "You should have seen his face when I told him about the stories on it. Like it was the best thing he ever heard."

"Hold on. *Stories*, as in plural. What do you mean?"

Luke offered the tale of two similar stories, one on the front, the other on the tablet's back. Both ran through similar events, and both referenced being *doomed* if a wrong decision was made on the trail. To her ear, it sounded like a myth.

"I could see Harry Fox wanted it," Luke said. "Didn't expect him to pay for it. If that's what you're after, you better find him. Can't imagine he let it go."

The story was more convoluted than she'd realized. Harry Fox hadn't turned out to be a typical trafficker. He had enough integrity, if you could call it that, to pay for the tablet even though the seller had tried to rob him. What that said about him, Nora still wasn't sure. More important, what made Harry so interested in the tablet? It was valuable, yes. A window into one of Persia's forgotten myths, perhaps. But why did it grab Harry?

Luke had started talking again.

"Stop," Nora said. "Say that again."

"I said you're the second person to call me about this today," Luke said. "My attorney got a call from a guy hell-bent on talking to me. He offered money for our defense. Which I am gonna need."

"Who was it?" Nora asked. "And what did he want to know?"

Luke drew in a slow breath. "Remind me, do we have a deal? Sounds like you want to know about this guy too. I bet my lawyer would say to keep quiet right now."

Steel threaded her response. "If you don't answer, you're not getting any deal. Ever. I'll make sure of it."

"Jeez, lady. I have no idea who the guy was. That's the truth. Said he was an *interested party* willing to pay if I told him what I just told you."

"The stories on the tablet."

"You got it," Luke said. "Told him the same thing you heard. That's it. Now, what about that deal?"

"Tell your attorney to call me," she said before hanging up and falling back into her chair. A long time ago Nora's father had given her advice she'd never forgotten. In his role as a prosecutor with the city, her father had said he'd learned that very few things are certain.

One of those few certainties was that coincidences didn't exist.

Luke had received another call about the tablet today. It was possible someone in the artifact underworld had heard about what happened in Greece. Probable, in fact. Except who both cared enough about the tablet and had the contacts to get Luke's attorney on the phone? The *interested party* didn't align with her experience. In situations where law enforcement showed up, smugglers and dealers vanished. Never had she heard of any of them contacting their jailed colleagues, trying to learn about an artifact. That was a blaring siren of a coincidence if she'd ever heard one. Someone with serious pull had gone to the trouble of getting Luke's attorney on the phone to ask about the tablet. That meant only one thing: there was more to this tablet than anyone realized. She picked up the phone, her foot tapping rapidly on the floor. The tablet *mattered*. Time to find out why.

Chapter Six

Yellow taxicabs buzzed like tiny ants along the street, locked in a maze of their own choosing as they stopped and started through gridlocked traffic alongside tiny pedestrians. At least that's what they looked like to a man standing seventy-six stories high. The man looking down swept his gaze up, across the harbor, skipping over the French statue on Liberty Island to study the sparkling waters stretching into the distance.

Guy Joyce was not a man given to introspection. Guy focused on the more practical things in life, such as how to ensure that his place in the world grew stronger every day. A focus he'd maintained with admirable consistency over decades. You didn't become C.E.O. of a pharmaceuticals company by chance. Guy saw what he wanted and worked to get it. Once he achieved his main goal, he didn't stop, cash out and buy a beachfront house to while away the days. He set a new goal. A bigger one. There are more successful companies around? Chase them down.

Which meant he had to adapt and find new ways to win. A path that occasionally resulted in strange bedfellows. But the end always justified the means, which was why he'd funded the legal defense of an antiquities smuggler just arrested in Toronto. The man had information that could chart a new course for Bergen Inc., the company Guy had led from its origins as a small-market producer of generic drugs to a major force in international pharmaceuticals. His

45

rise from the accounting department to running the company was a standard part of the company's pitch to recruits. You can achieve anything at Bergen, if you're willing to work for it.

He turned. Books lined the shelf behind his desk. The titles weren't what most leaders in the city displayed; no Warren Buffet or Henry Ford treatises on business. Guy molded his actions on leaders of a different caliber. The books he displayed were biographies of Napoleon, Winston Churchill, Genghis Khan. They had chased domination, a mindset Guy appreciated, and one necessary for success. He reached out and touched one specific book. *The Persian Empire.* Records of dynasties whose empires stretched across the known world, and the book in which Guy had first read a strange, captivating story. That story was the reason he had spoken with the Greek smuggler earlier today.

A buzzer sounded on his desk and Guy pushed a button. "Is he here?" Guy asked.

"Yes, Mr. Joyce."

"Send him in."

Guy looked to his office door, which opened to reveal a man wholly unlike Guy, though in truth this man was the closest to him in the world. His brother Brian.

"You wanted to see me?" Brian asked. He stood in front of Guy's desk, back straight, legs wide, arms behind his back. To Guy, it always seemed Brian was on the verge of saluting.

"Have a seat."

Where Guy was tall and thin, Brian was short and squat. Guy's quick smile had bypassed his older brother, who recognized charm but had decided it didn't suit him. Lines creased Brian's forehead. "What's wrong? If it's those hippie bastards again, tell me where to find them. I'll make sure they don't protest Bergen anymore."

"Easy, Brian." Guy leaned forward and touched his brother's shoulder. The damn thing was hard as stone. "There's no trouble. And protesting is legal. You beat up one of *those hippie bastards* again, you'll be back in the papers, and the board won't take kindly to another negative headline."

"You make them too much money," Brian shot back. "They'll bitch. That's it. And the hippies will be gone."

For once, Brian had a point. "Let's not test that theory," Guy said. "I need your help, and not with protestors."

Brian's posture somehow straightened further. "What's the mission?"

Guy groaned inwardly. Brian had never let go of the military, even after it had let go of him with a dishonorable discharge in his file. No private security contractor would touch him with his record. Which was how Brian had come to be Bergen Inc.'s executive security consultant. If it weren't for Guy, Brian wouldn't have had a shot at the job. It was the best Guy could do for him.

"Intelligence gathering," Guy said. "You and I have a meeting with the D.A.'s anti-trafficking unit this afternoon. As far as they know, I'm interested in helping preserve historical artifacts as part of our charitable efforts."

"You promised them money and you want something."

Brian might not have known his way around a boardroom, but he missed little. Brian had been a lot more like his brother before he'd joined the Marines and headed to Iraq in the Gulf War. Guy had gone on to business school, while Brian had chased Saddam and his men. That was where it had all changed for him. Where *he'd* changed.

"That's right," Guy said. "Earlier today I learned an item I've been tracking for years popped up again. The D.A.'s team somehow located the man trying to sell it, and they gave the information to Canadian authorities, who arrested him."

Brian frowned. "How do you know all this?"

"Friends in the D.A.'s office. We donate to the D.A.'s campaign. Heavily. The money gets me information when I need it."

Brian shook his head. "Politicians are the worst crooks of all."

Guy shrugged. "Better to have them on your side than not. Today

47

you and I are meeting with the agent who located this seller, who's Greek. Less than a week ago this Greek had the item I want."

"Does he have it now?"

Guy shook his head. "No. A second man either bought it or stole it. We need to find out who he is and track him down."

Brian scratched his clean-shaven chin. "Why are you sending me after it?"

Guy looked past his brother to an oil painting of William the Conqueror on his wall. "Let me tell you a story."

Brian grimaced. Guy ignored it. "Hippocrates was a Greek physician who lived over two thousand years ago. He is considered the father of modern medicine. Even today doctors still use techniques he created, and you've heard of the Hippocratic oath every physician takes. During his lifetime powerful rulers came from around the world to seek medical advice. Inevitably, stories would spring up about his miraculous deeds. Fabrications mostly, but with a kernel of truth." Guy looked back to his brother. "I believe one in particular. It describes a physician training under Hippocrates who showed such promise that Hippocrates believed the young man would one day exceed his own talents. However, the young man became sickly and frail. Eventually Hippocrates realized this young man suffered from a disease for which there was no known cure. Hippocrates was determined to heal him."

"Let me guess," Brian said. "He did it."

Guy narrowed his eyes. "Hippocrates supposedly created a cure for this disease. Not only did the young man recover, but he went on to live for over a century, carrying on Hippocrates' work long after his mentor died."

"That's a long life back then."

Heat rose in Guy's chest. "*Exactly*. In 450 B.C. the life expectancy was around thirty-five years. This man supposedly lived to be well over one hundred."

Brian was not impressed. "You really think this happened? And who was this guy?"

As much as Brian's disbelief dampened him, it gave Guy perspective. "No one knows. I'm not certain the story is true, but even the possibility it could be rooted in truth justifies us checking. The value of such a drug is priceless."

Brian laughed. "How could a medicine that old be useful today?"

"Hippocrates first prescribed willow bark for pain relief. In the mid-1800s scientists refined willow bark into the compound salicin, which fifty years later became acetylsalicylic acid. Today we call it aspirin, the most commonly used drug in the world." Guy looked at Brian until his brother looked away. "Tell me again how old knowledge is useless."

"Fine," Brian said. "You want to find this, I'm your guy." He looked up. "What does this thing look like and who has it?"

"It's a Persian tablet connected to Xerxes II," Guy said. "Rumors about it have been around for years. This morning, I spoke with the Greek man who used to own it. Xerxes II knew Hippocrates. It appears Hippocrates treated the king, and after Hippocrates' death his students continued to care for the king."

"How do you know this tablet has anything to do with the medicine?" Brian asked.

"I don't," Guy said. "That's what we're going to find out." He stood, and his brother did the same. "There's a chance this artifact is connected to Hippocrates. It may not be, but we have to follow it."

"Bergen's stock will skyrocket if anything pans out."

Guy walked around the desk and clapped a hand on Brian's bicep. "Correct." He pulled out his phone. "Time to go. We have a meeting with," he checked his calendar, "Agent Nora Doyle. She doesn't know we're coming." He led Brian out past his secretary's office and toward the elevators. "Let's see what she knows about Xerxes II and his tablet."

Chapter Seven

Manhattan

Anyone unfortunate enough to walk into Nora Doyle's office now would never be the same. She prided herself on maintaining equanimity, on never letting anyone get to her. But fifteen minutes earlier her boss had appeared, stood inside her door, and given an order she could scarcely believe. Nora briefly considered whether she could throw her desk lamp through the wall. If it managed to hit the district attorney as it flew, all the better.

This was *her* case. She had uncovered the trio of Greek smugglers in Toronto and gift-wrapped their arrest for the Canadian authorities. Nora should have been the one to run point on this, free of interference, as they unraveled the links between Luke and his black-market associates. Until someone with serious pull had called the D.A., and now Nora had two hangers-on with full permission to follow her investigation. This was bad, but she still couldn't believe the parting instructions from her boss.

"Help them, Nora." The D.A. had stood in her doorway, flashing that megawatt smile. The one he not-so-secretly hoped would one day land him in the mayor's office. "They're friends of this department. If they need information, they get it. Understood?" He'd turned and left without waiting for an answer. Now not only did Nora have to tolerate their involvement, she had been told to actively assist them with any questions. Her jaw tightened. Two *civilians*. What the hell did the D.A. think this was?

A knock on her door derailed her train of thought.

"Ms. Doyle?" Nora looked up to find her secretary watching her, a file folder clutched to her chest. "Two men are here to see you. They said you were expecting them."

"Send them in." She boxed up every bit of feeling and stowed it away. These two would be sorry they tried to intrude on her investigation. Nora propped her arms on the desk, her face a blank slate. The men darkened her door.

"Agent Doyle?" A man made entirely of sharp angles and capped teeth so white they nearly hurt her eyes when he grinned. "Guy Joyce." He strode in and offered his hand. She did not stand when she took it. "Thank you for seeing us," Guy said. He waited for a beat, and when she didn't offer him a seat, he slid smoothly into one. The smile stayed on his face throughout.

Nora got a look at the second man. A head shorter, a decade of bench presses wider, the second man still resembled the first. He noted her sizing him up. "Brian Joyce. Executive Security Liaison for Bergen." Brian took the other chair across from her desk.

Security made sense. Whereas Guy Joyce had the expensive haircut of a well-heeled executive, Brian Joyce wore his hair like a disease.

"Thank you for agreeing to see us," Guy said. "My company is proud to support the district attorney's office, and we know your time is valuable."

Nora hadn't moved an inch. "I understand you have some questions for me."

"Yes," Guy said. "I'm not sure how much you know about Bergen, Inc." He waited. She didn't bite. "We are a pharmaceuticals company, and as the C.E.O., I'm in a position to support your operation. I'm also a passionate advocate of the need to keep the past alive, and I have a strong interest in assuring that artifacts of cultural significance are treated with the proper respect."

He paused. Nora didn't say a word.

Guy was good. He went on without a hitch. "A significant artifact was recently identified in Greece. One with ties to the Achaemenid empire and King Xerxes II."

Nora had heard enough. "So your money buys you information from this office. As of an hour ago, it also bought you access to my investigation. Save us both time and tell me what you want."

"Now, Agent Doyle, we're on the same team." Guy indicated the silent man sitting next to him. "Brian, me, you. We want the same thing."

"I'm not here to argue," Nora said. "You're an executive at a large pharmaceutical company. What you could possibly have to offer me besides money is unclear."

Guy's face never changed. "I'm not here to get in your way. I want to help; that's all."

Brian Joyce finally spoke. "My tactical experience from the military will be an asset to your investigation."

She caught the first crack in Guy's armor. *Disappointment.* She stuck her hand in the wedge and pushed. "How are the two of you related?" Nora uncrossed her arms and leaned closer. "Same last name, and I see a resemblance."

"Brothers," Guy said softly.

"I'm older, he's younger. I handle his security."

"I see." Nora let that linger. "It must be nice to work so closely together."

Brian Joyce dipped his chin in agreement. Guy Joyce, she noted, did not.

Interesting dynamic. "Fortunately," Nora said, "the D.A.'s anti-trafficking team is well versed in handling investigations. I understand you are here for information."

"That's correct," Guy said. "In no way do we wish to impede your investigation. I only want to assist in any way possible."

"Which starts with me telling you whatever I know."

Guy had the grace not to respond.

"The artifact from Greece first came to my attention during another case." Nora detailed how her sting operation involving another trafficker selling a Marcus Aurelius statue had eventually resulted in the trafficker providing her with information on the Greek sellers, who were then arrested by Toronto authorities. "The tablet tied to Xerxes II was lost several days earlier in Athens."

Guy's face changed, the mirage of concerned antiquities lover gone. "What happened to it?"

"The Greek dealer sold it. Though not by choice." Nora recounted how Luke had tried to rob his buyer, but didn't account for the buyer's resourcefulness. "The man who Luke tried to rob actually paid him for the tablet. At a discount, but he still paid."

"Where are he and the tablet now?" Guy asked.

Nora bit her lip. "Information goes both ways," she said. "Why has this specific artifact brought you to my office? What's so special about a tablet tied to Xerxes II?"

"I have a personal interest in the tablet," Guy said. "That is all I can say."

"I'm opening my investigation to you. Not by choice, which we both know, yet here you are. Tell me why you are so concerned that I find this tablet."

Guy leaned back from her desk, kicking one leg over another. "Alright. I believe there is more to this tablet than anyone realizes. I can't say with certainty until I see it. It's possible I'm wrong. But I won't know until we find it, Agent Doyle."

Nora tried to get more out of him, but Guy was either telling the truth or dead set on keeping her in the dark. In the end she didn't have much choice. "I see." Nora looked out her window, following a plane as it approached the city for landing. "Right now, I don't have more to share. My investigation is in the early stages, though I'm confident my leads will result in progress sooner rather than later."

"What leads do you have?" Brian asked.

Nora hesitated. "We have a name. Of the man who purchased this tablet."

The brothers Joyce went still. "Which is?" Guy asked.

Nora debated. Now wasn't the time to fight. Not yet. "Harry Fox," she said. "He's a known associate of the Morello crime family. Harry is the only person we have positively identified as tied to this case." She stopped there. These interlopers didn't need to know they weren't the only people interested in the tablet yet. Not until she had a chance to find out who had called Luke the Greek's lawyer with an interest in the case.

Guy seemed to read her mind. "Has anyone else asked about this tablet in any capacity? Beyond me, of course."

Guy rested his chin on a hand, tilting his head to one side as he waited. Nora opened her mouth. She closed it. When the truth hit her, it took every bit of her self-control to maintain a blank face.

You called Luke's lawyer. Guy Joyce was the other man, the one Luke had mentioned, the one willing to fund his defense. How had Guy come across the information? He had resources. Money didn't only buy access, it bought answers. To questions such as *Who is the Greek artifacts trafficker in Toronto, and what is his attorney's name?*

Nora made a rash decision. "Someone called the Greek smuggler's attorney, asking about the tablet. Except you already know, because you're the one who spoke with Luke's attorney. He told you exactly what I did."

Guy didn't duck her words. "I want to trust people, Agent Doyle. Then I verify what they say. I believe I can trust you now."

"And if I'd lied to you?"

"This case would be assigned to a new agent." Guy said. "As I said, we are generous supporters of the district attorney."

Nora bit her lip. "I see." She glanced at her watch. "That's all I have for you now. Unless there's anything else?" She stood as she spoke.

Guy waited a beat, then rose as well. "Thank you for your time,

Agent Doyle. I trust you'll be in touch with anything new."

"Anything at all," Brian said.

"Of course." A frigid look settled over her face. "It seems I'm at your disposal."

She let the brothers see themselves out, then she shut the door and collapsed into a chair. Those arrogant pricks. Thinking their money could buy anything. Well, it did buy them access, but it wouldn't get them everything. Nora's boss might have thrown them on her, but that didn't mean she had to roll over. This was her case. Even if she had to accept the Joyces' unwelcome presence, she could make sure they never got what they truly wanted. Guy Joyce had a serious interest in the tablet. Why, he wouldn't say, but Nora would bet her last dollar he wanted it for himself, not posterity. She reached for the phone. Nora had one thing on her side Guy Joyce could never take away.

She dialed a number. "It's me," she said. "Remember when I said you owed me one? I might cash it in soon. If I call you with a story about an artifact smuggler here in the city, can you get it on the front page?"

The only reporter she trusted at the *Times* assured her he could.

"Perfect," Nora said. "Keep your phone charged. I'll be in touch."

She set the phone down, and for the first time since her boss had told her about Guy Joyce, Nora felt better. Guy might have all the money in the world, but if she located his artifact and splashed it across the front page, he'd have a hell of a time keeping it for himself. *Two can play this game, Mr. Joyce.*

Now she just had to find the damn thing.

Chapter Eight

Brooklyn

A well-dressed man walked into the bar in Brooklyn, taking his sunglasses off before he stepped out of the bright afternoon light and into the bar's dim lighting. It was kept intentionally dim for several reasons, one of which was to make it harder for people to tell who was inside at any given point. Patrons who didn't know to look for him often missed the big, quiet man hunched in the corner seat near the door. He was one of a rotating cast of big men not fond of small talk who manned that post, because that's what it was – a security post.

Joey Morello hung the sunglasses on his shirt, nodding to the beefy man as he walked past and took a seat at the bar. Overhead fixtures threw muted light off a long mirror running behind the bar. Everyone in Joey's world knew this was a Morello bar, which made it an obvious target for an ambush for those at odds with the Morello family. The big men's job was to make sure that didn't happen. To that end, they kept a loaded shotgun hanging under a painting on the wall.

The bartender raised an eyebrow to Joey. "The usual, Mr. Morello?"

"Hey, Sal. I'll take a Peroni." Joey grabbed the beer bottle when Sal brought it over, the glass chilling his palm. He closed his eyes, pushing away the world for a moment to enjoy the crisp lager. His mind stopped swirling for a few blissful seconds.

"Look what the cat dragged in."

So much for that. Joey opened his eyes to a familiar face. "Tony. What brings you here?" He stood and wrapped his arms around the other man. "Sit."

Tony Grifo was part of the Gallo family operating out of the Bronx, and a made man Joey had known for years. "Sorry to interrupt, Joey." The diamonds on Tony's cufflinks sparkled.

"You want a drink?"

Bartender Sal materialized at Joey's words. Tony didn't say anything, but pointed at Joey's beer. He waited until the bottle arrived and took a long pull before continuing. "I'm here on behalf of an acquaintance."

"What about?" Joey asked.

"A friend of a friend is looking for information. He's asking around about something involving one of your men. My associates vouch for him, so I said I'd talk to you. That okay?"

"No problem with a few questions. If there's money in it, all the better."

Tony winked. "I appreciate it. I know you have," he waved his beer to encompass the world in general, "*other* things on your mind."

Joey frowned. "You mean Altin Cana."

Tony kept his face ahead, studying their reflections in the mirrored wall. "That's right."

"You know those Albanian pricks trashed another one of our washing operations?" Joey asked. "Chafes my skirts." Businesses the Morello family used to launder profits from their illicit operations were called *washing* operations, because they took the dirty money and laundered it through the legitimate business. The Internal Revenue Service would be surprised to know how many of Brooklyn's most unprofitable bars were owned by the same man. Through a number of false fronts and shell corporations, that is. "Couple of foreigners went in looking for trouble, and they found it. Two of my guys ended up in the hospital with broken bones. It's gonna cost twenty grand to fix up the place, and now the local beat cops are all over us."

"Altin Cana sent his men into your place?"

Joey waved a hand. "We can't prove they were his men, but why else would Balkan thugs cause trouble in one of our places? There's no way they'd go there unless someone told them to do it."

Tony nodded. "It's a way to slow down the cleaning."

"I'm worried about what happens next. Yesterday it's a bar fight. Tomorrow, what? Altin Cana doesn't have any respect. You get into this life, fine. You follow the rules, stay on your turf. Altin Cana thinks he's too big for his little patch of Brooklyn now."

Light flashed in the mirror as the front door opened. Joey and Tony watched as the big man stood, inspected whoever was coming in, and then sat back down. A local old-timer, no threat to anyone.

"Altin knows it won't sit well with the other families if he pushes your father too far," Tony said.

Joey didn't respond. Tony was right, but the unsaid part rang equally loud. *It won't sit well with the other families, but they won't stop him.* Families rarely got involved with other families' business. Vincent Morello himself had laid down the edict years ago in an effort to stop the incessant feuds and bloodshed, but if you couldn't defend your own turf, perhaps you didn't deserve to have it.

"How is your father?" Tony asked.

"He's fine," Joey said quickly.

"Give him my regards."

"I will," Joey said, then pivoted. "Tell me about this friend of a friend."

Tony didn't push the subject of Vincent or his health. "He knows you have Harry Fox."

"If he's looking to buy something, send him to Rose." Joey finished his beer and called for another. "He should already know that."

Rose Leroux was New York City's fence for antiquities. Or any other goods with questionable to nonexistent provenance. Rose had been a part of his life for over thirty years, back to when Joey was a toddler.

"Why are you coming to me?" Joey asked.

"I asked my guy the same thing," Tony said. "This friend of a friend is tied to the artifacts world somehow. Apparently, Harry acquired a piece a couple of days ago that he's very interested in seeing." Tony shrugged. "I'm not into that kind of stuff, but I know there's real money to be made. This guy is anxious to get ahead of the line, and he's willing to pay for the privilege."

Joey chewed on that for a moment. If this acquaintance really was connected to Harry Fox's world, it was possible he'd heard about Harry's acquisition. "This guy can pay?"

"He's for real," Tony said. "I asked. He has money."

Which was what it came down to. Harry Fox's business made money for Vincent Morello. If Joey put Harry in touch with a buyer willing to pay a premium, all the better. "You have a way to get in touch with this friend of a friend?"

"I can have him call Harry directly."

Joey shook his head. "Get his name and a number to me. I'll take it from there. I don't need this guy having a line to Harry, even if you vouch for him. No offense, Tony."

Tony Grifo lifted a hand. "None taken." He drained his beer. "You having another?"

"You sticking around?" Joey asked.

"Of course," Tony said. "I'll be right back."

Joey watched in the mirror as Tony stepped outside, his phone pressed to an ear. The door closed, slicing off the fading afternoon sunlight, a metaphor for the thoughts roiling in Joey's head. Altin Cana's crew was more than just a thorn in his side. Real trouble was on the horizon, and it couldn't have come at a worse time. For decades Vincent Morello had steered New York families on a relatively peaceful path, the informal *boss of all bosses*. Violence was bad for everyone's business, so everyone got along, more or less, and they all made money. Now the Albanians wanted in on the action. Normally it wouldn't be a problem. Joey took a long drink. Normally, Vincent Morello wasn't sick. Right now, there wasn't much normal going on in Joey's world.

As Joey Morello tried to convince himself his father's troubles would pass, a phone rang across the city, high above the streets. The man sitting behind a desk he hadn't earned answered it.

"Tell me you have good news, Gio." Brian Joyce tapped a finger on his desk. "I'm not paying for bad news."

"I'm on it," the man named Gio said. "I talked to Tony, convinced him I knew someone who wants to buy the artifact. He talked to Joey Morello."

"Is he going to sell it?"

Gio hesitated. "You know what'll happen to me if Tony finds out I'm lying to him? Tony doesn't joke around. Neither does Joey Morello."

"Relax, Gio."

"They want to know why you want to go right to the source instead of talking to a fence."

Brian Joyce gripped the phone harder. "Because I don't waste my time. I have money. That's all they should care about."

"We're talking about Vincent Morello. He's the big boss, Brian. You don't want to mess with him."

"Did you confirm it or not?"

"I convinced Tony you're legit and to tell Joey Morello's man to talk to you. Tony gave your number to Joey Morello. Their guy will call you."

Brian gritted his teeth. "His name?"

"Harry Fox."

Brian Joyce hung up. He stared at his desk, moving chess pieces only he could see. The artifacts hunter didn't yet know it, but he was playing against Brian Joyce, a formidable adversary. There was only one possible outcome: Brian obtained the artifact for his brother Guy. Whether Harry Fox survived the coming days was up to him. It all depended on how quickly Fox realized this was an unwinnable fight.

Brian Joyce stood and headed for his office door. He wanted to deliver the good news to Guy. Then he needed to call Gio's brother Ciro, whose luck at the card table had recently gone south. Brian had heard about it, spotted a connection to the Morellos he could use, and bought Ciro's debt. Now Brian was going to offer Ciro a chance to clear his debt in one swoop.

Chapter Nine

Brooklyn

Afternoon sunlight assaulted Harry's eyes when he walked out of his apartment. It had been a few days since he'd returned from Greece with the tablet, yet he'd made no real progress on deciphering its stories. He needed an expert to do that, the type of person who'd made a career of studying the Ancient Persian empires. Professor Manan Khalidi of Columbia University was a renowned scholar of Middle Eastern studies. The professor also had a professional association with Rose Leroux as one of her preferred artifact authenticators. Professor Khalidi only consulted when Rose brokered the sale of a legitimate artifact, having never been exposed to pieces of a more questionable origin.

Rose hadn't asked Harry why he needed to speak with the professor. She'd called Khalidi, and he had agreed to meet with Harry when he returned from a conference in Jerusalem. For two full days Harry had waited, spending hours studying the tablet himself. The murky storyline, the vague references – none of it made much sense. He needed Professor Khalidi's expertise, and as he had no intention of sharing any information electronically, Harry had waited until the professor's return to New York. The tablet was in Harry's messenger bag as he headed for the subway to make the trek from Brooklyn to Khalidi's office in Manhattan.

He made it halfway to the subway stop when a familiar face materialized in the passing crowd. Harry called the man's name.

"Hey, Ahmed." Harry called out again, and his friend turned around. "How are you?"

Ahmed took a long stride over. Hands with the strength of decades spent laboring gripped Harry's arms. "Harry, my friend. It is good to see you."

"Who let you escape from the restaurant?" Harry asked. "I thought you lived there."

Ahmed chuckled. "Not far from the truth. I'm running to get produce."

"Don't you have employees to do that?"

"Send them and miss a chance to enjoy this afternoon sunshine?" Ahmed lifted his face to the sky. "A restaurant owner doesn't get time off."

"Fair enough," Harry said. "How's business?"

Ahmed shook his head. "It's okay." He opened his mouth again, then seemed to think better of it.

"Anything I can help with?"

A bus rumbled by, the trailing exhaust fumes stinging Harry's nose. Ahmed watched as the bus turned a corner. "You know where my place is. On the invisible border."

Ahmed's restaurant, called Sanna, was located on the street that was the unofficial demarcation between Morello and Cana turf.

Ahmed nodded to Harry. "You guys don't come in much. The Cana crew doesn't come much either, for the same reason. When half the neighborhood is related to someone on either side, it spills over, and now no one shows up." He shook his head. "If things don't change, I'm not sure how long I'll last."

Harry had nothing to offer. Ahmed's place was collateral damage. Harry rubbed his chin. *I just made Vincent over a million dollars.* Ahmed was a good guy. It couldn't hurt to ask. "What if I say something to Vincent?"

Ahmed lifted both hands to his chest. "Would you do that?"

"Of course." He stuck a hand out, wondering exactly what he'd gotten himself into. "I'll be in touch. If you run into trouble before then, give me a call. You have my number?"

Ahmed assured him he did, thanking Harry profusely before Harry dashed down the subway steps, pushing his way onto the train just as the doors closed. Thirty minutes later Harry walked up the steps to Professor Khalidi's office on Columbia's campus. He found the professor's office door open, tucked at the end of a long hallway. The sound of his knocking echoed softly.

A man sat at a desk inside, his bald head fringed with silver hair. Sunlight from an open window made his hair shine. "Come in." The man didn't look up when he spoke.

"Professor Khalidi?" Harry asked.

Now the man's eyes rose from the desk. He was studying a tattered document. "Mr. Fox?" Harry confirmed it. "Welcome," Professor Khalidi said. "Have a seat."

Harry stepped through the door and into an office that could not have been more unlike its occupant. The man who now stood before him had a bushy steel-gray mustache. His shirt needed a good iron, and the Yankees baseball hat on the edge of his desk could have been Mickey Mantle's. An odd man to have an office of gleaming hardwood and polished floors. Manan Khalidi's appearance may have been an afterthought, but he was one of the world's foremost experts on the Achaemenid empire.

"Thank you for seeing me, Professor." Harry sat and set his messenger bag on an adjacent chair. He kept one hand on the strap. "I have a unique object. One I hope you can help me understand."

"The tablet you mentioned when you called earlier?" Khalidi asked, and Harry nodded. "What do you know about it?"

Harry nearly laughed. "Very little. A few days ago, I had an unexpected opportunity to acquire this piece, and I took it."

Khalidi raised an eyebrow. Harry didn't bite.

"It tells two stories, one on each side, neither of which I've ever heard before. But here." Harry opened his bag and removed the stone tablet, now covered in a protective cloth. "Have a look." He laid it atop Khalidi's desk.

Professor Khalidi lifted one side of the cover, then paused. "If this is authentic, it is quite valuable." Khalidi removed the wrapping cloth. Air whistled softly between his lips. "My goodness."

Harry watched as Khalidi read the chiseled text, murmuring to himself. When he looked up, half a century had dropped from his face.

Khalidi's finger hovered over the tablet, at the very end. "This is signed by Xerxes II. He affixed his signature as proof it came from the throne. Do you understand how rare this is?"

"If it's real," Harry said. "My research indicates roughly a dozen other pieces with Xerxes II's direct seal exist, but they're unverified."

"You do understand. This may be a direct line into Xerxes' thoughts, a glimpse of what the king believed to be true." Khalidi looked back down. "And if my quick translation is correct, what he feared."

"Look at the back," Harry said. "I think it's a second story. It's nearly the same, but with a different ending."

"Let us talk about the front side first," Khalidi said. "This is Old Persian."

"The language of the Achaemenid empire," Harry said.

"This language hasn't been spoken for two thousand years. The cuneiform script also fell out of use during that time."

"Is it hard to translate into modern language?" Harry asked.

Khalidi grinned beneath his mustache. "Not when you've studied it for as long as I have." He fell silent, his finger hovering over the engraved slashes at the beginning. He grabbed a pencil and began scribbling on a sheet of notepaper. "It is a story I have never heard. It reads like a myth."

"Why would Xerxes sign it? Does that give it legitimacy, show he believed the stories?"

Khalidi's finger stopped moving. "Insightful, Mr. Fox. It is contradictory, on the surface." The professor began reading the front side aloud. Harry's elbows found his knees as he leaned forward to listen.

"So is told this tale of Xerxes the strong king, the King of Kings, ruler of the world, an Achaemenian. Xerxes praises his allies from across the sea, the honored Greeks, healers of men. The knowledge of the worthy Greek physician Hippocrates, refined—"

Professor Khalidi looked up. "Hippocrates and Xerxes II were contemporaries." Harry had to lean closer to catch his words. "Scholars have speculated either Hippocrates or his disciples traveled to Xerxes' empire, but it has never been verified."

"It's a long distance," Harry said.

"Nearly two thousand miles," Khalidi said. "The reference to Hippocrates, combined with the word *refined*, indicates Hippocrates' ideas made the journey, and perhaps those who studied under him did as well." He turned back to the tablet and continued reading.

"—by age, is wondrous and deadly. The King of Kings decrees no ageless beings may exist. The emerald elixir of Hippocrates journeyed to our ruler. It brings life and danger and must be lost. The king made it a beacon to outlast the gods. This beacon illuminates Memphis, the tomb of the mighty general who led the armies of Darius to great victory against the Scythians. Any who seek this general must first follow the Greek's knowledge before the king's wealth to reap his reward. The incorrect path leads to doom."

Khalidi turned the tablet over to read the reverse. It was identical until the very end. "This is where the two stories diverge," Khalidi said. "The final line."

"Any who seek this general must follow the Greek's wealth to reap his generosity. The incorrect path leads to doom."

Khalidi fell silent. Harry pointed to the tablet. "What about the four symbols at the bottom of the front side, where it references *the king's wealth*?" Harry asked. "They look like cuneiform, but none I've seen, and they form a circle. Do they mean anything to you?"

"Unfortunately, no." Khalidi frowned. "These are not letters I have seen. Perhaps they are a code or a draftsman's mark. I will need to research further."

Harry felt a bit better. "What do you think about the story? It's so vague it's hard to interpret."

"I agree. For instance, *the king's wealth* at the end. Does it reference physical wealth, or perhaps knowledge or wisdom?" Khalidi stroked his mustache. "What is the *emerald elixir*? A metaphor, perhaps. But for what?" He stood without warning. "A fantastic find, Mr. Fox. I am grateful you brought it here."

"I'm told you're the best man for these questions," Harry said as the professor retrieved a book. "What do you think?"

Khalidi placed the book beside Harry's tablet, then winked. "Seeking the answers is both good and bad. Good, because one never wants to be short of ideas. Bad, because how will I choose the right path? In that way we are not unlike King Xerxes and his tablet. We must choose the proper course."

"Or meet our demise?" Harry said, only half-joking.

"Let us hope not." Khalidi crossed his arms over the book. "I am certain of several items. Someone, either Hippocrates himself or one of his students, traveled from Greece to Persia to meet with Xerxes II. I suspect the latter due to the *emerald elixir* being *refined by age*. To me, this suggests any one person – even Hippocrates – did not create this elixir alone."

"Perhaps it's an actual potion of some kind."

"Perhaps. Or this may reference knowledge, a truth or fact so powerful that Xerxes II did not want anyone to have it."

"The *beacon* part didn't make sense to me," Harry said. "At first I pictured a lighthouse out in the desert."

Khalidi raised a finger. "Unless you understand the nuances of Old Persian," Khalidi said. "*Beacon* could mean *marker* or *waypoint*. Centuries ago, the term did not connotate a shining light so much as a navigational device. The next sentence builds on this. A beacon to *outlast the gods*." He looked up to Harry. "Suggesting that, if this is a marker or waypoint, Xerxes made it to last. I will return to this. We move to the beacon illustrating *Memphis*, the capital of Ancient Egypt. Armed with this, I know whose *tomb* they speak of."

"You do?"

"And I know where to find it." Khalidi flipped open the book before Harry could make out the cover image or the upside-down title, written in Arabic. "This is a map of Ancient Persia," Khalidi said, pointing to a specific dot. "Here is the city of Memphis. South of Memphis," his finger slid down the map a fraction, "you have Saqqara, twenty miles south of modern-day Cairo."

The name rang a bell, though it took Harry a moment. "Saqqara is a necropolis. *The* necropolis for Memphis."

"Correct," Khalidi said. "Where kings and high-ranking members of society were buried. Sixteen kings built pyramids here, and burials continued on-site for over three thousand years." Delight danced on his face. "Including a famed general named Megabyzus who defeated the Scythians."

"You think that's who Xerxes is talking about?" Harry asked. "Megabyzus, who's buried in Saqqara?"

"His tomb exists as a reminder to the Egyptians that this general laid siege to Memphis, their capital city." Khalidi offered a smile. "Xerxes forced the Egyptians to build a tomb for this enemy general in their own great necropolis, a way for Megabyzus to watch them even from the grave. In truth, Megabyzus treated the Egyptians well after defeating them. His tomb is the only one known to feature both Egyptian hieroglyphs and Persian cuneiform on its walls. It has survived relatively unscathed over the millennia and remains largely intact." Khalidi continued on before Harry could speak. "As to the next portion, I do not know what *Greek's knowledge* or *king's wealth* references. Perhaps the philosophy of Plato and Aristotle? The literature of Homer? Or the mathematics of Euclid?"

"Or the study of medicine from Hippocrates," Harry said.

"Xerxes possessed unimaginable riches," Khalidi said. "Wealth so vast as to render this sentence's meaning impenetrable." He flipped the book closed without warning. "Even now, evidence attests to it. Look no further than this cover."

The image Harry hadn't seen earlier turned out to be a gold coin. The Arabic title translated to *Ancient Persia.* "Who's the man on the coin?"

"The coin is a *daric*, named for King Darius, who ruled Persia several centuries before Xerxes II. You can tell this is Darius by the distinctive Persian bow. Every daric featured one, and often a spear as well." Khalidi looked up and met Harry's gaze. "You were about to ask a question. I have the answer."

Harry's mouth opened a fraction. "You what?"

"When I told you Megabyzus's tomb still exists you reacted. Why?" Khalidi leaned back in his chair. "A collector does not *acquire* a tablet like this without first knowing what he is buying. Yet you did, which tells me you are either dim-witted or not a collector. Clearly, you are not dim-witted."

Khalidi was silent for long enough that Harry asked, "What do you think I am?"

"One who does not sit behind a desk waiting for artifacts to come to him. I suspect you are a man who has seen the field." Harry didn't deny it. "Which tells me you view this not as an artifact alone, but something more."

"A *map*."

"And you want me to tell you if this map is reliable," Khalidi said. He took a deep breath, rubbing his mustache as he considered the wall over Harry's shoulder. Harry waited. "It is possible," Khalidi eventually said. "I have not heard this story before. It is specific enough that I believe it was meant as a record. However, I cannot be certain. Possibly it is only a lost story dreamed by an aging, fanciful king for any number of reasons."

Harry spread his hands across the edge of Khalidi's desk. "You believe this is real, that Xerxes truly did meet with a man from

Greece, and that the *emerald elixir* isn't only a story."

"I do," Khalidi confessed. "What is it? I have no idea, and will not venture a guess." He waved a finger at Harry. "I will tell you the tomb of Megabyzus has been thoroughly studied by modern researchers. Anything valuable is now in a museum."

"Anything valuable they *found* is gone. Could be they missed something."

Khalidi's response was grave. "Perhaps. Either way, your journey is as Xerxes described. Dangerous. The ancient necropolis should not be taken lightly. Vandals, crumbling walls, unscrupulous authorities. There are real dangers you will face if you follow the tablet's path." He sighed. "If that does not discourage you—"

"It doesn't."

"—then I'll tell you that this tablet brings to mind a Greek legend. One about a student who studied with the masters of medicine, men such as Hippocrates. This student was brilliant, one his teachers believed would greatly advance their field. However, he was frail and sickly, unlikely to live long enough to realize his potential. The Greek masters tried everything to heal this student." Khalidi shook his head. "In this fantastic story the young man is miraculously healed and lives for centuries, making immense contributions to the medical field."

"What was the student's name?" Harry asked.

"No one knows. It is a legend, after all." Khalidi sat very still. "But I recall that the healed man, who was once so sickly, was described as a *beacon* of manhood."

The hair rose on Harry's arms.

"Be careful, Mr. Fox." Khalidi blinked, then tilted his head slightly. "Do you attend a house of worship?"

He thinks I'm Muslim. Harry didn't flinch. He hadn't been inside a mosque or any church in years, and thunder might actually roll if he walked into one now. He pointed to the rumpled Yankees hat on Khalidi's desk. "That's my temple. The House that Ruth built. Yankee Stadium."

The professor laughed, deep and long. "As fine a deity as was ever worshipped," he said after a moment. "Whatever you decide to do next, I support you. Xerxes may be proven correct when he writes that this knowledge is dangerous." Khalidi stood and offered his hand. "Be careful."

Harry shook it. "I will. You too." He winked. "If it's cursed, it could stick to anyone who touches the tablet."

"In that case, this curse will need to get in line."

Harry's footsteps echoed as he walked down the long hallway and back outside, where the breeze ruffled his hair. He squinted in the sunlight as he began to walk. A block down the street he checked his phone and found it dead. *Damn.* Not dead, but off. He had shut the device down before meeting with Professor Khalidi to make sure they weren't interrupted. It started buzzing as soon as he powered it on. A text from Joey – he'd found a buyer.

How did that happen? Joey wasn't involved with Harry's side of the operation. Vincent Morello's son spent his time learning the family business and keeping the Morello family at the top of New York's food chain. Joey didn't interfere with Harry's work, and Harry appreciated it. Someone must have come to him asking about the tablet. Whoever it was, Joey had texted Harry their number and asked him to check it out.

Harry pocketed the phone. After what he'd just learned from Professor Khalidi, it could wait. Harry needed to see about a flight to Egypt first.

Chapter Ten

Brooklyn

Stefan Rudovic put his phone down. He rubbed the bristly growth on his chin, staring at but not seeing the vacant walls. His apartment furnishings couldn't even be called spartan. One couch. A small table with two chairs. A television. A single bedroom with a single bed. A coffee maker. He viewed his home as what it was: a place to rest, a place to hide, and a place to leave each morning. Personal touches were not a thing he worried about. Even if he did, it was not as though he had any family left to hang photos of. A refugee of the Kosovo War, he'd fled with his mother, who had quickly vanished after they'd washed up on the shores of New York. He'd been on his own so long the thought of family was as foreign as the idea of that Pakistani-American punk Harry Fox fitting in with the Italians.

Harry Fox occupied his thoughts now. Harry had the Persian tablet, stolen from a group of Greek sellers. The same Greeks now in a Canadian jail after Stefan had tipped off the New York D.A.'s anti-trafficking team to their whereabouts. About that, he didn't feel bad at all. How else could he convince Agent Nora Doyle he was a valuable informant? Sending a few small-time Greeks to jail was all part of doing business.

Stefan wanted the tablet. Harry Fox wasn't going to speak with him, much less let Stefan see it. As competitors in the artifacts hunting world, they didn't work well together. Add in they were men from two crime families? Forget it. That's why Stefan had called the one person in New York who could predict where Harry would go for help decoding the tablet's message. Rose Leroux, a woman Stefan had known nearly his entire life.

Harry may have been in the wind, but Stefan could figure out where Harry had been, then pick up his trail from there. He couldn't simply ask Rose about Harry. She actually liked the guy, so chances were she'd dodge the question. What to do now? Deceive her. To that end, Stefan called Rose and asked who the best man in town was to ask about Ancient Persian artifacts. One name rose above the others.

"Professor Manan Khalidi." Stefan pulled the man's biography up on his phone. "Columbia University." He found a phone number and called. As he hoped, a secretary answered.

"Professor Khalidi's office."

"Yes, my name is Harry Fox. I spoke with Professor Khalidi recently."

The sound of keys clicking. "Yes, Mr. Fox. This afternoon. Did you forget something?"

Perfect. "No," Stefan said. "I wanted to ask the professor a few follow-up questions. Will he be in his office?"

"He's staying a bit later today," she said. "I'm leaving soon, but I can put you through now if you'd like."

"No need. I'll turn around and come back now." He paused. "And if you could, please don't tell him I'm coming. I have a thank-you gift and I'd like it to be a surprise. He's been so helpful."

"Of course," the secretary said. "I'm sure he will appreciate it."

"Thanks."

Stefan clicked off, put a light jacket on and walked out the door. An hour later he walked up the steps of Professor Manan Khalidi's office building, a ballcap pulled low over his eyes, head down as he chased his shadow. Evening commuters clogged the streets. Each person he passed on his way inside was headed in the opposite direction, until Stefan found himself in a long, empty hallway leading to Khalidi's office. The door stood open; the now-vacant secretary's desk was just inside. He glanced over his shoulder to find nothing but red sunlight painting the floor and walls.

Stefan walked in without knocking. "Professor Khalidi?"

The man seated behind the desk looked up, frowning beneath his silver mustache. The same color hair fringed his head. "May I help you?"

"I hope so." Stefan remained in the doorway. "I'm in need of an expert's opinion on Ancient Persia. I was told you may be able to assist."

The frown remained. "Expert opinion?" He glanced at his watch. "I was about to leave. If you call tomorrow and make an appointment, perhaps I can help you then."

"It will only take a moment," Stefan said. "I'm willing to pay for your time." As proof, he removed a roll of bills from his pocket. "Please, Professor. I've come a long way."

Khalidi sighed, rubbing the bridge of his nose. "Come in. I can spare five minutes. What is your name?"

"Basheer Abbas." Stefan didn't offer his hand as he slipped the money back into his pocket and sat. "Thank you, Professor. I am grateful."

"What do you need an opinion on?" Khalidi asked.

"I'm interested in Xerxes II."

Khalidi stiffened. "I see."

"I am a collector, Professor Khalidi. Unfortunately, fakes outnumber authentic pieces by a wide margin." Stefan shook his head, offering Khalidi what he hoped was an exasperated, unthreatening look. "Before I spend money on a piece, I do everything I can to confirm it is real."

"My experience is limited with regards to artifacts verification."

"This piece is unique," Stefan said. "It contains a narrative that has never been seen before. I would like to know if you believe it is real."

A shadow passed over Khalidi's face. "What did you say your name was again?"

"Basheer Abbas." A common enough name among vaguely Balkan men.

"Mr. Abbas, you are the second person to ask me about just such an item recently. Is there anything else you can tell me about this piece?"

Stefan grinned. "My faith in your knowledge is well placed if the seller came to you." When Khalidi didn't respond, he plunged on. "I'm willing to pay for your knowledge, Professor." He pulled the rolled bills from his pocket and set them on Khalidi's desk. "Five thousand dollars. If I buy the piece, I'll double that."

Khalidi stared at the money. He didn't touch it. "I'm not comfortable taking your money."

"Then donate it to charity," Stefan said. "I can't take your time for free." He waited as warring emotions crossed Khalidi's face.

The professor relented. "That money will provide thousands of meals for abandoned pets. For that, I agree. However, I cannot discuss anyone else's interest." Stefan nodded, and Khalidi finally appeared to relax. "You understand this is only my opinion, correct? I cannot give guarantees." Stefan assured him he did. "What are your questions?" Khalidi asked.

"Do you think Xerxes signed it?" A softball to get things started.

"I do."

"What about the story? Or *stories*. Do you think they are true?"

The professor stood from his chair and pulled a book from his shelf. A large golden circle was on the front, what could have been a coin. "Nothing is certain. However, I believe it is possible."

Stefan paid close attention as Manan Khalidi laid out the two nearly identical stories, unwittingly giving Stefan what he needed to track Harry Fox. Fading light turned the buildings outside Khalidi's window a soft red; the light had vanished by the time he finished. Stefan listened in silence, though when Khalidi stopped talking, things had changed. Professor Khalidi had moved from asset to liability. He was the only person other than Harry Fox who knew what the tablet said. The only other person capable of spreading the idea it all could be real.

"Fascinating," Stefan said. "Thank you for such a thorough overview." Khalidi marked his place in the book as Stefan's eyes went to a wall clock. "I've taken far more than my five minutes. Forgive me. I'm sure you now have a long journey home."

"The subway is always crowded," Khalidi said with the resignation of a true New Yorker.

Stefan stood and bowed slightly, again not offering his hand. "I will be in touch if I'm able to make a deal."

Khalidi put the roll of money in his pocket. "The local animal shelter thanks you, Mr. Abbas. Good luck to you."

The building was empty as Stefan again pulled his hat low over his eyes and hurried out. Anyone leaving for the subway would likely come out the front exit, so Stefan crossed the street to stand beside a bus stop shelter with a direct line of sight to the front door. A solitary woman sat beneath the shelter, plastic grocery bags between her legs. Stefan leaned against a streetlight, keeping the metal pole between himself and Khalidi's building. He waited.

Manan Khalidi walked out the front door not five minutes later. Stefan ran to catch the green light, then fell into step a dozen paces behind Khalidi. Full sidewalks made it unlikely Khalidi would spot him. Khalidi stopped at the curb's edge, waiting for a green light. The light changed. Stefan dropped back even farther as they crossed, then he veered to follow Khalidi as he headed for the subway entrance ahead. The heavy flow of commuters took them both below ground.

A train had just departed, leaving Stefan little choice but to hang back near the entrance while Khalidi walked ahead to an open spot in front of the yellow line. There Khalidi stood, hands in his pockets. Stefan turned one ear to the tunnel. No telltale rumble of an approaching train. More passengers filed past, and now Stefan slid into the crowd until he reached a pillar behind and to the right of Khalidi.

"*Cambio de repuesto?*" A homeless woman stuck her hands out, nearly touching Stefan's shirt as she repeated her pathetic entreaty. "*Cambio de repuesto?*" She switched to English. "Spare change?"

He ignored her, turning his body to face Khalidi. Professor Khalidi was looking his way.

Stefan ducked his head, quickly stepping around the pillar and keeping his chin down. The rumble of an approaching train sounded. Stefan looked up. Khalidi had turned back around and was looking down the tunnel toward where the train would appear.

By now the platform was full. Stefan edged his way through people standing shoulder to shoulder until only one person stood between him and Khalidi. Warm air filled the platform. Metal wheels clattered on rails in a rapid-fire assault on his eardrums. The cyclops glare of the train's headlight appeared in the dark tunnel. The crowd inched forward as those at the back pressed ahead. Stefan stepped around the person in front of him. His chest brushed against Khalidi's back.

The front railcar arrived with a deafening roar. Everyone turned to watch. Everyone except Stefan. He watched Khalidi as the train rumbled in, the lead car now two hundred feet away. Stefan breathed in the dank, heavy air. One hundred. Stefan braced himself. Fifty feet. *Now.*

He shoved Khalidi forward. The older man stumbled, his arms pinwheeling for balance before his foot disappeared into the void and he tumbled down to the tracks. Stefan quickly pushed back into the massed crowd, dodging between people with no idea a man had fallen onto the tracks an instant before the train flashed over him. Stefan kept moving until he reached the staircase and jogged up the steps toward the starry sky. He paused near the top, only for an instant. A woman was shrieking.

Chapter Eleven

Brooklyn

Harry's flight to Cairo left in two days. Barely enough time to gather what he needed and confirm as best he could what waited for him. Professor Khalidi had believed in the tablet. Now, Harry did too. Coupled with the fact he already had an unsolicited buyer calling him about the tablet, Harry knew two things. First, he wasn't selling this tablet right now, not for anything. Second, time was not on his side. People were interested in what he had and that made him wary. In his line of work, things could spiral quickly.

His trusty pair of ceramic knuckledusters in his pocket offered a measure of reassurance, as did the amulet around his neck. The morning was cool as he headed back to his apartment after grabbing a coffee and breakfast sandwich down the street, sticking with his tradition of enjoying the best food Brooklyn had to offer before heading overseas. He walked slowly, taking it all in, because who knew when he'd be back?

He stopped at a red light and sipped coffee until the light changed. Leaves just starting to reveal their fall colors rustled as he looked up at the cloudy sky. Chances were good that his time in Egypt would consist of burning sunlight and not much else.

Harry turned the corner by his apartment, walking past a parked car as a man exited the driver's side and went to the nearby parking kiosk to pay. The muscle car demanded another look, especially the lime-green paint job. A classic car defaced by a garish color. Harry passed by as the man pulled out a phone and spoke in Italian, too softly for Harry to pick up despite being fluent in the language thanks to the private tutors his father had hired to teach Harry not only Italian, but also Arabic and Spanish. Supplemented by a childhood among first- and second-generation Italian immigrants, Harry occasionally found himself dreaming in Italian. It was said that was how one knew they had mastered a language. He also dreamed in Arabic, the language of his mother's homeland.

And the native language of Sara Hamed, professor of Egyptology at the University of Trier. Sara's face sprang to his mind now, the single most memorable aspect of his recent trip to Germany. Harry planned to lean on her knowledge of Egypt in his upcoming search. It was also an excuse to call her again.

Whatever it was, the easy pace or thoughts of Sara Hamed or something else entirely, Harry never saw it coming. He heard the Italian conversation continuing behind him, but he didn't pay attention. The words hung like so much background noise as he stopped at his front door, pulled out the key, and opened the lock. He took one step inside when a thunderous blow took him down, his kidneys exploding in pain as he fell to his knees and collapsed through the open door. The door slammed shut, the lock *snicked*, then another hammer blow landed. Harry curled up, arms over his head as he tried to twist away and failed. A man stood over him. The one with the muscle car who spoke Italian.

The man lifted a hand, but didn't punch again. "Where is it?"

Harry gasped for breath. "What?" he finally managed.

"The tablet. Tell me where it is."

Harry didn't answer. The man kicked him in his ribs, though Harry deflected some of the blow with his arm. "I know who you are, Fox. You have the stone tablet. Tell me where it is or I'll shoot you and find it myself."

The guy didn't have a gun out. Maybe he was bluffing.

"Okay, okay. Stop kicking me." A coughing fit came next as Harry scooted against the wall, buying time. He pulled himself up, one eye on the intruder, who had covered his face with a gaiter mask. The face cover ran across his nose, leaving only his eyes visible, eyes that darted back and forth.

You're not used to this. Harry pointed over the man's shoulder. "It's through there. My office." He stood, pretending to stumble and getting closer to the intruder. The man jumped back, dug in his pocket and came out with a handgun. A big one. And considering how shaky the hand was that held it, that thing could go off by accident.

"Whoa, easy." Harry darted back and put his hands up. "No need for that. You can have it."

"Get the tablet or you're done."

Harry pointed to the hallway. "Down there."

The intruder flicked his gun, telling Harry to move. "Go."

Harry got to it, his mind churning. Who was this guy? Was he from a rival gang? Unless this tablet led to the Holy Grail, it wasn't worth starting a war with the Morellos. Which was what would happen if this goon shot Harry. Vincent Morello was old-school that way.

Which family is stupid enough to send an idiot like this after me?

The intruder walked beside Harry, his gun poking Harry's ribs as they moved. Floorboards creaked as they moved past the kitchen and into Harry's office. Closed blinds left the room in murky darkness. Harry did not turn on the lights as he walked in. He went directly to his desk, walking around to stand behind it. The gunman stayed close, though he remained on the other side. A single book was atop the desk. A bookmark stuck out of it.

"I have to get the key," Harry said. "It unlocks my wall safe."

"No fast moves," the intruder said.

Harry didn't test the man's skittish trigger finger, moving with exaggerated slowness to open the drawer and remove a key. The man didn't notice that Harry's free right hand remained on the desk. Harry held the key up with his left hand. "The safe is behind that painting," Harry said, tossing the key as he spoke. He deliberately left it short. The intruder glanced first toward the wall, then followed the key in flight, actually moving forward a step trying to catch the bad throw. Harry kept his eyes on the gun, now aimed at the ground as the intruder bent over.

The key hadn't landed before Harry's right hand flashed under the desk to grab the loaded pistol secured there. Legs apart, the pistol in a two-handed grip, Harry took aim and then dropped to the floor when the intruder's gun went off. Harry fell behind the desk, firing all the while, then twisted to one side and pressed his back against the desk's drawers.

The desk *thumped* as bullets hit it. Harry kept still, waiting for the intruder to stop shooting or run out of bullets. Eight shots later, the firing ceased. Harry stuck his pistol around the side of the desk to fire blindly. The intruder screamed in pain. Harry fired under the table, aiming for a pair of shoes that quickly vanished around the corner.

Return fire came back at a rapid pace, the reports fading as footsteps pounded down the hallway. Harry heard his front door smack off the wall, flung open as the intruder raced out. Not that Harry could hear much of anything right now. He scrambled on his stomach to a window overlooking the street. No bullets shattered the window, so he hauled himself carefully up and lifted the blind to risk a look outside, in time to see the intruder reach his car, hop in and speed away.

Harry watched until the green car roared out of sight before he collapsed back to the floor. A minute passed before he stood and surveyed the damage. Bullet holes in the walls. His desk looked like mutant woodpeckers had attacked it. Thank goodness he had brick exterior walls to catch the slugs. His neighbors were safe. Likely scared to death, but safe.

Harry's phone buzzed. He hastily reloaded before running to the open front door and slamming it closed. The deadbolt shot home, then he stopped. *Think, Harry.* Who did this? Where he lived wasn't common knowledge outside, though a determined hunter would eventually find him. He'd never had a problem in his own home until this tablet entered his life.

Harry ran up to his bedroom and checked his closet door before removing the door's false panel and pulling out the tablet. Then he stowed it in his messenger bag before packing clothes in a suitcase, his mind racing. Who had told the intruder that Harry had the tablet?

What clues did he have? The intruder had sounded Italian. The guy spoke the language flawlessly. His olive-hued complexion was not unlike Harry's own. The intruder had broken into his house and threatened to kill him. He knew where to find Harry, what to look for, yet clearly didn't have the entire picture. A rival gang or artifact hunter could have guessed Harry would keep the tablet close, may even have known Harry intended to follow the story.

Professor Manan Khalidi was another possibility, albeit unlikely. He knew the tablet existed, though he had no information on where Harry was keeping it. Khalidi also hardly seemed the kind of man to sell information or orchestrate an attack.

Rose Leroux was a woman he'd known nearly his whole life and whose reputation put her above reproach. Perhaps someone from the district attorney's anti-trafficking team? Agent Nora Doyle had approached him about the tablet, and her badge carried weight, the kind she could use to lean on sources for information. But why send a man to steal the tablet?

His phone buzzed again. Exhaustion settled on Harry's shoulders as adrenaline from the attack washed away. Until he saw who was texting him. *Sara Hamed.* His overworked nervous system came back to life. Last time they'd spoken, she had wanted to talk about his amulet.

But Harry put the phone back in his pocket. Dragging Sara into this mess was the last thing he wanted. Not because she couldn't handle it. She'd proven that in Trier, going nose-to-chest with a skinhead looking for a fight with Harry. The punk and his friends had quickly decided they wanted no part of the fierce woman with honey-tinted eyes. If she hadn't jumped in, Harry could well have ended up on the wrong side of their fists.

Harry grabbed his bag and went back downstairs. The splintered bullet holes in his desk confirmed his decision. Don't bring Sara into this. First, find the truth about Xerxes' tablet. Then he could worry about Sara and anything she'd discovered researching his amulet.

Harry locked the door behind him and walked away.

Chapter Twelve

Manhattan

The NYC district attorney's anti-trafficking team had a modest budget, with little earmarked for office furniture. It certainly didn't include money for extra items, though at the rate Nora Doyle was going she would be putting in for a new desk phone soon. For the second time that morning she slammed the receiver down. Nearly twenty-four hours spent chasing that Persian tablet artifact, and Nora had zilch to show for it.

She'd cajoled, threatened and flattered her sources, on the books and off. Nothing. Nobody knew where to find Harry Fox and his tablet, or so they said. Nora leaned back and rubbed her eyes; she was far too stressed for so early in the day. She'd love to knock on Harry's door with a search warrant, but no judge in the city would sign it with what little evidence she could offer. Catching artifacts traffickers took patience. Nora had to wait for the right moment. Until then, she would work in a world of shadows and whispers. Whatever it took to deliver results.

Nora made it halfway out of her office door with an empty coffee cup before the phone rang. She darted back in. "Doyle."

"Good morning. This is Guy Joyce."

Nora gritted her teeth. "I'm busy."

"I'm checking to see if you've made any progress," Guy said. "It sounds like you're hard at work."

She took two deep breaths. "As I said yesterday, I'll be in touch."

"The district attorney is lucky to have people like you on his team. I'll be sure to tell him how diligent his employees are the next time we chat."

She didn't dignify the remark. "Anything else?" she asked.

"Hope to hear from you soon."

The beleaguered phone smashed down for a third time. Nora considered throwing it against the wall. The nerve of that guy. She didn't give a tinker's damn how much money he donated or who he played golf with. Guy Joyce wasn't running this operation.

The phone trilled. Nora's hand was still on it and she started, then ripped it from the cradle. "Doyle."

"Anything wrong, Agent Doyle?"

Oops. "No, sir."

The district attorney chuckled. "Have you heard the news?"

The D.A. never called to chat. "What news is that?"

"A man died in a subway accident near Columbia University last night. A professor at the university. He has assisted your office with past investigations."

She racked her brain. "We have a number of—oh my." Her stomach dropped. "Not Manan Khalidi. Was it him?"

"I'm afraid so," the D.A. said. "I saw his name and it jogged a thought. You are working on a case involving a Middle Eastern artifact, correct?"

As though you ever forget anything. "Yes, sir. Persian, tied to King Xerxes. We believe the tablet is here in the city, and we are trying to locate it now." Nora kept her tone neutral. "An associate of yours has taken an interest in the case. Guy Joyce."

"I'm sure you'll afford him every courtesy."

"Of course, sir."

"Excellent. I'm sorry about Professor Khalidi."

"Is there reason to suspect foul play?" she asked. The D.A. wouldn't have called just to tell her a man she sometimes worked with had died. There was always another layer with him.

"The police termed his death suspicious. It's still under investigation."

Nora sensed opportunity. It was a long shot, but what the hell? "Are you able to get me access to the crime scene and his office? I'd like to see if anything jumps out at me."

"Have you consulted with him on this Persian tablet case?"

"No. But he's a renowned expert on the Middle East. There is no one better suited to consult on the tablet." She frowned. "*Was* no one."

"And if we know that, so would anyone else looking for information on the tablet." The D.A. laughed. "You'd make a good prosecutor," he said. "The crime scene has been released, but I'll make a call and get you unrestricted access to his office."

"Thank you, sir."

"You'll notify Guy Joyce of this?"

Nora grimaced. "Yes, sir."

"Good luck."

The line went dead. Nora set the phone down, gently this time, then grabbed her keys and an extra magazine of ammunition before heading out the door. She couldn't disobey an order from the D.A., not if she wanted to stay on this case. What she could do was be considerate of Guy Joyce's valuable time. Sending him into morning traffic without first confirming the D.A. had secured her access? That would be downright rude. She'd get to the scene first. Then call him. If it meant she had to inspect it alone before he arrived, so be it.

Thirty minutes of horrific Manhattan traffic later, Nora stood outside Professor Khalidi's office building. A uniformed officer waited at the top of the steps leading inside. Nora charged up, going right for him.

"Agent Doyle?" he asked.

"Yes."

He touched the brim of his cap. "Pleasure. I'm Officer Iannazzo. Follow me."

The cop didn't make small talk. He marched her up to Khalidi's office, offering a concise summary of what they knew so far. "The deceased worked down this hallway," Iannazzo said. "So far we haven't found anything suspicious."

"What happened at the subway?"

"Witnesses offered conflicting testimony. Some say he jumped, others say he fell, and at least one person says he was pushed. Security cameras didn't get a great look at it. Khalidi fell near the center of the crowded platform."

"Thank you for the information."

Iannazzo stopped at the end of a long hallway. He pointed to a camera overhead. "The detective is waiting on the security footage. The college is putting up a fight about releasing it."

"Wouldn't want us to actually solve the crime or anything."

Professor Khalidi had a corner office, a quiet place to work in the middle of an incessantly busy island.

"I'll wait outside," Iannazzo said. "Shout if you need anything."

Nora stepped into the outer reception room. An empty desk sat to one side. Further in, a door with *Professor M. Khalidi* on it was open. She walked through to find the two chairs in front of Khalidi's desk off-center, with several drawers in his desk pulled out, and a book on the shelf sticking out from the others. As though the somewhat disinterested police investigator had rifled the deceased's possessions with one eye on the clock.

A book lying atop the desk caught her eye, one with a stunning gold coin on the cover. A delicate fabric strip marked Khalidi's spot. Nora tilted her head, her eyes drawn to the title running across the cover in elegant script. Written in Arabic, which she couldn't read. Bookshelves lined the walls, yet only this one had been marked and left on his desk. *Which page had your eye, Professor?*

A loud voice sounded outside Khalidi's office. "Call the district attorney, Officer. He'll set you straight."

Nora shuddered. *Brian Joyce.* Someone in the D.A.'s office must have an open line to Guy Joyce. She turned around as he walked into Khalidi's office.

"Agent Doyle." Brian nodded at her. "Did you forget to call me?"

"Good morning, Mr. Joyce." She crossed her arms. "No, I didn't. I wasn't sure if it would be worth the trip."

He didn't blink. "I prefer to be included."

"Your brother made that clear. I'm only trying to do my job." She held his gaze until he looked away.

"Why don't you tell me everything?" Brian asked.

She resisted the urge to smack him. "Manan Khalidi was a professor of Middle Eastern studies. He died last night at a subway station a few blocks away. Witness accounts of the exact circumstances are contradictory."

"Some say he jumped, others say he tripped, and a few say he was pushed." Brian Joyce looked beyond her as he spoke, to the walls lined with bookshelves and the windows between them. "That is also the extent of my information."

"So we're on the same page." Nora raised an arm, encompassing the office. "Not much here. Professor Khalidi was neat."

"What did forensics find?"

She raised an eyebrow. "*Forensics* consisted of two uniformed officers. What do you think they found, Mr. Joyce?"

Lines creased his forehead. "I don't know. What?"

"They found nothing, Mr. Joyce. Two untrained uniformed officers did not find any useful evidence."

Brian nodded slowly, absorbing this revelation as he began circling the room, arms behind him, back straight. He didn't look at her, though she watched him. Nora played a hunch. "Did you have investigative experience in the military?"

Brian shot her a fleeting look. "Not as such. Infantry. Targeted engagement. My duties did not include investigations."

"I'm sure your experience helps in your executive security role." She kept her eyes on him. "Your brother didn't get where he is in life by playing favorites. You earned your position."

"Guy is brilliant." Brian Joyce studied a row of textbooks with indecipherable titles on the spines. "He's always succeeded. Not everyone knows he started in the accounting department."

Yes, they do. Nora didn't voice the thought.

"Barely twenty years later, he's running the entire company." Brian's words picked up steam, and he turned toward her. "Bergen's share of the domestic pharmaceuticals market increased tenfold in that time. Guy made it happen."

Brian Joyce sounded like a brochure. "Impressive."

"Yes." Brian cleared his throat, turning back to the shelves. "He's taken an interest in this case. I'm here to help, that's all."

"I appreciate it, Mr. Joyce." Nora waited a beat before looking away. "From what I can see, there's not much here." She walked around Khalidi's desk, running one finger along the rows of books as she moved. She did not look at the one on his desk. "I spoke with the lead detective on my way here. Initial interviews with Khalidi's family and colleagues revealed no known enemies. He was unmarried, had no kids, and traveled extensively. From everything we've found, he was dedicated to his job."

Brian agreed. "I'm told he was an expert in his field."

Nora stopped walking. "You're conducting a separate investigation?" She managed to sound hurt.

"No, not at all." Brian spoke quickly. "Background research from our internal security team." He waited for her to speak. She didn't. "Bergen's security division is excellent. If you need any assistance, just ask."

"I'm sure with you running that division it won't be a problem."

Brian looked down. "I don't run the division. I'm the chief consultant."

"Forgive me." Nora almost felt bad. "I appreciate the offer," she said, and made an exaggerated glance at her watch. "I think I'm done here."

"Agreed," he said. "What's your next move?"

She led him out, past the waiting Officer Iannazzo. "I have calls out to several contacts in the antiquities scene," Nora said. "As part of – darn." She stopped short and snapped her fingers. "I left my phone in his office."

She darted back through the open door without waiting for a response, past the stolid Officer Iannazzo, and snapped a photo of the book on Khalidi's desk, including the pages around his bookmark before she hurried back to the hallway. To her eye, Brian Joyce had scarcely moved when she re-emerged.

"As I was saying..." Nora rattled off nonexistent plans as they walked, not giving Brian a chance to do anything but listen. Finally, they stepped outside again. "Thank you for coming by, Mr. Joyce." She stopped on the front steps and stuck a hand out. "I'll contact you as soon as I learn anything. Or if I need to tap into your security resources."

Brian Joyce looked like he didn't quite understand what had just happened. "Call me directly."

"Appreciate it." Nora turned on a heel and called over her shoulder. "Take care, Mr. Joyce." Only after she was behind the wheel of her illegally parked car and had roared into traffic did Nora laugh. Brian Joyce, hired lackey for his brother, was thoroughly inept at handling aggressive women. She would have felt sorry for him if he weren't trying to mess with her case.

She made a mental note to check into his background. He had reacted when she'd brought up the military. From how he'd trumpeted his military experience when they'd first met, she had thought tossing it out was a good way to get him unfocused, talking about his time in uniform instead of inspecting at the scene. It had worked, though not as she'd intended. Brian had been guarded, reserved when he should have been boastful. Rarely did a man who wore service on his sleeve not enjoy talking about it.

Nora veered out of traffic into an empty slot alongside the

sidewalk. A *No Parking* sign stared her in the face. She ignored it and pulled out her phone. Woe unto the traffic cop who came knocking on her window.

She pulled up the pictures from Khalidi's office, enlarging and turning each one all around. It didn't matter that she hardly spoke a word of Arabic. The images were clear, the writing legible. She fired off an email to a colleague who spoke Arabic, promising a bottle of his favorite bourbon if he could tell her the book's title and what the marked pages said. That done, she played with the final image, a shot of the page Khalidi had marked. It was a map. A place called *Saqqara*.

"What's so special about this place, Professor Khalidi?"

It could be nothing. Or everything. Her gut said the latter, and more than anyone else in the world, Nora trusted herself.

Chapter Thirteen

Brooklyn

No ostentatious green muscle cars lurked on the street. No men with fresh bandages leaned against trees. Nothing set off Harry's internal alarm as he went two blocks past his destination before telling the cabbie to let him out. He darted into a doorway as the taxi buzzed off, fading into the shadows. A woman carrying bags of groceries walked within feet of him and never noticed, bouncing her head to the rhythmic, tinny beat coming from her earbuds.

Only after she turned the corner ahead did Harry step out. Messenger bag over his shoulder, he walked briskly to the Morello family headquarters with his rolling suitcase bumping over the sidewalk behind him. He'd never acted like this in Vincent's neighborhood. The old man had lived here forever, growing rich under the protective eyes of his neighbors, never shy when it came to sharing his fortune. Someone in the neighborhood got sick and didn't have health insurance? Vincent paid the bill. A water heater broke and the owner couldn't afford a repair? Vincent handled it. He passed out envelopes stuffed with hundreds at graduation parties, gave gold necklaces and diamond earrings at first communions. He took care of his people, and in return, they watched his back. Nobody made a move around here without Vincent's army of watchdogs noticing.

Yet Harry checked all the same. Knowing the neighborhood had his back didn't carry as much weight after a gunman had barged into his house. The tension in his neck hadn't dissipated during his surveillance detection run; he had walked at speed past Vincent's building without stopping. As he looked over his shoulder one last time, Harry wondered if his sense of the familiar streets would ever return to normal.

Nobody had followed him. Nothing caught his eye as wrong, so he turned and walked up Vincent's front steps and through the door. He was happier than he cared to admit to see the familiar face seated just inside. "Mack, it's good to see you."

A shadow beyond the doorframe rose, turning into a mountain that moved at surprising speed. Arms like tree trunks spread wide to envelop him. "If it isn't my pal Aladdin. How are ya?"

Harry laughed for the first time all day. "You ever going to get new jokes?" He tensed for the crushing embrace. Mack had the courtesy to keep it brief.

"Never. That's a promise." Mack let Harry go and stepped back. His face clouded. "You okay? Looks like somethin' got you down."

"Rough morning. I'm headed out tomorrow and need to see Vincent and Joey before I leave."

Mack's concern grew. "Somebody botherin' you? Tell me and they'll stop." Knuckles cracked with the sound of falling boulders. "Nobody messes with you. Except me."

"I might take you up on that, my friend." Harry leaned closer to the big man. "I have to talk to Vincent first. Then I'll tell you what's going on."

For the briefest of moments, Harry felt sorry for the man with the green muscle car. Mack was about the worst enemy you could have, and judging from the red shade Mack's face turned when he realized Harry was serious, life would get difficult for whoever had broken into Harry's apartment. Difficult, and short.

Vincent's office door swung open when Harry knocked on it. A familiar voice came from inside. "Come in, Harry."

He entered with his roller bag in tow to find Joey Morello seated in front of his father's desk. Behind the desk sat the head of their empire, the man who ran New York's organized crime families with a wise but unforgiving hand. Vincent Morello, the *Capo dei capi*. The boss of bosses.

Vincent did not stand. "Harry. Have a seat."

Harry left his bag by the door. First, he walked over to Vincent and clasped the old man's hand in his own. You always paid your respects to Vincent. "Mr. Morello. It is good to see you."

A grin creased Vincent's lined face. "It is Vincent, son. How many times must I tell you?"

At least one more. Harry's father had made it clear. *No matter what he says, it's Mr. Morello to start. Out of respect.* "Of course, Vincent."

Harry went back around the desk into the embrace of the man who would one day sit behind it. Joey Morello, Vincent's only son and heir.

"Good to see you," Joey said. He pointed to Harry's bag. "I thought you weren't leaving until tomorrow?"

"I'm not," Harry said as he took a seat. "Only I can't stay at my apartment tonight. It's not safe."

"What do you mean?"

Harry set the messenger bag down and rubbed his shoulder. The tablet got heavy after a while. "A man attacked me today in my apartment. He wanted the tablet."

Harry relayed the encounter in full, starting with when he'd walked past the muscle car to the intruder racing off in it again.

"Are you certain he spoke Italian?" Vincent asked at the conclusion. Harry said he was. "But you did not recognize him?"

"I didn't," Harry said. "I can't imagine his car will be hard to find. It was one of those muscle cars from the sixties or seventies. I don't know the name, but you've seen them. This one had the *SS* on its grille."

"A Chevelle," Joey said. "Two doors with a hard top?" Harry nodded. "What condition?"

"Mint."

Joey shook his head. "I'll know by tonight if he's connected to any family in the city. What kind of goon brings that car to a job?"

"A man who does not respect our family." Vincent's words dropped like iron plates. "This man will be punished. Harry is one of our own."

"I'm on it," Joey said. "Let me make some calls." He retreated to a corner, phone pressed to his ear.

"Is it wise to continue your search?" Vincent asked. "Clearly this tablet is more—"

The words cut off as Vincent began wheezing, drawing in ragged breaths. Harry stood, but Vincent waved him back into his seat. After a few deep breaths Vincent pulled a silk handkerchief from his pocket.

"Forgive me, Harry." Vincent dabbed at the corner of his mouth. "My allergies."

Harry wondered how many people had allergies this bad in the fall. Or what kind of allergies made Vincent pale of skin and weak of voice. He knew better than to ask. "Do you want a drink?"

Vincent shook his head. "I am fine, thank you. As I was saying, the tablet search. Clearly you have gained unwelcome attention. Is it wise to move ahead? Perhaps it is best to wait."

"The thought crossed my mind," Harry said. "Someone wants that tablet badly enough to kill for it. My question is who? Not many people know we have it."

"True," Vincent said. "Though this includes the authorities. There is no telling who is aware now that they are involved."

Harry hadn't thought of that. "Good point." He frowned. "It's hard to even guess who's after it."

"The attack is informative." Vincent paused, his chest rising and falling rapidly. Harry looked away until Vincent spoke again. "The tablet is valuable on several levels. First, its association with Xerxes. And it could have greater value not for *who* it speaks of, but for *what* it says." Vincent's hedgerow eyebrows lifted. "You already know this."

"You're right," Harry said. "What if the story it tells is the true prize?" He spoke quickly, the words tumbling out. "A tablet with Xerxes' signature and a myth is one thing. A true story about a healing elixir? That's entirely different."

"It is difficult to believe the story can have impact today," Vincent pointed out. "It is thousands of years old."

"So why are people trying to kill me for it?" Harry asked. "I need an answer."

A grin cracked Vincent's face. "Your father's spirit is within you. Fred Fox would do the same thing you intend."

"What would you have me do?"

"Follow your instincts. This attack will not drive you away. Quite the opposite." Vincent pointed to the suitcase by his door. "You will follow this trail, uncover what it hides. And you have my support."

Was it that obvious? Harry didn't think so, yet Vincent had read his mind. Harry's father had been the Morellos' antiquities hunter for years. Maybe all that time spent with his father gave Vincent insight Harry didn't understand.

"It is your curiosity," Vincent said, again reading his thoughts. "Your father had the same thirst to know, to understand. I know nothing will stop you from going to Egypt."

"Thank you, Vincent. I wouldn't go against your wishes."

"I know."

The unique chill of glimpsing the steel behind Vincent's grandfatherly manner shot up Harry's spine. Harry turned as Joey returned from across the room.

"I have people on it now," Joey said, lowering himself into the leather-covered chair. "I have a contact in the Department of Motor Vehicles. We'll find that punk."

"Harry will stay here tonight," Vincent said. "No reason to take chances before he leaves tomorrow."

"Thank you," Harry said. He looked at Joey, then to the old man. "There's one more thing I'd like to talk about."

Vincent waved a hand. "Of course."

"It's about Sanna, the Middle Eastern restaurant,"

"Best baklava in the city," Joey said. "You're friends with the guy who owns it, right?"

"Ahmed." Harry hadn't considered the best way to attack the issue. He decided on a bull rush. "His business is struggling."

"No doubt due to the location," Vincent said. "Men from rival operations do not dine together. Not when Altin Cana looks to rise beyond his station."

"*Bastardo.*" Joey spat the word out. "Albanian thug thinks he can push us around."

"I have seen his kind come and go," Vincent said. "Do you remember the Romano gang?"

Joey frowned. "No."

"Exactly my point," Vincent said. "Years ago, a man named Gaspar Romano decided he did not like how our five families cooperated in the city. Gaspar thought he should have more say in matters. I warned him such behavior is not tolerated for the good of us all. He did not listen."

"Which is why I've never heard of him," Joey said.

"The current disagreements between the Cana family and our men hurt Ahmed's business," Harry said. "If things don't pick up, he'll have to close his doors."

"You hope to change his fortunes," Vincent said.

How did he know that? Harry opened his mouth and asked him.

"You have your father's heart," Vincent said. "Fred Fox would have been a terrible captain in our family. His heart was open to others. Which some would say is an indictment on me." Vincent shrugged. "I do what I must."

"You're right, Vincent. I thought I could help. A loan, or a truce with the Canas about Ahmed's place?"

Vincent spread his hands across the desk. "Harry, let us consider. First, a possible truce. This requires me to acknowledge Altin Cana is a threat to my oversight of our informal arrangement between families that makes us all richer. Do you know why it works, why the man who controls Queens does not try to move in on Brooklyn and disrupt my operations?" Vincent tapped his chest. "Because of fear. The men in Queens fear crossing me. Not only because my family is strong, but because an attack on me is an affront to their territory as well."

"Unity makes us all stronger," Joey said. "We become greater than the sum of our parts."

"Which leads to the second point," Vincent said. "The families across all five boroughs are unified to a degree. However, how strong is our agreement, truly? It depends. Should a relationship fracture, I must rely on a stronger bond, one more solid than an arrangement based on mutual profit."

"Shared heritage," Joey said. He pointed out the window toward Manhattan. "All five families are Italian. We understand the rules and how to settle differences. Now an Albanian thinks he's on the same level as us? That can't happen. You've seen what they do. The violence, the pointless murders."

Harry did not point out he knew a number of Morello associates who'd been charged with murder.

"We project strength," Joey said. "People respect us. They fear crossing us. If we admit we actually see Altin Cana as a threat, then what's to stop people from thinking the Morellos aren't so tough after all? If that happens, we're done."

"That is why we cannot negotiate with Altin Cana," Vincent said. "I am sorry for your friend Ahmed. His is an unfortunate casualty of holding our position."

"I hope he doesn't go under," Joey said. "If he does, though, it's a chance for us to move a loyal Italian family into his place. People we trust."

Harry spoke up. "A person on the border between the Cana and Morello territories. A first line of defense."

Vincent nodded. "Yes."

Harry didn't like it, but he knew better than to argue. "I understand."

"I admire your wish to aid him," Vincent said. "However, if Ahmed's business survives, it must do so on its own. Do you agree?"

Harry did. No helping Ahmed, even out of his own pocket. A pocket that overflowed thanks to the massive diamond Vincent had given him in gratitude for his recent acquisition and sale of a religious manuscript. The buyers had paid in cut diamonds, and a choice one had made its way to Harry. "I won't interfere."

"Excellent," Vincent said. "Now, you have a long journey ahead. Let my son find the man who attacked you, and let us handle him. You focus on uncovering the truth behind the tablet."

"I will," Harry said.

"Use any guest room you like," Vincent said. "One of the men will take you to the airport tomorrow morning."

Harry left them with his thanks and the promise of updates on progress. After leaving his bags and the tablet in a guest room, he ventured back outside in search of food. Tonight, Harry had eggplant parmesan and baklava on his mind. The best in the city.

Harry had a blissfully uneventful walk to Ahmed's restaurant. Inside, he spotted his friend watching over the sparse crowd. "You guys do to-go orders?"

Ahmed looked up. "Harry, welcome." White teeth glistened above his trim beard. "Want a drink?"

"Always," Harry said. "I'll take the usual, to go."

Ahmed put in the order before following Harry to a seat at the bar. Ahmed ducked behind it, and two bottles of beer came out of the cooler. "Wouldn't want you to drink alone."

"Appreciate it." Harry took a long pull of his beer. On the walk over he'd considered every way to handle this. None seemed right, which left one option. Honesty. "I just spoke with Vincent Morello." He practically felt Ahmed's body tighten. "I'm sorry. There's nothing I can do."

"I suspected as much," Ahmed said. He spun his bottle between two fingers. "Helping me validates Cana as a rival. The Morellos won't do that."

Harry looked over. "That's exactly what Vincent said. It's not personal."

Ahmed shook his head. "I should have chosen a different location." He lifted his bottle to Harry. "Thank you for asking, my friend. Not many people would do even that."

"You're a good guy. I don't want to see you or your place go away."

Ahmed looked at Harry, but he didn't see him. He was lost in a thousand-yard-stare that went well beyond Sanna's walls.

"I'm really sorry," Harry said. "Vincent strictly forbade me from helping, even out of my own pocket."

"One of Altin Cana's men came here earlier today. Asked how business was."

"What did you tell him?"

"The truth." Ahmed lifted a hand toward the empty tables. "I have little business. Italians stopped coming here so they don't get into trouble with the Albanians, and the Albanians did the same. None of the neighborhood people come any longer, because everyone is tied to either the Morellos or the Canas. A friend, a cousin, a bookie. Which leaves me without customers." He drank deeply. "I believe the next time they come it will be with an offer."

"To buy you out," Harry said. *To plant an Albanian flag on this beachhead instead of an Italian one.* "If that happens, let me know. And don't accept right away."

"Men without money have little bargaining power." A waitress dropped off Harry's food, bundled in a paper bag. "Perhaps we will find a miracle."

"They happen every day." Harry finished his beer and stuck out a hand. "I'm headed out of town for a bit. If they come back, call me. And remember, don't take their offer until we talk."

Ahmed's eyes carried the weight of falling dreams when he shook Harry's hand. "I won't. Safe travels, Harry. And if you see any of these miracles, put one in your pocket for me."

Chapter Fourteen

Cairo, Egypt

Egypt was a country caught between old and new, balancing the traditions of those who had come before with the incessant clamor for change from the next generation. Today's Egypt offered hope for those citizens yearning for more freedom, yet the increasingly authoritarian government threatened to quash those hopes.

The relentless sun beat down on the dust-covered Toyota four-wheel drive now rumbling over a bridge in Cairo. Harry Fox had both hands on the wheel as he looked out over the Nile. Sluggish, silty water that was nothing like the river of legend. Not surprising, given the twenty million people living near its banks whose presence had turned the once-clear waters into a muddy scar slicing through the city. Harry slipped on his sunglasses and aimed his rental vehicle due south, on a path for Memphis, capital city of Ancient Egypt. Harry made his living from the past, yet Saqqara, the ancient burial site, was almost unimaginably old. Its earliest graves dated from the First Dynasty, established around 3100 B.C.

Over five thousand years ago. Through the centuries thousands had been buried there, including kings and other nobles, nearly all now forgotten. A few names still rang from the past, be it for their exploits in life or the grand monuments they had built for themselves. These included an Achaemenid Persian general named Megabyzus, the *mighty general who led the armies of Darius to great victory against the Scythians.* If Professor Khalidi was correct, Megabyzus was the man whose tomb held the clue to understanding Xerxes' tablet.

The Nile's turgid waters had not yet disappeared from view when Harry crested a rise and spotted the most famous pyramids ever constructed. The Giza Necropolis stood as a bulwark against the future, three stone towers unbowed by sand or sun, standing guard over the lifeblood of Egypt for nearly five thousand years. The mythical Sphinx stood vigilant beside them on an eternal watch. One day Harry would come back here and properly enjoy the Giza Necropolis. But not today.

Harry accelerated around a slow-moving truck, then nearly hit a string of camels being herded alongside the road. The Toyota rattled as he veered onto the dirty shoulder and whizzed past the plodding animals before swerving back onto the roadway. The truck blasted its horn and the camel herder waved a staff. Harry let his foot off the gas. *Camels. You have to be kidding me.*

He wasn't about to dodge bullets in Brooklyn only to have a bunch of slow, hairy horses derail him now. His jaw tightened at the memory of his bullet-riddled apartment. Unless Joey's search turned up the gunman with the green muscle car, Harry had no idea who to even suspect for the attempted hit. The list was too long. Which was why he pulled out his phone now and dialed a number.

An idea had taken root in his head on the flight over. Joey did have connections across the city, yet there might be a faster way. Someone whose reach exceeded even that of Vincent and Joey Morello.

Rose Leroux. Biggest fence in the city. He punched in her number and waited.

"If it isn't Harry Fox."

The familiar voice with an accent he could never quite place brought a smile to his face. "Hello, Rose. Is this a bad time?"

"I always have time for you, Harry." Burning tobacco crackled in his ear, followed by a long exhale. Harry could almost smell the acrid smoke floating from Rose's cigarette, lodged in the end of a slender holder. "Are you out in the field?"

"I'm in Cairo."

"A beautiful city in the fall. Is this tied to your request for an expert on Persia?"

Rose Leroux had been a fence for Vincent Morello and the rest of New York for decades, perhaps the only person capable of brokering deals between families. She was the antiquities world's version of Switzerland. Which meant she had worked with Harry's father on nearly every sale he had made. Harry had known Rose since he was in grade school, before Harry knew what Fred Fox did for a living, or how his mother had died, or why Fred and Harry had spent so much time around the local Italian families. Many of whom didn't like him, for reasons he didn't understand. Xenophobia wasn't in twelve-year-old Harry's dictionary. Harry knew his father had fully trusted Rose, so Harry trusted her. In all matters.

"Yes," he said. "It is connected."

Harry laid it out for her from the very beginning, starting with the botched robbery attempt in Athens, the anti-trafficking team's attempted recruitment, his meeting with Professor Khalidi, and the attack at his apartment. "I landed here in Cairo two hours ago."

"You will tempt fate one too many times. Your father would turn over in his grave if he knew what you were doing." More tobacco burned. "He would also be proud of you."

A warmth spread through Harry's chest. Traffic thinned as Cairo grew smaller in his rearview mirror. Harry stepped on the accelerator. "I'm trying to figure out who told that intruder about the tablet. Only a few people know I have it."

"The Greeks likely didn't talk," Rose said. "Acknowledging they lost an artifact while attempting to rob you would not be good for their business."

"Maybe someone close to them knew. Our world is a small one."

"It's possible. *Someone* knew the Greeks were selling to a Brooklyn buyer. It's not hard to identify the Morellos or their antiquities man as the probable target. Especially if they had a description."

"My Pakistani heritage wasn't so good for Athens," Harry said. "It's better in Cairo."

"You may pass for an Egyptian. Let us hope no one asks you to quote the Koran."

Harry laughed.

"Be cautious, Harry. You aren't in Brooklyn."

Harry adjusted knobs until cold air flowed into his vehicle, fighting off the sun's heat beating through the windshield. "Joey will find the guy who attacked me," he said. "I don't envy that guy once the Morellos get to him."

Rose didn't respond. Harry caught the sounds of ice clinking on glass, a bottle top coming off, and then the ice crackling as though warm liquid was poured on it. Vodka, in this case. Harry glanced at his watch. *It's only noon in New York.*

"Joey finding your assailant will not be the end of this," Rose said. She took a long drink. "You don't know about Professor Khalidi."

Harry's stomach went cold. "What about him?"

"He died two days ago. Fell off a subway platform as a train arrived."

Khalidi was dead. The academic who deciphered Xerxes II's message, who had been visibly moved by the tablet Harry showed him. He couldn't have jumped in front of a train. "Are you sure he fell?"

"From what I know it was an accident," Rose said. "Professor Khalidi was not a suicidal man. Though his thoughts lived with the dead, he was not eager to join them."

"Are they sure he wasn't pushed?"

"I am waiting on more from a friend within the police," Rose said. Another swallow from her martini. And martini it was, because Rose drank nothing else. "Do you think his death had anything to do with my going to see him?" he asked.

"I do not believe your one conversation is enough to make

anyone want to kill him. But his death coupled with your near-miss practically shouts that the tablet is somehow involved. Two attempts have been made on your life since the acquisition. This tells me someone believes the tablet is worth killing you for. And, perhaps, killing Manan Khalidi."

Harry's eyes went to the mirror as a car roared up behind him, engine growling, the driver gesticulating.

They found me. Harry gunned it, nearly rear-ended the car in front of him, hit the brakes and then checked his speed. He'd fallen well below the limit as he cruised in the passing lane. After he moved over, the angry driver zipped past, weaving in and out of traffic. Harry's breathing slowed. There was nobody on his tail.

"Are you alright, Harry?"

"What?" He looked all around. Sand, dirty cars and more camels. No one trying to kill him. "Yes, I'm fine."

"You must be careful in Saqqara," Rose said. "Searching the tomb of Megabyzus will involve going beyond the guiderails. The authorities are always on high alert at their historic cultural sites. Don't get yourself sent to an Egyptian prison. There are fewer places you would rather be." Her voice grew softer. "Your father would suggest reconnoitering Saqqara first. Check the guards, the layout, and give yourself time. No need to rush."

"Unless one of those people I can't identify shows up. They won't worry about killing me if it gets them the tablet."

"Impatience will also get you killed, Harry."

Harry chewed his lip. "I'll check the place out before I do anything. Who knows, it could be the next chapter in Xerxes' story is right out in the open, but no one knew to look for it."

"You sound like Fred. He saw things others didn't, same as your mother. Always thinking, planning two steps ahead, not diving in head first."

Harry's knuckles whitened on the wheel. "You knew my mother? I thought she was dead before you met my father?"

"What I know came from your father." The sound of high heels clicking on a marble floor sounded in Harry's ear. "Fred never spoke of her with you around. Before you joined him at work, he spoke about her on occasion."

"What did he say?"

Rose didn't speak for a long time. "Perhaps this is better left for another time."

Rose had never mentioned his mother. Dani Fox had died just as her young son began forming memories. He treasured the precious few he had more than any artifact in the world.

"Dani was exotic," Rose said. "And enchanting. Fred once said the Pakistani half pulled him in, and the British half kept him there. He appreciated the dichotomy, the merging of two cultures to produce a unique woman."

"Like artifacts," Harry said. "He always talked about how an item came to be. Artifacts are so often tied to the clash of cultures, to the intersection of two worlds meeting. Each artifact offers a story, as long as you know how to listen."

"That sounds like Fred."

"What else did he say about my mother?"

Rose's reply was quiet. "Fred Fox never let Dani go. Her memory fueled him."

"Did he tell you anything else about her?"

"Patience, Harry. Now is not the time. You are chasing ancient ghosts who have become all too real. Focus." Another draw on her cigarette. "It's what Fred would do."

Rose's truth cut through his reverie. "I'll be in touch."

Harry clicked off as a speck on the horizon slowly gained substance. Mountains of dirt spiked from the sandy expanse. The stepped Pyramid of Djoser, a tiered structure constructed twenty-seven centuries before Christ. Two other pyramids stood on either side, the smooth Pyramid of Unas and the deceptive Pyramid of Userkaf, constructed in such a manner that the exterior resembled a pile of rubble.

Other funerary monuments dotted the dusty landscape between and around the three major pyramids. The landscape changed dramatically as Harry approached the city of El Badrashin, which sat beside the banks of the Nile. One moment, nothing but dust and sand. Look a bit further and you saw verdant foliage, modern buildings and vibrant civilization. All made possible by the Nile, yet even that great river could only push the desert back so far.

Four miles long and nearly a mile wide, this ancient necropolis held thousands of the dead, as well as millions of animal remains. Archaeologists uncovered tombs, sarcophagi and mummies seemingly on a monthly basis. Saqqara was one of the largest and most active excavation sites in Egypt. Which made Harry's plan for a private excavation in plain sight a tad challenging.

Driving onto the necropolis grounds, Harry passed the first policeman at a sign pointing to the Imhotep Museum, a sparkling white stone structure. The next officer stood near a cluster of vehicles parked by the site's main attraction, the stepped pyramid. The armed officer didn't react as Harry drove by. A tour bus passed in the opposite direction, followed by a trio of men on bicycles. The most practical way to get around was by vehicle, motorized if possible, and the sheer scope of the grounds hid Harry in plain sight as he navigated to the lone tomb on his itinerary: the one containing General Megabyzus, keeper of the truth behind King Xerxes' obscure story. Stone statues of terrifying deities and human–animal amalgams watched over this city of the dead, their fierce eyes on Harry as he passed. A city guarded by mythical beasts alongside very much alive Egyptian police.

Police officers with guns and an entire country where he could be made to disappear.

Rose Leroux crushed her cigarette in a sparkling glass ashtray.

Moving with the unhurried ease of one for whom the world waits, she poured another martini, speared two olives and let the vodka chill. Then she picked up her phone and dialed, leaning on her bar. She really shouldn't make this call. Rose never mixed personal feelings with business. But in this situation, her rules couldn't apply.

She lit another cigarette as the phone rang. A gruff voice answered. "It's Stefan."

"Hello, Stefan."

"Good afternoon, Rose."

"I have a question, Stefan, and I need you to be honest with me. Understand?"

Stefan Rudovic, Cana family underboss and Altin Cana's most trusted soldier, said he did.

"You asked me for the best man in New York to tell you about Ancient Persian artifacts. I sent you to Manan Khalidi at Columbia. I did not ask why you wanted to see him, as that was none of my concern. Correct?"

Stefan waited a long time to respond. Long even by the standards of a cautious gangster. "Yes."

Ash fell from the end of her cigarette, which had been lodged at the far end of its slender holder. Rose eyed herself in a tall mirror on the wall. *Do not let your feelings interfere. This boy is not his mother.* "If your inquiry had anything to do with a Persian artifact now owned by Harry Fox, you must stop. Whatever you are doing, it ends now. I do not care what anyone else told you or how much money they have promised." A stream of smoke flew at the ceiling. "Do you understand?"

This time his answer came quickly. And, to her ear, with much less weight. "I do." A pause. "Why is Harry Fox important to you? First, the Geoffrey of Monmouth book business not long ago. Now you want me to leave his Persian tablet alone. Why?"

"My concerns are none of yours. If it is Harry earning a profit on the tablet that concerns you, and it should not, know he does not face an easy road. The Manhattan district attorney has taken an interest in the tablet. Harry is on their anti-trafficking unit's radar. Now, repeat this. You will not go after Harry Fox and his tablet."

Stefan repeated his orders, and Rose decided he was telling the truth. Of all the dangerous, hard men who had crossed her path, Stefan had the greatest chance of any to oppose her and survive. History was littered with the bones of men who had challenged Rose Leroux and lost. Stefan, for a reason known only to Rose, would not be among them.

"I appreciate your cooperation," Rose said, and clicked off.

Her cigarette turned to ash while she watched the cirrus clouds flitting across a pale blue sky. She loved Stefan dearly. She also could not trust him, not fully. Rose hadn't mentioned Professor Khalidi's demise, and Stefan had not given any indication he knew. Perhaps he didn't know, and had nothing to do with it. Or he did know and was keeping it to himself. Either way, the wrong person knew Harry Fox had the tablet. They had sent a man to his Brooklyn home to retrieve it, casualties be damned. If that someone was Stefan Rudovic, then Rose had just made Harry's path slightly safer.

Rose tilted her martini glass back, savoring the cool burn in her throat. She set the glass down and played with the choker of diamonds around her neck. She might have smoothed Harry's path to uncovering the truth behind Xerxes' message. Or she might have achieved nothing, because someone other than the Cana family knew of Harry's tablet and would kill him to get it. In that case, Harry was in danger and Rose Leroux could do nothing more to help him.

Chapter Fifteen

Brooklyn

A soccer match played soundlessly on the television in a room deep inside Altin Cana's headquarters. Stefan Rudovic watched it without seeing, the conversation with Rose dominating his thoughts. This was a new one. Stefan had his sights on an artifact and he knew where to find it, but now he couldn't give chase, thanks to a roadblock from a woman with no obvious motive to create it.

Why did Rose care about Harry Fox or the tablet? Stefan's was a world of gray with very few exceptions. Rose Leroux was one of those exceptions. A black-and-white woman in the murky reality of artifacts hunting and trafficking. Rose was an outlier because one goal motivated her every action: profit. She never deviated. Which told Stefan she had a financial stake in Harry Fox uncovering the truth behind Xerxes' tablet; otherwise, she wouldn't have told Stefan to stay away. At least that would make sense. Except for one glaring point. Rose didn't care who brought her items to fence, only that they came. She made money all the same, so what motivated her to warn him off Harry's trail? Had Harry promised her a bigger cut? Stefan had been at this since shortly after he'd washed up on America's shores as a youngster soon to be without a mother. He'd seen much of how the world operated. None of it had indicated that Rose would stand in his way today. Yet she had.

One of the teams scored a goal, their arms shooting skyward in celebration. Stefan flicked the remote and they vanished. He replayed the phone conversation in his head again. He must have missed something, a tell as to why Rose wanted him to back off. All the way through, then once more. It hit him right near the end.

The anti-trafficking unit.

How had he missed that? Stefan grabbed his phone, tapping it against his chin. He'd missed it because Rose Leroux had thrown a curveball and buckled his knees. She had never interfered until today, and it was such a change that Stefan had missed the obvious way to find out why. Not only why, but *who*. Rose hadn't told him why she stood in the way, but she had inadvertently told him how to find out. He dialed a number.

She answered immediately. "Agent Doyle speaking."

"Are you free to talk?"

Nora Doyle grumbled. "I'm busy, Stefan. You have two minutes."

"I heard you're having trouble finding Harry Fox and that tablet."

"That's none of your concern."

"I can help. I know things you don't," Stefan said. He didn't add *Just not about this tablet.*

"I'm listening."

"First, I need to know if you have anyone else looking for this tablet, because this is dangerous."

"We're past that," Nora said. "The tablet may be responsible for a murder here in the city."

"What are you talking about?"

"A college professor died under suspicious circumstances. There may be a connection."

Stefan's hand tightened. *Khalidi.* "Who was it?"

"A local professor of Ancient Middle Eastern studies," Nora said. "An internationally recognized authority on the subject."

"What happened?"

"A subway car cut him into pieces." Her next words came much more slowly. "Can you tell me where you were two days ago between six and eight in the evening?"

He forced a laugh that came up short. "You think I ran a subway car over this guy? Give me a break."

"I'm serious, Stefan. Professor Khalidi met with someone twenty minutes before he died. And they found five thousand dollars cash in his pocket. I think that meeting was tied to Harry Fox's tablet."

"Ask Harry Fox." Stefan stood, then sat again. "Don't they have cameras in the subway station? You should be able to see what happened."

"The station platform was crowded," Nora said. "Witness accounts are conflicting. Even an amateur like me thought of checking surveillance cameras."

Stefan fell back in his chair. *Praise the gods.* He took a second to compose himself. "Why aren't you bugging Harry Fox about this instead of me?"

"I'm working on it," Nora said. "He's hard to track down."

"I'd say I'm sorry for your bad luck, Agent Doyle, but I'd be lying."

"Did you have anything useful to tell me?"

"Maybe. You never answered my question. Is anyone else looking for this tablet? I've heard a few things. Could be I can tell you where to find it."

"Hold on." A door closed, then Nora spoke in lowered tones. "Yes, someone else is searching for it. We've enlisted an outside party to aid my team in the investigation."

"Outside party, as in the feds?"

"It's a private party."

Stefan frowned. "Help from the private sector?"

"One of the D.A.'s big donors wanted to tag along for reasons I don't quite believe. Bergen Incorporated."

"The pharmaceutical company?" he asked. Nora said it was. "Why does a drug company want to find an ancient stone tablet?"

"No idea, and I'm not allowed to ask," Nora said. "Their C.E.O.

is involved, along with his head of security, who is his brother. There – I just compromised the integrity of my already-compromised investigation. Do you have anything useful for me or not?"

He had to give her something. Anything, really, as long as she got off the phone and didn't figure out Stefan's call had been a fishing expedition. "Harry Fox isn't going to sell the tablet. Word is he hasn't contacted his usual fence about it. She'd know if he planned to sell. Add that to his meeting with the dead professor and I can tell you if you want the tablet, look for Harry Fox."

Nora seemed to chew on it. "Maybe," she finally said. "If you help me find him before the pharmaceutical guys do, I won't forget it."

Stefan said he would see what he could find and then clicked off. He would help find Harry Fox. He just wasn't going to help *Agent Doyle* find Harry. No, Agent Doyle had been helpful in figuring out how Stefan could walk the fine line between foiling Harry Fox and keeping Altin Cana happy. Altin wasn't keen on Stefan chasing down the tablet. He'd made that clear during their last conversation. Despite being invested in this tablet hunt up to the point of having eliminated Professor Khalidi, Stefan had no intention of crossing Altin Cana. No artifact was worth risking what he'd worked for, what Altin could take away with a few words. And if Stefan couldn't get his hands on the tablet to unravel the real story and profit from it, then Harry Fox wouldn't either. The problem had been how to make that happen without Altin Cana finding out. Or now Rose. Thanks to Agent Doyle, he had the answer.

It didn't take long to find the name on Bergen Inc.'s website. Brian Joyce, Chief Security Liaison. Whatever that was. The brother of Bergen C.E.O. Guy Joyce, who was a prominent supporter of the district attorney and the man who had forced his way into Agent Doyle's investigation. If Brian Joyce was any kind of security man, he would be loath to turn down help, even from an anonymous source.

A woman answered when he called Brian Joyce's listed number. "I have urgent information for Mr. Joyce regarding an artifact," Stefan told her. "No, I won't leave a message. Tell Brian Joyce if he wants to find the tablet, I know where it is. I'll call again in ten minutes."

Stefan clicked off, turned the soccer game back on, then flicked the set off ten minutes later and redialed. This time a man answered on the first ring.

"Brian Joyce speaking."

"You're looking for a Persian tablet tied to King Xerxes."

"Who is this?"

"A friend who wants to see you get that tablet," Stefan said.

"How do I know you're not sending me down the wrong path?"

"We have a mutual interest. You want the tablet. I don't want the man who has it now to benefit from it. You can make sure that doesn't happen."

"There's no way for me to know you're telling the truth."

"Fine," Stefan said. "Don't take my advice. I'll find someone else who's interested in making the money. The person I call next won't care about the tablet. He'll be in it for the money. And he won't care who gets in his way."

"I hope you're not threatening me. We had a name for guys like you in the Marines. Dead."

Stefan rolled his eyes. *Real tough guy.* "No threats, Brian. I'm only showing you this can be easy if you just listen."

"What do you want from this?" Brian asked.

"I want someone other than Harry Fox to have the tablet."

"Who's Harry Fox?"

"You're not a good liar, Brian. Harry has the tablet and I want him to lose it. You can make it happen."

Brian Joyce fell silent. When he finally spoke, he sounded like a man who has just been told he won the lottery when he didn't even buy a ticket. "I'm listening."

Listen he did, for several long minutes as Stefan told him to look for Harry Fox in Egypt, in or around the Giza or Saqqara necropoli, starting at the tomb of General Megabyzus.

"What's special about Megabyzus?" Brian asked when Stefan finished.

"I'm not sure," he admitted. "One interpretation of the tablet is it points to Megabyzus's grave. That's where to start if you want to find the tablet."

Brian grunted. "I'll check this out. There's no way I—"

Stefan cut him off. "You want to waste time and let Harry Fox get away, be my guest. If I hear he's been in and out of Egypt and you guys didn't find him, I'm sharing what I know with someone who will listen."

"There's no need to do that."

"Then I suggest you get to Egypt. You already know the tablet is valuable. You wouldn't have spent all that political goodwill by muscling in on the D.A.'s investigation if you didn't."

"How do you know—"

"Stop worrying about what I know. Start acting on what I told you. And don't try to find me. All your brother's money won't help you if I think you're a threat."

"I'm not interested in finding you," Brian said. "How do I reach you?"

"You don't," Stefan said and hung up. He quickly disassembled the burner phone, the parts destined for several sewer drains. Now all he could do was wait. For Brian Joyce and Nora Doyle to catch Harry Fox. For them to figure out what the tablet was truly about and perhaps even uncover the path it might or might not describe. If that happened, Stefan might have a new target to follow, a prize truly worth stealing. Nora would give him information. All he had to do was feed her the same low-level garbage he'd been handing over since their arrangement began. Nora got enough to keep her happy, and Stefan took over the business of his competitors when Nora arrested them. Wins all around.

Stefan stood and headed outside, nodding to the guard at the door as he left the Cana family headquarters. He turned his collar up against a cool breeze, his stomach rumbling when he passed the corner pizza shop. New concerns pushed any thoughts of Harry Fox aside. Recently rumors had churned through Altin Cana's organization. Whispers, none confirmed, but all saying Altin Cana wasn't sitting back any longer. He had plans to expand the family territory, to let their closest rival know the Albanians were no longer second fiddle in Brooklyn. Word was Altin Cana had plans. Plans to pick a fight with Vincent Morello.

Chapter Sixteen

Manhattan

Nora Doyle closed the folder and laid it on her desk. It stayed there for one full second before she made the prudent choice and fed the entire contents into her shredder. She wouldn't put it past Brian Joyce or his brother to go through her office when she wasn't around. The thought of Brian Joyce coming across the dishonorable discharge paperwork from his stint in the Marines made her nervous. A man who had reportedly shot unarmed Iraqi civilians during the first Gulf War was a man you didn't cross lightly. Lucky for Brian Joyce, the military had found no witnesses willing to testify.

A knock sounded on her door. She looked up to find one of the I.T. geniuses standing in the hall with a flash drive in one hand.

"Have a second?" He wiggled the drive. "Surveillance footage from the traffic camera near Columbia University you asked for."

Nora jumped up. "Finally." She took the drive he held out.

"You can keep it. Want me to stick around while you watch?"

Nora shook her head. "No thanks. I'll call if I have any questions."

He walked out as she stuck the USB drive into her computer and opened the file. A still image flashed onscreen, taken from the vantage point of a streetlight across from the entrance to Manan Khalidi's office. A time and date stamp in the lower corner showed this was twenty minutes before the unidentified second man Khalidi met on the day of his death arrived. She hit the fast forward button.

The image jumped, frames moving ahead as people walked at normal speed.

"You're kidding me." Nora leaned over until her nose nearly touched the screen. "That's Harry Fox." She manipulated the image, zooming in on the man walking in front of Khalidi's building. It was a slightly grainy, long-distance view of a man whose face you couldn't see clearly. A man with dark hair, ruffled by the breeze. A man whose face was shrouded in shadow until the clouds parted for an instant and sunlight lit his face, illuminating his features. A face she knew.

Harry Fox was walking out of Manan Khalidi's building the same day he'd died. Twenty minutes *before* the man she was looking for had walked in for Khalidi's final meeting.

"What were you doing at Khalidi's office?" Nora watched him walk out of screen, then grabbed her phone.

A bored voice answered after five rings. "Evidence department."

"This is Agent Doyle with the anti-trafficking unit. I need everything you have on a case." She rattled off Khalidi's file name and number. "How soon can it be here?"

The man on the other end didn't conceal his sigh. "As soon as possible, Agent Doyle." He hung up without waiting for her response.

Her phone survived the crash landing. *No wonder you're stuck down in Evidence.*

Eyes closed, she kneaded the bridge of her nose. Khalidi had a secretary. The two uniforms who had checked his office would have checked for scheduled appointments that day. If Harry Fox's name was listed, there would be a record of it. Nora's finger tap-danced on her desk. Why had Harry Fox been there? Had they met? If so, what had they talked about? And who else knew Fox had been there?

The *ding* of an email interrupted her train of thought. A message from the Arabic-speaking investigator the D.A.'s office used from time to time. She had sent him two images from the marked pages in the book on Khalidi's desk. His message supplied the translations, along with where she could deliver the promised bourbon.

Finally, progress. His first summary explained the map, which was of Saqqara, the burial grounds for people who died in Memphis when it was the capital of Egypt. She had managed to learn that on her own, though confirmation from the investigator eased her mind. Next, the opposite page, one she couldn't read a word of. The page noted royalty and other prominent persons buried at Saqqara.

A knock sounded on her door. Nora looked up to find Brian Joyce standing there, doing the oddest thing. Smiling.

"Good afternoon, Agent Doyle." He walked in without asking. "I have good news."

"Come in. Have a seat." She waved at one of the chairs across from her. "You could have called and saved yourself a trip." Brian either didn't care about or didn't pick up on the jab.

"Not with news like this." Joyce crossed overly muscled arms on his chest. "We have a lead on the tablet."

Through supreme force of will, Nora appeared unimpressed. "Is that so?"

Brian Joyce powered on. "Harry Fox will soon be in Egypt. Specifically, at a necropolis, either Giza or Saqqara. With the tablet."

Now Nora let her true feelings show. "How do you know?"

Brian kept his lips shut. Nora glared at him. He got the message. "We have contacts close to the Italian mob. One of them heard that Harry left town for Egypt. He may already be there."

Nora grabbed her mouse and clicked until an image of the book from Khalidi's desk came onscreen. She flipped the monitor around so Brian could see. "Remember this book? It was on Professor Khalidi's desk with a bookmark inside. Care to guess what the page is about?"

Brian Joyce's face made it clear how he felt about guessing games.

"One page was a map of Saqqara," Nora said. "The other was a list of notable people buried there."

Brian aimed a thick finger at her ceiling. "That proves it. Harry

Fox is headed to Saqqara."

"*Proves* is a strong word," Nora said. "I'll go with *suggests* for now." His face fell and she spoke quickly. "Which is more than we had an hour ago. Combine what your source said with these marked pages and we may have something."

"Do you think Fox was the one who met Khalidi before he died?" Brian asked. "None of my intel points to Fox as a killer. He's an artifacts guy, a softie. Not the kind to take a man out up close."

Nora didn't point out that, by Brian's definition, she was also a softie. "I don't think Harry Fox is a killer. We still don't know if Manan Khalidi's death was a homicide or an accident, and may never know for sure."

Nora told Brian about the traffic camera footage showing Harry Fox leaving Khalidi's office at least twenty minutes before the unidentified visitor arrived. "I'm having the secretary's day planner checked to see if Fox had an appointment. I suspect his reason for visiting an expert on Ancient Persia was to ask about the tablet. Not to kill anyone."

"Fox wouldn't want anyone else to know about the tablet," Brian said. "He could have been cleaning up loose ends. Maybe the professor knew too much."

"Professor Khalidi was an academic. He traveled the world speaking at conferences on the subject he loved. It's more likely he would have treated Harry's inquiry as an intellectual exercise, not a chance to rob Harry."

Brian's jaw tightened. "You've already made up your mind."

Jeez. Mr. Tough Guy was more sensitive than he let on. "I'm not criticizing your idea. Without your source I'd still have nothing but guesswork. Your information makes a convincing case for Harry being the connection."

The glowering stopped. "You think so?" he asked with a dash of hesitation.

"I do." Nora spread her arms out. "When we catch up to Harry

Fox, you can ask him about Manan Khalidi and see if you don't agree with me. Best to face him man-to-man, right?"

"That's right. Get his measure that way."

I'm sure you think so. "Excellent," Nora said. "Now, I have to plead with my boss for a plane ticket to Cairo. If Harry Fox is there right now, we can't wait."

She reached for the phone and nearly jumped when Brian Joyce touched her hand. "No need for that," he said. "We already obtained permission for this next step. You can ride with me."

"To *Cairo?*"

Brian nodded. "And wherever else we have to go. On a Bergen jet. My brother gave us one from our fleet. It's ready now."

Nora opened her mouth, failed to get anything out, then regrouped. "You got us a plane?"

"A Gulfstream G550. It will get us to Cairo in ten hours."

Nora Doyle was the daughter of a city prosecutor and a homemaker. She'd never been on a private jet in her life. "*Us* as in you and me?"

"And two members of my security team familiar with the Middle East."

Nora shook her head. "Okay, that's great. When do we leave?"

Brian stood. "As soon as you pack your bag. I'll have a car come to your home."

Nora stood as well. Her entire body buzzed. "Give me thirty minutes."

Brian Joyce turned to leave, then stopped. "I suggest leaving your duty weapon here."

She looked up from stuffing her computer into a bag. "You're right. Egyptian security won't let me bring it into the country."

"They won't. That's why I'll bring you an extra one." He rapped a knuckle on the door. "See you at the airport."

Chapter Seventeen

Saqqara, Egypt

A Toyota four-wheel drive entered the Saqqara necropolis, skirting the busier sections where tourists gathered and teams of archaeologists turned earth. The vehicle wound through the site until it reached a secondary tomb that did not receive many visitors. The tomb of a Persian general from the Achaemenid empire who had once crushed a revolt, and whose tomb could hold the key to unraveling a centuries-old mystery.

Harry ground to a stop outside the entrance to the tomb of Megabyzus. Moments later the dust cloud in his wake caught up, enshrouding his vehicle in hazy darkness. The tomb was cut out of a hillside and accessed solely by this unpaved road. Harry had passed a pair of motorcycles moments earlier, each with a passenger and driver. Tourists, from the look of them. He turned and watched the road behind him, counting to a hundred. They did not reappear. Harry reached for his door handle as another vehicle crested the hill in front of him. He choked on the dry air.

Police.

A squad car. Lights atop the roof. Uniformed officer behind the wheel. The police officer drove past Harry's stopped car and parked not far away, near the tomb's base. Harry watched as the officer got out and walked to the front of his car to lean against the hood, arms crossed on his chest, eyes hidden behind mirrored sunglasses. The policeman's face didn't turn toward Harry's car. In fact, the officer took no notice of him. The officer stood looking over the necropolis grounds toward the lush green trees and fields less than a mile distant, where the Nile flowed past the city of El Badrashin.

"Keep sitting here and he'll get suspicious," Harry said to himself. His was the only car in sight. The officer didn't show any interest in the Toyota, but if he stuck around long enough that could change. Harry grabbed a flashlight and his phone, which had images of the tablet stored on it. The ceramic knuckledusters he took on every mission went into another pocket in case things got hairy. Suitably equipped, he opened the door and was promptly assaulted by a blast furnace of heat. Dusty air coated his throat as a light, scorching breeze carried particulate into his eyeballs. Harry cursed and pulled the neck gaiter up over his mouth and nose. He grabbed a bottle of water and closed the car door, checking twice that it was locked before walking toward the tomb's entrance. He paused, looking down the gently sloping hill back to the main entrance, with El Badrashin beyond it. Two bicyclists cruised slowly in his direction, the only other people around other than the police officer. Harry kept one eye on the cop as he walked, though the man never once looked Harry's way.

Harry pushed the cop from his thoughts and moved toward the tomb, truly looking at it for the first time. His steps slowed as he approached. Stone giants guarded the entrance, three fearsome soldiers on either side carved into the hill, all six clad in unique garb and carrying different weapons as they stood watch over the general. One from each of the successful campaigns Megabyzus led, each soldier representing a vanquished opponent. Harry inspected each in turn, pretending to take pictures.

Through it all the nearby police officer did nothing more than get into his car and blast the air conditioning. Harry took that as a sign and stepped through the tomb's only door, a dark hole in the hillside scarcely large enough for two people to enter together. One moment

Harry stood under Ra's flaming orb; the next, he disappeared into the darkness.

Dim electric lights lined the walls of Megabyzus's tomb as Harry descended two steps to the stone floor. Dim to Harry because the sun had ruined his vision, rendering him virtually blind as he entered the darkened interior. Rapid blinking brought the world back into focus. A rectangular chapel stretched before him, carved deep into the hillside where Megabyzus's life and exploits were recounted on every available surface. Hieroglyphs covered the walls, surrounding recessed statues of men, gods and other beings Harry knew not, telling a story he couldn't read very well of a man he knew little about. Harry turned back to face the entrance, looking to where the floor met the wall. He'd start there. Engravings covered every inch of the place. If there was a message to find, he couldn't skip a single one. The statues would be last.

Harry flicked his flashlight on, bent down and started reading, using his rudimentary knowledge of hieroglyphs and cuneiform. Many of the glyphs had paint on them, dark blues and light greens under Harry's flashlight, visible even after thousands of years. The glyphs repeated themselves, stating the general's name over and over, along with the major Egyptian and Persian deities. Nothing stood out on the front wall, and Harry turned ninety degrees to move down the longer side wall, which had statues set in recessed alcoves. A lioness watched him from one side, while a stone soldier stood opposite.

Sweat stung his eyes. It was *hot* in here. The narrow front door kept air from flowing in or out. Dust motes floated in Harry's flashlight beam as he went. More hieroglyphs mixed with cuneiform. Most of the writings were hieroglyphics, the names of prominent gods such as Ra, the sun god or Osiris, the god of death. Those he knew. Others he didn't.

There were carvings behind the statues in the alcoves. The sweat soaking his shirt acted as a lubricant, letting him slide around to the narrow space behind these stone soldiers to get a better look at the walls. Dirt smeared his face, arms and legs. What would the police officer say when he came out looking as though he'd dug a trench? Harry stepped out from behind a statue and took a long drink of water. Find the hidden message first. Worry about that cop later.

As he sweated and choked on dust, Harry's thoughts turned to another problem with no solution, this one gathering steam in Brooklyn. Vincent Morello was not a young man, though in the nearly three decades Harry had known him, Vincent had been a rock, a constant in Harry's world. Years earlier Vincent had survived an assassination attempt in jail. Survived with the help of Harry's father. After jail, Vincent had navigated to the top of New York's organized crime hierarchy, yet still went to church on Sundays. For an entire generation, Vincent Morello had been the bedrock on which New York's crime families were built. Now cracks had formed in that foundation, and only trouble could come next.

Unless Vincent got ahead of it. How? His son. Joey had been groomed to take over the family business, had spent time as an associate below the soldiers. Joey got his hands dirty alongside the other men looking to make a name for themselves, though he was the only one with a prep school education and a degree in Finance. Now Joey was the Morello family underboss, his father's right-hand man and next in line to the seat of power. Of course, the other families had to accept Joey as the heir apparent, or chaos would reign.

For now, those problems existed half a world away. Harry reached the corner where one long wall met a shorter one at the chapel's rear. Nothing he'd seen yet seemed tied to the tablet. Xerxes himself was mentioned many times, but Harry decoded enough to conclude none of it was tied to the tablet.

A dark shadow raced across the wall. Harry jumped and dropped his flashlight. The beam flashed wildly around the room. The white light hit him square in the eyes, leaving white circles in his vision. He scrabbled in the dirt, grasping for his flashlight as he rubbed his eyes with one hand. Bad move. The gritty dirt and sand brought tears to his eyes. His roving hand found the flashlight. Harry turned in a circle, heart pounding.

Stop it. The room held only shadows circling around a guy who'd dropped his flashlight. The narrow doorway was a searing rectangle of light far behind him. No police officer was standing outside of it watching him. The only danger here was Harry's imagination. He moved toward the rear wall and tripped. Oh, and that. A stone cover had been bolted over the shaft leading to Megabyzus's burial chamber, a smaller room below this chapel where his body had once been, mummified and sealed in an intricately carved stone coffin. Coffin and mummy were now in the Imhotep Museum at the necropolis complex entrance. He looked down at the stone manhole cover that sealed the shaft. Too bad it wasn't quite level with the floor.

He stepped over the cover and faced a lone statue along the back wall. Bigger than the others, more than life-sized, the engraving above the recessed alcove told Harry this was Megabyzus, resplendent in full battle gear. A curved sword in one hand, a circular shield in the other, Megabyzus glared at his visitors from beneath a pointed helmet, a bearded, fearsome warrior challenging any who entered. His smooth, rounded eyes watched with an eternal gaze. A tremor crawled up Harry's back. This was one mean-looking bastard. Who had died thousands of years ago. *Stop worrying and get on with it.* The tablet had brought him here, because Megabyzus had been buried in this necropolis for a reason. Xerxes wouldn't have done that simply to taunt his vanquished enemies. Harry's light played over the statue's shield. Xerxes had done this with *purpose.*

Harry grabbed the water bottle and tilted it up, playing his flashlight into the alcove as he drank. A dark corner of the alcove came to life. Harry stopped drinking. He blinked. *No way.*

He slipped past the stone statue of Megabyzus and into the alcove. The cutout behind it was nearly big enough for a second statue. Partially hidden behind the statue of this tomb's occupant was a carving, a circular design etched into the wall that looked exactly like the shield Megabyzus carried. Hieroglyphs and cuneiform writing stretched from floor to ceiling even back here. He knelt, scraped his knee on a stone, launched an expletive and then kept reading. More about Megabyzus the conquering hero, how he owed it all to King Xerxes, the mighty and powerful, on and on. More of the same, as though gaining access to the afterlife had depended on how often he praised Xerxes. Perhaps to Megabyzus, it had.

The glyphs told the story of Megabyzus's triumphs in battle, words swerving around the carved shield on their way to the ceiling. Harry stopped reading. Nothing had been carved into the shield's surface, a circle of unblemished stone that seemed out of place when every other available surface had been scrawled upon. The shield actually stuck out from the wall, as though it were a separate carving placed there after the wall was cut. He could slip his fingers into the gap, though his probing hand found nothing but caked dirt.

Why was the shield nearly barren of carvings? Four cuneiform glyphs at regular intervals around the circumference were the sole decoration. The four glyphs were placed like cardinal direction points. The sound of a distant engine rumbled at the edge of hearing, and Harry stepped back to peer around the statue, looking back to the entrance. It remained empty; there was nothing other than hazy orange light falling onto the floor. He turned back to the shield. He stopped.

I know those glyphs. Four separate inscriptions. The Achaemenid version of a compass, though these weren't directional. Indecipherable, but not unrecognizable. Harry had seen them carved into Xerxes' tablet. The ones Professor Khalidi couldn't identify.

"Why are these here?"

A renowned scholar couldn't identify the glyphs. Yet here they were again, carved in stone and tucked behind a statue on walls with Persian imagery. He reached out and touched the topmost object, a mix of horizontal and vertical slashes. Harry traced them once, twice. These cuneiform carvings weren't exactly the same as those on the tablet. Close, but not quite.

He pulled his phone out and opened a snapshot of Xerxes' tablet, zooming in on the glyphs. There was one difference: they weren't in the same order. The four carvings on the tablet formed a ring, with one at each cardinal direction. He swung his flashlight up and illuminated the carvings on the shield in Megabyzus's tomb, the same carvings but in a different order. The top and bottom tablet images were reversed, and the ones to either side had also switched places — as though the shield had been rotated a hundred-eighty degrees before these images were carved. Since the tablet referenced the tomb, the tomb had been built sometime before the tablet. Whoever had created the tablet had made an upturned version of the glyphs on it. Why?

Harry looked at the stone shield, then back at his phone, turning it upside down to compare. When he touched his phone again his finger left a streak of dirt across it from when he'd been digging around the shield. A shield far enough out of the wall for someone to get a solid grip on it.

Inspiration struck. Sticking the flashlight between his teeth, Harry reached into the dark recesses around the shield's circumference, flexing each fingertip to clear the dirt away and reveal ridges on the rear surface. As though whoever built this had intended for it to offer a solid grip. The kind needed to twist a three-foot-tall shield halfway round so it matched the glyphs on Xerxes' tablet. His body tensed, teeth clenched tight on the flashlight as he grabbed the shield, set his feet, and twisted. Legs and back, he put everything into it, pushing and straining until, without warning, his hands slipped and he fell to his knees, leaving a streak of sweat and skin on the shield where his face bounced off it on the way down.

Damn. The flashlight had fallen, and when Harry picked it up a drop of blood slipped from his nose onto the handle. So much for not leaving evidence behind. Blood dripped down the shield as well, the thin, dark streak turning the light stone black. The glyphs hadn't budged an inch.

He grabbed the outer edges again, took a deep breath, and twisted. Arms screaming, back burning, he twisted until the cut on his nose burned where sweat streamed over the wound. Harry stood back, leaning against the statue behind him. He couldn't call for help. His closest friends were across an ocean. Except Sarah, who was in Germany, nearly two thousand miles away. Not much closer than Brooklyn.

If this shield was actually meant to be turned, Harry was on his own. He grabbed the outer edges again, jamming his fingers around the lip, then shoved his foot against the wall for better leverage, kicking up a cloud of dust in the process. A deep breath before twisting sucked in the dusty cloud, sending him into a coughing fit until he dropped the flashlight from between his teeth. He tried to stop it rolling away with one foot but managed only to step on it and lose his balance. His foot slipped out from under him and he tumbled, only able to stay up due to his death-grip on the shield.

Which moved.

Harry let go of the stone and fell to his backside. "That's *it*. Clockwise. It goes the *other way*."

Every time Harry had grabbed the wheel and twisted, he'd tried to move it counterclockwise, the same way he'd loosened anything his entire life. The Egyptians must have done it differently. The shield made a half-revolution, bringing the glyphs into alignment with Xerxes' tablet. Harry blinked away dripping sweat. Now what?

A low rumble began at Harry's feet and worked through his bones, felt more than heard. Dirt trickled from the ceiling, cascading in shimmering waves from between stone blocks. He dove under the statue of Megabyzus. The rumbling seemed to last forever, though it was no more than a few seconds. The world stopped vibrating. Harry peered out from between his fingers into a translucent film of dust hovering in the suddenly still air.

The cop. He had to have heard the rumbling. Harry jumped up and looked to the front entrance. Was the policeman already standing outside, calling for backup? Was he about to walk in, arrest Harry and throw him in an Egyptian prison? This and more seared across his mind as he stepped back from the statue, his flashlight bringing the chapel's interior to life. He took another step back and found nothing but air. He fell, tumbling into the netherworld below, arms flailing before his backside hit rock and he skidded down a sloped floor to smack on level ground. The complete absence of sound and light told him what had happened. He was flat on his stomach, face pressed into what felt like another dirt floor. Harry sneezed, his body shifted, and the flashlight beneath him gave a sliver of light. He'd been lying on it. Staying prone, he reached for the light and his arm shouted in protest. Whatever he had hit on the way down had done a number on every part of his body. Cautious this time, he moved with care, shining his light ahead to see what type of underworld he had entered.

Angry gods surrounded him, deities with animal heads and human bodies, falcon and jackal heads atop human shoulders on the walls. Brilliant green and blue paints brought the fierce creatures to life, their purpose to shepherd the deceased's soul safely to the afterlife. But Megabyzus's coffin had been found long ago. Which meant this was not his tomb.

Then what was it? No more than ten feet wide or long, it was an antechamber of sorts, below the actual tomb, and its entrance had been covered by a stone plate. This room had shared a wall with the tomb through its discovery and excavation, yet it clearly remained undiscovered.

Harry turned in a circle. No statues here, only paintings on the wall. No glyphs or cuneiform letters either. A dull white mound in one corner caught his eyes, which narrowed. *Bones.* A pile of them. He picked one up, then dropped it in shock. Not animal bones.

Human. He could see several femurs and a pair of ribcages laying on top of each other, as though a number of bodies had been stacked there, time having turned them to dry bone and strips of cloth. Harry's flashlight beam caught a square edge beside the pile. He flicked the light over. It was a stone pedestal, almost as high as his waist. Something rested atop it. Small, and thin. Almost the size of…*a tablet.*

He took a step toward it before his brain kicked in and he stopped, nearly tumbling over as his arms swirled for balance. Don't move. *Think.* If Xerxes had hidden this room, he had a reason. It wasn't hard to believe he would also protect it. Traps, open pits, any number of terrible contraptions Harry had seen before could be in here. He played the light around, first to the side, where he saw a large stone block on the ground. Not a pedestal. A counterweight. Judging from where it lay, this stone had been balanced on an edge until Harry had twisted the shield above it, knocking it off-kilter and sending it tumbling. That had opened the entrance above by way of the heavy rope attached to it.

The counterweight stone now lay beneath the chute that had opened and deposited Harry down here. It wouldn't be easy, but if he could get on top of the counterweight, he could scrabble back up the angled chute to the chapel. Harry stepped toward the pedestal. No trap doors opened; no axes swung from the ceiling. That being handled, an object resting atop the pedestal demanded his attention. Rectangular and smooth-edged, it looked about the same size as Xerxes' tablet. Or, Xerxes' *first* tablet, he should say now. Because he'd just found a second one.

Cuneiform ran across part of the tablet's front side, and an image stretched across the bottom. An engraving of a building, wide and flat, with five pillars across the front. Harry pulled his phone out and snapped several pictures. No writing was visible on the pedestal, no sign that removing the tablet would trigger any reaction. Harry swallowed to no effect; his mouth and throat were dry as the tomb.

He reached for the tablet, gingerly slipping his hand under the edge, and lifted it. He stopped. Nothing tried to kill him.

Dust swirled in his light as Harry exhaled. He read the tablet's first few lines, deciphering what he could. One name appeared time and again. *Xerxes*. And this wasn't written *about* the great king. It was written *by* him.

A different phrase caught his eye. *City of Persians*. Not the most specific name, given the Achaemenid empire had covered over two million square miles. How many cities were in that vast area? But hope sparked as he read on. *"You must follow the Greek's knowledge before the king's wealth."* The same phrase found on Xerxes' first tablet. Professor Khalidi had said it might be tied to Homer, Plato or Euclid, or even Hippocrates. As for the *beacon* that could outlast the gods, did it also tie into the legend of a once-sickly physician who had ultimately lived for over a century?

A distant voice sounded from above as a man called out in Arabic. Harry moved over to stand beneath the chute. The voice rang out again, louder now. Closer.

"Marhabaan? Hal 'ant huna?" Hello? Are you in here?

Someone was searching for Harry. It had to be the cop, the only person who had seen Harry come in here. The man's voice was louder now. As though he was right next to the opening.

"Hello? I felt the ground—"

The man's words cut off, turning to a scream as he crashed down the chute and slid out, one arm clipping Harry's shoulder as he tumbled into the antechamber. Harry flicked his light off and didn't move. Neither did the man who had fallen in, who now lay unmoving on the ground. Harry set the tablet back on the pedestal and crept over, where his light revealed it was the cop from outside, last seen escaping the heat in his car. A cop now unconscious and not moving on the dirt floor of this antechamber. Harry checked for a pulse. Strong and steady, same as his breathing. The cop had hit his head, even had a small gash, but overall seemed okay.

Time to go. The cop should be fine. He was a bit overweight and not exactly young, so climbing out of here might not be in the cards for him without help. But Harry had no plans to be around when the man woke up. Harry grabbed the tablet, jumped on the counterweight stone and reached for the chute. He paused. He didn't want the man to suffer until help came, so Harry grabbed his water bottle, took a last drink, then set it in plain sight within reach of the unconscious man. He stuck the new tablet in his waistband and hopped into the chute, managing to pull himself to the top and into the empty chapel. Sunlight still cut across the dirt floor, falling through the door in a narrow strip. Saqqara's main entrance was nearly a half mile distant on unpaved dirt and sand paths. Should the cop prove enterprising, he might have time to get out of the antechamber, find his radio, and call for assistance before Harry made his escape.

But there was one way to slow that process. Harry stepped outside into the Egyptian sun. The cop's car was where he'd last seen it. Disabling the guy's radio would buy him time. Harry was reaching for the door handle when two motorcycles buzzed past the tomb entrance.

He pivoted and walked to his car. One of the riders turned his way, long enough to get a good look at his face. *Damn.* Now someone could identify him. Forgetting stealth, he jumped into his vehicle, grabbed the wheel – and swore at full volume when it burned the skin off his raw hands. He wrapped his shirt around the wheel. The interior of the car was now like a blast furnace, even hotter than the tomb. More carefully now, he started the car and set off.

Bouncing and jarring over the uneven road, he reached over and put Xerxes' new tablet in his messenger bag, which he tucked under the seat. The two motorcyclists buzzed past again, now going in the opposite direction, seemingly not paying him any mind. Harry ducked his head anyway. He sped down a sloping hill and back up the other side, then swung around a long curve before checking his rearview mirror; he was finally able to see the entrance to Megabyzus's tomb. He looked twice, then hit the gas. The two motorcycles had parked outside the tomb.

Heatwaves shimmered off the ground as Harry now raced toward the exit, dust clouds billowing in his wake. A quarter mile to go, none of it straight. Down a sloping curve, he lost sight of the tomb until he was up the other side, just in time to see one motorcyclist run out of the tomb entrance. The one who had looked him square in the face minutes ago. The man leaned inside the police car and then stood up with the portable radio in his hand. Harry's eyes went to Saqqara's entrance, where two police cars sat side by side, officers standing in front of them, heads bowed in conversation. A beat passed, then another. One of the cops glanced into his police car as though his radio had squawked for attention.

Harry couldn't get out through the front gate now. Venturing into the desert wasn't an option. His only way out was through that front entrance, where the police officers were now moving with a purpose they hadn't had before. He slowed, easing around a curve that dipped to hide him from both the front and back. He couldn't see the tomb or the entrance, and for the moment, no one could see him. At the bottom of this slight depression a tent stood on one side of the road. Likely a staging point for one of the ongoing excavations. Two cars and a handful of motorcycles were parked near the large tent, all of them a good hundred feet from the tent's front flap. A front flap that was closed.

The occupants likely wouldn't hear the sound of one engine. A motorcycle engine. Harry wheeled over, parked between the tent and the group of motorcycles. Emptying the car's glove compartment, he stuffed everything into the messenger bag and looped it around his torso. The Toyota's keys came with him. He needed a spot of luck. Harry looked toward the tent. *One of you has to be the trusting sort.*

Of the six bikes, one grabbed his eye. A Triumph Bonneville, one of the British manufacturer's most popular bikes and a mainstay in the world of motorcycles. A 750 cc from the looks of it, thirty years old if a day. Harry had ridden Triumphs, though he hadn't been on one since before his father's death. Harry checked the ignition: no keys. He leaned over and stuck his hand under the front mudguard. *Bingo.*

He grabbed a helmet from another bike as he pushed his new ride onto the road. He fired the engine, strapped the helmet on and slipped the bike into gear, heading toward the exit. A glance over his shoulder revealed nothing amiss. No angry bike owners running after him, no police car moving in to catch him. Harry rode through the entrance gate, let off the gas and slowed to a more meandering pace. Just another tourist enjoying Saqqara, driving cautiously back to his hotel. Nothing to see here.

A black Range Rover passed him on the way in. Harry sat at the light as a man exited the passenger side and went straight for the officers standing guard, brandishing a folder that he stuck in one cop's face. Thickly muscled, short hair, pale skin. He couldn't be anything other than American.

Harry shot across traffic and pulled off a block from the entrance. He kept the helmet on and watched. Watched the American gesturing at the police officer. Watched as the harangued officer spoke into a radio moments before a second police car appeared. The second car headed for Megabyzus's tomb. Then Harry watched the American jump back into his Range Rover, which shot into Saqqara, racing up the road leading to Megabyzus.

Harry pulled out his phone and dialed Joey Morello's number.

Joey answered at once. "I hope you're in Cairo by now."

"Better than that," Harry said. "I'm outside the necropolis. Listen to what I found." He gave an abbreviated version of uncovering the tablet. "I'll explain more later, but right now I may have a problem. I think someone followed me here." Harry described what he'd witnessed. "That Range Rover just stopped in front of Megabyzus's tomb," Harry said. "Either he's helping rescue the cop from the antechamber, or he intended to go there all along."

"Who outside our family knows you're in Egypt?"

"No one other than Rose. I told her about the connection with Saqqara."

"Hold on," Joey said. "My father wants to talk." Joey put the call on speaker. Vincent Morello's voice sounded. Weakly.

"Harry, are you in danger?"

"Not immediate," Harry said. "I borrowed a motorcycle and got out of the area."

"Quick on your feet," Vincent said. "Just like your father. How much does Rose Leroux know?"

"Pretty much everything," Harry said. "What's on the first tablet, what I thought it meant, and its ties to Saqqara."

"What about the anti-trafficking unit and the agent who contacted you?" Vincent asked.

"They might have an idea that I'm here," Harry said. "Depends on how much they got from the Greeks. It's possible that detective could connect the dots. Let's say the agent suspects I traveled here. If the D.A. sent people to Egypt, wouldn't they coordinate with law enforcement agencies here? They'd be visible, not hidden."

"True," Vincent said. "Meaning Rose is the only other person you know who is aware of the Saqqara connection."

Harry shook his head. "We've done business with her for decades. She knew my father."

"Rose is driven by profit. Never forget that." Vincent coughed. "She has risen to a high place in our world, yet she could not have come from more humble beginnings. Tragedy had a profound effect on her."

The buzz of traffic faded to nothing. "What do you mean?" Harry asked. He'd never heard anything about Rose Leroux's life before she became New York's biggest fence. He assumed she'd been born into it. "I don't know anything about her past."

"Rose immigrated to America under terrible conditions. I know she came to this country to escape conflict in the former Soviet Republics. I believe she is Ukrainian, though I am not certain. Her family was killed in the turmoil of the Soviet collapse. It happened when she was a younger woman, though I do not know where she lived before coming to America."

"I always thought she was French," Harry said.

"Rose never dispels inaccurate thoughts on her past," Vincent said. "She left Europe to escape the horrors of a collapsing world, using whatever influence she possessed." A rattling wheeze. "She has experienced the very worst of this world. To forget that is to fail to understand who she is, and what she may be capable of."

"You think she might have sold us out," Harry said.

"I doubt she would betray you, for two reasons. You are under my protection, and we pay her very well. The Rose Leroux I know would only betray a man for one thing: more money."

"And you have the most," Harry said. "Not to mention how much steady business we give her."

"Both true."

"I can't see her selling me out. When I told her about the tablet she was intrigued, and not just about her commission. She actually likes hunting for artifacts, same as me."

"Yet I hope you are cautious around Rose," Vincent said. "Assuming you can read her is a fool's errand." More muted coughing, which went on longer this time. "Excuse me," Vincent said. "The air is dry today." Another cough. "Rose is impossible to read. She did not come to America alone. Rose traveled with another woman and that woman's infant. They left their homeland together. Their journey could not have been easy, but Rose did not abandon her friend. She brought the woman and child with her, securing their passage across the sea. Rose risked her life to save those of her friend and the infant. Do not underestimate what she can do."

Harry grunted. "So she's a suspect until proven otherwise. Thanks, Mr. Morello."

"It is Vincent. You know that."

Joey spoke up. "Keep your eyes open, Harry. Where are you going next?"

"I have to decode this new tablet," Harry said. "The message on it is shorter than the first one."

"Let us know what you need," Joey said.

"I will," Harry said. "Don't tell anyone I'm here or that I found a second tablet." He squinted against the sunlight. "Someone followed me here. I know it."

"How?"

"Because that Range Rover just stopped in front of Megabyzus's tomb."

Harry clicked off, turned the bike's key and reached for the start button. Tires screeched as a car suddenly accelerated out of traffic and veered directly at him. Harry scrambled to back up, overbalanced and fell off the bike. The car stopped on screeching tires as the driver's door flew open. Harry twisted, got up and took one step before his feet went from under him. He crashed to the sidewalk. A hand grabbed hold of his collar to flip him around. Harry cocked a fist as he looked up into a black oval, his assailant's face backlit by the sun.

An assailant holding a gun.

Chapter Eighteen

Cairo, Egypt

A black Range Rover raced out of the hotel parking lot, its engine roaring as it vanished into traffic. Nora Doyle looked out of her hotel window and briefly thought about throwing a chair through it, followed by her desk, bed and anything else she could lift. Never had she imagined this happening when her boss had told her to allow Brian Joyce to *assist* in the investigation. Not when they'd jetted to Egypt on Bergen Inc.'s private jet. Not even when she had overheard Brian Joyce on a call several minutes ago in the lobby, a call she wasn't supposed to hear.

Brian Joyce and his two associates had just ditched her in a Cairo hotel, supposedly while she waited for "approval" from her superior as Brian and his men conducted off-the-books reconnaissance. *It will be faster this way*, Brian had told her. *You have to play by the rules.* She had no idea what rules he meant to break, and right now she couldn't reach her boss. Everything about it reeked of a setup, a play by Joyce to get Nora out of his hair.

Then Nora overheard Brian talking near the elevator banks. After checking in, Nora and Brian's two men had taken the elevator up to their rooms while Brian stayed downstairs to make a call. The elevator had stopped one floor up, at the same time Nora realized she hadn't received a room key. She took the stairs back down, emerging around the corner from where Brian stood talking, loudly enough for her to overhear him say her name. She stopped, mere feet away, hidden from view.

"Nora Doyle served her purpose," Brian had said. "We're leaving her behind. Should you tell the D.A.?"

Leaving me behind?

"No, good point. The D.A. doesn't need to know everything. Tell him you want us to have space in order to give him plausible deniability if anything goes wrong. He won't argue," Brian said.

Brian was almost certainly talking to his brother, Guy. Nora clenched her fist. This was her mission. Nobody left her behind.

Brian kept talking, his words more subdued. "You're right. Strongarming the D.A. is a bad idea. A quiet chat is better. You sure he'll go along?"

Guy must have agreed.

"Good," Brian said. "Wait thirty minutes after we go. I'll be in touch once we secure the tomb. Once we find Mr. Fox, he won't tell anyone about the tablet."

Nora's jaw was clenched so tight she couldn't speak. She barely managed to duck into the stairwell before Brian appeared from around the corner and stepped onto an elevator. Nora waited in the stairwell until he disappeared. So the Joyce brothers were double-crossing her, making Nora a pawn? It sounded like they planned to get rid of Harry Fox. *Won't tell anyone what he knows?* This investigation wasn't aimed specifically at Harry Fox. Why was Joyce threatening him?

Rumbling filled the stairwell. Her phone, buzzing like mad. Nora checked the screen, took a deep breath and answered. "Doyle speaking."

Her boss spoke lightly. "You make it to Cairo?"

"Yes," she said, then endured a round of pleasantries. It took him a minute to get to the point. As though he were avoiding it.

"A notification came from upstairs," he said. The district attorney. "He's checking on jurisdictional issues. You need to hold off on going anywhere for now. I expect it will be taken care of shortly."

"Brian Joyce and the Bergen security team will be disappointed to hear it."

"Technically, they're private citizens. Tourists, really. They can go about their business. I'll be in touch as soon as we have clearance for you to continue your investigation."

"I won't be able to provide support if the Bergen team runs into resistance. My ties to the office would be useful in securing local cooperation."

"Appreciate the concern, Agent Doyle, but wait until I have this handled before continuing the operation." He hesitated. "Any questions?"

"No, sir. I understand. No official investigation until I hear from you."

"Excellent. We'll speak soon." Her boss clicked off.

It took her a minute, but when Nora walked out of the stairwell and got on an elevator to her room, her poker face was back. Or at least as good a poker face as she could manage. Her Irish father's ancestral temper ran hot in her veins.

She made it to her room, tossed her bag in a corner, then two thumping knocks rattled the door. She didn't bother looking through the peephole before flinging it open. Brian Joyce stood outside, one hand raised. "Yes?"

He stepped back. "I just got the news of the delay. Sorry, Agent Doyle. I hate it when red tape gets involved."

She kept an even tone. "We need to stay here until we receive clearance to move."

It knocked Brian off-kilter. "Yes. I mean no," he said quickly. "Not exactly. We still have a chance to get ahead of this, see if the tablet is pointing to Saqqara."

"You're going out while I wait here." She didn't blink as she said it.

Brian did. "This isn't ideal, I know." He rallied. "One good point is my men and I don't have the red tape to worry about. We'll get boots on the ground in Saqqara, do some recon and see what we're up against. Once you get the all-clear, we'll be that much further ahead."

I'm not holding my breath. "I see."

Brian Joyce looked to the floor, then back to Nora, where he found no quarter. "Right. We're moving out. Keep your phone handy. I'll call as soon as we know anything, or you let me know when you're on the way." Something akin to concern crossed his face. "You can get a rental car here. The hotel offers them."

"I'm sure I'll manage. Won't be a Range Rover."

"Best operational car I've found," Brian said. "I always use them. Ask if they can find one for you."

Nora shut the door to cut off any further replies.

Now she watched the Range Rover disappear, taking with it a team she couldn't trust bankrolled by men using their money to manipulate the D.A.'s office. Her best chance at a source was still Harry, and despite how her first try had gone, she knew she could cultivate him. She crossed her arms, looking out over the brief stretch of greenery along the Nile's banks to the expanse of arid desert beyond. The parameters had changed. Nora would follow orders. She would not investigate until given full clearance. For now, she was a tourist. And what did tourists do? They went sightseeing.

Nora grabbed some essentials from her bag and hurried to the elevator. She needed a car and the front desk was happy to assist. "Bill it to my room," she said. The concierge took down the room number she rattled off. Brian Joyce's room number. Nora flashed a smile. "You have anything that goes fast?"

Ten minutes later a BMW 3 Series burst out of the hotel parking lot at full steam for Saqqara. The car's rich leather upholstery smelled of oil and money. Nora took a small measure of satisfaction knowing how much it cost to rent. Brian Joyce could shove it. Everything he'd done pointed to one thing: Brian had a private agenda, one that didn't involve playing by the rules.

She went heavy on the gas, bobbing and weaving through traffic, headed to Saqqara. Alongside and over the Nile, past the Sphinx and Great Pyramids at Giza, she kept the engine buzzing to catch Brian's team. A half-hour head start would have put them almost to the site by now.

An hour had passed and she had yet to receive a call from headquarters clearing her to proceed. Odd, considering their agent was halfway around the world and supposedly leading the search. Could be it really was taking time to cut through the red tape, though. Even the district attorney answered to someone, though chances were he was answering to money right now. And that money was saying *slow down.*

She fumed over this for the next twenty minutes. By the time a new set of pyramids rose on the horizon, Nora was doing one hundred forty kilometers per hour. What that equated to in miles per hour she had no idea, but it was fast. The GPS shouted her exit was ahead. Tires squealed as she veered across traffic and down the ramp, smashing her brakes at a light. She gunned it to the next light, racing past the vast expanse of Saqqara on one side and the Nile's lush banks on the other.

She approached the necropolis and spotted several dark vehicles, none close enough to verify as Brian Joyce's Range Rover. She'd have to track them down inside, which could take ages. This place was *huge.* Sitting at another light, she noted a pair of police officers inside the front entrance. They might help a fellow law enforcement agent. Excuse me, officers. Did you see a black Range Rover come through recently? You did? Tell me where to find him.

Or maybe they call the D.A. to verify this story and rat me out. Scratch that idea. Nora tapped her fingers on the steering wheel. She pulled out her phone and looked down the cross street. Her gaze flitted over a motorcyclist near the intersection, parked next to the sidewalk. The man stared toward Saqqara with a phone pressed to his ear. She looked past him, then her eyes went back to him for reasons she couldn't quite articulate. He looked familiar. Which was crazy. Her gaze narrowed. *Hold on.*

The man put his phone away and gave Nora an unimpeded view of his face. He slipped on his helmet and buttoned the chin strap. Nora looked in her side mirror and hammered the gas, red light be damned. The man tried to start his motorcycle. Nora couldn't let that happen. Harry Fox had just fallen into her lap. The BMW darted across traffic, slicing through a narrow opening between moving cars before one tire vaulted the curb and she stood on the brakes. It was that or run over Harry Fox. He turned as she jumped out and tripped him up, sending him to the sidewalk. Nora grabbed his collar with one hand, flipping him over. Harry cocked a fist.

"Harry, stop. It's Nora Doyle." She let go of his collar. "It's me, Harry." Nora raised her hands to show they were empty, except she still had her phone in one of them. She jammed it into her pocket.

Harry drew ragged breaths, lying on the sidewalk with one fist pulled back. He kicked back from her, then shielded his eyes. "*Doyle?*"

He couldn't see her. Not with the sun at her back. Nora stepped to one side, giving him more distance. Not enough to get away, though. "Take it easy, Harry. We need to talk."

Harry scrambled to his feet. He didn't run away, but adjusted his shirt to hide a metallic necklace as he leaned closer. "You're in Egypt?" Harry looked over her shoulder into the necropolis. "Are you with them?"

"Them? Who are you talking about? I'm –" *Them.* Nora spun around. "Did you see a group of Americans drive into Saqqara in a black Range Rover?"

"Yes. You know them," Harry said, taking a step back. "You're here for the tablet." He looked to the motorcycle between them. "Get out of my—"

She lifted her hands. "No, I'm not. I didn't come for you. Just *listen* to me." Harry took a step toward the bike. "Look." She grabbed her phone and held it out. "Take this if you don't believe me. I only want to talk."

"You're lying."

"I'm not. If you want to leave when I'm finished, I won't stop you." Nora tossed him the phone, which he caught. "Take these too." The BMW started beeping when she threw him the keys, though the engine still ran. "There. If you leave, I'm stuck here."

Harry kicked a leg over the bike. "Back up," he said. Only after her rear end touched the car and he was safely astride the bike did he speak again. "Two minutes."

Nora crossed her arms on her chest. "First, tell me who you think I'm with?"

"The guys in a black Range Rover." He pointed behind her. "The one parked outside Megabyzus's tomb."

Nora turned and looked into the necropolis. People moved about, some in cars, others on bikes or motorcycles, and many on foot. It was a maze she couldn't interpret. "Where's the tomb?"

"On top of the ridge. See the two cop cars sitting up there?"

She did. And right beside them, a black Range Rover with two men standing beside it. Brian Joyce's men. "Yes. I did come to Egypt with them, but I swear I'm not here to steal anything from you." She looked over her shoulder at Harry. "We came here to find you. There's more to that tablet than you realize. A lot more."

Harry laughed. "You're way behind, Agent Doyle."

She pointed toward the Range Rover. "Those two guys work for Brian Joyce. His brother is Guy Joyce, the C.E.O. of Bergen Incorporated."

Harry frowned. "The pharmaceutical company?"

"Yes. Brian Joyce gave me a ride to Egypt on their corporate jet. He's a top security man for his brother. Ex-military, same as the men with him."

"But you're with the district attorney's office," Harry said. "Unless you were lying about that when you tried to steal the tablet."

"I wasn't lying. And for the last time, I wasn't trying to steal anything." Her voice dropped. "You admit you have it?"

"You know I do or you wouldn't be here. Before you ask, it's not here. Don't bother asking where it is now."

"Somewhere I'll never get it, I'm sure." She turned back to the necropolis, watching Joyce's men do a whole lot of nothing. Their boss was nowhere to be seen. "You deciphered the message."

"Same as you," Harry shot back. "Or did those guys do it for you?"

Nora bit off a sharp retort. "They hired an expert. He suspected the *general* was Megabyzus, and that the tablet pointed here, to his tomb. Joyce had another contact too, but before you ask, I have no idea who it is. All I know is it was a man, and Brian Joyce spoke with him directly." She pointed a finger at his chest. "How did you figure it out?"

He ignored her. "Why aren't you up there with them?" She didn't respond, and to his credit, Harry figured it out in a snap. "You flew here with them, but you're not working with them."

Her expression answered his question. "I'm right," Harry said. "They're leaving you behind."

"Yes. *And* I don't trust them." She played a hunch, though why, she had no idea. Nora clearly couldn't read people as well as she thought. "All they're doing is using me for my connection to the D.A.'s office. If they find you, chances are you won't get out of Egypt."

"I'm not afraid of a few corporate thugs."

"Then you're not as bright as I thought. Those men won't hesitate to kill you, Harry."

"What, you're working with murderers now?"

"I didn't realize what these men were after. I overheard Brian talking in the lobby. He called his brother and made it clear if they find you it won't end well."

Harry never took his eyes off her face. "What do they think is so valuable about the tablet?"

"I'm not certain," she said. "And to be honest, I don't think they are either. The C.E.O. is the one driving this. He's certain that tablet is a marker, part of some larger path tied to King Xerxes, and perhaps the Ancient Greeks as well." She shook her head. "Some of that is guesswork on my part. They don't have all the answers, even after they hired a professor in Washington, D.C. He's the reason we made it this far. Not me, and sure as hell not Brian Joyce."

"Morons," Harry said softly. "I didn't even leave the city to figure out what it meant."

"And look how that turned out," Nora said. A bus pulled up beside them, dropping off passengers who streamed around Harry and his motorcycle. Several of the men stared at her bare arms. She glared back. "I know you met with Professor Khalidi. That happens, and a few hours later he's dead." She failed to mention the other visitor after Harry, the unidentified one she'd truly been searching for.

"I saw him right before I left. He's why I came here." Harry put a hand on his helmet, shaking his head. "I talked to him just a few days ago. He was *excited* about the tablet. Not just excited, but thrilled. Was it an accident?"

Had Harry already known Khalidi was dead? Hard to say, and she didn't push it. "We're not sure." She recounted his fall from the subway platform. "We can't tell if he fell, if he was pushed, or even if he jumped."

"He wouldn't have jumped," Harry said. "I'm telling you, the guy was stoked about this tablet. He wanted to know what I found here."

"I believe you," she said.

Now he looked past her again. "You don't trust these guys?" he asked. Nora nodded. "Then why are you skulking around? Go up there and tell them to piss off."

"It's not that easy. Guy Joyce is a big donor to the D.A. Guy asked to have his security team tag along with me as a personal favor.

Joyce is footing the bill for this trip and offering to pay for experts to help with anything we need, all under the guise of disrupting antiquities trafficking in the city. He convinced the D.A. this will be a front-page headline if we get the tablet. The kind of good publicity elected officials can't live without."

"Politicians are worse than the mob," Harry said. "What are you going to do now?"

The only people Nora trusted were five thousand miles away. Her investigation, and it was hers, make no mistake, was falling to pieces because the D.A. needed big donors more than he needed to stop antiquities trafficking. The legwork had all been done because Nora had done her job the right way. She had caught the smugglers who led them to the tablet, she had put Harry Fox on their radar, and she had got them to Saqqara. Only Nora was no longer really in charge, not from the moment Guy Joyce had called the D.A. and got Brian assigned as a liaison. She hadn't worked this hard, traveled halfway around the world and *actually found* Harry Fox to let it be buried. Dusty air burned in her throat as she looked from Harry Fox back to the treacherous Brian Joyce's team atop Saqqara's rising hillside. She had to do this alone. Certainly without these lying partners from Bergen Incorporated. "Harry, you've already been inside Megabyzus's tomb," Nora said.

Harry didn't respond.

"What did you find?" Still no response. "Whatever it is, I want to help."

Harry laughed. "You really must think I'm dumb."

"No, I think you have no idea how close you are to getting killed." She pointed into Saqqara. "Those men tricked me. They want to bury you. We have the same problem."

"What, you want to recruit me? You tried that. My answer hasn't changed."

"I'm an agent charged with preventing antiquities trafficking, to arrest and help prosecute offenders, and to recover artifacts. I have wide leeway to do so in a manner I deem proper." Nora stepped toward Harry and pointed at his chest. "Those men over there are part of the problem. It's my opinion there are additional artifacts associated with the original tablet, items of cultural and historical significance which will be lost if those men get to them before I do. Right now, the best way to prevent that is by working with you as a confidential source."

Harry shook his head. "Same story, different wrapping."

"In return for immunity, I'm asking you to help me find anything else tied to Xerxes' tablet. A side benefit of this is you'll stay alive."

"I don't even know if those guys are after me," Harry said. "The only person who said that is you."

"Professor Khalidi is dead. Who's to say they weren't involved in that, and they won't come after you next? They know your name, Harry. I didn't give it to them. Think about that."

His face had twitched, only for an instant. Something she'd just said had hit home. "Brian Joyce has resources," Nora said. "A jet, ruthless men, piles of cash. Could be a different person shows up, one you never see coming." His mouth twitched again. Nora made a guess. "Someone already *did* come after you."

Harry rubbed his chin. "When did you guys leave the city?"

"Yesterday." She waited, but he kept rubbing his chin. "What happened?"

A low rumble sounded in Harry's throat. "A man broke into my house and tried to kill me." He looked anywhere but at her. She let him stew. It was working.

"Let's say there is more to this path idea," he finally said. "Say that the tablet is a marker to something else. Your guys seem to know as much as I do. Who's to say they won't be right on my tail no matter what you do?"

"If there's more, they don't have it right now. You do, so we follow the trail. Delaying now gives them time to catch up."

"If I get to the end, you'll take anything I find and then you'll arrest me. Isn't that how it works?"

"Immunity, remember?"

"This is my job, Doyle. I do this to survive. Handing over what I find doesn't get me paid."

Nora uncrossed her arms, lifting a hand to shield her eyes against the sun as she glanced back to Saqqara. She was buying time, weighing options. None of them good. She turned back to Harry. "I'll give you a hypothetical. Say I determine the best course is moving ahead with my confidential source. I get to the end of this trail and find out I'm not the first to the finish line. Whatever's at the end is gone. In that case, the original tablet would be a welcome reward for my efforts." She couldn't believe she was saying this. *Get him on your side now. Worry about the rest later.* "The original tablet will make headlines. If nothing else is found, my word on the matter would be final."

Harry sat on the bike and grabbed one handlebar. "How do I know this immunity will hold?"

"You have a lawyer in New York?" she asked. Harry nodded. "I'll have my office draft an agreement and send it to your attorney. You can call to make sure it's real."

That seemed to work. "What if you're right and there are more artifacts on this trail? I don't think for a second you'll let me keep them."

"We'll talk about that on the way," Nora said. "Look, this is personal for me. Those asshats," she pointed her finger at Saqqara as though it were loaded, "are stealing my case. I need your help to take it back. If it costs me an immunity agreement and maybe another artifact, so be it." Her voice dropped, and Harry leaned closer to catch what came next. "I trusted the process and look how that's turning out."

"I'll consider your offer. Now, we need to move. We're not exactly hidden here."

Nora pointed to her BMW. "Get in. I'll drive."

"Where'd you get the nice ride?" Nora told him, and he laughed. "You rented it with that guy's credit card, and you think I'm getting in? These cars have tracking equipment in them. You may as well steal a cop car."

She should have thought of that. "I'm not riding on that deathtrap bike with you."

Harry smirked. "I have a car, only you have to go get it. I stole the bike and left my car in there." He indicated a worksite between Megabyzus's tomb and the main entrance. "You know how to ride a motorcycle?"

"What makes you think I would know how to do that?"

Harry shrugged. "City girls can surprise you sometimes. Too bad. You'll have to take your car up there and switch it for mine." He tossed her the BMW keys. "Try not to let anyone see—"

Harry nearly toppled off the bike when she whipped the keys back at him. "What's wrong with you?" he said.

"You have a helmet," Nora said. She grabbed one handlebar and shoved him off the bike. "Give it to me."

His mouth opened. "Okay. Leave the bike keys under the front mudguard."

Harry gave her the helmet, his mouth moving like a fish's, with no words escaping.

"City girls can surprise you sometimes," Nora said as the bike engine burbled.

Nora held out her hand, and Harry handed over his car keys. "Park this car somewhere out of sight. And try not to let anyone see you." She hit the clutch and shot off, leaving him staring.

Don't underestimate a city girl.

The rich scent of new leather filled Harry's nose when he slid behind the wheel of Nora's BMW and moved it down the street, well away from Saqqara's entrance. Eventually the hotel would track it down from the GPS after Harry and Nora were long gone.

This new development didn't sit well with him. Carrying on his search with a *government agent?* It went against every instinct in his body. A few months ago, when he had uncovered an original manuscript introducing King Arthur that had landed him in all manner of trouble, he had made it out alive by listening to his gut. That was one lesson his father taught him. Another? Guard your trust. Never hand it out freely. Which is exactly what he felt he was doing now. Harry reached for the amulet tucked under his shirt. He could use luck right now. He didn't trust Nora. If her immunity deal checked out? Maybe then. He gripped the amulet, checking that it was tucked out of sight beneath his shirt. No need to let Agent Doyle see it. Who knew what questions she'd have then.

He watched as Nora came back into sight after going through the entrance and dipping below the horizon. She handled the bike easily, moving at pace to the parking area where Harry's car waited alongside other vehicles and motorcycles that likely belonged to the team working the site. A tent stood a hundred yards from the parking lot, far enough away for them not to notice Nora's engine.

He saw her reach down and cut the engine, then coast the last fifty feet before hopping off to push the bike alongside Harry's car, which she jumped into after ducking down by the front mudguard. She drove through Saqqara to the front entrance, where two police cars were parked, with officers standing in front of them. As she approached, one of the officers lifted a hand and motioned for her to stop.

Harry's gut clenched when the officer motioned for Nora to roll down her window. A brief conversation later the officer stepped back and waved Nora through. She exited and made a left turn. The officers did not watch her go.

She's smarter than I thought. Harry turned around to confirm it. Sure enough, his white Toyota appeared from around the corner behind him. Nora parked well back, leaving the engine running.

"What was that at the gate?" Harry asked when he walked alongside the Toyota.

Nora slid over to the passenger seat. "They told me to slow down."

"They didn't ask for identification?" Harry climbed into the driver's seat, unslung the messenger bag and put it in Nora's footwell.

"Of course they did. They lost interest when I told them I worked for the Ministry of Antiquities, and I was late to pick up an executive."

Harry stopped moving, his hand on the gear shift. "They bought that?"

"After I fired off a few Egyptian curses."

"In *Arabic?*"

Nora's lip turned up at the corner. "*Hal 'ant mutafaji 'iinaa 'atakalam alearabia?*" She said it again, in English. "Are you surprised I speak Arabic?"

Harry felt his mouth fall open again. "Uh, yes. Yes, I am."

Nora shrugged. "My mother is from Saudi Arabia."

That explained the soft mocha skin tone, but not the hair, which was the color of cool fire. "I just thought you spent a lot of time outside," Harry said. "The red hair matches the name Doyle."

She patted her auburn ponytail. "My father is Irish."

"Look at me. America the melting pot," Harry said. "Smart move not coming straight to me." Harry buckled himself in and pulled away from the curb. He used a turn signal at the stop sign ahead.

Harry pulled into traffic, giving one last look up at the tomb of Megabyzus. Two men walked out into the sunlight a moment before it vanished from sight. One was almost certainly Brian Joyce. The other was a bedraggled man in an Egyptian police uniform. Walking upright, on his own power. At least he wasn't badly injured.

Nora spoke up. "You have to be straight with me. What did you find in the tomb?"

"Call your office and have the immunity agreement drafted, then send it to my attorney." He rattled off a name. "We'll talk once I get confirmation it's set."

She didn't argue. Harry half-listened as she picked up her phone, punched in a number and gave orders to someone back in New York. The immunity agreement mattered because once Harry signed it, he could do whatever he needed to in this search. Which included double-crossing Nora if necessary.

He'd worry about that later; their immediate concern was finding a safe place to inspect the new tablet. He gripped the wheel harder and stepped on the gas. The only Ancient Middle Eastern expert he knew had died after their sole meeting. Unless Nora Doyle could read Persian cuneiform and Egyptian hieroglyphs a lot better than he could, Harry had zero options for people he trusted. He wasn't letting Nora call anyone about this. But he really didn't know anyone who could help them.

Harry stopped at a red light. He bit his lip. That wasn't true. He did know one person. He even trusted them, except with this person there was a different problem. One Harry couldn't do anything about.

The light turned green. Harry didn't move.

"It's green," Nora said. She started talking into the phone again. Harry didn't move. "Hey," Nora said and jabbed his arm. "Move it."

"What?" Harry shook his head. "Right." He gassed it.

Nora put her phone away. "The agreement is headed to your attorney."

The cityscape around them shifted from low-slung residential buildings to commercial stores and wide parking lots. A massive structure loomed ahead of them, all concrete and shining glass. Harry signaled to change lanes, then drove into a towering parking deck attached to one of the bigger malls he'd seen in Egypt. The place was huge. "We can sit in here for a bit," Harry said. He pulled into an end spot that offered quick access to the exit and a clear line of sight in all directions.

He left the engine running. Cool air ruffled his hair, though that's not what caused the gooseflesh on his arms. Harry unbuckled his seatbelt. "I'm calling my attorney."

Nora waved a hand. "Have at it."

Harry made the call, confirming with his slightly unsettled attorney that an immunity agreement for Harry was now sitting on his desk. "It's real?" Harry asked. The attorney assured him it covered any illegal antiquities trafficking activities Harry had engaged in through the present day. "What about the future?" Harry asked. The agreement also cleared him of any wrongdoing associated with the investigation currently underway involving Ancient Persian artifacts. "Thanks," Harry said. He clicked off before his attorney could ask him any questions.

"Satisfied?" Nora asked.

"I am." Harry lapsed into silence.

"You *do* have something else?" Nora asked. "I'd hate to think you lied to me just to get immunity."

"I do. The original tablet pointed to Megabyzus's tomb here in Saqqara. There's more to that tomb than archaeologists realize."

Nora's mouth slowly opened as Harry described uncovering the hidden antechamber. "What was in it?" she asked.

"Another tablet." Harry pointed to his messenger bag. "It's in there. There's writing on it, but I can't read much of it. Any chance you can read Ancient Persian?"

"No," Nora said. "We had Brian Joyce's expert decipher the writing on the first one." She reached for the bag. "Let me see it."

"Hold on," Harry said. "I'm still thinking."

"About what?" Nora spread her arms out, banging one on the window. She swore.

"If I want to put a person I care about at risk," Harry snapped, "I know someone who can decipher this. A person who won't sell me out. You know anyone like that?"

"I can find someone," she shot back. "I'm a government agent, remember? I don't work with criminals." She lowered her voice. "Usually."

"Smooth," Harry said. "Pick a fight with me. That'll get us far."

"I'm not the one who works for a mobster."

"You think I had a choice in the matter?" Harry barked. He turned from her, looking out his window. His breath fogged the glass. He didn't turn around, clenching one fist until it hurt. The silence stretched on before Nora spoke again, her words soft.

"You're right," she said. "I have no idea what your life is like, or how you got here. What I do know is right now you and I are in a foreign country unraveling a trail tied to Xerxes while people with a whole lot more money and resources than we have do the same thing. We're here together, like it or not. You think I'd offer you immunity if I had any other choice?" He looked over as Nora stuck a finger in his ribs. "I'm in a hard place, same as you, and we're each other's best hope." She picked up steam. "I'm sure life hasn't been easy for you. Try being a female special agent in New York City."

"Fair enough. We'll complain about who has it worse after we figure out our next steps."

Nora glared at him. "Fine," she eventually said. "But enough of this crap. You're not stupid. If I wanted to steal your tablets, either one of them, I wouldn't put myself in a solo situation where you can turn the tables. I can handle myself. But I'd be stupid to bet on a guy who works for the mob as my only hope. Unless I had no other choice. So now I'm all in. I give you access to all my resources. You help me figure out why Bergen Inc. is so interested in these ancient tablets."

Harry hated to admit it, but she made sense, and she had access to resources he didn't. "Deal. The person I know who can help isn't in my world. She's a friend. I don't want to get her involved after what happened to Professor Khalidi."

Nora's eyes softened. "I don't think you had anything to do with Khalidi's death." She looked out her window. "It was pure luck I even found out you went to see him. When I found out he'd died, with the whole Xerxes tablet investigation going on, I checked security footage from his office. That's how I found out you went to see him. You weren't the last person in his office before he died."

Harry sat upright. "Who else did he meet?"

"We can't identify the guy. He knew where the cameras were and kept his head down."

"Which is why you're back looking at me," Harry said. "The last person to see him alive."

"Other than three hundred people in a train station," Nora said, and shook her head. "Professor Khalidi is dead. Homicide, accident – right now it doesn't matter. What matters is what we do next. We're one step ahead of everyone else who's after Xerxes' tablet. Do you want to waste that advantage?"

Damn Nora Doyle and her logic. "The problem is the person who can help us never asked to be involved. It's not fair to them."

Nora pointed at his chest. "You said this is a person you trust. The question now is if you want to lean on them, or if I'm calling one of my people." She pulled her phone out. "Your choice. Do you make a call, and I'll protect them any way I can, or do I handle this?"

Harry sighed. There wasn't a question. *Sara is not going to like this.* She would jump at the chance to help. It was what came next that he worried about. Once Sara heard about the adventure, he had a feeling her next stop would be an airport.

"We use my person."

"Fine with me." Nora put her phone away, then jumped when it buzzed. She pulled it out again and glanced at the screen. "Damn. It's my office." She put the phone away again. "They can wait. Who is this person we're using?"

"Her name is Sara Hamed. She's an Egyptologist at Trier University in Germany." All true. "I've known her a long time. We can count on her discretion." That part wasn't so true.

When Nora spoke, all the combativeness in her tone was gone. "May I see the second tablet before we call her? I'd like to know what we're talking about first."

"Sure," Harry said. "I haven't studied it. Any context we can give Sara makes her job easier."

He reached for his bag. When he looked up, Nora held her head in both hands. "You okay?" he asked.

"I'm fine." She hurriedly rubbed her eyes. "I'm sorry. It's very unprofessional." Harry let her take a beat. "This reminds me of my grandparents," she went on. She turned to face him, rubbing again at her red, damp eyes. "My mother is from Saudi Arabia. Her father was a soldier and a policeman in the army. Her mother was a nurse. They were both killed during the Al-Wadiah War in 1969. My mother was young, and she didn't have other family. Fortunately, she was adopted by an American couple." Nora cleared her throat. "Anyway, my grandparents' deaths gave my mother a chance at a new life. Being in Egypt reminds me of all of them."

Harry nodded. "Family is important."

"I like to think they'd be proud of me for doing what I do." She met his gaze, and for the first time Harry felt as though he was really seeing her. Nora rubbed the back of a hand across her eyes one last time. "Enough of that. Let's see the tablet."

A car drove past his window, headed toward the parking garage entrance. After it disappeared Harry opened the messenger bag. Nora had her phone out with the flashlight app on when he slid Xerxes' second tablet out and set it on his lap. The light wavered; Nora's hand was trembling.

"Can you read it?" she asked.

Harry pointed to the first line. "That says *King Xerxes*. I believe this tablet is a direct message from the king telling us where to go next."

Chapter Nineteen

Brooklyn

Clouds of smoke twisted below the ceiling, drawn in snake-like curls toward an open window. Stefan walked into Altin's office, accustomed to but by no means immune to the health hazards of meeting in this room. He wrinkled his nose. *Why does he smoke those things?* The office smelled like a stink bomb had gone off.

Of course, Stefan kept his mouth shut. "You called, Mr. Cana?"

"Have a seat." Altin pointed his cigar at a chair across his desk. "It is time for us to expand our operation."

A jolt of energy raced up Stefan's back. His plan to steal Harry Fox's tablet was on hold after Professor Khalidi's death. That situation needed to cool off. Now it seemed Altin had other plans to keep Stefan busy. "Last I heard, you were considering how to best make that expansion happen."

"Fate presented us with an opportunity. Vincent Morello is unwell."

"Unwell?"

"He is dying. An informant in the medical practice where Vincent receives care has seen him several times recently. He has cancer. Often deadly for men of his age."

"So we move now," Stefan said. "While he is weak. Joey isn't ready to run his father's organization. Forcing the issue will cause mistakes on their part and expose Joey's shortcomings. Other families will notice. Then it's only a matter of time until they decide the Morellos are no longer in charge."

Altin might have grinned. It was hard to tell with him. "We push them now. If they are strong, maybe they survive. If they are weak, they fall. Either way, we strike a blow to their reputation." The end of Altin's cigar glowed red as he puffed. "Find me the right place and time to attack."

"Who is the target?"

"Tell me who you think it should be."

Stefan looked to the ceiling. This wasn't just Altin asking him to plan. This was an interview. A chance to show he had what it took to lead. Altin had no children. Who would guide the Cana family after Altin? If this attack on the Morellos succeeded, the chances of that person being Stefan went up considerably.

"Vincent Morello is ill," Stefan said. "And less likely to handle adversity well. I suggest going after his son, Joey. If we eliminate Joey, the Morellos are left with a weak old man and no heir. Vincent will respond quickly. His attack will be rash, short-sighted, made by a man intent on vengeance. As long as we come out on top, he looks weak, and it's not long until the Morellos are finished."

"I agree. Attack Joey, not Vincent. Removing Joey leaves his father lashing out at ghosts." Altin expelled a stream of smog. "The Morellos cannot know who is after them. You cannot use our soldiers. These must be outside men in case any are killed and tied to our family. We avoid a direct war with the Morellos for now. That comes later."

"Of course, Mr. Cana. Thank you for your guidance."

"You will do well, Stefan. Find Joey's weak spot. Plan. Come back when you know how we will bring him down."

Stefan rose from his chair. Altin pointed the cigar at Stefan's chest. "*As-salaamu Alaikum.*" May peace be unto you.

"*Va-alaikum As-salaam.*" Peace be unto you too.

Odd words for two men intent on death and destruction. Yet to Altin, they fit.

Stefan walked outside, his phone pressed to his ear. Surveilling Joey Morello required new faces, people no one recognized. The Morellos kept tabs on Cana men, same as the Canas did on them. Which was why Stefan called a woman who worked for the Cana family, kept on retainer to provide services as needed. To get next to Joey required a subtle touch. In this case, a woman's.

He spoke in Arabic when she answered. "Iris, it's Stefan. Be at my place in thirty minutes. Bring Cici too." Now he switched to English. "Don't dress flashy. Bring hats and sunglasses. You're going to help me tail someone. I'll explain when you get there."

The woman didn't ask questions, didn't argue. She did as ordered. That was why they paid her, and why thirty minutes later Iris stood outside his front door with Cici. Neither flinched as Stefan cast an appraising eye over the two women. Two attractive women, casually dressed, not looking for attention. Tools in his arsenal to take down the Morellos. "Come inside."

The women followed him in. He didn't acknowledge when they took in the empty walls, the sparse furnishings. He had few visitors, but guests always responded in some way to the impersonal living space, even if they didn't say anything. Stefan didn't mind. He had bigger things to worry about than making his apartment nice for people he didn't care to impress.

"Have a seat." He indicated a table with four chairs. The women waited until he sat first. "I need your help tailing this man." Stefan showed them a snapshot on his phone. Dark hair, bright white teeth, an expensive gold chain around his neck. "Joey Morello."

Cici's head snapped up. "The Morello family?"

"Is that a problem?"

Her eyes dropped. "No."

He glared at the top of Cici's head for a moment. "I'm working on finding out where he goes, what he does. If he goes someplace where I think you can get close to him, I'll call you. Be available."

Stefan opened a drawer tucked under the tabletop. Out came a pair of cell phones. "On these. Don't give out the numbers to anyone. Don't make any calls. Understood?"

The cell phones disappeared into their purses without comment. "What do you want us to do with him?" Iris asked as the bracelets around her wrist jangled.

"Get close to him. Listen carefully to what Joey is saying. He often eats out at local restaurants. My hope is we can overhear whatever plans he's making at dinner or in a bar."

"You want to know where he'll be and what he's doing," Iris said. "When do we start?"

Stefan's phone vibrated on the table as a text message came through. "Right now," he said after reading the message. "I already have two men watching him. Joey Morello just left his home."

He stood. The girls followed him outside and they all got into his car. He was barely able to get buckled in before he smashed the gas pedal, headed to where his men were currently tailing Joey. Traffic was light through Brooklyn, and by the time Stefan pulled alongside the car with the other two Cana men, Joey Morello had already parked outside a barber shop. Stefan rolled down his window.

"Did he make any stops?"

"One," the other driver answered. "A couple blocks back, stopped at some old lady's house. He gave her something wrapped in foil."

Could be his great-aunt. Half the neighborhood was tied to the Morellos. Didn't matter. "How many men are with him?"

"Two."

"How's he dressed?"

"Nice clothes," the driver said. "Same as always."

"We'll take it from here," Stefan said. "I'll call when we need you."

The other driver nodded and pulled away. Stefan turned to Iris. "You have a hat and shades?" he asked. Iris opened her purse to reveal a folded pink ballcap and a pair of sunglasses. "Good. You may need them if he's on the move. He needs to eat sooner or later."

"We'll sit beside him, listen in on what he's saying."

Stefan watched the barber shop door. "That's a good plan."

"What if we can't get close enough?" Cici asked.

"That's what this is for." Stefan opened his glove compartment and pulled out what looked like a tiny glue gun, no larger than the palm of his hand. The tip had a circular cone around it.

"What is that, Marvin the Martian's gun?"

"Very funny. You should tell jokes." He handed the contraption to Iris. "This is a parabolic listening device. It fits in your purse." He handed each of them a tiny earbud, so small they were hard to hold. "Aim the device at Joey's table and listen through the earpieces. The range is up to fifty feet."

Cici was impressed. "Neat."

"Yes. It is neat." He made them test it on a couple walking by outside. "Hear anything?" he asked.

Iris smiled. "Like I am standing next to them."

"Same here," Cici added. "This is great."

"Neat and great," Stefan said. "Yes. Now be quiet." He pointed through the windshield. "That's Joey's car. The Tesla SUV. Not many of them in the city, let alone rolling around this neighborhood." He pointed again. "That's the barber shop Joey went to."

"How do you know that?" Cici asked.

"That's Joey leaving."

Joey Morello and two well-built men stepped out of the barber shop. Joey looked to the sky, where a cool sun had started to break through the clouds. The three men were two hundred yards away, much too far for the listening device, so Stefan could only wait. He frowned when Joey and his companions walked down the sidewalk in the opposite direction from where they were parked. *Guards,* Stefan chided himself. Bodyguards who would break Stefan's neck if they felt he were threatening Joey. Iris and Cici wouldn't fare much better should their listening device be discovered.

Stefan watched as the trio continued walking away. "This is the edge of Morello turf," Stefan told the girls. "For some reason they're walking toward Cana territory."

He reached for the ignition, then stopped. Let it play out.

Cici, of all people, called it first. "There's a great restaurant up there," she said. "Sanna. I bet they're going out to eat."

No sooner had she spoken than Joey Morello and his guards turned and walked through the restaurant's front door. "It's time to eat," Stefan said as he started the car. "Get close to Joey and his friends if you can. If he makes plans, mentions anything about where he's going next, text me. Don't rush. Have a drink or two. You are not to leave before Joey Morello is done."

"We understand," Iris said.

Stefan pulled a roll of hundred-dollar bills from his pocket as he drove to the restaurant. "Tip well. And don't let them see the ear buds."

He dropped the girls a block away, then circled around to a street parking spot with a clear view of the front door. Stefan removed a third earpiece from his pocket, one he hadn't told the girls about, tucked it into his ear, and settled in to wait. A minute later his earpiece came alive with the sound of men talking. Thankfully the men used names frequently enough that he could pick out who was who. Chad and Zach were the two men with Joey, talking about nothing useful at first. Baseball, girls, soccer, girls. Typical stuff, until Zach took note of his surroundings.

"Hey." Zach's voice had dropped, forcing Stefan to turn up the volume. "Look at the pair sitting over there. Not bad, huh?"

"Nice-looking," Chad said. "Good thing they came in here for some peace and quiet."

"What's that supposed to mean?" Zach asked.

"You're too chicken to chat them up," Chad said. "They're safe as can be."

"Funny guy. I don't see you heading over there."

"I'm here for the food," Chad said. "And you're a chump. Maybe you can get movie-star over here to help you out."

"You're jealous," Zach said. "The ladies can't say no to a guy like me."

"You talk a big game," Joey said. "You wanna bet on it? Hundred bucks says I can get the tall one's number. I like girls with red hair."

Stefan jolted upright in his seat. *He's talking about Iris.*

"You're on," Zach said. "Let's see it happen."

A chair scraped. Iris swore. Silence, until Joey's voice sounded in Stefan's ear. Much clearer. Much closer.

"How are you ladies doing today?"

"Fine," Iris said.

"I haven't seen you around here before. You live in the area?"

"Yes," Cici said.

"Same here. What street do you live on?"

Damn. If the girls told him a street on the Morello side of town, chances were Joey would know someone else who lived nearby. He'd ask about the person, and if the girls couldn't give him a real answer, Joey would get suspicious. And if Joey heard they lived on Cana turf, he might get really suspicious.

"Western and twenty-first," Iris said. That was on the Cana side. "We just moved in last week."

Nice work, Iris.

"Have you been here before?" Joey asked. "Either of you?" The girls said they hadn't. "A friend of mine owns the place," Joey said. "I'm coming back tomorrow for dinner. Trying to help support him, you know? If you're free, you should join me."

Iris laughed. "Perhaps," she said. "But we don't even know your name."

"It's Joey. Joey Morello."

"Nice to meet you, Mr. Morello."

"What are your names?"

Iris and Cici gave him fake names before their back and forth continued, until out of nowhere Joey's voice dropped. "What's that in your purse? Looks like some kind of spy equipment."

Silence. Stefan started the car. If Joey suspected the girls were following him, were actually eavesdropping, he could call in reinforcements. It wouldn't take much for them to connect Stefan to the gambit, sitting by himself in a car with a direct view of the restaurant. He put one hand on the gear shifter.

"What, this toy?" Rumbling as Iris must have pulled it partway out of her purse. "This is for my son. He's six. He loves Marvin the Martian cartoons."

"Your son? You don't look old enough to have a six-year-old kid."

"Sometimes we are lucky in life, even if we don't understand when it happens," Iris said. "Do you have children?"

"No, no kids." Joey sounded as though he'd taken a step back. "No time."

"Children are a blessing," Cici said. "Her son and mine are best friends."

Now Joey couldn't get away fast enough. "That's wonderful. It was nice to meet you girls. I hope your son likes his present."

Joey must have left, because Iris let out a few choice words in Arabic. Stefan laughed out loud in the car. He texted Iris, telling her to get a cab back to the Cana headquarters, then he started the car and drove away. Today couldn't have gone better. Joey Morello had given him exactly what he needed. Stefan had an opening tomorrow night. Now he needed to figure out how to use it.

Chapter Twenty

Outside Saqqara, Egypt

Nora Doyle looked from the tablet to Harry's face and back again. "How do you know what it says?" she asked.

"I can read Egyptian hieroglyphs," Harry said.

Her head shot back up. "You *can?*"

"Well, some of them." He pointed to the tablet. "Like this one. It represents a location. A city."

"Which one?"

Harry frowned. "I'm working on that. This is the first time I've examined the tablet too. Hieroglyphs aren't always straightforward. The language evolved over time, as dynasties came and went. Sometimes meanings are different based on the age."

Nora sat back. "Why don't you call someone who actually knows how to read *all* of them?"

Harry wanted to say *Because the last person who helped me read a tablet is dead.* But he had no choice. Either call Sara or turn this over to Nora's expert. He pulled his phone out and dialed.

"Egypt is one hour ahead of Germany time," Harry said. "She may still be in her office."

Another ring, then Sara's voice filled the car. "*Hallo, Sara Hamed.*"

"Hey, Sara. It's Harry."

It sounded as though Sara had dropped something. "Harry? *Heiliger Strohsack!* How are you?"

"Not bad."

"I texted you a few days ago. Is everything okay?"

"Sorry about that. I've been buried with work lately." By work he meant avoiding double-crossing black-market dealers in Greece, a gun-toting intruder in Brooklyn, and police officers in Egypt. "Is this a good time to talk?"

"Of course," Sara said. "I'm still researching the scarab language from your amul—"

"That's not why I'm calling." Harry cut Sara off, then avoided Nora's questioning stare. "Something else came up."

"More urgent than the amu—"

"Yes," Harry said quickly. "More than that. Are you alone?"

"I am," Sara said.

"Before I go on, there's someone you should meet. A colleague who's helping me with a new artifact."

"A new artifact?" Sara asked. "Wonderful. Who's the new guy on your team?"

"Her name is Nora," Harry said. "She's connected to the artifacts trade. It's best I leave it at that. She's here with me now."

Sara's voice became decidedly guarded. "Where is here?"

Nora spoke up. "Egypt. It's nice to speak with you, Dr. Hamed. I'm Nora, and I appreciate your willingness to assist us. It sounds as though you and Harry have done this before."

"Not exactly," Sara said. "What do you need to know?"

"We have an artifact from the Achaemenid empire," Nora said before Harry could respond. "A tablet we believe was written or dictated by King Xerxes II."

"Xerxes?" Sara asked. "That would be an incredible find. I don't know of a single existing example of Xerxes' writing."

"It's the second tablet we've found that Xerxes wrote," Nora said. "Harry will share details on the first one soon, but right now we're short on time and need your help."

Silence greeted her question. "Harry, are you making this up?" Sara finally asked.

"I'm not," Harry said quickly, before Nora could jump in. "I'll tell you all about it later. We need to decipher this tablet. You're the only person I trust to help us."

"Ancient Persians like Xerxes wrote in cuneiform, not hieroglyphics. He wouldn't have used that form of writing."

"Unless he paid for the tomb in Saqqara, where the Egyptians buried General Megabyzus," Harry said. "Which sounds crazy, I know." He struggled to catch Sara's response.

"The tomb in Saqqara has been extensively excavated. What you're saying seems impossible."

Harry gave her the short version of finding a hidden antechamber. "I found this second tablet in the antechamber. We think it's pointing somewhere else. I thought I could interpret it, but I was wrong. I need your help, Sara. If you're willing."

"If you think I'm going to pass on a Persian tablet tied to Xerxes, you are mistaken. I'm in. Put me on video."

Harry fiddled with his phone until Sara's face appeared on screen. A face he hadn't seen in weeks. "Hey, Sara. Good to see you."

"Hi. You too." She fiddled with her hair until Nora leaned into the picture. "You must be Nora."

"I am," Nora said. "Here's the tablet." She propped it up so Sara could see.

Sara said nothing for a long while. Her lips moved, occasionally letting out unfamiliar words. Nora fidgeted and twisted, scanning every car that passed as though it were the police coming to arrest them.

Eventually Sara broke the silence. "This is amazing."

"You can read it?" Nora asked.

"Yes, I can read it."

Nora's jaw tightened. "What does it say?"

"The first tablet was written as more of a story," Harry said. "The brevity of this one makes me think these are instructions. Plus, I thought I recognized a city in the text."

Sara's tone softened. "Well done, Harry."

"What city is it?" Nora asked.

"I'll get to that part," Sara said. "First, tell me about the other tablet."

"I'll send you pictures now," Harry said. "There are two sides."

Sara spent a minute examining them on her computer monitor. "The two stories are nearly identical. Where did you get this?"

"From a man in Greece."

"Is that why you were in Athens when we last spoke?" Harry said it was. "What type of provenance did they have?" Sara asked. "I'd be interested to know where this tablet came from."

Harry hesitated. "Their provenance was murky."

Sara turned her gaze to the phone. "I see. Anything you can learn about the first one is important."

Harry rubbed a hand over his eyes. For the first time he could recall, he felt odd about what he did. Not quite ashamed, but the sour feeling in his gut right now was within shouting distance of it. "What I know doesn't give a clear picture. All I can say for certain is a Greek man owned it for some time before it came to me."

"Sara," Nora asked, "what does the second tablet say? We have to focus on that."

"It sounds as though we do," Sara replied. "Before we talk about the message, I can tell you this second tablet could certainly have been dictated by King Xerxes. The geographic, societal and religious references all align with his time period."

"Does it say anything about *Greek knowledge* or *a Greek's knowledge?*" Harry asked.

"Yes, this second one does," Sara said. "In fact, that's the main focus. I'll read it to you from start to finish." Sara spoke in measured tones.

King Xerxes, the King of Kings, proclaims you have proven your worth. Having traveled the great distance to uncover this beacon, you uncovered the final resting place of the hero who defeated the Scythians, the great General Megabyzus.

Such bravery is required on this perilous journey. You are worthy to continue. Only the most learned and wise may possess the Greek emerald elixir, perfected by Hippocrates. A knowledge that makes demigods of men.

Now, worthy Persian, you must continue to prove deserving of what you seek. The five beacons in the city of the Persians call to you, voiced by the King of Kings. Any who seek this elixir must follow the king's wealth to reap his reward. The incorrect path leads to doom.

"You have to break it down," Sara told them. "The clues make sense if you know how to read and interpret them based on contemporary cultural references. Let's start at the beginning, with *the hero who defeated the Scythians.* He's talking about Megabyzus. You can tell Xerxes intended for another Persian to uncover this."

"He assumes a Persian man will have found the first tablet," Harry said. "Not just any Persian, but a man up to the task."

"Or Persian woman," Sara said. "Which is why I want to know where the tablet came from before a Greek owned it. This suggests Xerxes left the first tablet where a Persian would find it, prove their worth, and uncover this hidden journey."

"Why hide the path if this is so important?" Nora asked. "Xerxes was a king. Kings have power. Why not keep this Greek emerald elixir for himself?"

"I think this tablet tells us King Xerxes looked into the future," Sara said. "What he saw scared him. He hid the elixir to keep it from being used."

"The first tablet may relate to a legend from Xerxes' time," Harry said. He told Sara the story Professor Khalidi had shared with him about a promising young Greek physician, a man of immense intellect of whom even famed Greek physicians had been in awe. "According to the legend, an *elixir* of some sort changed him from weak and frail into a man who lived in good health for over a century."

"The legend refers to him as a *beacon* of hope," Sara said. "I've heard the story. It's always been seen as a fable."

"What about the last line?" Harry asked. "It's identical to the last line on the front of the first tablet."

"The dual story approach on the first tablet is odd. Identical stories, except for the last line, which substituted *Greek's wealth* for *King's wealth*. And the *Greek's wealth* side has four symbols carved into it. I don't recognize them."

Harry explained how those symbols had been a coded message on how to open the concealed antechamber in Megabyzus's tomb.

"You solved the riddle," Sara said. "I'm impressed."

Nora leaned in front of Harry, hiding his self-satisfied smirk. "Any idea why Xerxes would write two stories that are identical other than the final line?" Nora asked.

"I'm afraid not," Sara said. "But both paths warn of *doom*. Whatever that means."

Voices outside his window made Harry jump. Two women wearing traditional hijabs walked by outside, less than a foot from where he held a stolen Egyptian treasure in plain sight. They didn't look in as they passed.

"We're not exactly in a safe place right now," Harry said.

"Yes, right," Sara said. "Let's assume this *beacon*, or marker, was hidden in General Megabyzus's tomb at the order of King Xerxes. It references him in the beginning, and Xerxes paid for the tomb's construction in a part of the world far from where he lived. A good way to hide something you don't want just anyone to find. Stating the person who found it is on a *perilous journey* also makes me think the tomb is only a waypoint on the path to another destination."

Nora drummed a finger on the dashboard. "Which might be?"

"I'm not certain," Sara said. "I think it's telling you to go a long distance from Egypt." No one spoke. "The *five beacons in the City of Persians*. This time the word *beacons* doesn't mean marker. It is used in a more modern sense, that of a signal fire or lighthouse."

"The Lighthouse of Alexandria?" Nora asked.

"Perhaps, but my interpretation is that it's a metaphor for the entire Achaemenid empire. An empire reflecting the greatness of King Xerxes' people. Five examples." Sara took a long breath. "The five palaces at Persepolis, known in Xerxes' day as *the city of the Persians.*"

"Does Persepolis still exist?" Nora asked. "Or has it been buried in the desert?"

"It's still around, and I've actually been there." Sara's eyes darted away from the screen, looking at something Harry couldn't see. "Right now, you're roughly two thousand kilometers away."

Harry's mind whirred. "That's almost fifteen hundred miles."

"Sounds about right," Sara said. "Persepolis is in Iran."

Harry didn't move. "Iran. The United States assassinated Iran's top military leader last year. You really couldn't pick a worse country for us to search in."

"Oh, I wouldn't say that." Sara sounded almost cheerful. "Iran has a functioning government. Persepolis is protected from looting and preserved against the elements. To the Iranians it's culturally significant. Better yet, when I was there the place was basically deserted."

"The U.S. State Department has Iran on their list of countries no American should visit," Nora said. "Americans who go there have a high risk of being kidnapped, arrested without cause or even being killed because they're American."

"Fortunately, that ban doesn't apply to German citizens," Sara said. "I still have a valid visa from my last visit and I can go to Iran in a professional capacity. Nobody will suspect me of anything."

"Hold on," Harry said. "You can't go. It's not safe."

Nora suddenly found the parking lot very interesting. Harry had the urge to sink into his seat under Sara's unblinking eyes. "Then why are you going?" Sara asked. "It isn't safe for me, yet you two are going? I'm struggling with that part."

Harry made his smartest move all day and kept quiet.

"No thoughts? Good, because I have one to share." She jabbed a finger at the screen and Harry nearly jumped. "Not only am I the sole person who can help you unravel this mystery you've uncovered, but I am your best hope of actually finding anything when you get there. Which, I suspect, you have no idea how to do."

He opened his mouth, but Sara wasn't having any of it. "I told you the name of the city," she said, still going full-force. "Persepolis. What's next? Are you going to find a tour guide and ask for help?"

Harry felt compelled to answer. "No."

"Iran is dangerous, yes, but only if you're not careful. The best way of being careful is to go in with a plan, move quickly, and don't attract attention. Do you know how to do that on an archaeological site? I do." Now she grabbed the phone, the image bouncing as she paced the room. "What is it you do again? 'Buying and selling antiquities' was how you put it." Sara set the phone back down and crossed her arms. "Is a collector paying you to follow this trail?"

"No," Harry said. He tapped Nora's thigh, out of sight where Sara couldn't see, then made a rolling motion with his hand. *Play along.*

"There's more to it than travel restrictions," Harry said. "I had no idea authorities were watching the first tablet I acquired."

"What does that mean?" Sara asked.

Nora growled and pushed Harry aside. "It means Harry is assisting the city's anti-trafficking unit on an undercover investigation." A badge appeared from inside her shirt, which she shoved in Sara's digital face. "I'm a unit agent. Harry is working with us. Any objections?" Sara leaned back. "None?" Nora asked. "Good. Now, are you going to help us?"

Harry raised his voice. "She's not coming to—"

That was all he could get out before Nora grabbed his arm and put him in a wristlock. She didn't say a word, and all Sara could see was Harry diving out of screen as he dropped to keep his wrist from snapping.

"Ignore him," Nora said. "Where should we go in Persepolis to follow Xerxes' path?"

"I can help with that."

"Are you comfortable traveling to Iran?"

"I wouldn't miss it," Sara said. "When are you going?"

"Hold tight. We'll call you right back." Nora hung up, then released Harry's wrist a millimeter before it went from bad to worse. "Sit up and listen."

Harry rubbed the ache in his bones. "You're a lunatic."

"I said listen. First, I did you a favor. Second, don't ever tell a woman what she can and can't do. You'll live longer, and we need her. Without Sara we can't even read the tablet, let alone figure out where to go. Sara divined more from this rock in five minutes than either of us did in an hour, so don't act like you can do this alone. Third—"

Harry's voice boomed in the car. "Be quiet," he shouted. His wrist hurt, his pride ached, and Nora Doyle had one thing on her mind: follow the trail and solve this case, consequences be damned. "You don't care about Sara or me. I found the tablets. I connected with the right people to decode Xerxes' clues. Now you show up and think you can run the show?" He risked death and digit by shoving a finger in her face. "Sara is not getting involved. You'd throw us both under the bus in a heartbeat to solve this."

Nora didn't punch him. She didn't curse. To his ill-concealed disbelief, she agreed. "You're right. I want to solve this. Badly. And you're the person who can help me right now." She lifted her hands, palms toward him. "My boss forced me to work with a bunch of thugs who cut me out. I'm in a country where I don't speak the language, don't know anyone, and my supposed allies are chasing me. You're right that I'm trying to run the show. I'm out of my depth here, and I need help." She pointed at his chest. "*Your* help. And Sara's."

"Oh," was all Harry managed. "Okay."

"I'd never ask you to do anything I won't do. That's why I'm coming to Iran with you."

"You're a trained officer," Harry said. "Sara is an academic. She has no idea what she's getting into."

"Maybe you're correct," Nora said. "Or maybe she'll surprise you. I've only spoken with her once and I wouldn't bet against Sara Hamed. The girl has fire in her belly."

That she did. Sara was brilliant, worldly, and truth be told, a heck of a lot more qualified to follow an Ancient Persian trail than Harry. He bit his lip. Besides that, he liked the idea of having her along. As he sat there, an image of the first time he'd ever met Sara popped into his head.

Harry turned to Nora. "I met Sara in Trier, Germany. That's where her university is. I was walking past a bar and a couple of drunk skinheads saw me, an average-sized guy, darker skin, all alone. One of them gets in my face, starts mouthing off. Two of his buddies join him." Harry recalled reaching into his pocket and slipping the knuckledusters around his fingers. "I'm ready for a fight, looking for a place to run after I hit one of them. Out of nowhere this woman comes in, cursing the skinheads with the fury of a hurricane." He laughed at the memory. "This big tattooed bastard is a foot taller than her, but he backs down like the bully he is." Harry pointed to the phone. "The human hurricane was Sara. A total stranger, and she saved my bacon."

Nora laughed. "I knew I liked her. Tell me again why she can't handle this trip to Iran?"

"Fair point." Harry ran a hand through his hair. "We'll have a problem getting into the country. American passports aren't going to cut it. We need visas."

"I'm not worried."

His head jerked up. "Why not?"

"I know a guy who smuggles artifacts in and out of countries around the world. I bet he can get two people into Iran."

"I don't smuggle artifacts. I acquire them."

"You *hunt* them," Nora said. "For the mob. Your boss gives you free rein to go after whatever you like. He provides the resources, and you make him money. Sound about right?" His lack of response was answer enough. "Some of that was guesswork," Nora said. "The rest I knew. Our world isn't large, Harry. I protect artifacts; you exploit them." She kept going before he could respond. "I know two other points. Sara Hamed has no idea what you really do for a living. And that's because you don't want her to know."

"Sara is none of your business." Harry's chest got hot again, and before he knew it, his finger was in Nora's face once more. "You latched onto my search because those Bergen security guys used you. Your boss hung you out to dry as soon as his big money donors came calling. Don't think you can tell me what to do. You can't even count on your own department to help you." Nora's face contorted with anger. Harry was almost shouting now. "You're in over your head and you need me. Me, a mob flunky." He lowered his finger and looked out the windshield.

Nora didn't yell back. Her voice was soft when she spoke. "Feel better now?" she asked. Harry didn't look at her. His heart was still thudding too hard. "You're right about some of it."

Harry's gaze whipped back to her. He was *right?*

"I need your help because the D.A. seems to value donors over duty. It doesn't matter that it's probably because he thinks this trip to Egypt won't amount to anything. People like you are always two steps ahead. I don't expect to win every time, Harry. You're better funded, better informed, and you have one motivation I'll never have: this is your life. People act differently when it's all they have. I go home each night and put this world aside. If I missed out on an artifact?" Nora lifted her shoulders. "That stinks, but oh well. There will always be another one, another chance to preserve the past and make things right. You don't have that luxury. I get why you're upset."

Now Nora turned to look out the windshield. A sliver of clear blue sky showed between the parking garage levels. "I'm not going to say anything about what you do to Sara. Whatever your reasons, I respect them. She can make her own decisions. If she wants to fly to Iran with you, a man she's only met, what, one time?" Harry nodded. "Then she can do it. I hope you don't try to dissuade her, because we need her."

"You're right, too," Harry said. "I haven't been upfront with her." He left it at that.

"Your business. Not mine." Nora twisted around to check behind them. "We can't stay here. I was serious about you getting us into Iran. Any chance you can make it happen?"

He'd been thinking about that ever since Nora had said it. Since Nora was playing it straight now, he would too. "I know someone. If she can't get us in, nobody can."

Harry tapped his phone and called Rose Leroux. His father had trusted Rose. Harry would too. She answered on the first ring. "It's Harry," he said. "Is this a bad time?"

"I always have time for you, Harry. Are you interested in selling the Persian tablet? I have several buyers in mind."

Harry looked quickly to Nora, who had the decency to pretend she didn't hear. "Not right now," Harry said. "Actually, I could use your help."

"Anything I can do, ask."

"I'm in Egypt, following up on the first Persian tablet."

"*First* Persian tablet?"

Harry gave her a quick rundown of what had transpired from when he was attacked at his apartment until right now, including connecting with Nora after her betrayal by Brian Joyce. Nora began to protest, but he shushed her. Rose had never turned on him. "This trail is real. The next stop is in Iran. I can't get in there with an American passport. Any chance you can get us in?"

"Working with a government agent?" Rose asked. "I assume she is furious with you for telling me. Is she listening?" Harry said she was. "Ms. Doyle, I will never betray your confidence. I am more familiar with your unit than you realize. In my profession, allies and enemies often change rapidly. I have a relationship with your agency which has proven beneficial to both sides in the past."

Lines creased Nora's brow. "Are you an informant?"

"As I said, I have a relationship. Let us leave it at that. Now, how far are you from Cairo?"

"An hour, give or take."

"Can you leave tonight?"

"That won't give me time to get passports from Vincent. I was going to ask him for foreign identities for us both."

"I suggest you don't let the authorities stop you," Rose said.

"How will we get through customs?" Nora asked.

"Agent Doyle, I never deal with customs." A pause. "How are you with tight spaces?"

Chapter Twenty-One

Saqqara

Brian Joyce walked out of the oven that was Megabyzus's tomb into Saqqara's fiery air. Sweat stung his eyes, and his throat felt like the desert stretching in front of him. He lifted a hand to shade against the brutal sun. Harry Fox was close. Now Brian had to find him.

The inept police officer stepped out of the narrow tomb entrance and nearly bounced off Brian's meaty shoulder. The guy had been yapping nonstop in Arabic since Brian found him lying inside a subterranean antechamber a few minutes earlier. From the dust and fresh debris, the cop looked to have fallen in before knocking himself unconscious on the way down. Brian had hauled him up, tried to get a straight answer out of him, but the guy's wires were still crossed and his words were gibberish.

"English, buddy. Speak English." A bottle of water had been down in the antechamber, so Brian had stuck it in the guy's hand before slipping back into the tomb and vaulting down the hole. The place came alive under his light's beam. Brian immediately wished it hadn't. A pile of bones reflected dully against one wall. *Human* bones. At least three or four bodies' worth. The builders, perhaps?

A humorless grin cracked his dusty face. Brian could respect a man like that. Whatever it took to keep this place hidden. He turned to the tiered pedestal and stepped closer. A rectangle was etched into the top of what looked to be an empty shape. Brian reached out to touch it. His hand stopped. *It's not an engraving. It's an outline.* Of where something used to be, an object on which all the dust had settled over generations. Whatever the object was, it had been moved. Brian couldn't help but notice it had been about the same size as the tablet Harry Fox had used to find this place.

There's another tablet. It was right here.

Brian inspected the rest of the antechamber, seeing nothing but dust and sand. He jumped back up to the main level, where the befuddled officer had regained most of his wits. "Hey, buddy." Brian tapped the officer lightly on one shoulder. "You okay?"

More rapid-fire nonsense. "You speak English?" Brian asked.

This time the cop switched to English. "Yes. Thank you. The ground collapsed and I hit my head."

"You fell down a hole." Brian pointed helpfully. "Any idea how long you were in there?"

The officer checked his watch. "Less than ten minutes, I believe."

Harry Fox couldn't have gone far. Brian turned and walked outside. Maybe Fox was still here. He might be watching Brian right now.

That's when the cop following on Brian's heels ran into his shoulder and bounced off. Brian hardly budged. "Did you see anyone in this tomb?" Brian asked the cop without turning around.

"The ground shook, and a man was inside the tomb. I went to check on him." The officer frowned. "It was not you in there?"

"Not me," Brian said. "Do you remember what he looked like?"

"A tourist." The officer had been moving toward his vehicle when he stopped and turned around. "Why do you ask? Do you know him?"

Brian looked to his men standing beside the Range Rover. "We may have seen him," Brian lied. "We can help look if you can tell me what he looks like. The more people looking for him, the better. We want to be sure he's not hurt."

The policeman dipped his head. "You are kind. I did not see his face very well. I cannot even say if he is Egyptian or just very tan."

That had to be Harry. "Too bad," Brian said.

The officer went to his car and sat behind the wheel. "Sir, please move away from this tomb. I am not sure what caused the ground to shake. It could happen again, and more shafts could open."

Brian made to follow orders as the policeman spoke into his radio. "Let's go," he told his men, who jumped into their vehicle. "We just missed him."

They began to descend the long, sloping hill when a pair of police vehicles flew past them in the opposite direction. It wouldn't be long before the archaeologists and government officials arrived, eager to examine the newly discovered antechamber. And these cops could have questions for Brian he didn't want to answer. His protection under Bergen Incorporated went a long way in the United States. Here in Egypt, not so much. They made it out of the necropolis unscathed.

"Drive around and circle back on that street." Brian pointed to a side street across from the entrance. "We'll have a clear view of anyone leaving." His driver circled the block until they were headed back toward the entrance. They passed a line of ramshackle vehicles parked on the street, then an out-of-place BMW, before an open spot at the end of the street appeared. "Right there."

The Range Rover slid into a spot less than fifty yards from Saqqara's entrance. "Keep your eyes open," Brian said. "No telling what kind of car he has." He settled in to wait. Noon was well past. The site closed to tourists at sundown, only a few hours away, so if Fox was still in there somewhere, he couldn't stay much longer. Find Harry Fox, and he found the tablet. From what he'd seen in the tomb minutes ago, there was even more to uncover from that, which meant Guy would be pleased.

An hour later there had been no sign of Harry Fox. Brian looked at his watch for what felt like the hundredth time. He tapped a finger incessantly on the dashboard. His driver pretended not to notice, but the man started as Brian nearly jumped out of his seat when his phone buzzed. He answered without looking at the screen. "Joyce here."

"I'm looking for Brian Joyce. Do you know where I can find him?"

"Who is this?" He didn't recognize the voice. "This is Brian Joyce. How did you get my number?"

"This is Jim Reed. I'm with the district attorney's office in Manhattan."

"What do you want?" Brian asked.

"You're the only other contact on my list. I got the results back she asked for, but she's not answering."

"What results? And who are you talking about?"

"Agent Doyle," Jim said. "You're working on a case with her, aren't you? She put in a surveillance request. It came through. But if you're not on the case—"

"I am." Brian spoke quickly. "I'm working a case with her in Egypt." He had no idea what Jim was calling about, but he couldn't pass on getting it before Doyle had a chance to stick her nose into things again. He'd worked hard to cut her out. "What did you find?"

"All the details she requested. Should I send this to you?"

"Yes. And Jim, could you remind me who the request was on? I'm in the car and don't have my files."

"Someone named Harry Fox. Lives in Brooklyn."

Brian punched the air. "What do you have on him?"

"Call logs, text messages, the usual phone information. The guy doesn't make a lot of calls. Plenty of text messages, not many calls."

"Did you record his conversations?"

Brian sensed a pause. "Are you asking if we tapped his phone?" Jim asked. "No judge would issue a warrant to tap his phone for…hold on." The sound of keys being tapped. "For a possible artifacts trafficking case." Jim's voice carried a hint of suspicion. "Are you sure you're working with Agent Doyle?"

Brian smacked his thigh. "You're right, of course. I got the names mixed up."

"We have his call and text records, with names. You want me to forward them?"

"Yes. Send it to my email." Brian rattled off an address, then waited until the files landed in his inbox. "Thanks. I'll be sure Nora gets these."

"Oh, one other thing. Harry Fox's call logs cut out as of two days ago. Either his phone has been turned off, or he's out of the country where we can't track him."

"Thanks for the heads up," Brian said.

As his men watched the necropolis entrance, Brian opened the files and scanned for anything useful. Nothing jumped out, only lines of phone numbers Harry had called or texted, with information on who the numbers belonged to. All the calls and texts had been made over the past ten days, nearly all of them with New York area codes. All except one. An international number with the country prefix *49.*

Brian had no idea what country code that was. Good thing he had an entire team back home to figure it out. He fired off an email with instructions to call him as soon as it was received. His phone buzzed thirty seconds later. "You got it?" he asked at once.

"Opening it now," Dale said. Dale was part of a specialized team at Bergen's headquarters, all tech wizards reporting directly to him and who Brian suspected could take over a small country with a computer and an internet connection. "A bunch of phone numbers some guy called or texted," Dale said. "What do you need?"

"First, any movement on his Brooklyn number since I left?"

He had given Dale Harry Fox's phone number to trace before he'd left New York and instructions to track any movement.

"It hasn't been active for a few days. Whoever has the number either keeps it turned off or ditched it."

Or is in another country using a new number Brian didn't have. "I need everything you can find on the data I just sent," Brian said. "The guy is named Harry Fox."

"This is the same number I'm tracking."

Brian ignored him. "First you need to tell me if there's anything in those call logs that is tied to Egypt. Does anyone on that list own real estate in Egypt? Anyone have family here? Find something. Start with the number that has country code prefix *49*. I'm not sure which—"

"Germany." Dale cut him off. "And it's a cell phone. Give me twenty minutes and I'll have more."

Brian eyed the horizon. The sun had sunk close. "Hurry up."

Dale clicked off. Brian squeezed his phone. Not two minutes later it buzzed. Dale was already calling back. "You have something?" Brian demanded.

"The German number belongs to a Sara Hamed," Dale said. He let out a low whistle. "She's a looker. Want her photo?"

No, you little creep. "Can you tell why Fox called her?"

"No idea," Dale said. "From their text messages it sounds like they're friends. Sara texted him a couple of days ago saying she had more information. Doesn't say what it's about."

Interesting. "Anything else?"

"Sara called Harry the day after she texted him, but he didn't answer. After that, nothing. Radio silence for Harry Fox the past few days."

"Fox is in Egypt."

"Makes sense," Dale said. "I figured you'd want more on Sara Hamed, so I hacked into her work emails. Easier than her personal account, and guess what I found?"

"Messages from Fox?"

"Better. She stored her personal email login information in her work material," Dale said. "I had to run it through a translator, but I got into her personal account. Sara Hamed just booked a flight to Shiraz, Iran."

That made no sense. Why visit Iran? "Anything about why she's going?"

"Nothing," Dale said. "No conferences, meetings, nothing."

"When did she book her flight?"

"Thirty minutes ago. Paid with a personal credit card too, not a university one. She works at Trier University in Germany as a professor of Egyptology."

"Check her cell phone records," Brian said. "Get me every call she's made and received in the past twenty-four hours."

"That'll take a while," Dale told him. "I have to translate everything from German into something I can read."

"Make it happen." Brian tapped his chin. "Look for calls or texts from an Egyptian phone number. If you don't find that, tell me any calls she's made or received over the past forty-eight hours. Then look at her recent emails. Look for anything—"

"The country code for Egypt is twenty. Two-zero. Sara Hamed received a call forty minutes ago from an Egyptian phone number. She was still on it when she booked the flight to Iran."

Bingo. "Tell me about any ties between Iran and Persia."

"Persia, the ancient empire? I don't know, boss. Hold on." Keys clicked, then Dale laughed. "I'll say it does. Iran basically *is* Persia. Parts of the Persian empire were in Egypt, Turkey and Pakistan, but this map says nearly all of Iran was part of it."

Egypt *and* Iran. Harry Fox wasn't leaving Egypt. He was moving around within the Persian empire. The first tablet had brought him to Saqqara, where Brian was certain Fox had found something in the tomb. And that something was taking him to another part of the Persian empire in Iran.

"Send me her flight information."

"She doesn't leave until tomorrow," Dale said. "She's probably still in Germany."

"Do better than that. I need to know exactly where she is."

Dale went silent, though his keyboard clacked like mad. "Let's see what apps she has on her phone…okay, that's good. I can work with this."

"Can you track her?"

"I'm checking." More clicks. "Yes, I can track her. Two of the applications are vulnerable to tracking. Right now, Sara Hamed is still in Trier, Germany."

"Send me updates when she goes to Iran. I don't care what else you were working on or who it's for; this takes precedence."

"Got it, boss. I won't lose track of her."

"Keep me updated." Brian clicked off. "Go back to the hotel," he told his driver. "I think Fox is already gone. Look, they're closing the site now." Even as they spoke, a stream of vehicles exited the complex, tourists and archaeologists alike heading out for the evening. There was still a crowd surrounding Megabyzus's tomb. "Harry Fox found something in that antechamber and now he's headed to Iran. We need to get to Iran and wait for Sara Hamed to lead us to him. Sara Hamed is an Egyptologist." He ran through what Dale had told him. "She suddenly flies to Iran at the same time Harry Fox is on this adventure through the Ancient Persian empire? Harry and Sara know each other somehow. Maybe she's an expert he uses for Egyptian artifacts."

His driver hit the gas, shooting through a yellow light as he aimed for Cairo. Only after they were speeding along the highway did Brian give any thought to Nora Doyle. They couldn't take her to Iran. Another thought hit him. *How am I getting into Iran?* No matter. His brother had to know someone who could get them in without any issues.

He dialed Guy. "I found something," Brian said when Guy answered. He gave a recap of the antechamber, of getting Harry Fox's phone records and of finding a way to tap Sara Hamed's phone.

"She's the key, Guy. She'll lead us to Harry Fox. One problem, though," Brian concluded. "We need to go to Iran."

"Iran?" Guy asked.

"It's the next stop on Xerxes' trail. I'm sure Fox is headed there right now."

"How's he getting into Iran?"

"Same way he gets anywhere he doesn't belong. He'll sneak in. Or his boss will know a guy who will look the other way. It doesn't matter, because Sara Hamed will lead us right to him."

"What if you're wrong? Then Fox is gone and your chance of finding what Xerxes left behind is too."

"I'm not wrong."

Guy sighed. "Brian, you'd better be correct. Do you know why I sent you after this, why I called in every favor I had at the D.A.'s office to get you assigned as a liaison to this case?"

Brian Joyce had served his country. He didn't need a cop's permission to help Guy find a life-changing artifact. "The tablet is tied to King Xerxes and the Persian empire," Brian said. He grasped for more. "And tied to the Greeks."

"*Possibly* tied," Guy said. "The sources on this are thousands of years old. I hope that doesn't matter. If my research is correct, these tablets are markers on a path to the truth behind a Greek legend. A truth tied to Hippocrates, and one that could revolutionize modern medicine. It could change the course of history."

Brian was on the edge of his seat when Guy fell silent. "Because of a legend?"

"Yes. We think it's only a legend, but what if we're wrong? What if this really did happen, and these tablets are markers meant to keep the knowledge from being lost? If that's true, then we need it. And you're the one who will get it."

Brian frowned as the Cairo skyline came into view. "Why wouldn't Xerxes use it himself? You said he was old and dying when he wrote this message."

"It's hard to say. But you need to get to Iran. The Iranian government is in need of a supply of certain generic drugs due to ongoing international sanctions. I'm sure they would welcome you with open arms and closed eyes if I suggested Bergen will supply these drugs for humanitarian purposes. Through an intermediary, of course, so it can't be traced back to us. I'll make the calls. Be ready to leave."

"What about Doyle?" Brian asked quickly. "Do you really want her along?"

"No. I'll call the D.A. and have her recalled due to lack of progress."

"Understood," Brian said. "I'll provide updated intel once we're on the ground."

"Brian." Guy paused for a moment, and all Brian could hear was soft breathing. "Iran isn't like other Middle Eastern countries. Their Supreme Leader foments unadulterated hatred against Americans. I can get you in, but I can't guarantee you'll be safe."

Why was Guy saying this? Of course Brian knew. "Part of the mission," Brian said. "No concerns on our end." He didn't ask his men for their thoughts. They'd follow orders.

"You're not in the service any longer," Guy said. "Be careful." A pause. "I know I can count on you."

"You can." Brian bit off the *sir*. He waited until Guy ended the call. Yes, his brother could count on him.

They pulled into the hotel minutes later. "Pack your gear and be ready to move when the call comes," Brian told his men as they headed inside. "It won't be long."

Only after he was back in his hotel room did Brian try to call Nora. He'd give her the courtesy of a warning that their plans might change. Nora could take it up with her boss if she had a problem, not that it would do any good.

The call rang unanswered. *Too bad.* He'd tried, and now Nora was on her own. The Bergen jet was leaving without her. She'll be fine, Brian told himself as he refolded his clothes, careful to maintain the creases. Bergen would foot the bill for her flight home. First class, if he had to guess. Guy was generous that way.

Then his thoughts turned to locating the missing item from that infernally hot tomb in Saqqara. The Supreme Leader of Iran could kiss his ass. Brian had been a Marine, and if there was one thing he knew, it was that Marines never failed.

Chapter Twenty-Two

Brooklyn

New York City is composed of five boroughs, five distinct geographical areas sharing borders but yet completely unlike each other. Manhattan was a stone's throw from Queens, but the identity of one was wholly unlike that of the other. The financial empires in Manhattan often sneered at the former collection of Dutch towns and villages, who no doubt would tell their moneyed neighbors how they felt about the city. The Bronx and Brooklyn faced the world not just as two different counties, but more like two different countries, albeit both of them melting pots boasting residents from across the globe. And Staten Island wasn't about to let anyone forget the outsized cultural impact of the little island to the south.

Five boroughs, though in truth hundreds of unique neighborhoods, comprised each one. You could walk fifteen minutes and pass through what felt like six different cultures. Chinatown couldn't be more different than Little Italy, unless you walked by the Hasidic community in Williamsburg, when you'd be hard-pressed to find a clean-shaven man on the street. Such communities tended to be close-knit, the sorts of places where neighbors knew each other for blocks around and families had lived there for generations.

Which was why Stefan didn't want to hit Joey Morello at Sanna, the Mediterranean restaurant. It stood too close to the street dividing Morello and Cana territory and was a bad place to do this kind of business. Too many innocent people lived in the neighborhood, affiliated with either family, or in a few cases, both. Altin Cana wasn't looking to start a war. He needed Stefan to perform double duty: carry out a hit on Joey and maintain plausible deniability for the Canas. So Stefan Rudovic waited in the shadows of a park several blocks away from Sanna with his cell phone pressed to an ear. He stood beside a guy he barely knew, one of three toughs hired on short notice based on two qualities. One, their lack of Albanian ancestry. Two, an open mind toward hurting people for money.

Deniability came at a price. Namely, Stefan had to use unfamiliar faces. Offer these types of men five grand each to back Stefan on what he told them was a robbery and they were in. No questions asked when he handed each of them a ski mask and a pistol. *Don't shoot*, Stefan told them. *You're here to scare the guy into giving up what he's carrying.* They didn't care how Stefan knew a specific man in a certain car would be transporting a shipment of diamonds. A courier, Stefan said. An easy mark. Stefan had a plan, a way to distract the supposed courier from knowing what really hit him.

The other two hired thugs were each driving their own cars. Earlier in the night Stefan had taken his newly hired team past Morello headquarters, pointing out Joey Morello's electric SUV. Joey always rode shotgun, and Stefan told them how they would box the SUV in later that night, forcing it into a collision. Stefan failed to mention that the man riding shotgun in the SUV was the Italian mob's favorite son. He did tell the two how to stage the accident. One of them waited a couple blocks away, close to Sanna. The other parked near Morello headquarters. When Joey's car pulled out, they would follow it until they approached the park. At this point Stefan's hired men would be in front of and behind Joey's car, putting him in a box he couldn't see.

The lead guy would hit his brakes without warning. Maybe Joey's car stops in time, maybe it doesn't. Either way, the trail car doesn't stop. It slams into Joey's car, pushes it into the lead car, and now Joey

Morello isn't going anywhere. He's stuck, trapped between two hunks of metal, all of it happening near the entrance to a dark, quiet city park. A park where Stefan Rudovic and his third hired guy are waiting. The two drivers get out, words are exchanged, then Stefan and the other guy move in from the shadows to supposedly relieve Joey Morello of his diamonds before vanishing in the darkness.

At least that's what Stefan told the chumps he hired. In truth, things would get a touch more interesting than that. But these guys would all find out soon enough.

An evening breeze rustled the leaves above Stefan as he waited in the park. Streetlights dotted the empty sidewalk, their pools of light stopping just short of where Stefan and his hired thug waited. The man's name was Luke, and he was the quiet type. Stefan appreciated it.

Stefan glanced at his watch, turning it to catch the moonlight. "Not long now." He checked his phone, confirming it was on.

"Good," Luke said.

"Is your weapon loaded?" Stefan asked.

"Yes."

He could sense Luke didn't like questions. "Safety on?"

"Yes."

"Stay to my right. Al and Ryan" – those were the two drivers – "will get out on the far side. We stay on this side of the car." The passenger side, where Joey Morello would be sitting. "The diamonds should be in back. Keep your gun up. Make sure they see it."

"Got it. To your right. Gun up." Luke grunted, apparently exhausted from the monologue.

Could Stefan rely on Luke to keep the bullets in his magazine? He'd have to take it on faith that his sources were right, and that Luke could handle himself. Everything in Stefan's plan counted on Luke and the other hired guns doing what they were told. That was how they got to the end game, when Stefan's true plan kicked into gear.

Stefan's phone buzzed. It was the trail car parked outside Morello headquarters, driven by Al. "They're leaving," Al said when Stefan answered.

"You sure he's in the car?" Stefan asked.

"It's the fancy-ass SUV you pointed out," Al said. "He's in it."

"Are you behind them?"

"On his tail."

"Stay there. I'll call Ryan." Stefan conferenced in the lead car driver. "Ryan, I'm on with Al. Joey Morello just pulled out."

"I'm moving," Ryan said. Silence for a moment. "I see him now. He's one block behind me."

Stefan had laid out the route Joey would likely take and had driven it with all three of the hired guns over and over until each of them could follow it with ease. Now all they needed to do was stay with Joey's car until he passed the park where Stefan and Luke waited.

"When you're two blocks from the park, let the SUV get right on your backside. Al will be on his tail."

"I got it," Ryan said.

Both Al and Ryan kept the phone line open as ordered, calling out street names as they crossed them, until Stefan finally heard the street two blocks away. "Time to move," he said. Luke checked his pistol.

A pair of headlights appeared at an intersection to Joey's left. "Is that you, Ryan?" Stefan asked. The headlights flicked twice in response. "Jam the brakes halfway down this street, just outside the park entrance. Al, hit him hard. Luke and I will be there. And remember, no shots. This is a robbery. Nothing else."

Stefan clicked off. None of the men had sent off any vibes he didn't like, given any indication they didn't believe what Stefan had told them. Good thing, because his entire plan counted on them thinking Joey Morello had diamonds in the car. As far as Stefan knew, he had no such thing. What Joey had was about thirty seconds to live. Same as the three schmucks Stefan had hired.

Ryan's car drove alongside the park, nearing the entrance.

Rowhomes lined the opposite side of the street, tall houses with a view of the park's fountain. Porches in front, where the owners could sit outside on pleasant evenings. No kids were out now. No sun warmed the ground. No witnesses to see what came next.

"Let's go." Stefan stepped out from behind the tree, light from a streetlamp touching his shoes as Luke followed. Ryan's car passed, with Joey Morello's following. Al's trail car rumbled close behind. The park entrance was no more than twenty feet from the middle of the street. Stefan and Luke stepped onto the sidewalk as Ryan slammed on his brakes, the harsh squeal of rubber on asphalt making Stefan cringe.

Joey's car stopped just in time. *Good brakes.* A pool of light fell on the car, bringing Joey Morello's face into view. He rode shotgun, as Stefan had predicted. Al closed in hot on Joey's tail, heavy on the gas. Joey and his crew never saw it coming. One second, they barely avoided a guy stopping short in front of them, the next a second car smashed into their rear bumper, pushing them into the stopped car ahead. Metal crunched, glass shattered, and Joey Morello was trapped inside his vehicle.

"Take the passenger," Stefan said as he walked quickly to the accident. Walked, not ran, with what he hoped was a concerned look on his face. No doubt Morello and his men were armed. Anyone walking up waving a gun would get a bullet for their troubles. As Stefan neared the car, he caught a glimpse of movement above Joey's car. A door had opened across the street, cracks of light coming from inside the house to frame a small figure walking out. *Damn – a witness.*

"Is anyone hurt?" Stefan first went to Ryan's lead car. The passenger side window he approached was rolled down, as planned. "Hey, you okay in there?" Stefan looked inside. Ryan had his gun in hand, seatbelt unbuckled. The airbag hadn't deployed, a minor win. "I'll check on Al, then we move," he said quietly.

Ryan nodded his understanding as Stefan moved back to Al's car, skirting around Luke, who stood outside Joey's window asking if everyone was okay. Stefan kept one hand in the open, out wide as though showing concern for the men inside. The rear passenger side door on Joey's car opened as Stefan passed.

"You okay?" Stefan asked. He kept moving, getting behind Joey's car. "Anybody hurt?"

He didn't listen to the man's response, instead turning to confirm Al was getting out of his car, pistol in hand. Al nodded to Stefan. *Let's do this.*

Stefan closed his eyes, took a deep breath, then pulled out his gun and turned around. He stood five feet behind the man exiting Joey's car from the rear passenger seat. "You hurt?" Stefan asked. He held the gun behind his back. "I saw it all happen, this—"

"Gun!" The man shouted before he dove back into the Morello car. *How did he see it?*

Luke's pistol flashed under the streetlight. The moron had it out in plain sight. Joey's man hadn't seen Stefan's gun, he'd spotted Luke's weapon before diving back into the car's rear seat. Luke panicked, taking aim inside the vehicle and putting his finger on the trigger.

He didn't move fast enough. The car's interior lit up with two flashes and Luke crumpled to the street. More gunshots and the rear windshield disintegrated. Stefan hit the asphalt, cursing as he rolled away from Joey's car back toward the safety of Al's vehicle. He popped up to one knee in time to see a gun appear from the rear passenger window of Joey's car. Stefan fired twice and the gun vanished back inside.

This had all gone sideways. His plan was to get close enough to shoot Joey and then run. If Joey's men didn't take care of the three hired guns, Stefan would do it for them from a safer distance. No one on his team would be left alive to tie him to the killing. It was perfect. Until Luke had let Joey's men see his gun.

Stefan opened Al's passenger door and nearly got a bullet for his trouble.

"Damn, I nearly shot you." Al lowered his gun. "What's happening?"

"No idea," Stefan said. "Do you have a shot?"

Whatever Al said next, Stefan didn't hear. Far ahead, Ryan had taken cover behind one of his car doors, and as Stefan watched, Ryan unloaded a barrage into Joey's windshield. Joey's driver screamed as light flashed inside the car, the Morello men returning fire. Ryan stumbled backward before falling out of sight. The screams from inside Joey's car faded to silence. The Morello driver was down. So was Ryan. It was two against two now. Joey Morello and the guy in his back seat against Stefan and Al.

"Shoot into the rear window," Stefan said. This had to end now. Stefan glanced over to the porch where someone had walked out earlier, but they weren't in sight. The door remained open.

Al stood and fired until his magazine emptied. He swore, fumbling to reload. The rear occupant of Joey's car popped up and took aim.

Stefan shouted. "Get do—"

Bullets flew and Al went down. Stefan leveled his pistol and returned fire, taking out Joey's man. *You're the only one left now, Morello.*

Stefan dropped to the ground, fired twice at the passenger side of Joey's car, then scooted on his stomach around Al's wrecked vehicle until he was on the driver's side. Stepping over Al, Stefan hunched over and ran until he reached the driver's side door of Joey's car. The streetlight overhead cast a pool of yellow light around the scene. The dead Morello driver beside Stefan. The bullet-riddled Tesla doors. Broken pieces of tempered glass crunching under Stefan's shoes.

Stefan ripped open the driver's door. Joey Morello was turned in the passenger seat, one hand holding a pistol, his face looking back at Al's car. Surprised, he twisted as Stefan raised his gun.

A thunderous *boom* filled the air as the rear driver's side door was crunched inward by some giant, invisible fist. Stefan jumped onto Joey's roof and rolled down the cracked windshield to the hood, continuing onto the ground for a crash landing. A second massive *boom* shook the air. Stefan blinked. *What the hell?*

A white-haired woman, clad in a nightshirt that twisted in the soft breeze, walked toward them. She was the person Stefan had seen open the house door when the crash had happened, the house directly across from his ambush. She kept walking, toothpick legs ending in bedroom slippers marching directly at Stefan. She was carrying a shotgun. He dropped to the ground as she fired a third time, sending sparks showering off the Tesla's hood. This old lady was going to kill him.

Stefan ran, firing back at Joey's car. Legs pumping, he raced along the sidewalk. The window of a car he passed disintegrated when the old lady's shotgun blasted again. He sped up and turned a corner, sprinting two blocks to the getaway car he'd hidden earlier. The engine fired, and Stefan forced himself to drive slowly as he melted into neighborhood traffic, stopping only to drop his pistol down a sewer grate.

He'd badly underestimated Joey Morello. And he hadn't counted on fighting an entire neighborhood. *That's how it is?* Stefan's knuckles went white around the wheel. Joey would be expecting him now. *Fine. Next time I'll be ready.*

Chapter Twenty-Three

Four cramped hours behind a false wall in the vast hold of a cargo plane brought two people together in a hurry. The space was barely big enough to stand up in, situated beside the roaring propellers; the noise level was louder than a hurricane. Thank goodness for the hearing protection headphones they'd been given along with their uniforms. Harry touched the name patch sewn onto his shirt. *Ahmed*. At least Ahmed was about Harry's size, so it fit. Nora hadn't been so lucky. *Dina* not only had to wear a hijab, but the real Dina was shorter than Nora, which gave her disguise the appearance of having shrunk in the wash. Lucky for her, their pilot had provided a *manteua*, a thin sweater that women wore in Iran to cover their posterior.

It had all come together quickly. Rose Leroux had sent them to her contact in Cairo, a man who flew cargo planes in the Middle East and who let Rose's friends stow away in his cargo hold. A space that, judging from the wrinkled sheets on the fold-out cot and the dingy bucket in one corner, had seen much use. Rose had warned them of their host's spartan accommodations and they had prepared accordingly.

Harry and Nora had met the pilot at his office, where he had given them each a uniform of khaki pants and shirt, names included, along with noise-cancelling headphones with built-in radios. Absent those, they would have been forced to scream at each other once the engines started. Three hours of surprisingly smooth flight later, the plane smacked on a runway in Shiraz. They took the headphones off, sitting in silence until footsteps sounded outside the false panel. Harry's throat tightened as the panel opened. He stepped in front of Nora.

The pilot's head appeared. "Follow me."

Nora pushed roughly past Harry, a bookbag on her back. Harry followed them, the messenger bag over his shoulder as he stepped through the plane's dark, packed cargo area until they reached a door in the fuselage. The pilot touched the door handle and paused.

"There is a car in the north parking garage." The pilot handed Harry a set of keys. "Keep your heads down. The uniforms will prevent anyone from looking too closely. Get rid of them once you are away from the airport."

"Thank you for your help," Harry said.

The man grunted. "Rose said to give you this." He handed over a gym bag, which Harry opened to discover was filled with U.S. dollars and Iranian rial paper notes. "Ten thousand in dollars," the pilot said. "Five hundred million rials. Equivalent to ten thousand U.S. dollars."

The pilot had one more gift, handing over two pairs of aviator sunglasses and looking directly at Nora. "I do not know who you are, and I do not care. Do not let the authorities catch you. The jails here are no place for a woman." He considered. "Or a man. Good luck."

He pulled the fuselage door open. Sharp morning light assaulted Harry's eyes, and he scrambled to put the sunglasses on before descending the metal stairs that unfolded from inside. A sleek private jet roared in for landing as Harry and Nora walked with purpose across the tarmac to the door their pilot had pointed out, where Harry opened the door. The only people in sight were airline employees. *Keep going,* the pilot had told them. *Don't stop until you get to the parking garage.* Both of them spoke and read Arabic, so it was a matter of following the signs until they reached the parking structure. Twice they passed uniformed soldiers who never gave them a second look. Nora kept her eyes down, which worked with the hijab to make her blend in, another Muslim woman in a man's company.

Once they made it to the parking garage and found the nondescript domestic sedan, Harry's shoulders loosened by a fraction. They were in a hostile country without permission. "Mind if I drive?" Harry asked. He opened the glovebox to find an oversized flashlight with extra batteries.

"It would look suspicious if you didn't," Nora said. "Stay below the speed limit. That cargo plane leaves again in forty-eight hours with or without us. I'm not interested in finding our own way out of this country."

Silence filled the car as Harry drove out of the parking garage. Artificially green islands of grass and stubby trees surrounded the airport, quickly giving way to the urban sprawl and dusty hillsides of Shiraz. It was a city of nearly two million souls, located in the south of Iran. Modern buildings mixed with structures dating back hundreds of years passed by in succession as Harry balanced Nora's demand for both speed and prudent driving. As they drove, the city soon changed to countryside, the rocky hills dotted with hardy trees and mist-shrouded mountains in the distance. He followed signs which took them north toward the ancient ceremonial capital of the Achaemenid empire: Persepolis, which contained significant cultural artifacts in the Middle East. The ruins of five palaces and numerous great halls stood among well-preserved tombs. Five palaces. Or five *beacons* in the City of Persians.

Harry passed the exit ramp for the road to Persepolis, instead taking the next exit for the Persian Gulf Complex, which the sign noted as "The 12th Largest Shopping Mall in the World". Confronted with a monstrosity of concrete, shining glass and garish corporate logos, Harry drove into the parking garage closest to the main entrance and found a spot, where he lowered the windows and shut off the engine. They waited.

"You really think Sara will find us here?" Nora asked. "This place is massive."

"Twenty-five hundred stores massive. Yes, Sara will find us. I told her to get dropped off at this entrance."

Harry and Sara had connected via text message to coordinate their rendezvous in Iran. Sara's flight from Germany had left late last night, eight hours on a redeye putting her in Shiraz around the time Harry and Nora had landed. Given Sara had to go through customs and find a taxi to the shopping mall, he expected to see her in around twenty minutes. A straightforward plan. Harry tapped a tuneless beat on the steering wheel. If that were true, why was his heartrate accelerating?

He hadn't seen Sara since he'd been in Germany several months earlier. In the interim she had been digging into the mystery of his Egyptian amulet, the heirloom Harry's father had worn around his neck ever since Harry could remember. Sara had revealed to him that the amulet had ties to Mark Antony and Cleopatra, and was continuing to research the piece in Germany. Now, unexpectedly, she'd be at his side. Of course, he wanted to know what she'd found, but not with a near-stranger along as they followed an entirely different trail. The amulet was different. *Personal.* There would be a time and place for it, and now wasn't it. First, survive whatever Xerxes' trail had in store.

He shifted in his seat. It didn't help that Sara had told him she had news about the amulet. Maybe he could send Nora off for five minutes and have a private moment with Sara.

"She's here."

Nora's voice derailed his thoughts. Harry sat up like something had bitten him. *Stop losing focus, you dope.* Daydream like that in Persepolis and you'll get someone killed.

A woman appeared from the stairwell, descending from a level above. The hijab may have covered her hair, but it couldn't hide the honey-colored eyes scanning the parking garage.

"Smart girl," Nora said. "She didn't get dropped off at this entrance."

Harry didn't disclose he'd told Sara to do that. He put his hand out the window, waving until Sara spotted them. She stopped, bending down to tie a boot that wasn't unlaced, looking all around before she stood and made for Harry's car. Harry checked their surroundings. Nobody appeared in the stairwell, no cars hurried to catch up as Sara slipped into the back of Harry's vehicle. Which meant anyone tailing her was good.

"Do you think anybody followed you?" he asked.

"No," Sara said. "I got off the plane first, then waited for everyone else to leave before I caught a cab to a hotel. I went inside, changed my hijab and flipped my sweater inside out. Then I took a different cab here."

Harry saw Nora lift an eyebrow. "Smart," Nora said, and stuck her hand out. "Nora Doyle. Thanks for coming."

"Sara Hamed." A single, hard shake and then Harry drove out of the parking garage, taking a winding route to flush out anyone trailing Sara. Not much, but the best he could do. "Appreciate you having me along."

"It's in the bag beside you," Nora said.

Harry glanced in the rearview mirror. Sara's face lit up as she pulled the tablet out, holding it like a newborn. "*Mein Gott.*" Harry struggled to catch her words. "A Persian tablet in an Egyptian tomb built beside the graves of Egypt's elite. Fascinating, given Xerxes conquered Egypt but didn't hold it. Most nations would destroy a tomb built by their oppressor."

"Lucky for us they didn't," Nora said. "Still think we need to go to Persepolis?"

"I'm sure of it," Sara said.

Harry studied a well-used map provided by the pilot. A red line marked their route, which the pilot had assured him was the fastest route to Persepolis. "You do not want to miss the flight home," the man had said. He hadn't asked why Harry wanted to go to the ancient city.

"Is there any other city Xerxes could be talking about?" Harry asked. "What about a city of the same name before Xerxes' time? The empire lasted for centuries. Is it possible the *City of Persians* name was used before?"

"Fair idea," Sara said. "The empire lasted over two hundred years. For a time, they ruled from Central Asia across Europe. At its height, the empire counted forty-four percent of the world's population as its Persian subjects. The largest empire by share of population in history."

"But none of those other cities was called *the City of Persians.*"

"Correct," Sara said. "Combined with the reference to *five beacons,* it doesn't connect to anyplace else. Persepolis is known for its five palaces." Sara looked up from the tablet and caught his eye in the mirror. "I researched and found nothing else remotely possible. It's Persepolis."

"Any chance those five palaces are all still around?" Harry asked.

"Yes and no. Some have been refurbished or rebuilt, while others are in what's left of their original state after thousands of years."

"What other leads are there?" Nora asked. "The tablet has two paragraphs on it. Persepolis is big. We need more than a city name or we'll be searching for a long time."

"No need to worry," Sara said. "We'd be arrested in short order. Iran is quite serious about security at cultural sites." Nora didn't laugh. "Only a joke," Sara said. She cleared her throat. "You're correct. The tablet doesn't give us much to go on." The corners of her lips twitched. "But I think it gives us enough."

Nora kept her eyes ahead. "I'm listening."

Harry kept both hands on the wheel as a convoy of military vehicles rumbled past at speeds well over the posted limit. He didn't look at the soldiers sitting in the back under canvas flaps, didn't so much as let his tires touch the painted lines until the desert camouflage trucks were far ahead. A mountain range dotted the horizon ahead, while surprisingly green fields stretched out on either side, dotted by homesteads or farms. It was almost possible to think they were on a welcoming European country road instead of driving into the middle of a country where *Death to America* was a national motto.

"What makes you think we have enough information?" Harry asked. "Is it the lines about *Greek emerald elixir* or the *knowledge* they mention?"

"No. I have an idea about those, but I think the end tells us more."

Sara traced the words with her finger as she read. "*Any who seek this elixir must follow the king's wealth to reap his reward.*" She looked up. "This tablet is a guide. We're following it. The next step after Persepolis is to *follow the king's wealth.* Only then will we *reap his reward.* Which is what this is all about – finding what King Xerxes left behind."

"Unless we take the path leading to *doom*," Nora said.

Harry jumped in. "We should be careful, but I've done this enough to realize those warnings are mostly smoke. It's probably a way for the priest or whoever wrote this to reassure Xerxes his orders were protected by the gods."

"Xerxes practiced Zoroastrianism," Sara said. "The religion honors a single deity of wisdom, Ahura Mazda. It is one of the ₒoldest, continuously practiced religions in the world."

"*Continuously* practiced?" Harry asked.

"Very much so. It has over one hundred thousand adherents today."

"How does that help us figure out how to stay alive in Persepolis?" Nora asked.

Sara shrugged. "I'll tell you more when we get there."

Nora frowned. "Where is *there*? We can't wander the sites all day."

"Persepolis does have dozens of sites that could have been used either as a hiding place for another marker, or the final stop on this journey. However," Sara lifted a finger, "one stands out as the most likely by far. A tomb."

"Which tomb?" he asked.

"Xerxes'." Sara raised an eyebrow. "You didn't know he was buried here?"

"The same Xerxes who wrote this tablet?" Harry glanced at Nora. "I read about Xerxes' tomb after I left Greece but wasn't certain of the location. We didn't have time to study on our trip over."

"How *did* you get into Iran?" Sara asked.

"That story can wait," Nora said. "You're certain it's the same Xerxes?"

"Artaxerxes II," Sara said. "King of kings, ruler of the Achaemenid empire. The same. And I believe the tablet points us to his tomb, because Xerxes talks about a Persian following his trail and finding whatever Xerxes left at the end. He believed a Persian would complete the journey, so Xerxes would only leave the prize – the *Greek emerald elixir* – in a place known to and revered by Persians. A place like his tomb."

"What do you know about his tomb?" Nora asked.

"It's carved out of a hillside. More of a cliff, really, and it's over a hundred feet tall."

A car raced by them in the passing lane. Nora's eyes narrowed, and she followed the black sport utility vehicle as it flew up the road. A Range Rover. "Something wrong?" he asked.

"No. Just nerves." Nora turned to face Sara. "Have you been inside the tomb?"

"Yes, when I visited here before. I didn't get to see anything other than the first-level entrance. The rest was under repair."

"How will we know where to go once we're inside? It sounds massive."

"The façade cut into the hillside is tall," Sara said. "But the interior doesn't go up. It goes down."

"How far down?" Nora asked.

"Only several levels. I hope this tablet points us in the right direction after we get inside."

"What if it doesn't?"

Sara tapped Harry's shoulder. "Harry's done this sort of thing before. I trust he'll put us on the correct path."

Great. Now she was putting it all on him. "I've seen my share of maps and tablets," he said. "I haven't had to decode a Persian word-puzzle and find a king's hidden elixir."

"Then what sort of artifact hunts *have* you been on?"

His mirror revealed her eyes boring through the back of his skull. "Depends on the artifact."

"You'll have to tell me more sometime."

A fortuitous road sign appeared. "We're almost there. This is the last town before Persepolis."

Turned out it wasn't a town. Not as Harry knew them, anyway. More like a speck on the map. No streetlights, no stop signs, a few buildings crowding the road, with a large speed limit sign beside the first house. The road bent, and he rounded another turn to find more of the same. No one walking along the road or standing in the green fields on either side. A pair of motorcycles leaned against the side of a house. How had two classic bikes like those ended up out here?

A black car appeared in his rearview mirror.

"Who's back there?" Nora asked.

Harry shrugged. "Beats me."

She twisted in her seat. "Another one," she said.

"Another one of what?"

"Another black SUV." She squinted. "Looks like a Range Rover."

"Does that matter?"

"I'm not sure." Nora turned back around. A cross street bisected the main road ahead. As he approached it, the front end of another vehicle inched into sight. A black Range Rover.

He felt more than saw Nora tense before she shouted. "Hit the gas!"

Harry punched it as the Range Rover roared out from the cross street, aimed right at them. The trailing Range Rover grew in his rearview mirror. Their sedan jumped ahead, fast enough that the Rover coming from the side merely clipped Harry's rear. Harry held on as his world twisted. Airbags deployed like shotgun blasts before the car went eerily silent. Screams floated at the edge of hearing, either Sara or Nora; Harry couldn't say.

Their car spun halfway around, ending up facing oncoming traffic, but all Harry could see was the Rover that had clipped them, stopped in the middle of the street. He blinked, and the Rover went airborne, tossed like a child's toy. Glass sparkled after the trail car broadsided the first Rover and flipped it up over Harry's hood, the Rover's windshield spiderwebbing when it landed. Harry stared into the other driver's face, barely a foot away. Red liquid spattered the windshield. The choking scent of gasoline filled the air.

"Get out." Harry could barely hear himself talk. He fumbled with his seatbelt, managing to pull it loose. Nora did the same beside him. "Move," Harry said. "The gas."

Blood streaked down Nora's face as she worked herself free. Something *thunked* behind him: Sara kicking open her door. Nora had no such luck. "It's stuck." Nora grabbed the handle, fighting it with her entire body. "I can't open it."

Harry's door didn't budge. He laid a shoulder into it once. Twice. The third time failed as well.

"Jump back here." Sara squirmed out, slipping the tablet into Harry's messenger bag and over her shoulder.

He turned to Nora. "Can you make it?" In his head a clock was ticking down. Whoever had tried to smash them to bits could be getting up, coming to finish the job.

Nora pushed him back out of her way. "I know who did this." She tumbled into the back seat and fell out of the car. Harry followed more nimbly, landing on his feet outside Sara's door. One Range Rover lay atop the hood of their sedan, leaking gas. The other was hidden from view, pressed up against the flipped Rover, holding it there.

The driver who had flipped onto Harry's hood was probably dead. No way a man could lose that much blood. Harry didn't see anyone else inside that vehicle, which left the trailing Rover. Even if airbags and seatbelts had saved them, chances were anyone inside wasn't on top of their game. Which gave Harry an opening.

One look at their own sedan told the story. "Our car is finished," he told Nora. "Stay back. If this goes south, run to any house and call the cops." Then he remembered. "Who *are* these guys?"

"Brian Joyce only uses Range Rovers in the field. A black Range Rover passed us on the road not long ago." She pointed to the car that had flipped onto their hood. "I bet it was that one. Then a second one rams us from behind? That's no accident."

"You think the Bergen security team followed you here to kill you?" He reached into his pocket, slipping one hand into the ceramic knuckledusters hidden there. "Maybe you're right. I have to see if they're still moving." He took a deep breath. *Those guys better not have guns.*

The flipped Rover's rear end hung out enough to give him cover. Harry ducked down and crawled underneath the Rover's tail end until he was behind it. He pressed his back to the rear bumper and listened. Someone was moaning inside, up near the driver's seat. He circled to the other side and stopped at the passenger door, trying and failing to use the mirror to see inside. *Forget this.* He grabbed the door handle and pulled.

A man fell out. Harry stumbled back, landing on his backside with the guy's weight holding him down. The guy was *big*, trapping Harry beneath him. Harry punched him once, twice in the head, solid blows. The man didn't budge. Harry stopped fighting and started thinking. The guy was breathing, but only softly. He was out of commission for now, possibly forever.

The moaning inside turned to grunts. A man's head slowly came into view, and the engine turned over.

"Don't start it," Harry yelled. "You'll kill us all." Gas fumes permeated the air. In a small miracle, the engine noises stopped. Harry finally pushed the body off his own and saw the driver trying to get out of his door. He had a pistol in his hand. Then a shadow appeared behind him. Nora Doyle had joined the fight.

"Nora, get out of here." Harry moved around the Rover's rear bumper, knowing he could be running straight into a gun barrel. If he came from behind, the gunman had to turn around, away from Nora, to deal with Harry. He could give her a chance to run—

Harry came around the car and stopped. The gunman lay on the ground, unmoving. Nora stood over him, holding the heavy flashlight from inside their glovebox like a club. She looked up at Harry. "Are you okay?" she asked.

"Yeah, I'm fine." Harry looked from Nora to the man at her feet. "Did you do that?"

"Yeah." She looked at the flashlight in her hands. She lowered it. "This is one of Brian Joyce's men."

"Nice work." Harry pocketed the man's gun. He thought better of it, ejected the magazine, cleared the chamber, then threw the bullets in one direction and the pistol in another. "Where's Brian Joyce?"

"On the ground where you left him." She pointed through the open car to the man whose heavy body had trapped Harry. "This man was riding shotgun."

The clock in Harry's head struck zero. "We've been here too long," Harry said. "The cops should show up soon. Someone must have called them." Harry used the driver's belt to tie the unconscious man's hands together, then rolled him to the curb.

"How do we get out of here?" Nora pointed to their wrecked sedan. "Our car is smashed. One of these Range Rovers is leaking gas, and this other—"

The gas. Harry grabbed Nora by the arm and dragged her away. "Get away from here," he said. "The gas fumes could go off any second." They ran across the street to where Sara leaned against a dingy brick wall. "Are you hurt?" he asked Sara.

"No." She kept her eyes on his. Her voice didn't tremble.

"Good. That's good." He reached for her, and she reached back. For a reason he couldn't explain Harry turned quickly away and left her hand hanging. "We have to go." He looked around the corner of the house they huddled against, and, for the first time since they had arrived in town, saw another person. An old man, his head poking out of the adjacent house. An image popped into Harry's mind. "Stay here," he told Nora and Sara. He reached into the messenger bag around Sara's torso before heading off.

The man's trim white beard set off a sunbaked face. He didn't move as Harry moved quickly toward him. Harry stopped a few feet away. "*As-salaam 'alaykum.*" Peace be upon you.

The man blinked. "*Wa 'alaykum salaam.*" Upon you be peace.

Harry continued in Arabic. "Forgive our intrusion. There's been an accident. My car won't run any longer." He pointed to the wrecked sedan, as though this guy might not believe him. "My friends and I must leave immediately."

The man cleared his throat. "Are you in danger?"

Honesty? Or a more calculated response? The guy might want nothing to do with helping three strangers leave before the authorities showed up. Or he could be an ally.

He guessed. "Yes, we're in danger."

The man's gaze traveled up and down the main road, searching far in the distance. Harry fought the urge to do it as well. Finally, the man turned back to Harry. "How can I help?"

Phew. Harry pointed to the corner of the man's house. "There are two motorcycles leaning against this house. Are they yours?"

"Yes."

"I can pay you five thousand dollars for them." Average household income in Iran was under three thousand dollars annually. This guy lived in the middle of nowhere. His house looked like it was older than the dirt beneath it.

The man shook his head. "Go away. I cannot replace them with so little."

"Not rials. *Dollars.* U.S. dollars." Harry pulled out half the American money he'd taken from inside his bag moments ago. "Like these."

A hoarse rattle sounded in the man's throat as he sucked in air. The man's hand shot out. "Let me see it."

Harry might have been desperate, but he wasn't dumb. "Show me the keys first. I don't know if those bikes even work."

"Check for yourself." He reached into a pocket of his loose cotton trousers, pulled out a set of keys and handed them to Harry. "The money?"

Harry gave him half. "How much petrol is in them now?"

"The tanks are always full."

He ran over to the bikes and started each one. Their engines purred, the smooth sounds of cared-for motors belying their ragged exteriors. Both gas tanks showed as full, just like the man said. Harry walked back to the porch and handed him the other half of the cash. "Thank you."

Lines creased the old man's face as he reached out and touched Harry's arm. "May Allah watch over you."

"And you." Harry turned to find Nora and Sara had walked over and were standing near the bikes. "Our new rides," Harry said. "Come on."

He pried one key off the ring and gave it to Nora, who hopped on a bike. She looked up when Harry stood in front of her.

"How did those men follow us?" he asked Nora. "You didn't even know we were coming here until *after* you met me, so they couldn't have overheard you. How did they know?"

"I have no idea," Nora said. Her face turned hard. "You think I told them?"

"Of course not. The problem is they found us somehow." He

thought for a second. "Turn your phone off."

"You think they're tracking it?" Nora shook her head. "That's crazy."

"They're a private security force for an international corporation. You don't think they have the money or sophistication to track your phone?" He knew a couple of guys the Morello family used for such activities. Normal, mostly law-abiding computer wizards who liked extra cash.

She frowned, but powered her phone off. "What about yours? Brian Joyce knows who you are. They could hack your phone."

"Good point." Harry switched his phone off, then turned to Sara. "Yours too."

"How would they even know to look for me?" Sara asked.

"Are we willing to take the risk?" Harry asked. Off went her phone. "Thanks," Harry turned back to Nora. "Fire that bike up. You'll like the sound."

Nora's face lit up as the bike's engine came to life. "Someone takes care of this machine."

Sara flinched at the rumbling engine and took a step back. "I've never been on a motorcycle."

"They're fun. And better than waiting around for that guy to wake up."

"You mean the one whose hands you tied together and left beside a car that might explode?"

Harry nodded. "Yeah, him. The one who tried to kill us. And he's on the sidewalk now. Best I can do." Harry jumped on the second bike, motioning for Sara to join him. "Sit behind me and hang on tight. Persepolis is ten miles from here. It won't take long on these." He reached around and patted the seat. "Unless you want us to stay here."

Nora gunned her engine. "Those guys likely have more friends on the way."

That got Sara moving. She kicked a leg up, getting astride Harry's bike in one fluid motion. Harry grabbed her calf, but she didn't seem to mind. "Tuck your feet back." He guided her foot until it found purchase. "Stay close to me." She inched toward him. "Closer. This isn't a junior high dance." She pressed up against him, her body warm against his. "Hold around my waist. Not too tight," he said quickly when she latched on with a death-grip. "Better. Now try not to move too much. If I lean to turn, follow my lead." He turned around to face her, his nose brushing her hair. It smelled faintly of flowers. "We'll be fine."

"Forgive me if I'm anxious. Someone tried to kill me today." Her eyes narrowed. "You don't seem fazed."

Harry turned back around. Whatever thoughts he had about Sara, and he wasn't even sure *what* thoughts he had, none were like this. Now she thought he was a criminal, comfortable with dead bodies and not hesitant to tie up an unconscious man and leave him on the street. *He did try to kill us.* "Hold on." She latched on tightly and he slipped the bike into gear and moved off. Nora fell in behind him.

The old man stood on his porch, lifting one hand as they passed.

Chapter Twenty-Four

Persepolis

Ten nervy miles of empty roads brought them to Persepolis. The city's remains were a sprawling network of pillars, arches and intact structures sitting at the foot of a soft, slow rise that eventually led to mountains. Persepolis hadn't been forgotten, left to crumble in the middle of Iran. No, this city was managed and cared for, starting with the parking area, which led to an entrance gate where an attendant waited to collect the ticket fee.

Harry parked, and the absence of Sara's arms around his torso was more noticeable than expected. She stepped off the bike, took a second to find her land legs, then put both hands on her hips and looked at him squarely. *Uh-oh.*

"Why were those men chasing you?"

Harry did the only thing he could. He stalled. First by standing slowly and stretching his back. Then his legs. Fresh out of body parts to ease, he turned to face her and opened his mouth.

"Harry hasn't been totally open with you." Nora swooped in, jumping between him and Sara. She dug in her pocket and came out with a badge. Sunlight bounced off it like a weapon. "I'm an agent with the New York City district attorney's anti-trafficking team. On our first call, you said Harry's job is 'buying and selling antiquities'. That's true. Harry is an expert consultant I brought on to help stop an international smuggling ring involving Bergen Pharmaceuticals. I'm not at liberty to discuss the details. I spent a week undercover as a liaison with their security team in New York and Cairo. Harry has helped me extract information on the second Xerxes tablet, and he's vital to our effort."

Nora looked straight at Harry, turning so Sara couldn't see her face. "You can tell her now. We're into this and we have to trust Sara if she's going to be able to trust us."

Harry stood with his mouth open, fresh out of words.

"My goodness." Sara reached out and took hold of Harry's arm.

"I couldn't say anything," Harry managed.

Nora continued her explanation. "During my investigation into Persian artifacts we needed someone with Harry's expertise. There aren't many people who have both the historical knowledge and field experience Harry does. We're lucky to have him. Even more so now, since he knows you."

It was as though a new light shined on Harry, one only Sara could see. He felt bad not telling Sara the real truth. But he kept quiet.

"It makes sense now," Sara said. She squeezed his arm.

"Nora is the one who went undercover," Harry said.

"Part of the job," Nora said. She pointed to the expanse of Persepolis. "Let's go."

Harry pocketed his motorcycle keys and led the way, paying their entrance fee on the way in. He looked around. "No maps. How are we going to find our way around this place?"

Sara pushed past him. "Follow me. I studied the layout on my trip over."

Nora followed behind Sara. "Useful girl," she said softly.

"Thanks," Harry said. "I owe you."

"Damn right you do. Help me find whatever is in Xerxes' tomb and we're even."

Harry knew Nora wasn't joking, and for what she'd done, he would find it. Sara couldn't have been more thrilled to be helping them. Was it because she had become suspicious Harry was an antiquities trafficker, and Nora had dispelled the notion? If so, why would Sara react like she had? His thoughts on the matter could wait, though, for a couple of reasons. Not the least of which was that his redemption rested on a lie.

"See that cliff ahead?" Sara asked. Harry jogged to catch up, falling into step beside Nora as they approached a series of pillars standing side by side, supporting nothing. "It's hard to see from here," Sara continued. "But that's Xerxes' tomb carved into the face. We're headed there."

Nora pointed to the pillars beside them. "Did this used to be one of the palaces?"

"Yes, a smaller one. If you look ahead, you'll see what's known as the 'Palace of One Hundred Columns'. That was more along the lines of what we envision as a palace."

The first set of pillars fell behind as they followed gravel paths between demarcated sites within Persepolis. Stumps and remnants of formerly towering pillars stretched on either side of what would have been a soaring structure in its day, one fit for an emperor.

"We're lucky," Sara said, her voice dropping. "There aren't many visitors here right now."

Wooden planks formed a desert boardwalk, encircling some of the ruins while leading past others, as wide as a four-lane roadway. A handful of tourists dotted the thoroughfares, the furthest ones resembling tiny dolls in the far reaches of this former capital. The cliffside to which Sara led them overlooked the entire city, accessible via unpaved, dirt pathways leading from the flat main level up to Xerxes' tomb. A series of stepped walls fronted the tomb.

"What's it like inside the tomb?" Harry asked. "Any lights, or is it fairly primitive?"

"No lights as far as I know," Sara said. "We used portable lights connected to our generator."

"What are visitors supposed to do?" Nora asked. "We only have the one flashlight."

"When I visited, the tomb wasn't open to tourists. The only reason I could go in was my work."

Nora lifted her hand. "Hold on. You're telling me we might not even be allowed inside?"

Harry cut in. "When did following rules start concerning you?" Nora had no response. "First we find out if Sara's interpretation of the second tablet is correct. If she's right and this is the final stop, we find what's waiting and sort out the next steps later." He looked to Sara. "With the proper authorities, of course, including Nora's office."

Harry picked up the pace, ascending the sharply sloped hillside leading to the tomb's entrance. Past the stepped stone walls, which hid the entrance from view until Harry crested the rise to find a plateau, its flat area ending at the tomb's entrance. And it was an entrance fit not just for a king, but for a King of Kings. Ornamental columns fronted the vertical hillside, supporting a ledge cut to resemble a crenellated battlement. The relief above it depicted dozens of soldiers. Sara pointed to them.

"Those soldiers represent every ethnicity under the empire's control during Xerxes' reign. See how their arms are lifted up? They're carrying the emperor to his tomb."

Harry only had one ear for her words. He edged closer to Nora, inclining his head to the tour group standing in front of the tomb. "That's a problem."

No sooner had he spoken than the tour guide began walking toward Harry. Or rather, toward the path behind him.

"What problem?" Nora asked. "Stand aside. We won't hold them up."

Harry moved. The ledge fronting Xerxes' tomb offered a view he might call breathtaking. The sweeping vista of this once-mighty city dominated the foreground, before giving way to green foliage and square plots of farm land, all with a distant mountain range backing the view. Soft sunlight painted it all, the only sign of more visitors a single rattletrap blue pickup truck approaching the main entrance. Harry noted there were zero black Range Rovers in sight and that not a single person was moving toward the tomb. For now, they had it all to themselves.

"Time to go," he said after the tour group was halfway down the hillside. He made it two steps before skidding to a halt. "Is that a gate?"

His stomach dropped. It was a gate. Metal bars covered the open entrance to Xerxes' tomb, which, to his surprise, was so small he'd have to duck to get through. Clear plastic barriers prevented anyone from getting closer than ten feet from the tomb itself, the waist-high barricades stretching across the entire plateau. He leaned over to peer at the bars as though he could make them disappear through force of will.

Sara came up beside him. "The gate is new. Maybe it's not locked?"

"One way to find out." Harry didn't think there was a chance in the world it would open, but what choice did they have? He vaulted the plastic barrier and walked to the gate. Two horizontal metal bars had been welded to the vertical ones, all bolted into the rocks. An oversized padlock secured the gate to its frame. He pulled on it. No luck.

Nora heard the lock rattle and she cursed. They'd come all this way for nothing. Harry's head dropped, increasingly ridiculous ideas taking shape. Could Sara use her academic credentials to get inside? Nora's authority didn't extend to Iran, and should she somehow secure local cooperation, her boss had actively undermined their investigation for a donor who'd tried to have them killed today. They'd come so close, but were now well and truly done. Harry leaned against the warm metal, resting his head on a horizontal bar, and closed his eyes.

His shoulder pressed against a vertical bar. His foot slipped, sending him off balance. He twisted, his feet tangled, and before he knew what happened his chest was lodged in the gate. He managed to squeeze out as excitement arced through his body.

I can slip through this gate.

He'd never even considered it. The metal bars weren't close together, and only two horizontal bars ran across the gate at the top and bottom. That left the middle part wide open. He twisted again, pushing one shoulder through first. He pushed until he was halfway through, his chest catching before he dug into the dirt and a final burst saw him through. He fell, the lower metal bar serving as a perfect tripping hazard to send him sprawling. His shin barked on the bar, dirt filled his nose, and Harry had never felt better.

Nora had already followed him by hopping the barriers and stood at the gate when he turned around. "I can't believe they made a gate you can slip through," she said before doing just that. "Come on." She urged Sara to join them. "Before someone comes."

To her credit, Sara only hesitated a moment before leaping the barrier and squeezing through. Harry stuck out his hand. "May I have the flashlight?"

Sara dug in her pocket and came out with a small light. "We're in my world now, Harry. Let me lead." She handed the oversized flashlight from his bag to Nora. "I prefer Nora holds this. I've seen how she can use it."

Nora actually laughed. "Lead the way."

Sara shielded her light before flicking it on. "Follow me, and don't turn the other light on until we're well inside." With that, she headed into the gloom.

Nora turned to Harry. "I like her." She turned and followed Sara, leaving Harry to wonder whether it was luck or skill that he'd managed to find the perfect team to uncover the truth behind Xerxes' mysterious path.

Chapter Twenty-Five

The man's name was Farhad. He had survived the Islamic Revolution in 1979 by sensing which way the winds blew and setting his sail to follow them. A farmer for whom dirt-poor was a goal, he had been born in this small village and never left. As he watched his two prized motorcycles being driven away, Farhad sent thanks to Allah for his generosity.

The foreigner who spoke excellent Arabic had paid him twenty times their worth. To Farhad, those motorcycles had represented freedom and the ability to stretch his world beyond the horizon, if only for a day. The money that man had paid him for two motorcycles would fix his tractor, repair his roof, and protect against several poor harvests. Last year Farhad had earned the equivalent of one thousand U.S. dollars. This man with American money had paid him that ten times over.

Movement beside one of the crashed vehicles caught Farhad's eye. He blinked, the winds shifted, and the scent of gasoline hit his nose. The one who had bought his motorcycles had left another man lying near the wrecked vehicle. No one else in the village so much as stepped outside when Farhad ran over and pulled the man farther away. Only then did Farhad realize the man's hands were bound. Farhad tried not to consider why that was necessary as he went back into the wreckage to discover a body on the other side. The second man hadn't survived this crash. Judging by the amount of blood covering the windshield of the second vehicle, the one that had flipped up and over, it seemed there were no more survivors.

A noise came from inside the upended car. A human noise. Farhad jumped when one of the crushed doors creaked open and a man fell out. The man pulled himself to his feet and immediately pointed a pistol at Farhad. It wasn't the first time a gun had been aimed at Farhad. He barely blinked. "Are you hurt?" he asked the man in English.

The man lowered his pistol slightly. "My head."

Blood dripped off his chin as the man pulled a bandanna from one pocket and wrapped it around his head. When the bloodied man looked again at Farhad, he did so with the eyes of a hunter, not one being hunted. The violence of a car crash would throw most people completely off balance. Not this man. Farhad took a step back.

"One man is dead." He pointed to the other vehicle. "Another injured. I pulled him away from the vehicle."

The wounded man moved slowly to his bound colleague, kneeling to loosen the belt, and spoke to him in English. Farhad listened.

"Brian, are you hurt? Why are your hands tied?"

"I don't know." The man called Brian rubbed his wrists. "Help me up." Brian gained his feet, cursing as he tested both legs. "How bad is your head, Clay?"

Clay touched his head, wrapped with a bandanna. "Head wounds bleed. I'm fine. Can't say the same for Ian. His neck is broken."

"We'll come back for his body. Harry Fox and the women are gone." Brian turned and looked at Farhad, then walked over to him. "Did you pull me out of the car?" Brian asked, again in English. Farhad nodded. Brian indicated the wrecked sedan. The one Farhad suspected they had deliberately rammed. "There were three more people in that car. What happened to them?"

"They left."

Brian waited until he realized nothing else was forthcoming. "Where did they go?"

"I do not know."

"Which direction?"

"Why do you wish to know?"

Clay glowered and reached around behind his back. "Tell us, old man."

"Your gun does not frighten me," Farhad said. "Be careful what you do." He looked over each of his shoulders in turn, back and forth, to the houses where curtains had been drawn aside. "This is my village. *My* village. You are strangers, and far from home."

Brian lifted a hand to stay Clay. "We're disoriented from the crash." Brian opened his wallet. "Here. For your troubles." He pushed a stack of U.S. hundred-dollar bills into Farhad's unresisting hand. "Those three have stolen something that belongs to us. I have to find them."

Farhad pocketed the cash. "They offered a different story."

"They were lying," Brian said. "I'll pay you for any information." A wad of U.S. bills bound with a rubber band came out of another pocket. "Five thousand in cash. Tell me where they went and it's yours."

Allah is truly generous. "I accept your offer." Farhad stuck his hand out and took the money. Years of security, now in his grasp. "They went north." He pointed to the road out of town, down which his two motorcycles had vanished. "On two motorcycles that I sold them."

Brian frowned. "Do you have any other bikes?"

"No. I have a truck."

"How much did they pay you for the motorcycles?"

Farhad didn't hesitate. "Ten thousand."

Brian didn't blink at the figure. "Will you sell me your truck?"

"It is my only vehicle," Farhad said.

Brian held out his arm. "See this?" He tapped the watch on his wrist. "It's a Rolex Submariner. I paid fifteen thousand dollars for it. I'll trade you for the truck."

Farhad put his other hand out. Brian handed over the watch for his inspection. To Farhad's complete surprise, he recognized the timepiece. "This is a James Bond watch. Sean Connery. I like him the best."

"Me too," Brian said. "Do we have a deal?"

Farhad had no personal use for a watch. He did, however, have a cousin who worked in Tehran and knew men who wanted a watch like this. Men who could afford to pay fifteen thousand dollars for it. "We have a deal."

Brian didn't balk when Farhad showed him a rusty truck parked behind his house. He took the keys from Farhad, sat behind the wheel and turned the engine over. "Where do you think they are going now?" Brian asked as Clay got in the passenger side.

"Persepolis is in that direction. If it is not Persepolis, the road travels hundreds of miles to Tehran."

"They're not going that far on motorcycles," Clay said.

"Agreed," Brian said. He looked at Farhad. "Thanks." Brian pointed to the wreckage still clogging the village street. "I appreciate what you did for me."

Farhad dipped his snowy beard. The truck's engine rumbled, and the last Farhad saw of his beloved red vehicle was as it faded to a speck in the distance, the same way his motorcycles had vanished minutes earlier. Farhad sent another silent prayer to Allah, this time begging forgiveness. Wherever the man and the two women were going, they had better hurry.

Chapter Twenty-Six

Persepolis, Iran

A lone passageway led to Xerxes' tomb. Rooms had been carved out of the stone walls on either side, the ceilings not much taller than Harry. Along the passageway they passed vacant sarcophagi, open graves whose occupants had been removed, and empty rooms with artwork and carvings adorning the walls. All related to Xerxes, extolling his virtues and power, but none of it appeared to be tied to either tablet. The main hallway split into two walkways. One fork led to the right, the other to the left.

"Which one?" Nora directed the question to Sara.

"I don't know," Sara said. Her flashlight brought the walls to life: fearsome mythical creatures were interspersed with images of Xerxes, some realistic, others of an imagined form, blending man with beast or god. Xerxes with a lion's head. Xerxes with cypress trees, which Sara said symbolized eternal life. Harry took one step into a tunnel and stopped at an image of Xerxes with the Egyptian sun god Ra, depicted as a man's body with the head of a falcon.

"Guess he hedged his bets," Harry said. "In case the Egyptians had it right all along and Zoroastrianism didn't pan out."

"A king cares about his people if he's a good man. If he's not, he only cares about himself. But all kings care about their name and exploits living on through the ages. If it took Ra's protection to ensure his legacy, Xerxes wouldn't anger him by not honoring his name."

"Should we be looking for a Greek reference?" Nora asked. "The tablets describe a *Greek emerald elixir*."

"It's possible," Sara said. "We may need to find a demigod, or possibly Hippocrates or Megabyzus. They were both mentioned by name, although I suspect we've already found what Megabyzus was meant for."

"Hold on," Harry said. He put his hand out toward Nora. "Mind if I borrow the flashlight? I want to make sure there's nothing dangerous down these tunnels. I can't see very far."

"Good idea," Sara said.

Nora didn't agree. "If you're worried, stay behind me." She pushed past Harry without giving up her light.

"Watch the floor." Harry caught up and walked beside her. "There could be trip stones or levers, things you step on that might spring a trap. Traps are typically activated by your weight."

Nora stopped. "What do you mean, typically? How many booby-trapped tombs have you been in?"

Harry lowered his voice. Maybe Sara wouldn't hear. "My fair share. If you trip one it could kill all of us."

Nora didn't respond, but she did slow her pace. The walls lit up under her beam, while the ceiling appeared to press down even closer as they walked on. No alcoves had been carved to either side on this route; the only decorations were figures of gods and men interspersed with blocks of text.

"Sara," Harry called, "we have a good bit of writing over here, but I can't read most of it. I see lots of references to Xerxes." The ceiling arced up as he kept walking, though not until his foot scuffed on the ground and he nearly fell did he realize that the tunnel sloped upward.

He dropped to one knee, motioning Nora aside as he set a coin from his pocket on edge. "We're walking uphill." Sure enough, the quarter rolled down the gently sloping floor past his footprints. Harry ran back down and scooped it up. "Sara," he called at the junction.

"Are you walking uphill? This tunnel goes up."

"This other tunnel goes down," Sara called out from deeper inside her tunnel. "Get back here. You two need to see this."

"Nora, come back down here," he called back up the other tunnel. "Sara found something."

They found Sara a good distance down the other tunnel, one that definitely sloped down. She aimed her light at the wall. "What does that look like to you?"

The carving depicted a man in flowing robes. Under one arm he held a book, while the other cradled a tall staff. "He doesn't look Persian," Harry said as he touched Sara's hand. She drew in a quick breath as he moved her light closer to the wall, focusing on a specific area of the image. "I recognize his staff. That carving at the top with a snake winding around it."

"Good eyes," Sara said. "That's not any staff. It's a mythological symbol still used today. The Rod of Asclepius."

"It's the international symbol for medicine," Harry said.

"Asclepius is the Greek god most associated with healing, or medicine."

Harry snapped his fingers. "What if this is a message? I haven't seen a single other reference to Greece. This could be Xerxes pointing us not to the Greek *god* most associated with medicine, but the Greek *man*."

Sara grabbed his hand. "Hippocrates. This is the tunnel we should follow."

Nora didn't sound convinced. "Don't you want to check the other tunnel as well? Harry couldn't read most of the writing."

"Fair point. You two keep going in this tunnel. Look for any other Greek text or imagery. I'll only be a minute." Sara jogged down the tunnel, turning to inspect the one leading upward.

It didn't take Harry long. "Look at this. Greek letters."

"Any idea what it says?" Nora asked.

Harry had none, and told Sara this when she appeared around the corner a moment later.

"The upward-sloping tunnel ends with a room for a sarcophagus," she said. "Xerxes may have been buried there before they removed his body. I didn't—" Sara caught sight of the Greek words. Her eyes beamed in the false light. "This is fantastic." She walked past Harry, getting closer to the wall. "Greek writing in the tomb of a Persian emperor. The Persians and Greeks were at war for fifty years in Xerxes' time, a war the Greeks won decisively. When Xerxes died the defeat would still have stung. So why is there Greek writing here?"

"Maybe it's a marker," Harry said. "I can read one word. *Five.*"

"Correct," Sara said.

"You read Greek?" Nora asked.

"Not as well as Arabic or German, but yes."

Nora leaned closer. "Hold on. You're fluent in all those languages? I thought you were an Egyptologist."

"I am," Sara said. "I can also read Egyptian hieroglyphs."

"You're a good person to have along," Nora said.

"I hope so." Sara pointed to the Greek script. "You're correct, Harry. That's the Greek word for *five*, spelled out instead of written as a numeral, and you'll recognize what it's referencing." She pointed to each word as she translated, her voice loud in the narrow corridor.

"*Xerxes, King of Kings, honors you with his presence among the five beacons, worthy Persian.*"

"He's referencing the tablet," Harry said. "Except you'd never know it unless you had the tablet. Anyone else reading this wouldn't guess it's a message."

"It gets better," Sara said.

"*Your native bravery led to the city of the Persians. Use the King of Kings acinaces as Set once did. Raise Osiris to the heavens and stand back from his glory to visit his kingdom. Beware the false wealth as you seek the elixir of my words. The emerald awaits.*"

"*Native bravery,*" Harry said when she fell silent. "A reference to the second tablet. We're in the right place." He frowned. "The rest of it's odd. Osiris is an Egyptian god. So is Set. Why mention them?"

Sara put a hand on her chin. "Good questions. Osiris is the Egyptian god of the afterlife, the dead, and resurrection. Set was his brother. He murdered Osiris and stole his throne, but Isis, Osiris's wife, reassembled his dismembered corpse and brought him back to life so they could have a child, Horus. The child avenged his father's murder. It's a major story in Egyptian mythology."

"Why would Xerxes care about an Egyptian myth already several thousand years old when he built this tomb?"

Nora aimed her light past Harry. "I think I know. Look."

Harry turned to find a solid wall ahead of them. The end of the passage. And on that wall? An engraved figure. He didn't believe in ghosts, yet Harry found himself reaching for the amulet tucked beneath his shirt, his good-luck omen. "Is that Osiris?" he asked. "What in the world?"

"It's him," Sara said. "Only he's inverted. Look – he's wearing the atef crown and holding a crook and flail. You can see his legs are partially mummified. The embalmer's wrappings end at his waist." She touched the carving as she spoke. "This is a classic depiction of Osiris, except he's upside down. That doesn't make any sense."

"Why not?" Harry asked.

"I've seen Osiris depicted many times in my career. Not once have I seen him inverted."

"You're talking about a guy who was supposedly chopped to pieces then brought back to life," Nora said. "Logic isn't a big part of the story."

"An excellent point. But what's the purpose? A Persian king who followed Zoroastrianism has an Egyptian god in his tomb? Why?"

Harry frowned. What if Nora was right? The reason Xerxes had put an Egyptian god in his tomb didn't have to be logical. Except to Xerxes.

"Tell me again what happened to Osiris?" Harry asked. "And his brother, Set."

"Set coveted Osiris's throne. The story begins with Osiris ruling Egypt along with his queen, Isis. The legend tells us Set killed Osiris so he could become king. He cut Osiris' body into pieces, which Isis later reassembled into the first mummy before getting help from the gods to reanimate him. They had a child, Horus, who eventually avenged his father." Shadows danced as Sara's light flitted around the god's image. "There are variations on the story, though none involve Osiris depicted with his head on the ground."

A shape flashed in the dark. "Move your light back up," Harry said. "There, above his feet. What is that?"

"That, Harry, is an *acinaces*. A Persian sword from Xerxes' time."

"What are those grooves under it?" Nora asked. She walked over and touched the wall. "They run between Osiris and the sword."

Harry closed his eyes. Xerxes wouldn't have brought them so far for nothing. *Think like a man in Xerxes' time.* What did all of this mean to Xerxes? He had envisioned an educated man following this trail, an elite like him. A Persian who knew the myth of Osiris and could discern the messages given on both tablets and now on this wall.

Harry's eyes snapped open. *Orders.*

"Those are orders. *Directions.*" He slipped past Sara. "It's Xerxes talking directly to us. He's telling us what to do, the same as he did with the tablet. We just have to know how to read it."

"What is he telling us to do?" Sara asked. "There's no tangible event, no next step, and we still have no idea what the *emerald* reference means."

"We do what Xerxes told us to do. Stand back." The two women did so, aiming their lights while Harry stood in front of the wall. "The grooves aren't decorative." Two parallel lines cut into the stone ran from below the Persian sword to Osiris's feet, perpendicular to the floor. "They're purposeful. Part of Xerxes' message. He's telling us to do what Set did. Which was?"

"Kill his brother," Sara said. "How do you kill a stone carving?"

"I have an idea." The sword's blade pointed down to Osiris's feet.

Harry ran his fingers over the grooves, stopping as he reached the god's feet. He scratched his fingernail over the stone surface. It caught in an almost invisible line, one running in a circle around the inverted carving of Osiris, now nearly completely filled with dust. If Harry's guess was correct, that was. He took a breath.

Harry reached up, standing on his toes until he grasped the sword's handle with both hands. A stubby cross-guard offered better grip. Harry leaned back and tugged on the carved sword, pulling with everything he had.

Sara ran over. "You'll break it."

"Watch out," he said between clenched teeth.

She didn't listen, instead grabbing his arm. "Harry, you'll damage it. That carving is price—"

"I get it." Nora ran over to stand beside Harry. "He's giving us *instructions*. Xerxes told us to do this." She shoved her light into Sara's hand. "Get a better grip," Nora told him. "I'll grab your waist and pull."

Harry didn't have a chance to argue before Nora latched onto his waist. "Ready?" she asked. Her legs splayed out around his, one of her feet on the wall for purchase.

"Ready – pull."

Harry's shoulders screamed as he again pulled down on the carved sword and Nora pulled on his waist. Rock cut into his palms like daggers, his shirt ripped somewhere, and Nora's cursing filled the chamber. She pulled hard, trying to rip him in half as Harry kicked the wall, tasting dirt and dust and the tomb's stale air.

Rock grated like tectonic plates shifting in the tunnel. The sword slid downward an inch.

"Keep pulling." Harry could barely get the words out. Sara dropped her light, the beam bouncing like mad as the wall went dark, and Harry held on as Sara grabbed him by the shoulders and heaved down. Harry bit his tongue, and the sword moved. It dropped, slamming down to kill the god Osiris, Harry now playing the role of the murderous brother as he plunged the stone sword into Osiris's feet. Harry didn't let go. He leaned to one side, both women still hanging on. "Keep pulling," he yelled again. "I think we have to twist it."

They kept dragging Harry down to the ground as he kept hold of the sword, which had become a handle that turned the carving of Osiris counterclockwise. It righted the god's image, his head now skyward. They had taken Osiris and *raised him to the heavens.*

Osiris now stood straight up. The tunnel walls rattled. Harry reached for the flashlight, but his grasp fell short as the floor underneath disappeared and darkness consumed them all.

Chapter Twenty-Seven

A black hole swallowed Harry Fox, the ground opening beneath him. Light swirled and down he went, rolling ass-over-elbows down a stepped hillside until he smacked into level ground and finally stopped. He blinked, finding nothing but darkness.

Where am I? He was alive. No way dying hurt this bad. Daggers of pain knifed into his back and legs, first as he tried to sit up, then again when his hand slipped on a loose rock and he slammed back down. The rock skittered away to parts unknown, but en route it must have bounced off one of the flashlights either Sara or Nora had dropped, for a blinding beam of light appeared to bring Harry back from whatever underworld he'd discovered into the land of the living.

Sara. Nora. He called their names. Nothing. No response. No shouts for help. Harry scrambled to one elbow, reached for the flashlight as it rolled beside him, missed and knocked it away. He tried again and pain arced up his arm.

"Stop knocking the light around."

"Nora. Are you hurt?"

"Of course I am. I won't know how bad until I get my flashlight."

"Where's Sara?"

"I'm here." Now a second light appeared as Sara retrieved her own. "You turned Osiris around and the floor collapsed."

"It wasn't a floor." Nora had managed to get to her feet, flashlight in hand. "These are *steps*."

Nora's beam gave shape to the formless chasm into which they had fallen. The ground had collapsed, turning from level into a series of steps. Harry sat nearly at the bottom, having tumbled from halfway down. He looked up to find the newly turned carving of Osiris a good ten feet above his head.

Sara aimed her light up and pointed. "Turning the carving must have acted as a lever. It released a counterweight or some kind of support that had kept the floor level."

Nora pointed to either side. "These were support columns. Nothing but fallen rock now."

Perfectly square rocks lay scattered to either side, clearly cut with precision by men's hands. Harry didn't study the rocks for long. If there was room for those rocks to tumble sideways, that meant whatever chamber they'd fallen into was wider than the tunnel. A *lot* wider.

"Those stones were carved," Sara said. "They were balanced to keep the floor level. When we turned the carving, it moved the stones and allowed them to drop onto this staircase."

"How would you ever build a thing like this?" Nora asked. "The people who set the support pillars wouldn't have a way to get out."

"Unless there's another exit," Harry said. "Shine your light around us."

Both women did, and the scope of what they'd uncovered become apparent. Sara and Nora took tentative steps forward to reveal smooth stone walls set far back from the staircase. Their pockmarked surfaces told Harry no man had carved out this room. "This is a natural cavern," Harry said. "A cave inside the mountain."

"How did Xerxes know to send us here?" Nora asked.

"Kings often chose their tombs long before dying," Sara said. "Persepolis was already home to other royal tombs, so Xerxes likely chose this spot and ordered construction of his tomb during his lifetime. It would explain why the exterior is grand, but what we've seen until now is a series of tunnels. The workers uncovered this cave and it fit his plans perfectly."

"So, Xerxes uses this natural cave to hide something," Harry said. "The Greek emerald elixir." He stepped down to the cavern floor. "Shine your lights ahead."

Dust coated his throat. He coughed, waving his hand to clear away the dust clouds as he walked. White light from behind shimmered off particulate floating in the air. Sara moved to his side, through the hanging dust cloud, which parted just enough to reveal a scene that stopped them both in their tracks. Stubby stalactites hung from the cave's ceiling, which rounded where it met the walls far overhead. Rope-like tendrils ran along the ceiling, as though great vines had crept across it in thick, fibrous strands to hang from an oblong shape he couldn't quite make out in the dark. A massive stalactite, perhaps. Or it could be a shadow. A natural gulley ran down the middle of the cave; the floor sloped slightly upward in either direction to the walls. What could have been carvings on each wall were hidden in the murky depths, too far away to be seen clearly.

"Xerxes went to all the trouble of concealing this place," Harry said. "He wouldn't have left it empty. There has to be—"

Sara pointed ahead. "What are those?"

Two rows of rising columns stood in front of them. The first columns, set twenty feet apart, were at knee height. Behind them, about the length of a stride away, were another pair of columns, these ones waist-high. Beyond that, a higher set. On it continued, the columns rising until they reached the cavern's rear, where each column nearly touched the ceiling far overhead.

"Those are amazing," Sara said. "Xerxes carved interlocking stones and stacked them into columns." Her light flickered in the cavern's darkness. "Why?"

"What's on top of that last column to the right?" Nora asked, aiming her flashlight. "It's gold," she said. "There's some type of golden object on the last column."

Now that his eyes had adjusted, Harry could make out a pedestal atop the final column on the right, the one that nearly backed up against the far cave wall. An image flashed across his mind's eye. "I found a similar pedestal in Megabyzus's tomb in Egypt. It had the second tablet on it."

"And nothing else was there but the tablet." Sara chewed at her lip. "So what's up there?"

"One way to find out." Nora pushed past them. "I'm climbing it."

Harry and Sara leapt as one. "No chance," Harry said as he grabbed for her.

Nora twisted away.

"Do not step on the column," Sara said. "Not until we inspect it."

Nora huffed, pulling away from them both. "Xerxes built these for a reason. He's telling us to climb them."

"Don't rush this," Harry said.

"What just happened with Osiris?" Nora asked. "Is that your definition of taking it slow?"

"We could have been killed when that floor collapsed," Harry said. "Don't make the same mistake I did." Nora glared at him, and he glared right back. "If it is safe, you can run up there first, I promise."

"I want out of this cave." Nora looked around, at the ceiling far above, at the dry walls all around.

"It's been here for thousands of years," Harry said. "It's not falling down any time soon."

Sara aimed her light at the closest step. "There's a carving."

"It's almost like a cameo," Harry said.

A face was etched into the center of the step. The person wore a decorative hair covering, possibly a helmet, and had large eyes, with styled hair falling from under the head covering. Harry stepped closer. "I think it's a woman."

"Not just any woman," Sara said. "A goddess. Athena, the patron goddess of Athens. I've seen this image on Greek coins."

"Why carve it on this step?"

"Not only on here. Look at the next one." Sara aimed her light at the next column, the one a step higher and further into the cave. "It's on there as well. And the next one after that." She moved to the third column in this row, which rose to her sternum.

Images of the Greek goddess, rising to the very top of the cave, where an unidentified golden object waited. If Xerxes had carved these images on the steps, it meant something. Standing in darkness, barely able to see his hands in front of his face, Harry had an idea. He turned around, looking at the other row of columns. If Greek coins adorned these pillars on the right, the others could have a message as well. "Come over here," he told Sara. "We should check—"

"Don't move."

A new voice cut through the cave. Blinding light erupted by the stairs. Harry raised an arm, turning away from the intense beam. Sara did the same. Harry was in the open and couldn't see a thing. He moved toward the far pillars to take cover.

A bullet thundered off the cave floor. Sparks erupted by his feet. Harry stopped moving.

Nora shouted from near the steps. She had her light on the intruder. "Dammit, Brian, it's me. Put that gun away."

Brian? Harry slowly turned. Nora's flashlight lit up the intruder, a man Harry recognized. Brian Joyce. The Bergen security man, formerly of Nora Doyle's investigation team.

"Are you hurt?" Brian spoke to Nora, though his eyes stayed on Harry. The gun stayed up. "Did these two force you to come with them?"

"Force me?" Nora threw a hand up. "No, they didn't force me. Put the gun down, you fool."

"I'm worried for your safety." Brian kept speaking as though Nora hadn't responded. "We lost you in Cairo. I had no idea Harry Fox took you." Brian turned and barked a command. "Clay, make sure Agent Doyle is safe."

Another man stepped from the gloom behind Brian Joyce. Clay slipped past Brian and walked to Nora. Harry's stomach tightened.

Two armed men stood between them and the exit. Men who had no qualms about trying to kill them. Men who had already lost one colleague hours earlier. *You're not fighting your way out of this one, Harry. Think.*

"We didn't kidnap her," Harry said.

Clay stopped beside Nora and received a two-handed shove for his efforts. To his credit, he barely stumbled.

"I told you I'm fine," Nora said. "*You* two left me in Cairo. And what about the car accident? You don't think I know it was you?" Nora had a full head of steam now, her chest bumping into Clay's. "You nearly killed us. Why don't you tell me the real reason you're here in Iran? You're the ones I'm worried about." Harry flinched as she slapped Clay's hand.

Brian Joyce wasn't having any of it. "You're confused, Agent Doyle. We lost contact with you in Cairo. I left instructions at the hotel for them to inform you of our extenuating circumstances. You must have been waylaid by Harry Fox." The gun stayed aimed at Harry. "And I have no idea what accident you're talking about."

Clay grabbed Nora's arm and held tight. "Are you armed, Agent Doyle?" Clay asked. He reached for her pockets. "I have to check for our safety."

Nora told him in no uncertain terms what he could do with his probing hand an instant before she headbutted him. The *thunk* of shattered nose cartilage crackled in Harry's ear. Clay screamed, Nora twisted to get free, and then Clay ripped her arm back to send Nora airborne. She crashed to the ground head first and didn't move.

In the time it took Harry to process what had happened, Brian Joyce's gun was touching his forehead. Harry was average height at best, yet he stood several inches above Brian Joyce. Who was a thick man. The guy was wide, all of it muscle.

"What did you do to her?" Harry shouted.

Brian ignored him. "Agent Doyle is confused," he told Clay. "Secure her for her own safety." Clay produced a pair of handcuffs and locked Nora's wrists in front of her as blood leaked from his nose. "Is Agent Doyle alert?" Brian asked.

"No, sir. Unconscious." Clay laid her on the ground, one hand keeping pressure on his nose as he touched her neck. "Pulse is steady. Breathing normal. She'll wake up soon."

"Good." Brian's voice changed. He looked at Harry. The gun stayed between Harry's eyes. "I'm glad we finally caught up with you."

"Look, we're not after trouble. I'm unarmed. Could you put that gun down before it goes off?"

"You should have planned better." Brian took a step back, out of Harry's reach. "Clay, get the other woman over here."

"Don't bother with your tough-guy act," Sara said. "I'll come on my own." She marched to Harry's side. "We don't have any weapons."

"Check them," Brian said.

He took another step back as Clay gave them each a quick pat-down, pulling out Harry's amulet in the process. Harry's body tensed, but Clay merely shrugged and let it fall back under Harry's shirt.

"They're clean," he said, taking Brian's flashlight to aim it at Harry and Sara. He tilted his head up, cursing all the while.

Brian lowered his gun and ran a hand through his hair, taking time to study the vast cavern. His eyes ran up one set of graduated pillars, then back down the other. He studied the walls. Then he looked at Harry. "What did you find in Cairo in the antechamber?" he asked.

Harry ran a finger over his pocket. Clay hadn't found his knuckledusters. "Nothing. The chamber was empty."

"The pedestal inside had an outline in the dust." Brian lifted the gun. Now it pointed at Sara. "Lie again and I shoot her."

The words spilled out. "A second tablet."

"Do you have it?"

Sara lifted the messenger bag around her neck. "It's in here."

Brian made no move to take it. "What is on it?"

"Ancient Persian. A message from King Xerxes."

"I'm listening."

Why didn't he want to see the tablet? Only one answer made sense: Brian couldn't read Ancient Persian. For the first time since these two had barged in here, Harry had a small advantage. "I don't read Persian very well," Harry said.

"Then how did you know what it says?"

"I can read it," Sara said. "Get out of my way." Sara went to Nora's side, glaring at Clay, daring him to intercede. Clay didn't move, his light on Sara all the while. Sara leaned down as Nora's eyelids fluttered. "Nora, can you hear me?" She brushed a lock of Nora's hair aside, checking for damage, seeming to find none. "No cuts I can see." Sara shot up and got right in Clay's face. "You're lucky she's not seriously injured."

"Dr. Hamed, back away."

Hearing her name must have surprised her, because Sara did just that. "How do you know me?"

"I prepare for missions," Brian said. "I know you are a professor in Trier, and I needed to confirm you could read Persian as well as Egyptian before we go any further."

So Brian knew she was an Egyptologist. What else did he know? Harry bent down as Nora moaned, lifting her shackled hands to her face. It took her a second to remember what had happened.

"Take it easy," Harry said. "Don't sit up too quickly."

Nora immediately sat up. The handcuffs rattled. "Who put these on me?" Now she looked up and spotted Clay standing nearby. "Take these things off me right now." She pushed Harry's helping hand aside and stood, making right for Clay. "I'll have you locked up for years."

"You've been injured," Clay said, deftly sidestepping Nora's attempted blows. "We believe you are a danger to yourself, Agent Doyle."

"Danger to myself?" Nora's voice echoed off the walls. "I'll show you what danger is—"

"Settle down, Agent Doyle." Brian moved with unnatural quickness and grabbed hold of her handcuffs. "If you don't, I'll have to shoot your captors."

That got her attention. "You're not a murderer."

"No, I'm not. What I am is concerned for your well-being. I'm worried these two are plotting to release you from these handcuffs against our judgment. The same two people who kidnapped you."

"You are out of your mind," Nora said. "If you don't—"

Harry cut her off. "Listen to him, Nora. He's not lying. Who is the D.A. going to believe? Us, or the lead security man for his biggest donor?" Harry saw a flash of anger run across Brian's face. "It's not as though the D.A. has jurisdiction here anyway."

"He's right," Brian said. His voice had dropped; the false concern vanished. "Harry Fox is a crook, a tomb raider. Not worth dying for. We're running out of time. We came to rescue you from Harry Fox and Dr. Hamed. It's only a matter of time before the Iranians appear."

"They may never come," Sara said. "Odds are no one saw us come in here, and if they did, they won't call the police. Iranian citizens don't all love their heavy-handed government."

Brian Joyce did the oddest thing. He smiled. "I hope you're right."

The knot in Harry's stomach tightened. "Why have you been following us?" he asked. Better to keep Brian talking. The longer he did that, the more chance they'd find a way out of here. "Why does a pharmaceutical company care about these ancient tablets?"

"You've read them," Brian said. "You figure it out." He pointed the gun at Sara's chest. "Tell me what the second tablet says."

Sara crossed her arms. "No."

Brian fired.

The gunshot rattled stone from the walls. Sara fell, arms over her head. Harry lunged for her, skidding on the dirt floor as he crashed into her. He couldn't see a wound, couldn't tell what had happened.

"Give me light," he shouted over the ringing in his ears. "Over here." His hands ran across her chest, stomach, legs, yet he found no bullet holes.

Brian's voice came through at the edge of hearing. "Next time I won't miss. Get up."

The adrenaline coursing through Harry's body ebbed. His shoulders sagged as Sara looked at him from between her fingers. "It's okay," he whispered in her ear. He pulled her close, holding tight as he stood and lifted her with him. "Tell him what it says."

Sara held his gaze. She nodded. Her chest went out, air blew softly from her nose, and Sara calmly turned to Brian. "King Xerxes congratulates the person holding it for their bravery in uncovering both tablets. Xerxes says whoever found it is worthy to continue on the journey to find the Greek emerald elixir."

"The Greek emerald elixir?"

"Yes, though I don't know what that means."

"Tell me what you think it means."

Sara shrugged. "My guess is it refers to a legend, though I can't say for certain which one. It's possible both of the tablets tie to some forgotten tale."

"Is that all it says?" Brian asked.

"Xerxes says that the Persian, because clearly he believed a Persian would uncover his trail, must continue on to prove they are deserving. They have to find the five beacons in the city of the Persians, and follow the *king's wealth* to reap their reward. Which Xerxes makes clear is the elixir. And the wrong path leads to doom."

"What does all of it mean?"

"You already know part of it," Sara said. She lifted her arms, pointing all around. "Persepolis is the *city of the Persians*. As to the *king's wealth*, I'm not sure."

Brian pulled out a penlight and aimed it at the two rising sets of columns. "What are those?"

Sara lifted her shoulders. "Look like steps to me."

Brian's light went all the way up. Gold flashed on one of the tallest pillars, some fifty feet above the floor. "And that?"

"I won't know until I get up there."

Harry edged closer to the nearest column. Brian's flashlight lit up the image of Athena carved onto the top of it, though neither Brian nor Clay seemed to have noticed it. A ghostly image on the other short column flashed briefly as Brian's light moved over it. Harry knew that image, though he struggled to place it. An image of a bearded man.

"What's that?" Clay aimed his light at the nearby column. "There's something on top."

Brian stepped closer. "It's a person." He turned to Harry, paused for a beat, then looked to Sara. "Who is it?"

"Athena, protectress of Athens."

"Why would a Persian king choose a Greek goddess for his tomb?"

"Look over here." Clay flicked his light at the other set of columns. "There's another carving."

Harry took several steps over to get a look. Under Clay's light he saw the outline of a bearded man. A crown sat atop the man's head. In one hand he carried a long spear. In the other, a curved bow. Harry started. *It all makes sense.*

"What is it?" Brian aimed his penlight at Harry's face. "Tell me."

Harry blinked. "It's a man. A Persian man."

"How can you tell?"

"The bow," Harry said. He showed Brian his palms and walked slowly to the column. "Shine the light over here. This is a spear." He pointed as he spoke, then looked at Brian's eyes. They followed every move of Harry's hand. "It's a Persian spear. Same with the beard and the crown." Harry outlined each in turn, his gaze flitting over to Sara, catching her eye. He lifted an eyebrow.

"The bow is curved," Harry continued. "A distinctive Persian style. I'm sure of it."

"He's right," Sara said.

"What does that have to do with the tablets?" Brian asked.

Sara hesitated. Harry jumped in. "Both contain one phrase that tells us what to do." He let Brian stew on it for a moment. "*King's wealth*. That's the key. *Follow the king's wealth to reap his reward.* The tablets are guides for the path Xerxes laid. Guides, or maps."

"Follow the wealth?" Brian asked. "To the gold up there?" He pointed up the long set of columns, to the ones with Athena's image.

"No."

"The elixir is the prize, then," Brian said. "Where is it?"

"What do you mean?" Harry asked.

"Hippocrates is the father of medicine. He lived at the same time as Xerxes, and Xerxes must have learned about Hippocrates' greatest secret – a healing elixir."

Harry listened as Brian told them of the brilliant but sickly man whose ailments were miraculously cured, a man who went on to become Hippocrates' greatest student. A man whose story they had heard before. Harry and Sara kept silent until Brian stopped talking.

"I've heard stories like that before," Sara said. "You think the elixir Xerxes talks about was real."

"My brother is certain, and he's never wrong."

"Guy, the C.E.O. of Bergen?" Harry forced a laugh he didn't feel. "You expect us to believe he sent you across the world to chase an old legend? You may as well go searching for the Holy Grail."

Brian's voice was deadly calm. "This may *be* the Holy Grail. Or at least the closest we will ever get to it." He pointed up the columnar staircase. "It could be right there, written in gold."

"Athena." Harry paused. "The patron goddess of Athens," Harry said. "The daughter of Zeus, *king* of the gods. Athena was Zeus's greatest treasure, his true *wealth*."

"Is that what Xerxes meant by *follow the king's wealth?*" Brian nodded to himself. "Could be."

"There's more," Harry said. "Let these two go and I'll tell you the rest."

"You and Dr. Hamed are going to an Iranian jail," Brian said. "Agent Doyle is coming back home with us for specialized care." He continued over Nora's protestations. "She may not realize it yet, but she needs help." Brian leveled the gun at Harry's knee. "Talk, or your knee won't work anymore."

As if Brian were really going to let any of them out of here.

"That's the image of Athena on the *drachma*, the Greek coin that's been used for thousands of years." Harry's hand slipped into his knuckledusters as he spoke. He'd need every bit of power the ceramic weapon packed if he wanted to take Brian down. He needed to get Brian's weapon without getting shot.

"The Athena image is the path," Brian said. He aimed his penlight at the uppermost column, where a golden rectangle lay. "That must be a third tablet. The golden tablet. The king's final message."

Brian cupped his chin in thought with the hand holding the penlight, which briefly illuminated the ceiling. Harry looked up into the shadows. A long shadow stretched across the ceiling, with some kind of vines hanging from it. Odd. Was it a stalactite?

"Stand back," Brian barked. Harry looked down to find Brian's gun aimed directly at him again. "Out of the way," Brian said.

Harry backed up to the first set of columns, the one with a Persian *daric* carved into them. Brian motioned for Sara to do the same, giving him room to walk past them to Clay, where he lowered his head close to Clay's ear and spoke in hushed tones.

Sara's lips scarcely moved as she whispered to Harry. "I've never heard Athena referred to as a *king's treasure*."

"Me neither," Harry whispered back. "Do you recognize the Persian image?"

"It's a *daric*."

"I've seen it before." He flashed back to the office of Dr. Khalidi at Columbia. The book Khalidi referenced during their conversation had a stunning golden *daric* gracing the cover.

Any further conversation was cut off when Clay pulled a knife from his pocket. Harry stepped in front of Sara when Clay moved closer to them. Harry stood his ground, looking up at the taller man until the knife's business end was only inches from his nose.

"Are you sure about this?" Clay asked. "Athena is the clue?"

"Yes," Harry said. He didn't move in order to avoid impaling himself. "It's the answer that makes sense."

"It better be," Clay growled. He turned and strode away, stopping to exchange his larger flashlight for Brian's penlight before heading to the first pillar that had Athena carved on it.

A hand closed around Harry's wrist. Sara's, her skin cool on his. "Can Nora handle herself?" she whispered in his ear.

"I hope so," Harry said. "I'm getting closer to Brian. Stay behind me, and if this goes bad, run."

Harry hadn't taken a step before Sara pushed past him. Brian jerked at the sudden movement, but Sara ignored him, walking past the barrel of his gun as though it didn't exist to kneel beside Nora. "How's your head?" she asked.

Brian put himself between Harry and the two women. Harry closed the gap, step by tiny step. Brian didn't notice, because everyone's eyes were on Clay as he climbed onto the first column.

"It's solid," Clay said. He jumped up and down to show it.

"Can you step to the next one?" Brian asked.

Clay's penlight cut through the gloom. "Yes. It's only a couple feet higher." A long stride put him atop the second column. "It's solid too."

He moved on to the third and fourth columns, rising in elevation until he was ten columns in and over twenty feet off the ground. Brian's heavy light stayed trained on Clay. As the beam aimed ahead, the darkness edged closer to Harry, who moved in the shadows until he stood only ten feet from Brian. Harry edged sideways. A few more steps and he'd be out of Brian's peripheral vision and close enough to attack.

"Take one more step and I shoot you." Brian whipped his pistol around to aim at Harry. "Get back near the other columns. Now."

Brian's gun remained steady as Harry moved back close to the *daric*-emblazoned columns. Clay continued his ascent, now more than halfway to the end. His flashlight bounced as he hopped from one column to the next, taking each step carefully, now forty feet in the air with nothing but solid rock waiting at the end of a fall. Brian kept one eye and the gun on Harry, the other eye and his light on Clay. He seemed to have forgotten about Sara, who remained on one knee beside Nora.

"One more to go." Clay's voice called from across the cave, fifty yards distant. "The columns didn't get any bigger this far in. It's tight standing on the last one."

"What's up there?" Brian shouted.

"There's a pedestal on the last tomb. About two feet wide, half as deep, and as high as my waist. A tablet is inset in the rock. Its face is gold." Clay's light bounced. "Check that. The tablet has to be *solid gold.*"

"What's on the tablet?" Brian asked.

"A design," Clay shouted back. "I don't recognize it."

It looked as though Clay put the penlight in his mouth and began moving around. It was hard to see him standing so far above floor level with the shorter pillars blocking most of the view. Harry looked over to see Brian engrossed with Clay's search. Nora still sat on her tailbone, Sara beside her. *Come on, look at me.* He willed Sara to catch his eye. Now was their best chance.

"It's a figure," Clay said. "Human body. With some kind of animal head. A wolf, I think." The light rattled. "The tablet is stuck. I can't lift it out."

"Is there any writing on it?" Brian asked. He looked over a beat before Harry could move closer. The gun stayed on Harry's chest.

"I don't see any," Clay said. "I think I can pull it out. Maybe there's writing on the back side."

"A man with a wolf's head?" Brian asked. "But no writing at all?"

"None. The head might not be a wolf – it could be a dog. There's a stick in one of the man's hands."

Sara gasped. "That's not a dog." Everyone looked at her. Harry frantically shook his head. *Don't say it.*

"How do you know?" Brian asked.

Sara opened her mouth. She caught Harry's look. She turned to Brian, mouth still open. "It's not a deity I recognize," she finally said. "I should know them all, certainly one with a wolf or canine head."

Brian bought it. "Describe the figure again," he called out. "The head."

Clay wasn't listening. "I think I can pull it out. The tablet is moving."

If Brian noticed Sara pulling Nora away, he didn't say anything. He definitely didn't see Harry inching back toward the entrance. Had he done so, he would have seen the identical looks on Harry and Sara's faces. Two people who knew Sara had lied, that an Egyptian god with the body of a man and the head of a wolf *did* exist.

Anubis. The Egyptian god of death.

Clay kept shouting. "It's coming out. If I twist it—"

Thunder split the air. Tons of rock moved from somewhere out of sight, rattling the walls as debris fell, sending pebbles skittering across the ground. Clay shouted, his words lost as deafening noise filled the cave. Brian spun around, his light twisting in a full circle that ended up back on Clay and the golden tablet clutched in Clay's hands as he stood atop the farthest column. The cacophony subsided for a beat, just long enough to let Clay's words come across.

"There's nothing on the back," Clay shouted. "It's blank. I can't—"

A tectonic plate shifted overhead. One sharp *crack*, loud enough to reach the heavens. Harry looked up. Brian must have too, because his light aimed skyward to show the entire ceiling shifting. Harry squinted. *That's the shadow.* The long, dark spot he'd noted earlier with vines hanging from it. Only those weren't vines; they were ropes, and the shape he'd mistaken for a shadow now detached from the ceiling and swung down. The shadow was a massive rock, the vines were ropes securing it to the ceiling, and the entire contraption became a battering ram that fell, swinging on screaming ropes as it hurtled at the back wall, a giant missile curving directly above the columns Clay had just ascended.

The first column shattered at the halfway point. The swinging missile clipped the top of one column in an explosion of dust and debris before smashing into the next column and the one after it, each blowing up as though a bomb had gone off. The missile gained speed. As the columns disintegrated, shards of rock flew, and Clay's mouth opened in a silent scream. The beam from his flashlight filtered through the dusty haze for a long moment before the swinging missile landed and Clay vanished.

The deafening roar shook the cave. Harry dropped to one knee as the missile thundered into the high back wall, flying through it and continuing outside, leaving a massive hole in its wake. Sunlight, painful in its intensity, poured through the opening, lighting up the cave for the first time. The curved walls with their natural fissures turned a greenish hue. Mineral specks flashed in the light; tiny, geologic gemstones were embedded in the rock. With a start, Harry realized what those strange carvings on the wall to one side really were. Not Persian artwork or religious symbols. They were doors, and one of them had opened.

A huge boulder waited behind the door. Harry took a step back as it started rolling down the sloped floor. The vehicle-sized boulder gained speed as it rumbled toward them.

"Move!" Harry's feet skidded for purchase. "Get back." He looked up and hit the brakes. Brian Joyce had his pistol aimed at Harry's chest.

"You did this!" Brian shouted, wild-eyed, struggling to keep the gun level. "You knew that path wasn't—"

The words stopped abruptly and Brian's eyes rolled up in the back of his head as he collapsed. Nora stood behind him, cuffed hands clutched together into one heavy fist she'd just smashed Brian senseless with.

"Where's the key?" Nora knelt down, rummaging through Brian's pockets. "He must have one. I can't—"

"Get out of the way!" Harry launched himself, tackling both women to the ground. The boulder rumbled past, crunching something in a collision Harry felt in his bones. He looked up to find the first pillar with a *daric* on it had been steamrolled.

Sara pushed him aside and sat up. Dust coated her face. "Where did that massive rock come from?"

"The wall." Harry pointed. "Those aren't carvings. They're doors with boulders sitting behind them. Boulders that roll downhill."

A sharp snapping noise made Harry look up. The ropes that had guided the destructive ceiling rock were now straining under the weight of other enormous stones held in their grasp, stones that were now slowly dropping to the ground like clock weights. Harry watched as the doors carved into each side began to open.

"The ropes are opening the doors," he said. "It's some type of pulley system."

"There's another boulder behind that one," Sara said, pointing.

"I can't find the handcuff key." Nora was still digging frantically through Brian's pockets.

"We don't have time," Harry said. "We have to get back outside now."

"Harry," Nora said. "Look behind us."

He did and his stomach clenched. The cave entrance was buried under tons of rock.

Rumbling noises grabbed his ear. "The boulder." Harry spun around as the second boulder gained speed before it crashed into the second and third *daric* columns. "The boulders are taking out the taller columns."

How could they get out? He squinted at the sunlight flowing in from where the massive ceiling rock had taken Clay on a one-way ride through the wall. Clay had been standing on the tallest of the other columns, which was now smashed to bits. Harry blinked. *Sunlight.*

The ground shook again. "This cave is collapsing," Harry said. "We have to climb the columns and out through that hole. We don't have much time." Harry grabbed Nora's arm and pushed Sara ahead of him toward the lowest surviving column. "We'll have to jump to grab the top of the column. I'll boost you—"

A hand latched onto his ankle. Harry turned and stared into the crazed eyes of Brian Joyce, wounded and lying on the ground, still holding his pistol. Which he brought to bear on Harry once more. "You're not leaving me in this cave." Blood dripped down Brian's forehead as he started pulling the trigger. Harry kicked, unable to get free.

Nora's foot lashed out. Brian dropped the gun with a yelp of pain, and Nora grabbed it. Brian lunged for Harry as Nora fired. The pressure on Harry's ankle disappeared. Brian Joyce lay slumped, unmoving.

Nora turned to Harry. Her face was white. "I had to shoot him."

"You did," Harry said. "Thanks." He reached for her arm. "We have to get up to that opening."

Sara had moved on to the closest standing column, waiting at the base for them. "I can't reach it," she said. "It's too high."

The column stood nearly ten feet high. "Get on my shoulders." Harry pressed his back to the column and bent down. "I'll boost you up."

"But how will you get up?" she asked.

"I can jump up there. Climb on." Harry half-dragged her onto his shoulders before standing up. Sara grabbed a handhold and her weight vanished. Harry looked up to see her feet disappearing over the lip. "Keep moving," he said. "We're right behind." He turned to Nora. "You next. Get on my shoulders." They repeated the process, Nora managing to get hold of the upper lip with her manacled hands and haul herself over. "Keep going," he shouted up. "I'm coming."

He stepped back and leapt, kicking at the column's side for purchase as he went up, up high enough to get his fingers on to the lip, where he hung, suspended above the ground.

His grip broke and he crashed back to the ground. *Damn.*

"Grab our hands!"

He turned. Hands stuck out from above the column. Sara and Nora, side by side, reaching down for him. "Move it," Sara hollered. "You'll get us all killed."

He scrambled up, jumped again, and two strong hands caught his. The women hauled him up more easily than he would ever admit until they all stood together on top of a narrow column meant for one.

The cave's ceiling cracked with tectonic fury. Chunks of rock bigger than cars broke off, crashing onto the ground around them.

"Sara first," Harry yelled. "Then Nora. I'm last. Go go *go!*"

No one argued. Sara cleared the long step to the next pillar and kept moving. Splits appeared in the cave walls as the entire room shook. The column beneath their feet shuddered. Nora went next, stumbling as she moved, but Sara grabbed hold of her.

"Keep going," Harry yelled.

Sara moved on. Nora waited, hesitating at the edge. Harry jumped over as the column beneath him turned to rubble. He lost his balance and leaned out over the chasm all around him, fifteen feet in the air, too high to ever get back up.

Nora grabbed him. "Move it." She smacked his chest, right on the amulet beneath his shirt.

"I'm moving."

Nora turned and stayed one column behind Sara. Harry waited until the next column was clear before jumping on. He made it one column before the ground rumbled again. Louder. Deeper. He turned and watched as the side walls began to collapse entirely.

Harry touched his amulet. "Run!"

Sara took off at full speed with Nora and Harry behind. They ran, climbing higher and higher, knowing a fall would doom them. Sara gained the final column, the one with a pedestal on it. And a golden tablet.

Sara stopped. She grabbed the tablet. "It's stuck," she yelled over her shoulder.

"Forget it." Nora jumped onto the final pillar as well. "Jump outside."

Harry stepped onto the next to last pillar. Light poured through the hole not three feet beyond Sara, revealing a sloped hillside. It was the back of the mountain. Harry couldn't see ground. There could be a sheer drop right there, deadly at this height. "We're out of time."

Sara pulled at the tablet. Green sparks flashed. "I'm not leaving it."

Nora looked back at Harry. A message passed between them.

"Let me try," Nora shouted. Sara stopped struggling with the tablet, which now had streaks of green shining from it. Nora looped her cuffed hands over Sara's head, clutched her tight as Sara shouted, and jumped through the hole before falling out of sight.

Harry leapt the gap. The final column cracked beneath his feet as he landed, one side shearing off. He stumbled, arms pinwheeling, then caught his balance. The tablet sat atop the pedestal, lodged into an indentation perfectly cut to hold it, glowing green. Sara's voice played through his head.

Cursing himself, Harry grabbed the tablet and pulled. Nothing happened. He tried again. One try too many.

The column dropped from beneath Harry's feet as he jumped and went airborne, a rocket shot straight out of Brooklyn into the Iranian sunlight.

Epilogue

Brooklyn
One Week Later

The man who waited in Vincent Morello's office must have stepped out of a time machine.

It was the only explanation. Harry failed to suppress his reaction. "Mr. Morello?"

Vincent smiled broadly. "It's Vincent, Harry. And do not look so surprised." The mob boss stood from his chair, clapped Harry on the shoulder, then stepped around the desk and pulled him close for a hearty embrace. "There is life in me yet. Welcome back, my son."

Harry didn't resist as Vincent's arms wrapped around him. Gone were the sallow complexion, the liver spots prominent on sagging skin. No more did Vincent hobble about on weak legs, drawing raspy breaths after each sentence. Vincent had appeared to have one foot in the grave when Harry had left on his hunt for Xerxes' tablet. The man now crushing him in a bear hug had returned to life with a vengeance. Vincent Morello in all his glory.

Vincent released him and Harry stepped back and regarded him, trying not to stare.

"You look different, Vincent."

"Go ahead, Harry. You can say it. I look alive." He went back around his desk and sat in the big swivel chair.

"Very much so." Harry sat down in his usual chair across from Vincent's.

"Praise to God, and to my oncologist." Vincent frowned. "Can you believe it? I have an oncologist. He found the lymphoma and gave me pills. They saved my life. It is night and day, Harry. Before, I could scarcely walk. Now…" He snatched a baseball off his desk and tossed it into the air. "Life is a mystery. They say I will make a full recovery." Vincent set the baseball down as a knock sounded on his door. Joey Morello stood outside. "I am trying to focus on the positive aspects of life," Vincent said to Harry. "They are far too few."

"Harry, thanks for coming over," Joey said as he walked through the door. Harry stood, but Joey swept past him and went directly to the window behind his father's desk. Standing to one side of the frame, he peered out, then closed the blinds. Only after repeating this process at every unshaded window did he wrap Harry in an embrace. "It's good to see you."

"I haven't heard from you since I got back last week," Harry said. "But I know you've been busy." Joey stepped back but didn't respond. "Damn shame what happened to Zach and Chad when you were ambushed."

Joey's voice was soft when he responded. "I'd be dead if it weren't for Mrs. Reyna. That sweet grandmother keeps a shotgun by her door. She's from the old school of Italian ladies. The reason I'm alive is that whoever came after us was stupid enough to make their move on our turf."

"They came for you," Vincent pointed at Joey, "because of me. Word of my condition leaked. How, I am not certain. When our rivals saw me as weak, they attacked. Remove you, and the Morello family would never recover." He waited. Joey didn't look up. "Because you are the last of our line."

"I should have seen it coming."

What Joey left unsaid spoke volumes. The last Morello. Harry jumped in.

"Any idea who was behind it?"

"Who do you think?" Disdain tinged Joey's reply. "Those bastard Albanians."

"We cannot prove Altin Cana ordered those men to kill you," Vincent said.

"Proof?" Joey's eyes caught fire. "Nobody else is that stupid. It's that bastard Altin, and you know it."

"Anger can be useful if you control it." Vincent's quiet words brooked no argument, and Joey didn't respond, merely holding his father's gaze. "Whoever sent those men wants us to lash out, to behave irrationally. Doing so plays into their hands. Now is the time to consider our options, identify who is responsible, and make them pay. Carefully, cautiously. And only when the time is right."

"When's that going to be?" Joey asked. "After they try to kill me again?"

"No." Vincent stood and went to his son's side, laying a hand on the younger man's shoulder. "When they least expect it. An overwhelming response without mercy from which they will never recover. Look at me, son." Joey did. "Long after I am gone, you will face these challenges. *Think* before you act. Otherwise, nothing I or anyone else can do will keep this family safe."

Harry almost shrank back when Vincent turned to him. "You are one of us, Harry Fox. Your father saved my life. Perhaps one day you will save my son's. Do not let him forget what I said."

Harry had no idea what to say. "I won't," he managed.

"I know you will not." The Morello family leader turned abruptly from them. "My inquiries are ongoing," he said, walking to the fully stocked bar along one wall. "So far, your suspicions appear to be correct, Joey. The most likely person to have done this is Altin Cana. Once I have proof, we plan our response. Until then, we remain vigilant. We do not retaliate." Vincent poured a glass of wine. "Is that understood?"

Harry now knew how a vengeful god appeared in the flesh. He would never forget the look on Vincent's face.

Vincent held his glass to the light, swirling the deep purple liquid. His face changed, a kindly smile pushing away the fury. "Harry, I spoke with a contact of mine in the police department." He walked back over to his desk and picked up a manila folder. "This is everything they have on the case in which your father was framed. There is very little – just the officers' names and some notes."

Harry accepted the folder without opening it. "Thank you, Vincent. Did they name the informant?"

"No," Vincent said. "However, I believe you will uncover it. Investigate, Harry, but do it quietly. The truth will be revealed; I am sure of it."

A feeling he couldn't name and had no desire to share ran hot through Harry's chest. "This means the world to me."

"Make your father proud," Vincent said. "But enough of this. Joey has a new car. Perhaps he will show it to you?"

Joey's face brightened for the first time since he'd walked in. "Come on, Harry. It's out back. You're going to love it."

New car? What was that all about? Harry tucked the manila folder inside his coat and forced himself to follow Joey's lead. They walked down the long hallways of Vincent Morello's sprawling headquarters in silence. Harry followed as Joey stepped outside, giving him no warning of what waited for them. Harry took one step out and went still.

"That car." The memories flooded back. An unseen punch sending him to the ground. A pistol in his face. Shots fired inside his home. This lime-green car roaring off, his assailant at the wheel. "The guy who attacked me. That's the car he drove."

"He doesn't need it now," Joey said. "I thought you might want it. A new paint job and this ride will be special."

"Who was he?" Harry asked.

Joey's face darkened. "His name was Ciro." Harry waited. "You remember Gio?" he finally asked.

"Gio, the bouncer at the social club?" Harry asked. Joey nodded. "I remember him."

"Ciro was Gio's half-brother."

Harry noted the past tense. "Gio's a good guy. Why would his brother come after me?"

"Half-brother," Joey said. "They weren't close. Ciro owed some Russians a pile of money. Bad luck at the card table. When I asked around, I found out someone bought all of Ciro's debt not long ago. No idea who yet, so don't ask."

"You think whoever bought his debt made Ciro come after me?"

"I think someone found out Ciro was related to the bartender at a bar our family likes, and they saw an opportunity. To get information, keep an eye on us, who knows. Maybe they heard you were after those tablets. I have no idea, but it's no coincidence. They tried to get at you through Ciro. It almost worked."

"Does Sal know?" Harry asked.

"No, and he never will." Joey tapped the car's hood. "I know you're not a car guy, but this is a 1970 Chevy Chevelle SS 456. Four hundred and fifty horsepower. I'm thinking red with black stripes would look nice."

Harry considered it. "I like it."

"I'll set you up with a guy," Joey said. "The paint job is on me."

"I can't accept that, Joey. You're already giving me the damn car."

Joey waved the protests off. "Think about how much money you made for our family. Fresh paint is the least I can do."

"Alright."

"Speaking of money and the tablet, I haven't heard the whole story. How did you get out of Iran?" Joey leaned against the lime-green vehicle and lifted an eyebrow. "You mind?"

Harry joined him. "Not at all."

"Tell me the story, then tell me about that tablet. My father wouldn't say much. He said to ask you."

Birds chirped as Harry recounted their journey, beginning with the smuggler ferrying them into Iran, to buying motorcycles after nearly being flattened by Range Rovers outside Persepolis, to the discovery of King Xerxes' hidden cave in which a swinging rock and car-sized boulders had nearly finished the job Brian Joyce couldn't.

Joey listened in silence the entire time. "You guys climbed those columns while the whole cave was collapsing?" he asked after Harry finished. "How close was it?"

"The last column—"

"The forty-foot one."

"That one," Harry said. "It disintegrated a half-second after I pulled the tablet out of its pedestal. I jumped, but honestly, luck got me through the hole in the back of that mountain. And, if it had been much steeper, we'd have been killed."

"What about Brian Joyce and his man?"

"They didn't make it." Harry cleared his throat. "After we got out, we walked around the mountain to the motorcycles and went straight to the airport in Shiraz. The smuggler met us as planned and flew us back to Egypt. From there we all headed home."

"Sara is in Germany?"

"Yes."

Joey tilted his head. "You've talked to her?"

"We've texted."

"And Agent Doyle?"

"Told her boss what happened, and he said he'd look into it. Nothing else from him so far. Funny thing, though. She got promoted yesterday to lead a brand-new department. She reports directly to the district attorney now."

Joey shook his head. "Imagine that. Some of those people are more crooked than any criminals I know."

"She told me to call if I ever need a favor. Seems the immunity offer is still on the table."

"A fair trade, considering you gave her the first two tablets. I saw that article in the *Times*. Big stuff in her world."

"It never hurts to have friends in high places," Harry said with a laugh.

Joey managed to hold off for all of five seconds. "What about the last tablet? The one you still have."

Harry looked at the trees. Leaves rustled on a breeze, and the sparkling surface filled his mind's eye. "It's solid emerald. There was clay covering it so we couldn't tell until Sara knocked a chunk off. The tablet has another message from Xerxes. First, it tells why he hid the elixir."

"Xerxes realized how dangerous it was," Joey said. "And he didn't think he should be the one to use it to extend his life."

Harry's eyes narrowed. "That's right. How did you know?"

"Lucky guess. And I know a thing or two about the pressure that comes with being on top."

"I guess you do," Harry said. "Xerxes wanted to be sure only a worthy man found it. A worthy Persian who could unravel the mystery of his tablets."

"Did it say anything else?"

Harry nodded. "It describes a physician named Nebrus, who studied under Hippocrates. Nebrus visited Xerxes when the king was dying and offered to give the king medicine to heal him, what he called an *emerald elixir*. The same elixir that had cured him as a sickly young man."

"Nebrus was the sickly youth from the first tablet."

"Want to know what else the tablet said?" Harry asked.

"You have my attention."

Harry's voice barely carried between them. "It gives the formula for the emerald elixir."

"Can you understand it?"

"I can."

"Can we recreate it?"

"The formula requires gland secretions produced by a species of frog found in the Aegean Islands. That's a problem, because this species of frog went extinct three centuries ago when the Greek government diverted a river to supply water to cities. The process destroyed the frog's sole habitat."

Joey nearly fell back onto the green hood. "So, the formula for a life-extending elixir has been hidden in an Iranian cave for three thousand years, and it's useless because someone *dammed a river?*"

Harry shrugged. Joey cursed in Italian. Then he laughed, and cursed again.

"My thoughts too," Harry said. The leaves rustled and Harry realized that right then he had no desire to talk about Xerxes or the solid emerald tablet any longer. "Hey, are you hungry? I'm dying for some baba ghanoush from Sanna. It'd be nice to see Ahmed."

Joey peered at him out of the corner of an eye. "Ahmed took on a partner. He needed the cash to stay open."

"Did they change the menu? You can't get Mediterranean food like that anywhere else."

"Worse. The new partners are Albanian. Now Cana men are crawling all over Sanna. We need to stay away while my father figures out who tried to kill me."

"Ahmed sold out to the Albanians?"

"Needed cash," Joey said again. "Last you told me, he was in a tough spot."

And I tried to loan him the money. "Yeah," Harry said. "He was." Harry's phone vibrated in his pocket. He glanced at the screen. "Joey, I have to take this."

Joey walked back inside as Harry connected the call. One from a German number.

"Sara?"

"Hello, Harry."

He hadn't heard her voice in several days. For reasons he wouldn't quite acknowledge, his nerves tingled. "Everything okay?"

"Everything is fine. You?"

Harry looked at the green car. "I'm good."

"That's great to hear." A pause. "You have a second?"

"Of course."

"I just spoke with an acquaintance. She is an expert on Roman culture and is sometimes asked to verify the authenticity of items sold between private sellers."

"Collectors."

"Correct. Do you remember when I told you I had more information on your amulet? You were in Greece the first time. Egypt the second."

Harry picked up on and ignored the implicit rebuke. "I remember. Did this acquaintance know something about it?"

"Not about the amulet. I haven't told anyone it exists. I promised you I wouldn't. But she did have information on the scarabs I told you about."

"The scarabs Mark Antony and Cleopatra gave as gifts during a victory celebration."

"Their last military triumph. Those scarabs were more than extravagant gifts."

Harry gripped the phone so hard his hand hurt. "What do you mean?"

"My acquaintance verified the authenticity of a scarab artifact for a private sale. It's one of the scarabs given out by Antony and Cleopatra." Sara's voice quickened. "She discovered an inscription on the piece that she could not explain."

Harry's chest tightened. *Easy, Harry.* "Inscription?"

"I told you about the writing on the exterior of each scarab. Those inscriptions are well documented and are on each known scarab. What's not documented is what she found *inside* the scarab. It wasn't one solid piece, but actually two interlocking pieces. When she opened it, there was a message inside." Sara took a breath. "And guess what? One line is nearly identical to part of your amulet."

Harry held his breath. "What does it say?"

"That we were right. Your amulet isn't just an amulet. It's part of a coded message from Mark Antony and Cleopatra. And the best part? I understand what it says."

Author's Note

Though *The Emerald Tablet* is a work of fiction, real events inspired many portions of the novel, some of which I was hard-pressed to believe were true. Though in my research for this and other tales, one phrase that I found resonates more clearly with each book is "Truth is stranger than fiction." Below are several which you may find interesting.

While I refer to the central artifact in this story as the Emerald Tablet, you may know of another Emerald Tablet from the annals of history which is real and in no way resembles the artifact Harry Fox tracked to Persepolis. Historians referring to the Emerald Tablet do not have an actual tablet in mind. In fact, they're not even talking about a physical object at all, but instead a text (or recipe of sorts) attributed to the legendary and mythical figure known as Hermes Trismegustus. Hermes is a combination of the Greek god Hermes and Egyptian god Thoth who formed over time, and allegedly the author of the *Hermetica*, a series of texts and treatises covering such wide-ranging topics as astrology, medicine and alchemy to more philosophical musings regarding the relationship between man and god.

Despite this attribution, the first incident of the historical Emerald Tablet dates to medieval Arabic texts from the eighth century. These were then translated into Latin, and other versions in different languages followed. The original content of the historical Emerald Tablet claims to provide an alchemical recipe for producing *the greatest power*, an undefined idea which *ascends from the earth to the heavens and becomes ruler over that which is above and that which is below.*

As you can see, the entire idea is light on specifics, which is why this myth became a favorite of alchemists across the centuries, the tinkerers and scientists seeking the philosophers' stone, that mythical alchemical substance able to turn base metals into gold. To date, this has never been achieved, though perhaps it is because all alchemists through history merely haven't managed to mix the ingredients properly. While the name of this story ties to a fanciful text allegedly written by what happens when you smash a Greek god and an Egyptian god together, much more of this story is based in fact.

A three-foot tall, two-hundred-pound marble statue of Marcus Aurelius *(Ch. 3)* truly was stolen from an Algerian museum in the late nineties, though neither Nora Doyle or the antiquities trafficking unit of the Manhattan district attorney's office – a real unit comprised of lawyers and a team of antiquities trafficking analysts created in 2017 – played a role in the recovery. Members of the Cultural Property, Art and Antiquities Investigations team operating under the U.S. Department of Homeland Security's Immigration and Customs Enforcement tracked down the missing statue as it was being readied for sale at Christie's.

Looking further back into the past, Hippocrates truly did prescribe willow bark to patients for pain relief, though it is unlikely he could have foreseen what this natural remedy would later contribute to modern medicine. As mentioned, willow bark was refined in the mid-1800s into the compound salicin, which fifty years later became acetylsalicylic acid. Today we call it aspirin, and it is the most commonly used drug in the world.

The driving question in this tale is what, if anything, did Xerxes II learn from Hippocrates or his pupils? Could the father of medicine truly have shared any advanced knowledge of how to heal the body with King Xerxes *(Ch. 9)*? Unlikely, but not impossible, as Xerxes II was born in 440 BCE and lived until 358 BCE. Hippocrates lived from 460 BCE until 350 BCE, which means that in theory, at least, it is possible their paths may have crossed. Given that Hippocrates spent most of his life in Greece, over 2,500 miles from Iran, it's unlikely – but who knows?

The Persian general Megabyzus plays a prominent role in Harry's journey from Brooklyn to modern-day Iran, and he truly did defeat several nations while leading Achaemenid forces *(Ch. 9)*, including Egyptian and Athenian armies. However, Megabyzus only served his country until 440 BCE, the year Xerxes II was born. His tomb is not located in the Saqqara necropolis, though his final resting place is not known, so it could be waiting in the necropolis, yet to be uncovered.

The description of Megabyzus's tomb *(Ch. 17)* was inspired by the tomb of Wahtye, a real tomb in Saqqara, and one which is the subject of a wonderful Netflix documentary titled *Secrets of the Saqqara Tomb*. The documentary follows along from when the tomb is first unearthed to the end of the excavation, and it is in this magnificent burial structure that I found inspiration for the vivid depictions of my imagined tomb for our Persian general. I strongly recommend the documentary if you want to learn more about the real Saqqara, or simply to get a look at how excavations occur in Egypt when Harry Fox isn't around causing trouble.

Across the world, since humankind began gathering in villages, tribes, cities, states and empires, none have exceeded the size of the Persian empire when measured as a percentage of the world's population at the time *(Ch. 24)*. The Persian empire truly is the largest in history by percentage of world's population. One of the empires crown jewels was Persepolis, known at the time as the city of Persians, and Persepolis had five palaces. In terms of religious affiliations, Xerxes did practice Zoroastranism, and the faith is one of the world's oldest continuously practiced religions, with over one hundred thousand adherents today, most of them in India, Iran and North America.

The city of Persepolis exists today as described *(Ch. 25)*, as does Xerxes tomb. Unfortunately, visitors cannot go inside the tomb, and as far as I know there are no secret caverns contained within holding forgotten artifacts which men like Harry Fox pursue.

Excerpt from The Next Harry Fox Adventure

Visit Andrew's website for more information and purchase details.

andrewclawson.com

Prologue

Roman Britain, outside of Londinium
AD 61

A lone hawk darted across the sky, never once looking down at the massed armies gathered below. A discordant symphony rattled as ten thousand armored Roman soldiers craned their necks skyward, following the predator as it soared over an open field. Horses stamped, soldiers offered prayers to their personal gods, and every soldier in the two legions considered the omen. Good or bad? They would soon learn, for battle cries erupted from the throats of the tattooed, blue-painted army across the field as one hundred thousand Celtic warriors made ready to attack.

Emperor Nero's horse bucked at the thunderous noise. Nero barely held on, cursing the beast as a servant struggled to calm it. "Control this wretch," he shouted. The servant didn't look up as he held the bridle with an iron grip. Nero had ordered men executed for much less, though today would be different. Nero, the fifth emperor of Rome and an unrepentant tyrant, stared across the field as a foreign sensation grew in his chest. An emotion he'd rarely felt in his decades as the world's most powerful man. *Fear.*

A fear of one person. A fear he would never admit to for many reasons, though one stood above all: Nero was afraid of a *woman*.

A female barbarian, the heathen leader of the unwashed rabble standing across from Rome's finest soldiers. A woman who so far had resisted Nero's every attempt to crush the insufferable rebellion she had instigated a year earlier after Rome broke an agreement made with her husband, one of the Celtic kings subdued decades ago by Roman legions during their conquering march across Brittania. A woman who called herself Queen, who led one hundred thousand rebels against the ten thousand Roman soldiers arrayed before her.

Boudica, Queen of the Iceni. A rebel queen who represented the first true threat to Roman rule in Brittania for two decades. In under a year she had led a revolt which topped cities, slaughtered an entire legion, and directly caused the deaths of over seventy thousand Roman subjects. Survivors of battle with the Celts were rare, and surviving legionnaires almost non-existent. Of the handful who survived defeat at Boudica's hand, several had recently come to Nero's court in Rome. Each carried with them the scars of defeat, and a common, horrific tale.

How had Boudica's ragged army of wild savages with little military training or proper weaponry defeated the most disciplined, successful army in the world? According to the surviving soldiers, by magic.

Nero spat at the ground as sweat beaded on his forehead, the sun beating mercilessly on the gathered forces. He scarcely believed the first man to offer this fanciful reason for their defeat, threatening to behead him for his lies. The soldier never recanted, though, right up to the point when Nero pressed a sword against the man's neck himself. Nero spared the man, hard-pressed to believe any soldier would lie to his emperor with their life in the balance.

His disbelief turned to curiosity before the second survivor offered a nearly identical story. Then another surviving Roman from a different defeat again gave a mystical reason for their legion's defeat. Curiosity turned to concern, followed quickly by fright when a final survivor from Boudica's most recent victory repeated the outrageous claims verbatim. Now Nero did not doubt his men. No, he believed them, and that belief made him fear that today would prove to be Nero's folly, a miscalculated risk that would leave Rome in need of a new emperor. For if what his soldiers said were true, no horse in the world could run fast enough to save Nero from Boudica's wrath.

Nero closed his eyes. The raw, crisped skin on the final soldier's arm flashed across his mind's eye. Caused by the magical weapon each man claimed Boudica used, one so powerful it cut down swathes of armored troops as a scythe cut wheat. If such a weapon existed, no man could stand up to it, no army could defeat the one wielded such power. For all his might, Nero would stand helpless in the face of this weapon. Rumors already spread through his troops. That the Celt gods came down from the skies to crush her enemies. That she could channel the elements in battle, bend nature to her will, laying waste to the Roman forces. Despite Nero's edict promising death to any who dared speak such heresy, reports told that every Roman on the field today had heard the whispers, knew of Boudica's supposed vengeance and her confirmed thirst for blood. If it were true, Rome's time atop the world order would soon end.

A general named Quintus rode to Nero's side and saluted. "Augustus."

Nero tore his gaze from the seemingly endless expanse of screaming Celts. "Speak."

"What are your orders, sir?"

Nero studied Quintus, a grizzled veteran of countless campaigns, one of his most experienced leaders and a man Nero would trust with his life, were he so foolish as to do such a thing. "You are a general. Counsel me. What would you have me do?"

The stone-faced general blinked. "I trust in your leadership, Augustus."

Augustus, official title of the Roman emperor, the undisputed leader of all Romans. The leader who ordered when to attack, and when to give quarter. None would be offered today, though in Nero's heart, he did not know which army would instead offer death to their enemy. "We are outnumbered," Nero said. "Ten-to-one, the scouts tell me."

"A correct count," Quintus said. "We are outnumbered by an enemy with little armor, no cavalry, no true soldiers, poor discipline and little experience."

Nero turned to stare at the Celts. "An enemy which overran our garrison at Camulodunum, annihilated the Ninth Legion and conquered Londinium. They have killed over seventy thousand Romans, soldiers and citizens alike. Tell me, Quintus." Now he looked to his trusted general again. Nero did not like what he saw. "Rumor says this enemy is led by a sorceress who harnesses the power of earth and sky. A demon in human form. Tell me why you are not concerned?"

General Quintus spoke to Nero as few others dared – honestly. "I am terrified, Augustus. But a Roman soldier does not run from battle."

Nero nodded. "Well said. Now, how do you suggest we attack?"

"*Cuneum Formate,*" Quintus said without hesitation. "Drive a wedge through the heart of an untrained force and they will run. As we push in further, the wedge spreads them apart, distancing the troops from their leaders to leave them incapable of receiving orders or mounting anything beyond a discordant response. Once their line breaks, our reserves attack."

"And victory is ours," Nero said. "A Roman victory, as your instructors taught you."

General Quintus made no reply.

"Unless Boudica resists our attack," Nero said.

"Our men will prevail."

"Who will lead them?" Nero asked.

Quintus had spent his entire adult life in the military. He knew there was only one correct answer. "It would be my honor to lead the charge."

"And I would be a fool to put you at the tip of the spear," Nero said. "You will remain by my side."

Quintus, for a reason Nero could not possibly fathom, seemed disappointed. "As you command, Augustus."

"Give the orders," Nero said. "We attack now."

Quintus wheeled, his horse snorting as he rode a short distance and conveyed the orders to his senior staff, who dispersed through the troops to tell men some of them would soon die. The noisy Celts fell quiet as the Legion moved efficiently, and within minutes soldiers had formed into attack formation, with reserve lines set to deploy in the second wave, an unstoppable ocean of Roman force crashing on the massed Celts. Nero removed his helmet, took a towel from a servant and ran it across his brow. When he looked back up, a hole had opened in the Celtic line. A solitary figure stepped through, paused, and then began crossing the field.

The sweat running down his chest turned icy. A lone woman approached the Romans. Luminescent hair twirled riotously around her shoulders as she walked, crimson locks burning under the sunlight. Blue paint lined her face. A metal breastplate on her chest had been weathered to a dull gray, though the sword belted across her waist gleamed with a razor's edge. Nero tried to look away and failed, the sight of a single woman marching into the teeth of his army unnerving in a way he had never imagined possible.

Queen Boudica, leader of the Celts, slayer of Romans across Brittania, had come for battle. Nero squinted. What was in her hands? A bag of some kind, smaller than a soldier's rucksack. Quintus returned to Nero's side and raised an eyebrow, but Nero stayed him with an upraised hand.

"Let her come to us," Nero said. "Perhaps she wishes to negotiate."

"Will you speak with her, Augustus?"

Nero forced the familiar cruel smile to his face. "No. I will kill her first, then cut down her troops like animals."

Quintus nodded. "We await your orders, Augustus."

At that moment Boudica stopped walking. One hundred yards from the Roman front line, she stood and stared directly at Nero. Emperor Nero, unmistakable on his towering warhorse, clad in gold-plated armor polished to outshine Mars himself. A warlord in all his glory, the man who had come to crush Boudica's rebellion. The Celtic queen stared at Nero a moment longer, then set her bag down and lifted a hand, pointing one finger at Nero. In case there was any doubt, she then shouted his name, her voice carrying across the fields.

Nero could not understand what came next. Harsh words, a language native to Brittania which Nero did not understand. Whatever she said caused the Celts to erupt, a cacophonous cheer which hung on the heavy air for some time. Front line Roman's remained still, watching the infamous queen staring back at them until the noise died, when she bent down and opened the sack at her feet. Two objects came out. Boudica held one in each hand and raised her arms. The effect was immediate.

A roar of sound exploded from the Celtic army, twice as loud and long as the prior cries, carrying on with such force that Nero's horse rose on its hind legs and screamed. Nero slipped from his saddle, only managing to stay on top of the beast because his boots were in the stirrups. He berated the animal as his aides grabbed it again and calmed the beast. Sunlight painted the grassy plain a vibrant green as the roaring Celts fell silent. Nero looked up. Boudica had put one object back in the bag, now holding the remaining one in both hands. The black lump seemed to absorb any light hitting it, a dull half-circle of what looked like rock. Simple stone, though from a hundred yards away Nero couldn't tell.

Boudica began shouting once more as she lifted the stone skyward. A chanting, one her army mirrored, their strange and grating tongue sending cool dread from Nero's boots to his chest, forcing the air from his lungs. Nero watched the chanting queen, transfixed as she set the dark object down and removed a pair of leather gloves from the sack, dark and bulky leather which went up to her elbows. Then Boudica picked up the object and held it out toward Nero, turning it in a specific way so it angled directly at the closest Roman troops, soldiers who formed the tip of a spear which would shatter the Celtic lines.

The chanting increased in volume as the object in Boudica's hands seemed to *darken* while Nero watched, turning hazy as Boudica looked to the sky, adjusting her grip and angling the strange object toward the Romans. Nero started as flashes of light jumped from the stone, arcing like the bolts of light thrown from the night sky by the god Summanus, bolts which burned trees and set fire to the ground. The chanting fell away as larger sparks shot from the dark object. Nero tasted metal on his tongue. Boudica raised her hands and the air around them turned hazy, as heat waves shimmered from the item now sparking as though it would erupt in fire any moment. The hair on Nero's arms rose, his mouth dry as tinder.

A blackness enveloped the object like cloth covering an open door before a bolt of light exploded from the dark object. Nero covered his eyes against the brightness as men screamed and the sickening scent of burning flesh filled the air. Nero stared, dumbfounded. A hundred of his troops lay dead.

Then the world went dark. Soldiers gasped, men shrinking from the sky as the sun vanished, the god Sol cut down by an unknown hand. What sorcery was this? First, a hundred soldiers dead in a flash, then the sun vanishes. Only when Nero turned in fear to see what Queen Boudica would offer next did he realize: she had not made the sun disappear. Her mouth hung open. A stunned emptiness washed over her face as she struggled to hold the deadly object aloft.

The innate sense of self-preservation which had carried Nero from an orphanage to the pinnacle of Rome came alive. He grabbed

Quintus by the arm and shouted.

"Attack!"

Nero drew his sword, pointed it at Boudica's heart, and the full might of a Roman legion flew at the Celts.

Dead and dying men littered the field, precious few of them Romans. Thousands upon thousands of Celts covered the grass, their blood mixing with the ubiquitous blue paint to turn paint the ground a grisly gray, a color of death and Celtic defeat. Groups of Roman soldiers moved about the field in orderly fashion, dispatching survivors and pulling fallen comrades back to camp for a military burial. The first birds had arrived, circling lazily on hot air above the newly-created graveyard, waiting for the living to depart so they could gorge themselves.

Nero stood in front of his tent, watching the familiar scene unfold, as he had dozens of times before. Rome conquered all. At least, until now. Today, Rome had escaped for reasons Nero could not understand. The capricious will of the gods? Or perhaps Boudica's failure to wipe out Nero's legion was something else, a sinister victory offering Nero a glimpse of what was to come. A day when the Roman forces would no longer march with impunity across the world. Such thoughts had never seemed possible, not before today. Before Nero saw what could have been.

Quintus rode up in a rush and dismounted, falling to one knee after marching to Nero's tent. "Augustus."

Nero waved at him to stand. "Did you find her?"

"Yes," Quintus said. "She fell in the first attack."

The only attack. It had been a slaughter. The Roman troops overran a panicked force ten times their size with ease. Once Boudica's initial attack faltered as the sun was eclipsed by darkness, the Celts showed their true nature, a disorganized rabble incapable of withstanding the Roman onslaught. Rome's musicians would sing

276

odes to another of Nero's great victories, and Nero would bask in their praise. Yet he knew how close this battle had come to disaster. He saw what power Boudica wielded, and it had shaken Nero to his core.

"Did you find the object?"

Quintus lifted a satchel, offering it to Nero. "They are inside, Augustus?"

Nero hesitated. "What is it?"

Quintus emptied the bag, laying out in front of Nero a pair of the strangest rocks he had ever seen. Two which seemed to have once been one. Nero bent closer, angling his head to study the shifting, cloud-like swirls which appeared to drift over the surface even as he watched. A dull sheen emanated from the stones, a darkness hovering beneath the odd cloud-like surface. The rocks appeared to be *alive*.

"These were on the woman's corpse." Quintus laid a pair of leather gloves on the ground. The gloves Boudica had worn when she used the rocks to strike unforgettable terror in Nero's heart.

He picked one up. Blood dripped from it. "It is leather," Nero said. "No metal. And thick." The gloves would stretch nearly to his elbow were he to don it. "These must protect her hands when she uses these...*things*."

Nero dropped the glove. It landed, he blinked, and everything became clear. What he must do to protect himself. To protect his troops, and to ensure the empire was never defeated. "Take these stones and bury them." Nero stood, stepping back toward his tent. "Far from here. These rocks must be lost for eternity."

In response, Quintus did something Nero had never heard him do since Nero became emperor. He questioned an order. "Is that wise, Augustus? You saw what these are capable of." Quintus gestured to the mass graves being dug as they spoke. "With these, you would be invincible."

Nero, known across the world for his ruthless nature and

seemingly unquenchable desire for power, paused. Only for a moment. For the first time he could see fires burning in defeated cities and hear the cries of vanquished foes. Except this time, he worried he saw Rome burning, and heard his own shouts as he fell.

"I would. Which means anyone else who came to possess them would also. There is nothing but misery promised in those stones. Bury them deep, Quintus. And never tell a soul where to find them."

Chapter 1

Newark, NJ

It all began with a scarab. One crafted of solid gold, with sapphires and rubies dotting the wings. A scarab which turned out to not be so solid after all. Over two thousand years after Mark Antony and Cleopatra presented a number of the bejeweled scarabs as gifts commemorating a great military victory, a German historian discovered the scarab wasn't one solid piece, but instead a pair of intricately designed halves which locked together. When the historian opened it, a long-forgotten secret was revealed.

Harry Fox stood in a warehouse not far from the Port Newark-Elizabeth Marine Terminal. *Why do I always end up in a warehouse?* What was it with these antiquities traffickers? Of course, he knew the answer. Proximity. To water routes, major highways, international airports, to the places where goods entered and departed a country, occasionally without proper documentation. If Harry Fox wanted to move items across international borders without the authorities knowing about it, he'd operate near the same places. The ports, the highways, the airports. Except he'd have a real office, someplace where you didn't hear cranes running and ship horns blasting day and night.

A metal door banged open. Harry reached for the amulet around his neck without thinking, touching it as the man he'd spent weeks tracking down finally appeared. A man who specialized in acquiring

279

certain items, often without proper documentation. A man Harry worried might just kill him because it was easier that way.

"Mr. Fox." The man who called himself Charles walked in, trailed by a single guard. "Forgive me, I've kept you waiting."

Harry heard everything Charles said, but only after his brain added in the missing consonants and cut through the drawn-out words. *Cha-ahles*, as he called himself, came straight out of the Bayou in deep Louisiana. How he ended up as an artifacts dealer of questionable repute in New Jersey was a mystery. Though he'd come North, Charles brought with him the light blue seersucker suit and colorful bow tie. He eschewed socks with his bespoke footwear.

"I'm sure you're busy," Harry said. He eyed the guard who had taken up a post by the small room's only exterior door. Good thing Harry had the sense to open the closest window before Charles walked in. If this went south, the window became a quick exit.

"Never too busy for a friend of Ms. Leroux's." The *r*'s turned to *ah*'s on his drawl. "How is she?"

"Well," Harry said. "Rose sends her regards."

"You tell her I appreciate the business," Charles said, lifting the briefcase he'd walked in holding. "I believe this is what you are after."

Harry never turned his back on the guard as Charles set the briefcase on a metal table and motioned Harry over. Locks *snicked*, the briefcase opened, and Harry Fox took one more step on an ancient path laid out by Cleopatra, one-time ruler of Egypt. "That's it."

Charles stood next to Harry. "It is a beautiful piece, Mr. Fox. I can see why a man would want to own it."

Harry lifted a hand. "May I?" he asked.

"By all means." Charles gestured at the necklace and stepped back. "You won't break it."

A chain forged of golden links ran from either side of the pendant. Harry gently lifted it from the felt-lined briefcase, barely noticing the chain's weight, heavy enough to tell him the links were solid gold. Far too heavy for comfort. No, the piece was meant to impress, to make a statement. With a pendant like this, it succeeded in spectacular fashion.

"It's incredible," Harry said to himself.

Charles overheard. "A double-headed eagle," he said. "Wings spread out wide. Truly one of a kind."

"Not just that." Harry angled the weighty centerpiece, more of a sculpture than a pendant. The thing weighed a couple pounds. "There's a crown between the two heads. A crown made from a serpent."

The eagle boasted sharp talons, with its long wings spread out as though ready to take flight. Rubies dotted the curved claws, burning red even in the room's weak light. Rich sapphires stood in for the eagle's eye, while soft emeralds colored the serpent which coiled like a crown between the two eagle heads which jutted from the body, one looking in each direction.

"I have never seen such a creature." Charles again stood at Harry's side, with his head tilted at an angle. "No idea what would possess a man to make it. Man or woman, I suppose."

Harry didn't respond. Charles may speak slowly, but in truth he was a shark circling in the water, sniffing for something eat. Men didn't survive long in the international antiquities trafficking world if they weren't sharp. Charles might fool an amateur with his act. Let him try it on the next buyer.

"How did you find it?" Harry asked, if only for the sake of appearances.

"Now, Mr. Fox." Charles wagged a finger. "You know I cannot reveal my sources."

"Fair enough." Harry turned the double-headed eagle over. The rear portion was as exquisitely carved as the front, the eagles' plumage impeccably-crafted, down to the smallest feather. "I appreciate you acquiring this for me."

"Always happy to do business with a fellow collector," Charles said.

Harry frowned. Charles knew what Harry did, which meant more people like Charles also knew. People around the world, men and women Harry had to view as competitors, if not outright threats. Less than a year into his new role and already his face was known.

"I don't speak about Mr. Morello's business," Harry said. "Or my own."

Charles's face dropped. "Forgive me, Mr. Fox. I meant no offense."

Harry gritted his teeth to keep from laughing. "None taken."

He looked back to the pendant, letting Charles stew. Having the head of the New York Italian mob in as your boss proved useful at times. Once people heard Vincent Morello's name, they tended to show respect. Not surprising considering what happened to people who disrespected the Morello family.

"I'm satisfied," Harry said a moment later. Gently laying the pendant and chain down, he stepped back while Charles closed the latches. Harry reached into his pocket, slowly. "Here's the payment we discussed."

Charles took the black felt bag from Harry's grasp. It weighed practically nothing, made no noise, yet when Charles opened it to reveal the contents he went still. A pair of half-million-dollar cut diamonds did that to a person. A loupe materialized from inside his pocket.

"My goodness." Charles studied one of the diamonds for a moment, turning it to catch the light. "Mr. Fox, this is a beauty." He lowered the loupe. "Eight carats each, is it?"

"Nine," Harry said. "Appraised at a million wholesale in total. A fair price for your excellent piece."

"I agree." The diamonds vanished into a pocket. "Are you sure you don't have a pretty lady who will miss one of these?"

A face flashed into his mind. The face of a German historian. One who he'd promised could help him with this supposedly benign purchase. Harry grimaced. *Sara won't be happy.*

Charles misinterpreted his look. "She won't miss it," he said quickly. "Not when you show her that—"

A thunderous boom shook the metal building. The walls seemed to tremble, as though a bomb had gone off outside the front door, close enough for the shock waves to rattle Harry's brain. He grabbed the table for support, then on instinct took hold of the briefcase.

"Are you okay?" Harry asked. That's when the guard starting shouting.

"It's the cops," the guard shouted as he peered through the exterior door. "They busted down the fence. They're coming around now!" He slammed the door shut and flipped the lock.

Squealing tires and shouting voices reached Harry's ears through the open window. Charles ran toward his guard, but Harry had no illusions about getting out that way. Same with the window. He took the only option left: a door behind him leading deeper into the warehouse. Better that than the cops arresting him with a trafficked artifact. The metal door clanged open as Harry raced through it and into the warehouse's cavernous interior.

Slick floor glistened in the weak red light cast by *EXIT* signs over locked doors as he ran without direction, the briefcase still clutched in one hand. He'd glanced into this part of the warehouse a moment before Charles walked into the room, long enough to confirm it offered no immediate way out and nothing more. The creaking building stretched the length of a football field, with steps leading up to the second set at intervals down each side. Far overhead sodium lights flickered like dive bar beer signs as his footsteps bounced off the walls. A pair of doors waited ahead, eighty yards distant.

Doors which the cops would surely know about. Instinct told Harry to hit the brakes. He did, turning to run up the closest staircase a heartbeat before both of doors blasted off their hinges and went crashing across the concrete courtesy of police battering rams. Harry gained the second level as the first cops came pouring inside, ducking into the first door he found. Which, it turned out, weighed roughly one thousand pounds. He tugged on the metal handle and the door barely moved enough for him to slip inside.

Harry ran into a wall of darkness cut only by the slice of dingy, overworked light slipping through the cracked door. With the police coming quickly, he used his phone flashlight to push back the darkness. And then Harry stopped, phone held in the air, his mouth hanging open.

He stood amid a treasure hoard. Not gold or gemstones, but something better. *Artifacts*. Statues and scepters, scrolls and sarcophagi. An archaeologist's dream surrounded him, at least a dozen incredible pieces. The sounds of his impending arrest faded as the puzzle pieces clicked into place. The heavy door. The fantastic artifacts. A relic smuggler's warehouse. Harry nearly laughed. Charles had left his room-sized safe unlocked, and Harry had just stumbled inside.

Charles must have grabbed the necklace from in here minutes ago, expecting to return in a short while with Harry's diamonds. His light played around, falling on a fiendish mask of solid gold, and he moved over to find a demon looking up at him from a felt-covered table. The mask had been carved in the shape of an ape-like creature, its tongue lolling out to well below the jaw. Four pointed incisors struck fear in the heart of beholders, while a decorative engraving around the exterior told Harry this was a pre-Incan mask from South America. How Charles had come to possess it was beyond Harry. He hefted the piece: too heavy to carry away.

Shouting erupted outside the door and downstairs. Charles, berating the police as they took him into custody. Then a man shouted. "I'm going upstairs!"

Harry forgot the mask and spun around. More artifacts than he could hope to find in several years, but he'd trade them all for a way out. Four walls penned him in, with only the heavy door behind offering a way out, an escape leading directly to the cops. He stepped deeper into the room. He stopped. *What's that?*

A razor-thin shadow went up the back wall, a place his phone's light didn't seem to illuminate. Another step, and Harry realized. It was *another* room, one hidden by a door with no handle or hinges. But why was the door hanging ever-so-slightly open?

The darkness swirled as he ran for the slim hope of safety. This door moved weightlessly under his touch, falling back to reveal another room. Harry found a handle on the inside, so at least he wouldn't be stuck in here. He pulled the door shut, then stopped an instant before it closed. He wouldn't be stuck unless Charles had installed a lock secured by a passcode or key, a backup in case someone managed to find their way into this hidden room inside a veritable safe. What kind of man would do that? An artifacts trafficker who trusted no one. Harry pulled the door nearly shut, leaving only a sliver of space as he held the door and shoved his phone into a pocket, all without dropping the necklace briefcase.

Light exploded as someone entered the room outside, a shaft of light pouring through the narrow opening into Harry's eyes. He held his breath. If the intruder came too close, he'd spot Harry's hidden door and it was over. If the cop stayed back near the entrance, Harry had a chance.

Footsteps pounded as the man walked in. Harry tensed.

"Clear!"

The cop who'd come in shouted it again, this time right outside Harry's door, only to pound away a beat later. A radio squawked. "Repeat, this room is clear. But tell the boss to send someone up here. She's gotta see this."

A drop of cold sweat ran down Harry's back. *I'm still trapped.* He turned an ear to the door as the radio barked to life again. A woman's voice this time.

"What's up there?"

The man who stood outside responded. "Stuff. All kinds of fancy stuff." Harry's sliver of light turned to shadow as a flashlight beam ran across it. "A mask, a big-ass coffin, some kind of gold stick. You'll know more about it."

"Don't touch a thing," the woman said. "I'm on my way."

"Understood," the man said. His footsteps clicked on the metal walkway outside the room's door.

Harry's situation had not improved. The artifacts may have bought him time, but could he really close himself in here? What if he was right, and Charles had turned this into a panic room of some kind – one only Charles knew how to get out of? Then he'd be lucky to get out of here. It could be weeks before anyone found him. Holding the door in place, he pulled his phone out, shielding the light so it didn't alert anyone to his presence. What he found stopped him cold.

A table. Behind him, in the very center of the hidden room. The sounds of an artifact trafficker being arrested faded to nothing as he walked to the table, stopping in front of it. He set the briefcase down. A book rested atop the table. Not just any book. One without a cover. Harry leaned closer and the breath caught in his throat. *Papyrus*. The pages were papyrus, the favorite writing materials of ancient civilizations. Romans, Egyptians, Persians. And Greeks. Which was the language flowing across the visible first page. Precise hand-written Greek letters ran across the page, large enough for Harry to make out a few words he recognized in a dialect not spoken for thousands of years. This ancient book held the place of honor in the secret vault of a world-class trafficker. Harry didn't think twice.

Moving with a care belying his predicament, Harry slipped the Greek book into his briefcase, nestling it gently alongside the necklace. He gritted his teeth when a single page slipped free from the book, which he slid back inside before latching the briefcase. That's when the first words pushed through the fog of elation clouding his ears and Harry went still. The words of a woman in the room behind him, standing amid Charles's artifacts. Harry angled his head. *I know that voice.*

He listened a moment longer. Yes, he did. Pausing long enough to confirm nobody was answering the rhetorical questions the woman posed herself, he pulled up a number on his phone and paused, a finger hovering over the screen. He never expected to use this number again. *Life is funny.*

Harry hit *SEND*. A moment later, the woman outside fell silent. Rustling, as though she were digging in her pocket. A grunt of surprise. Then, she spoke. "Normally I'd never answer a call right now," she said. "But you cannot imagine where I am. What do you want?"

"You're in a warehouse at Port Newark." Harry spoke softly, his voice scarcely a whisper. "You just busted a trafficker."

"How the hell do you know that?" the woman replied sharply.

"I'm not done," Harry said. "Then you found a hidden room. One with more artifacts in it. Enough to get your team in the paper."

For once, the woman was speechless. Harry stepped closer to the door. "Do you have a gun?"

"Do I – what? Yes I have a gun."

"Then don't shoot me." Peering through the narrow opening, Harry looked out to see a woman's back toward him. In one hand she held a phone, and the other was empty. "Turn around."

To continue the story, visit Andrew Clawson's website at andrewclawson.com.

GET YOUR COPY OF THE PARKER CHASE STORY *A SPY'S REWARD*, AVAILABLE EXCLUSIVELY FOR MY VIP READER LIST

Sharing the writing journey with my readers is a special privilege. I love connecting with anyone who reads my stories, and one way I accomplish that is through my mailing list. I only send notices of new releases or the occasional special offer related to my novels.

If you sign up for my VIP reader mailing list, I'll send you a copy of *A Spy's Reward*, the Parker Chase adventure that's not sold in any store. You can get your copy of this exclusive novel by signing up here: DL.bookfunnel.com/uayd05okci

Did you enjoy this story? Let people know

Reviews are the most effective way to get my books noticed. I'm one guy, a small fish in a massive pond. Over time, I hope to change that, and I would love your help. The best thing you could do to help spread the word is leave a review on your platform of choice.

Honest reviews are like gold. If you've enjoyed this book I would be so grateful if you could take a few minutes leaving a review, short or long.

Thank you very much.

Dedication

To Spider and JJ,

for helping our kids discover that life is a wondrous adventure.

Also by Andrew Clawson

The Parker Chase Series

A Patriot's Betrayal

A dead man's letter draws Parker Chase into
a deadly search for a secret that could rewrite history.

The Crowns Vengeance

A Revolutionary era espionage report sends Parker
on a race to save American independence.

Dark Tides Rising

A centuries-old map bearing a cryptic poem sends Parker Chase
racing for his life and after buried treasure.

A Republic of Shadows

A long-lost royal letter sends Parker on a secret trail
with the I.R.A. and British agents close behind.

A Hollow Throne

Shattered after a tragic loss, Parker is thrust into
a race through Scottish history to save a priceless treasure.

A Tsar's Gold

Parker follows a trail through the past toward a lost treasure
which changed the course of two World Wars.

The TURN Series

TURN: *The Conflict Lands*

Reed Kimble battles a ruthless criminal gang
to save Tanzania and the animals he loves.

TURN: *A New Dawn*

A predator ravages the savanna. To stop it, Reed must be
what he fears most – the man he used to be.

TURN: *Endangered*

Tanzania's deadliest gangster is after everything Reed
built – and will stop at nothing to destroy him.

Harry Fox Adventures

The *Arthurian Relic*

The *Emerald Tablet*

The *Celtic Quest*

The *Achilles Legend*

The *Pagan Hammer*

Check my website AndrewClawson.com for
additional novels – I'm writing all the time.

About the Author

Andrew Clawson is the author of multiple series, including the Parker Chase and TURN thrillers, as well as the Harry Fox adventures.

You can find him at his website, AndrewClawson.com, or you can connect with him on Twitter at @clawsonbooks, on Facebook at facebook.com/AndrewClawsonnovels and you can always send him an email at andrew@andrewclawson.com.

Made in the USA
Monee, IL
24 April 2023

32389489R00166